Arcane
Arctic #1

Peter North

Contents

1. Frozen Feelings   1

2. Out Cold   12

3. Questionable Relief   20

4. The Witch Doctor   33

5. Golden-Eye   48

6. Integration   58

7. Dungeon-ess?   69

8. Broken Basics   81

9. Outcasts   94

10. Entering The Frozen Tomb   105

11. Snow Scorpions   119

12. Level Up   132

13. Beetle Guts   144

14. Well, That Didn't Go as Planned   155

15. It's Complicated   168

16. Safe   182

17. Cold Shower   192

18. Heart to Heart   204

19. Keys and Heroes   214

20. Bison Berries   226

21. The Forbidden Crypt   237

22. Stalkers in the Shadow   249

23. Secrets of the Crypt   260

24. Garden Harvest   272

25. Frigid Depths   283

26. The Pharoh's Tomb   297

27. Phar-oh-oh!   309

28. Where the Buffalo Roam   323

29. A Traveling Merchant   337

30. Busy Work   348

31. Medicine and Machinations   359

32. Molly's Confession   371

33. A First for Everything   384

34. Epilogue   398

Thanks for Reading!   402

Recommended Groups   404

Also by Peter North   406

1

Frozen Feelings

If Jay Morgan had known that "Arctic Expedition" was code for "overpriced frostbite," he might have reconsidered the whole enterprise. But there he was, shivering on the deck of a ship that seemed to be held together by sheer willpower and an optimistic coat of paint, staring at the endless expanse of ice that was Spitzbergen, Norway. Jay was pretty sure the brochure had left out the part about needing to be part polar bear to enjoy the trip.

Molly O'Brian, on the other hand, was like a kid in a candy store—if the store was freezing and made entirely out of ice. She had managed to wrap Jay around her little finger yet again, convincing him that this trip was essential for her future in environmental science. And Jay, ever the sucker for Molly's ambitions, had footed the bill.

Okay, her ambitions and maybe her smile… and that cute little crinkle on her freckled nose when she laughed, and… well, the list went on. It had been carefully curated since they were about eight years old, and Jay had gotten the first inklings of what true love felt like. He loved Molly with all his heart, and it made him happy just to see her happy, even if she never seemed to return his feelings in quite the same way.

Besides, she was busy with school and didn't have time for a boyfriend. And he had… work. Nothing but work, and the few blissful moments with Molly that she squeezed in between research projects, essays, and exams. Maybe this was his lot in life, to freeze his balls off in the Arctic just for the chance to see Molly smile. After all, what was the point of his soul-sucking corporate job if not to fund life-threatening escapades in the name of friendship and unacknowledged love?

"Isn't this amazing, Jay?" Molly's voice cut through the Arctic air, pulling him out of his reverie. She was decked out in every piece of winter gear known to mankind, a clipboard with a waterproof observation's checklist and a grease pencil clutched in her mittened hands, looking like an enthusiastic marshmallow with a penchant for science.

"Oh, absolutely," Jay replied, his voice dripping with sarcasm. "I always dreamed of becoming a human popsicle. Really, this is a bucket list moment for me."

Molly laughed, a sound that warmed him more effectively than his three layers of thermal wear. "Come on, grumpy. Where's your sense of adventure?"

"Left it back in the office, I think. It's probably hiding under a pile of spreadsheets."

Molly jumped up and wrapped her arms around him, squeezing him so hard he thought his ribs might break. Or his heart might stop. Or... maybe that wasn't the hug so much as being close to her, and smelling the sweet, herbal scent of her organic, eco-friendly shampoo. Jay didn't know. He just knew that he didn't want it to stop.

"I know this isn't your idea of a good time," she said, going up on her tiptoes to kiss him on the frozen cheek. "Thank you for coming with me, and for giving me the most incredible birthday present I've *ever* gotten. You're the best friend a girl could have, Jay Morgan."

Jay felt his heart beat harder even as the joy at her closeness withered slightly at that word. Friend. Yes, he was her friend. He would always be her friend, no matter what. But what he wouldn't give to have the rest of her heart, too. It wasn't like she was in love with someone else. Why couldn't she see how much she meant to him?

And why couldn't he bring himself to tell her?

Okay, technically he knew why.

Because once, when they were sixteen, shortly after he'd gotten his driver's license and a beat-up old

Honda Civic hatchback for them to cruise around in, Jay had gathered up all his courage and kissed Molly goodnight when he dropped her off at home after taking her to a movie. And she'd kissed him back. Passionately and so thoroughly he'd barely been able to concentrate enough to keep his car on the road as he drove home. Even the sight of her scowling step-father, Barry, shooting daggers at him through a crack in the front-window curtains hadn't been enough to knock him off cloud-nine.

Jay had thought it was the beginning of something new in their relationship. He'd thought it was true love.

But the next day, Molly had acted like nothing had happened. If anything, she was a little distant. It had crushed him, but Jay knew how to take a hint. He had never tried anything like that again, even when—in college—Molly had seemed like she might feel differently. He figured she could make the first move if she did. He wasn't going to risk making a mistake and pushing her away again. She knew how he felt, didn't she?

But she never did make a move, and soon school began to take up more and more of her time and work took up his and now they had... this. *Friend*ship.

And freezing cold balls that brought new meaning to the word blue. But that was a him problem, not a them problem. Jay winced as he tugged on the back of his parka, hoping to insulate himself from the icy wind. Who on earth came to places like this voluntarily? And *enjoyed* it?

Molly, judging by the current crinkle on her pink, freckled nose, and the sparkle in her sea-blue eyes. Jay sighed and resigned himself to a few more days of misery in order to bask in the glow of Molly's excitement. It was worth it.

"All right, folks," one of the tour guides slash scientists shouted across the din of waves hammering the side of their boat. "It's time for our first foray onto the ice floes. Gather your charts and clipboards and see your group leader if you have any questions about the survey. We're boarding the Zodiac now."

As part of "all the adventure of an Arctic expedition in a week," they were scheduled to cruise in a Zodiac to explore the glaciers. Jay wasn't entirely sure what a Zodiac was until he saw it—a small, inflatable boat that looked about as sea-worthy as a rubber duck. Apparently, they were expected to gather survey data for the scientists while attempting not to freeze to death—and this was *after* they'd paid for the privilege of joining this research expedition.

To Jay, it all seemed like a remarkably good deal for the scientists and a questionable one for anyone stupid enough to shell out money for the experience.

Stepping into the Zodiac with the enthusiasm of a man walking the plank, Jay wondered if his life insurance was up to date.

Then, he realized it didn't matter.

He didn't have anyone to leave his money to anyway. No siblings. His mom had never been in the picture and his dad—who had come to fatherhood late in life—had died of undiagnosed prostate cancer when Jay was halfway through his degree program. Molly was the only one who would care if Jay froze to death in the arctic, except, perhaps, for his boss during the ten minutes it would take to reassign his contracts to one of the other company lackeys.

And Molly....

Well, she was practically bouncing with excitement, completely heedless of any danger they might be in. Her red curls peeked out from under her beanie in a way that made Jay's heart do strange things.

Strange, all-too-familiar things.

He wished it wouldn't.

Their guide, a man who introduced himself as Erik but looked more like a Thor, began detailing the day's itinerary with a level of cheer that should be illegal in such cold conditions. "Today, we'll be getting up close and personal with glaciers, fjords, icebergs, and, if we're lucky, the majestic polar bear!"

Jay leaned over to Molly, whispering, "When he says 'up close and personal,' do you think he means 'inside the digestive system of'?"

Molly snorted, earning them a curious look from Erik/Thor. "Don't mind him," she told the guide. "He's just allergic to fun."

"Fun, she calls it," Jay muttered dryly under his

breath. "Whatever happened to pizza and beer and... I don't know... bowling? Next time we're going bowling."

As they set off, the Zodiac bobbing alarmingly in the icy waters, Jay decided that if he survived this trip, he'd need to reassess his life choices. Maybe it was time to stop agreeing to potentially lethal adventures just because Molly's eyes sparkled a certain way when she was excited about something.

Or maybe, he thought as he watched her face light up at the sight of a distant walrus, he just needed to find a more temperate way to win her over.

Love might warm the cockles of the heart, but it did absolutely nothing for frostbitten toes. He had evidence to prove it, aching in his oversized winter boots.

As the Zodiac sliced through the icy waters of Spitzbergen, Jay studied the odd group of people he felt certain he was going to die with. Molly was on the edge of her seat, her binoculars permanently glued to her face as she scanned the horizon for wildlife. Jay, trying his best to channel the spirit of an Arctic explorer, was mostly just channeling the spirit of someone deeply regretting his decisions. The rest of the paying members of the tour seemed to feel more like Molly than Jay. He'd never understand these nature types.

Erik, their Finnish guide, proudly spouted a fountain of knowledge, pointing out features of the landscape with a passion that rivaled Molly's. "And to your left, you'll see one of Spitzbergen's many glaciers. It's been here for thousands of years, shaping the land."

Jay, feeling the cold seep into his bones, muttered under his breath, "And yet there's still no hot tub? I'm beginning to think the evolution deniers have a point."

Not long afterward, the silence of the awed tourists was broken by an excited shout from their guide. "Polar bear! Straight ahead, by the edge of that 'berg!"

The mood in the Zodiac shifted instantly, the amazement at seeing one of the Arctic's most iconic creatures up close palpable. Even Jay, who had been more concerned about staying alive and warm, found himself caught up in the excitement. The bear, a magnificent male with a thick coat that seemed to glow in the weak sunlight, was a good distance away but clearly visible against the stark white of the snow.

Erik was almost vibrating with delight, quickly pulling out a camera and beginning to document the encounter. "This is incredible, folks! We'll need to gather as much data as we can. These encounters are crucial for our understanding of their movements and behavior. Ivan, can you bring us nearer to the edge of that floe? We need to get closer."

Ivan, the large man with a rifle who was driving the Zodiac, looked less than thrilled at the suggestion. His job, as he had gruffly explained at the beginning of the tour, was to ensure the safety of the group, which meant keeping a respectful—and considerable—distance from the polar bear. But his warnings did little to dampen Erik's enthusiasm, or Molly's, for that matter.

Ivan maneuvered the Zodiac close enough to the edge of the ice floe that any who wanted could climb out of the boat. The polar bear was walking away, still a safe distance from them, but Jay wasn't inclined to chase it.

Molly had other ideas.

"I'm going on the ice," she declared, her eyes alight with the kind of fervor that Jay knew all too well. It meant there was no stopping her.

"I don't think that's a great idea," Jay tried, even as he helped her up. His protests were met with a determined shake of her head. Erik and the others were already climbing out, and Molly was eagerly awaiting her turn. Jay shook his head as they prepared to disembark onto the ice.

As Molly stepped out of the Zodiac, Jay was right behind her, his hands ready to steady her. He glanced over the edge of the boat, feeling suddenly uneasy. The waves seemed to churn around the dingy, making eerie slapping noises that sounded a bit too much like laughter. Jay shivered, imagining kelp-haired sirens with sharp teeth rising up from the depths of the Arctic Ocean, ready to pull him under the icy waves.

He shook his head.

Where the hell had that idea come from?

Jay swallowed, attempting to push the thought from his mind. He was about to turn back to help Molly when a strange, swirling pattern in the water caught his attention.

"Hey, Ivan?" he asked, motioning toward the water with a gloved hand. "What's with the waves here?"

Below the boat, shifting shadows danced just beneath the surface. Jay had the sudden, horrifying insight that oceans hid big creatures under the waves. Anything could be lurking down there. Was it a whale? A shark? A giant squid?

Ivan peered over the edge of the boat and frowned. Jay didn't like the look on the guide's face. It was the look of an experienced man seeing something he couldn't explain. It was not a good look.

"Molly, wait—" Jay began, intending to pull her back into the boat.

But she was already scrambling onto the ice. The boat rocked, making it harder for her to reach the edge. The other tourists were already hurrying toward the polar bear, cameras clicking, so there was no one to help her up. Jay grabbed her by the waist, unsure if he should pull her back into the boat or push her up onto the ice floe.

Molly's foot slipped on the edge of the Zodiac, and in a frantic attempt to catch her, Jay lurched forward. Molly screamed. Jay's gloved hands slid on the fabric of her coat. There was a horrible crack as Molly's head clipped the edge of the ice floe and she went limp in his arms before they both tumbled into the freezing waters.

The cold was a shock, stealing the breath from his lungs. Jay's instincts kicked in, and he wrapped his arms around Molly, who was lifeless in his grasp. He kicked towards the surface, but the swirling pattern of the waves had grown into a whirlpool, pulling them down with irresistible force.

Ivan stared stoically after them, that same stunned look still on his face. Jay could see his shape flickering through the surface of the water.

Panic set in as Jay realized they weren't going to easily break free from the pull. He tightened his grip on Molly, determined not to let go, even as the cold began to numb his senses.

Below them, the water darkened, and the pull grew stronger. Jay's thoughts were a blur as fear and resolve warred for control of his body. He had to save Molly; he had to get them back to the surface. But no matter how hard he fought, the icy waters continued to drag them down, down, down, into the abyss.

As the light from the surface began to fade, Jay's last coherent thought was a desperate hope that this wasn't the end—that somehow, they'd find a way out of this. Then, darkness enveloped them, and the world above seemed like a distant memory, lost to the cold embrace of the Arctic depths.

2

Out Cold

J ay came to with a start, sitting straight up and gasping for breath before he remembered that he was underwater and was likely going to drown for his efforts.

Except he didn't drown.

He sucked in a lungful of icy, cold, but mercifully dry air as his eyes fought against an inky blackness that he couldn't blink away, and his brain ached with stabbing pain.

What had happened? Had they been rescued? Why didn't he feel wet?

Jay pressed his gloved fingers into his eyes and rubbed, trying to make them work again. He could hear nothing but the sound of his own heart hammering in his temples and the distant sound of birds cawing. Ravens or...

No, that didn't make sense. They were in the arctic, on the ocean. There shouldn't be any ravens around...

Jay dropped his hands and blinked rapidly, relieved when the inky clouds began to fade, revealing some shapes and colors that slowly came into focus. First, he saw his oversized snow boots, then as his gaze traveled along his legs he saw insulated black snowpants with reflective tape wrapped around the knees, and the bottom of his bright red parka. He wiggled his toes experimentally, and though he couldn't see the movement through his boots, everything felt okay. Cold but not broken.

Beyond his boots, an expanse of white—so flat and featureless that it looked like a video game that had failed to load properly—stretched as far as his bleary eyes could see. The cawing persisted, and Jay looked up to see he was sitting in a clearing, surrounded by a few scraggly trees. The overcast sky above him was filled with black birds, circling like vultures, and screaming their birdy-prayers that he was dead.

Jay picked up a handful of snow and threw it impotently at the birds.

"Fuck off, you filthy scavengers!" he shouted, mostly to make himself feel better. He was so surprised to be alive that he was shocked to actually hear his voice cutting through the cold winter air.

But where was he? What had happened? He'd been trying to help Molly climb out of the boat—

Jay's heart clenched in his chest. Molly. Where was Molly?

They'd fallen into the weird swirling water together. He remembered clinging to her and fighting to pull her to the surface even as the whirlpool sucked them deeper into the freezing depths of the ocean.

So how had he ended up here? Cold but dry, with not a wave nor whirlpool in sight? And what was with the trees and ravens? There were no trees in the artic. That was part of its charm, wasn't it, one of the things that made it such a unique environment? The glorious arctic... a place that you wanted to spend thousands and thousands of dollars to take your wannabe girlfriend for her birthday and then drop her in the ocean where you can both freeze to death, unhappy and unfulfilled?

Jay cursed under his breath and tried to roll onto his side to get his knees under him. His muscles and joints ached with cold, despite the multiple layers of arctic gear he was bundled in. He wondered how long he'd been laying in the clearing.

"Molly?" he called out in case she was somewhere nearby. There was no answer, and he cursed again. He couldn't see much past the stupid fur ruff of his hood—which the salesman had claimed to be wolf-tail but was probably scavenged from some mangy coyote that had been picked off a golf course. But he was too cold to take it down.

Finally, Jay managed to shove himself to his feet and look around, moving his entire torso and keeping his neck straight so that he could see through the frosted fur window around his face. He was in a sparse grove of black-trunked trees that looked like they were probably malnourished even at the best of times. Snow covered the ground, interspersed with a few boulders splashed with bright orange lichen like a muppet had thrown up on them.

"Molly?" he tried again, louder this time.

Jay winced as he took a step forward, feeling the weight of his body press into his frozen joints like a pile of bricks. Everything hurt. He could hardly force himself to take a step forward.

But there was something there, behind the orange-covered rock, a black lump that didn't quite fit the organic setting.

"Molly!" Jay rushed forward, no longer paying any attention to his crying muscles and tendons. He felt his heart leap into his throat and lodge there, where it refused to move until he made sure she was okay.

Molly wasn't moving.

The lump he saw was a boot, and that boot was connected to a pair of black snowpants just like his—they'd ended up buying the same set of gear at the overpriced outdoor store Molly loved so much, but couldn't afford... Or, rather, he'd bought a matching set *for* her, because she'd looked so damned cute in the oversized parka.

Now...

Jay swallowed against the lump in his throat as he took in the bright red jacket and the mittened hands that looked too small, even in their bulky covers.

"Shit, Molly, are you okay?" He fell onto his knees

and scrambled over to her, pushing back the fur of her hood to see an angry red gash on her forehead. Suddenly, he remembered the way she'd hit her head on the ice before they'd tumbled out of the boat, the horrible crack he'd heard before she went limp in his arms.

Jay ripped his gloves off, heedless of the cold, and pressed his fingers under her jaw to check her pulse. "Come on, Molly. Please be okay. Please."

His heart almost burst with relief as he felt hers beat weakly beneath his fingertips. Letting out a ragged sigh, he kept his fingers there counting between each beat. He couldn't remember much of the first aid training he'd taken back in his university days, but he knew her pulse was weak. Better than no pulse, but... not good.

"Okay, Mol. Stay with me, okay? Can you hear my voice? I'm going to find you some help. I'm going to—"

Jay's words cut off as he looked around, searching for some direction to go for help, some sign than they weren't the only two people out here in... wherever they were. How could this be possible? They'd fallen in the goddamned Arctic Ocean. If they'd been rescued, why would someone abandon them in the middle of the freakin' tundra? And if they hadn't been rescued... What the hell had happened?

He knew he wasn't supposed to move a person who had suffered a head injury. Molly may have broken her neck in the fall. He had no way of checking when she was unconscious.

But he couldn't leave her here while he went to look for help.

The circling ravens were one thing, but what if there were wolves out here? Or—Jay shuddered—one of those polar bears? There was no way he was going to abandon her when she was unable to protect herself. But there was nothing he could do for her when he didn't know what was wrong.

"Okay, I can do this," he muttered to himself, gazing at the distant horizon. "I can figure out what to do. Years of project management experience have honed my ability to make decisions under pressure. It says so on my resume and everything. Think, Jay, think..."

Something caught his attention at the far edge of his vision, a smudge of darker gray against the overcast sky. Was that smoke? Could there be a camp or a town that way?

Either that or this pitiful wasteland was suffering from a midwinter wildfire. While that would just be his luck, Jay had no choice but to check it out. And because he refused to leave Molly to freeze to death or be eaten by polar bears, that meant he was going to have to carry her—and pray to the powers that be that she was only suffering a concussion and not a spinal cord injury.

Jay felt sick as he tore his gaze away from the smoke and knelt next to his best friend. Her pretty face was paler than usual. Even her freckles seemed faded, and her cheeks—which should have been pink with cold—looked like they were carved from ivory. The curls of copper-red hair that peeked out from behind the fur ruff of her coat seemed duller than usual, too.

Jay was sure that was just his imagination. Even if she'd lost a lot of blood, which it didn't look like she had, her hair shouldn't have been affected by her injury. But she didn't look well, of that much he was certain.

It was as if the life was slowly seeping out of Molly O'Brian, and if Jay wanted to help her, he needed to move quickly.

Ignoring the aches and pains in his own tortured body, along with the nagging questions about how they had gotten into this mess, Jay gently slid an arm under Molly's knees and the other behind her shoulders, supporting her neck. When he stood, he was shocked at how weightless she felt, as if she were already half-ghost.

Jay pushed that idea out of his mind, reminding himself that he'd felt her heartbeat. She was still alive. She was just tiny. Molly had always been petite. He'd teased her about it before, when she'd demanded piggy-back rides at the end of a long hike or a night at the pub.

His heart ached at the memory of Molly's playful, goofy side that only seemed to come out when they were alone together.

He clutched her body to his chest and began to

walk, keeping his eyes on the blot of smoke across the frozen wasteland before him. All he had to do was get her there. Someone would be able to help them. And if they couldn't, he'd carry her to the next town if he had to.

Preferably, they'd let him rent a car, but he would carry her until he collapsed if that was what it took.

Jay wouldn't rest until he knew Molly was going to be okay. He had no choice. He wouldn't be able to live with himself if something happened to her. Not when it had been his stupid idea to take that trip to the arctic. Not when she never would have been on that boat in the first place if it hadn't been for him.

Gritting his teeth against the cold, Jay began the journey across the tundra. The ravens cawed their frustration at him as he carried away their free meal, and he sent a final curse their way before setting his mind to ignoring them too.

The only thing that mattered now was closing the distance between Molly and that little smudge of hope on the horizon.

3

Questionable Relief

By the time Jay reached the village he was delirious with cold and exhaustion. He must have been, because the scene that unfolded before him was like something from a dream. Wind had whipped across the open tundra, wailing like a screaming banshee the entire time he'd been walking. The dull gray overcast sky had deepened into a charcoal hue, which made seeing the smoke difficult at first. But soon, the night sky lit up with dancing lights of green and blue and even flashes of pink, and the smoke took on a silvery tone against the colors.

Jay hadn't paid that much attention to Molly's rattling-off of facts about the arctic, but he thought it was the wrong season for northern lights. Wasn't that a winter thing? Despite the cold, it was technically springtime. Or maybe the lights could be seen all year round, and they were only more spectacular in the winter months.

Jay wished Molly were awake so he could ask her. He promised himself he would pay attention this time. He would commit every word that came out of her mouth to memory, if she'd only wake up and say something.

When the village finally came into view after what felt like hours of shuffling across the frozen ground, Jay wished Molly would wake up for another reason. Because he needed her to tell him that he wasn't losing his mind.

The village—for that was what his mind insisted on labeling it—was little more than a scattered collection of saggy tents and some sad lean-to shacks arranged in a semicircle before an icy rise in the tundra. It was this rise that caught Jay's attention first. It was like a cliff, really. A plateau about twelve feet high that stretched as far as he could see in every direction. If he didn't know it was impossible, Jay would have said the cliff looked like it was made from ice—crystal clear, sparkling blue ice.

Stranger still, there were two massive doors carved in the icy cliff which seemed to be engraved with some kind of pictographic language, the syllabics of an indigenous culture maybe? Jay had no idea except that he knew they weren't in any kind of language he recognized.

The tents and huts were arranged in an arc before

the doors, almost reverently, as if whatever lay beyond the cryptically marked passage was integral to their lives. It was eerie. Almost a cultlike vibe, as far as Jay was concerned. If he had any other option, he might have skipped this town and gone onto the next, but Molly's health was more important than his case of the heebie-jeebies.

And as weird as the giant ice plateau was, and the ramshackle village cult, neither held a candle to the people who came out of their tents and shacks to stare at Jay as he stumbled off the tundra and into their midst.

People... they were people, weren't they? Not...

Jay shook his head. He was definitely delirious if he was imagining being greeted by human-sized animals, or even some kind of human-beast hybrid. As far as he knew, the government wasn't doing any tests on mutant animals in the arctic. He hadn't even heard any conspiracy theories to that effect.

But maybe that explained it. Maybe the government kept people distracted with rumors about UFOs and lizardmen and kept the real freaky stuff hush-hush?

No, no. He had to stop thinking crazy. He didn't want to act crazy and scare these people off, not when he needed their help.

And they were people, of course. What else would the be? They were just people with unsettling, animal-like clothing that made them look like they had wolf ears and tails. Or rabbits, or foxes, or snow leopards, or bears. Jay even saw a woman with a cloak made of huge white feathers and a beak-like mask on her face like she was dressed up as a snowy owl. Maybe it was some kind of festival or something?

Or some cult thing...

Never mind. Jay didn't really care why they were dressed up the way they were, or why they were staring at him like he was the weird one. He only cared that they were his best chance to help Molly.

Jay stumbled forward.

He'd long since lost feeling in his fingers and toes. Even his arms felt numb and dull, though he managed to keep holding onto Molly despite the fact that he couldn't feel his limbs. Or his face. Or his brain.

"Help," he rasped, surprised at how dry and hollow his voice sounded. Stumbling forward another couple of steps, he tried again, finding it difficult to push the words out through his numb lips and frozen tongue. "Need help."

One of the people, an older man wearing a gray fur cloak over his stooped shoulders, stepped forward to meet Jay. He appeared to have some kind of headdress or hood with huge wolf ears on it covering the top of his skull. The man's golden eyes—Contacts? Jay wondered—were narrowed with suspicion, his weathered face wrinkled with exaggerated dismay as he regarded the newcomers.

Jay felt he should be the one staring suspiciously. He wasn't the one dressed up like a werewolf, for fuckssake. But he'd couldn't afford to be too picky when Molly was laying like a deadweight in his arms.

"Please," he said, forcing the words out through his uncooperative mouth. His mind felt strange, as if he couldn't quite understand the words he was speaking, as if they were coming out in a language he didn't know. "My friend, she... she hit her head or something. I can't wake her up. She needs a doctor."

The old man took another step forward, and Jay noticed the large staff he was leaning on—made of twisted, gray wood and etched with runes that had been burned into its surface. His gnarled hand clenched the staff as if he was considering whether he was going to need to use it as a weapon. When he spoke, Jay startled backward in dismay.

"You come from across the tundra?" the wolf-man said. His voice was a deep growl far louder and more resonant that Jay would have expected given his ancient appearance. "Why do you seek aide with the Faunari and not in one of your human cities? Have you no hearthstone?"

His voice, too, seemed to lag in Jay's brain like his words were being translated before they arrived in his ears. But that was impossible. He must have hit his head, too, when they'd fallen... from where? The ocean? Nothing made sense anymore.

"My human..." Jay shook his head, trying to understand the words he was hearing. "I'm sorry but I have no idea what you're talking about. I don't know where we are or how we got here. I came to your village because I saw the smoke from your fires. I didn't know where else to go."

"Our *village*," the old man said, and his growl became a cavernous, frightening laugh. Jay caught a glimpse of yellowed, fang-like teeth behind his thin lips and took a step backward, suddenly doubting his decision to approach the strange people. Others were advancing now, all looking as hostile as the gray-furred man. Jay even heard someone in the back snarl, and he felt the hairs lift on the back of his neck at the purely unhuman sound.

The wolf-man spoke again, scorn dripping from his words. "This 'village' as you call it is an outpost for nomads and outcasts, nothing but a place for our kind to die out of the sight of yours, human. How dare you seek help from the Faunari when we have been cast aside like refuse by King Wenshire, our claim for Arcanicean citizenship rewarded with nothing but mockery from nobles such as yourself. No, you shall not find help nor hearth here. Begone!"

"Arcan...Arcanicea?" Jay stumbled over the unfamiliar word, his teeth beginning to chatter. "Is that in Finland? Are we still in the arctic circle?"

The wolf-man's eyes narrowed to slits, and his lips pulled back from his teeth to expose long, dagger-like canines.

Jay was certain now that he was hallucinating, but his mind wasn't quite ready to give in to it. He kept trying to rationalize the situation. "I don't know who this Wenshire guy is, but he sounds like an ass. I mean, I didn't think there were many kingdoms around anymore. I don't really follow world politics, I guess. I just... Even if you don't want to help me, could someone help her? I'll pay. I have money. Cash, credit... Do you take Amex?"

The man swung the staff at Jay, the gnarled wooden head sweeping in an expansive arc before him. Jay flinched, but breathed a sigh of relief when he noticed the wolf-man was too far away to hit him.

Or he should have been.

A concussive wave slammed into Jay a fraction of a second after he decided he was safe, knocking the wind out of him and forcing him to his knees.

Somehow, he managed to keep hold of Molly, clutching her against his chest.

Jay's mouth opened and closed as he fought to draw breath into his emptied lungs, his eyes watering. With a wheezing gasp, his throat opened and sucked in an icy breath of air. As he glanced down at Molly's pale face, checking to see if she'd been hurt by the mysterious blast, his attempts at diplomacy evaporated in a storm of rage.

"What the fuck, man?" he shouted, still fighting an invisible pressure that kept him on his knees. Jay didn't know what was going on, but he wasn't going to let some cosplaying nut job hurt Molly. "Enough with the shamanic cult bullshit, asshole. If you hurt her, I swear to God, I will take that stick and beat you to death with it."

Even as the words left his mouth, he realized

he had no reasonable expectation of being able to follow through on his threat. But he was pissed, and that didn't leave a bunch of room in his tired, cold-fogged brain for rational thoughts.

Jay struggled to get to his feet, feeling the continued pressure of invisible hands holding him down. He held Molly tighter against his chest and roared in frustration, his muscles screaming as he fought against whatever insanity was holding him there.

The wolf-man laughed, holding the staff in front of him and pointing it at Jay in mockery. "Not so powerful now, are you human?" he snarled. "All alone on the tundra with no crusading armies at your back... Perhaps I'll send pieces of you to your king as payment for his treatment of my people."

Jay cursed, closing his eyes, and willing his sanity to return. He knew that what he was experiencing was impossible. But what did that knowledge do to help him when there was nothing he could do to wake himself from the living nightmare that he seemed to have stumbled into?

"I just want to help Molly," he said through clenched teeth. "If you don't want to help her, fine. Point me in the right direction and I'll leave. Maybe I'll see this Wenshire character, if you think we're such good buddies. Maybe he's man enough to help an injured woman without turning it into a pissing contest."

The man snarled again, and Jay had a fraction of a second to regret his words before an older woman in similarly strange garb stepped forward, putting her hand on the wolf-man's shoulder.

"Runolf, stay your hand," she said, her voice low and gravelly. "He speaks the truth. Can't you see? He cannot be one of them."

"How can he not?" Runolf growled, refusing to lower the staff or to tear his gaze from Jay's. Jay kept his eyes locked on the wolf-man, too. It was the only thing he could do to demonstrate his refusal to submit to the bully.

"No power has awakened in him," the woman said. She, too, gazed at Jay, though her pale-yellow eyes were kinder. Jay wondered if he should be insulted by her words, but he couldn't muster the energy. She smiled at him. "What child has not set foot inside the dungeon and been awakened, even in these cursed parts? I know you can see for yourself that I am right. Heed me, Runolf. They are not from this land."

"Not from Arcanicea?" The old man's wolf-ears seemed to twitch, giving Jay a start. "You cannot believe the stories, Raina. They are old wives' tales at best."

"And yet, those old wives' tales have given us the roots of our magic and our medicine, Runolf," she said, turning her gaze back to the wolf-man. A tail, silvery-gray and bushy, swished behind her with a movement that Jay interpreted as amusement. He couldn't believe what he was seeing. The woman continued, "Just because a story is old does not make it untrue. There are others who claim to have come through the portal, remember..."

Runolf scoffed. "Ah, yes. Brunor the Ursari Barbarian and Skadi the Winged Giantess and all the other heroes of old. If you haven't noticed, there is nothing heroic about the Faunari people now, Raina. Our dungeon is as cursed as our people, and those stories are only proof of how far we have fallen—that there was ever a time we believed in heroes."

Jay listened to his words, barely understanding any of them. His mind was fixed on something the old woman had said.

"Portal..." he repeated, his mind whirling with images of the strange waves and the sucking sensation as he and Molly were swallowed by the cyclonic waters. "Yes, a portal! We fell into the ocean... I thought we'd drowned. But we woke up in a clearing of trees, completely dry and in the middle of nowhere. Has this happened before?"

Raina's pale-yellow eyes widened, and she flashed a toothy grin at Runolf. "You see?" She turned to Jay. "Tell us of this stand of trees, young man."

Jay shook his head. "They were thin and scraggly," he said. "Not much to look at. Like a circle of burned sticks more than trees. There were some boulders there, too, with bright orange lichen."

Runolf growled. "The Fallow Lands."

"There were ravens flying over head, like they were waiting to decide if we were dead enough to eat," Jay said, knowing he was rambling, but his mind was suddenly adrift with the strangeness of what had happened. "I was afraid bigger scavengers might follow their cawing. I couldn't leave her..." He glanced down at Molly, whose pale face was nearly the color of the surrounding snow. His heart ached. He turned to the woman, his earlier animosity dissolving as he realized how desperate Molly's situation was. "Please, I'm sorry for what I said before. I meant no disrespect to you or your people. I just... I need someone to help her. I'll do anything. Please."

The wolf-woman growled, and for a moment, Jay thought he'd made a mistake. Then he realized it wasn't him she was angry with.

"Runolf," she said. "Lower your staff. I am the medicine woman of this tribe and I accept the call of these wanderers. You insult me with your continued hostility to our guests."

"Guests?" Runolf spat the word like it tasted of something awful. "You insult *me* by calling them so. Have it your way, Raina. But do not ask for my help when this son of Wenshire double-crosses you for your kindness. Do not ask for mercy when your bleeding heart betrays you."

Behind the pair of wolf people, others in the crowd began to murmur, casting wary glances at one another. Runolf and Raina appeared to be two very powerful figures in the village, and it made the others uncomfortable that they were in disagreement. Jay could see them silently taking sides with one or the other of the elder wolf-people.

"Please," he begged again, loudly enough that all present could hear him. "I will make it up to you, to all of you. I will be indebted to your people. All I ask is for someone to help her. Please."

Finally, Runolf dropped his staff and Jay felt the pressure that had been pressing him into the ground ease. He gasped with relief, realizing suddenly how much harder it had been to breath with that invisible weight attempting to crush him. His muscles screamed with relief and trembled in exhaustion. Jay hadn't noticed how hard he'd been fighting the mysterious sensation until it was gone, and he didn't have to fight anymore.

"Come with me," Raina said, stepping in front of Runolf and holding out a hand to Jay—though he couldn't take it with his arms holding Molly. "I will examine her in my tent. Once we know what is wrong with her, we will discuss the payment for her healing."

Jay struggled to get to his feet, his vision going black and woozy again as the blood rushed, too slow, through his limbs. Raina lifted her eyebrows in bemusement as he stood, as if she'd expected him to keel over instead.

Jay blinked the sensation away, forcing himself to focus on the woman before him. "You *can* heal her, though?"

"There is very little a shaman of my skill cannot heal," she said, her smile twisting. "With the right ingredients. You'll do anything, you say?"

"Anything," he said, hope flooding through him for the first time since he'd awakened in this world. "Anything in my power to do, it's yours."

Raina grinned at him, flashing canines as long, yellowed, and knifelike as Runolf's were, and the hope he'd been feeling faltered.

"You are either very brave or very foolish to make a promise like that," the old woman said, her wolf-like ears twitching as they swivelled toward him. "But I admire your dedication to your companion... Follow me. Let's see if we can't come to some sort of understanding."

4

The Witch Doctor

J ay followed the wolf-woman through the ramshackle village, struggling not to stare at the fluffy
gray tail that—he had to admit—looked to be part
of her actual body rather than some costume. It
swayed back and forth as she walked, just as her ears
twitched and swivelled as if to pick up snippets of
conversation being whispered as they passed.

Despite her age, the woman was straight-backed
and muscular. She was shorter than Jay, but not by
much, making her quite tall for a woman, though
the ears added some to her height. He guessed she
was probably about five-foot-nine, which was impressive for a woman who was well into her seven-
ties if her brown, wrinkled skin was any indication.
The other people they passed—each with animalistic features of their own—shuffled aside when Raina

came through, some even bowing to her like royalty.

"I appreciate your help, Ma'am," Jay began, noticing again the strange delay in his speech as if his words were being translated as they left his mouth.

The woman laughed, her pale-yellow eyes darting to glance at him over her shoulder. "Now there is a word I've never been called," she said, flashing her teeth at Jay. "Save your 'Ma'ams' for if you ever do make it to Wenshire's court, or one of the other human kingdoms. We do not use such honorifics here. I am called Raina Frostmane, and that is all."

Jay didn't know how to address the fact that Raina, like Runolf, insisted upon treating him like he was a different kind of person—almost a different species—than they were. Despite the animal attributes, they seemed just as human as he was, certainly more so than an actual wolf.

"Well, Raina, then," he said, panting as he fought to keep up with her long, determined strides. "Thank you. It seems you are a powerful person here, and I'm honored that you're willing to help us."

"It has been a long time since anyone has come through the portal into Arcanicea," the wolf-woman said. "But I have heard of such injuries occurring. Some who pass through fail to regain consciousness on the other side. Healing your friend will be a miracle in the eyes of many around here, and I would be lying if I said my reputation would not benefit from the rumors of my success."

"You… you can heal her, though?"

"If any can do it, it is I."

"If you can heal Molly..." Jay searched his mind for some phrase that would highlight the depth of his feeling on the matter. "I'll owe you my life."

Raina snorted, and her yellow eyes returned forward. "So easily you say such a thing? I am a shamanic priestess, wanderer, a Witch Doctor who has delved farther into the cursed dungeon than almost any other on the tundra. If I wish to take your life as payment for this healing, I can and I will."

Jay swallowed hard. The words were being translated, if that was what was happening in his mind, so that he could understand the woman. But while he understood the words, they didn't make sense. Dungeons, Witch Doctors, Miracles. But he hadn't meant it lightly. Nothing about this place made sense, but he knew that he would do anything to save Molly.

"Even so," he said. "It is a price I will pay."

He noticed the wolf-woman's gaze dart back to him appraisingly before she turned down a narrow passage between two large tents made of rough hides painted in blue runes. Jay followed as best he could, though he didn't know how it was possible that his arm muscles were still holding on. He thought perhaps his joints had seized, and that was the only thing keeping Molly in his grasp.

"In here," Raina said, standing next to one of the painted walls. She reached across and pulled open a flap, revealing the warm, herbal scented interior of one of the tents. Jay ducked his head and stepped inside, grateful that he'd soon be able to share the burden of Molly's well-being with someone more knowledgeable than he was. He couldn't shake the guilty feeling that it was his fault she'd been hurt.

"Where should I put her?" he asked as Raina followed him inside the tent, letting the scrap of hide fall closed behind her.

"Over there," she said, indicating a slim cot next to a firepit where orange embers flickered in the cold air that had swept inside the tent alongside them. "Undress her, if you will."

Jay flushed. "I don't think she'd want me to—"

"She does not have to be naked, young man," the old wolf-woman said, chuckling with her low, gravelly voice. "But down to a single thin layer, if you can. Hurry now."

Jay crouched next to the coat and groaned as his arms finally gave out, allowing Molly to roll gently onto the narrow mattress. His wrists and elbows cried out in anguish as he straightened his limbs for the first time in hours. But he didn't pause to massage feeling back into them before he hurried to do the Witch Doctor's bidding.

It took longer than it should have to pull her winter boots off, to unzip the parka and slip her arms out of it, and to tug the snowpants down over her feet. He folded the outerwear as best he could before tackling the multiple layers of sweaters and pants she had on, until finally she was in nothing but a set of merino wool long underwear—baby blue and snug fitting enough that Jay's flushed cheeks felt like they were burning bright red by the time he was done.

Raina didn't say anything about his obvious discomfort, however. She had her nose buried in an ancient-looking book with ragged pages and bits and pieces of fabric, paper, and dried leaves poking out like makeshift bookmarks.

Now that he was inside and the biting wind of the tundra was safely locked outside the tent, Jay found himself sweating. Hurriedly, he removed his own outerwear and folded it haphazardly next to Molly's. The bulky jackets didn't want to cooperate, and he was fighting with them when Raina slammed the book shut with a crack. Jay's heart leaped in his chest, and he looked at the wolf-woman, who's wrinkled face was a mask of irritation.

"What is it?" Jay asked, afraid to hear the answer but knowing there was no sense in putting off the inevitable. "Can't you heal her?"

"I can," Raina Frostmane snapped, dropping the book on a cluttered desk with another loud noise. "I believe the ritual is quite simple, actually."

Jay stared at her, waiting for the rest.

The Witch Doctor's pale-yellow eyes met his and she grimaced ruefully. "Let me look at her. Move, human. Let me in there. I'm not going to bite her."

Jay shuffled aside, surprised by how wary he felt of the wolf-woman now that Molly was laying there, so pale and vulnerable. He cleared his throat. "Jay," he said. "My name is Jay, not 'human.' I'm Jay Morgan. And this is Molly O'Brian."

Raina snorted as she bent over the cot, tilting Molly's head to inspect the wound on her forehead. The scarlet gash, about two inches long, was surrounded by deep purple bruises. To Jay, it looked bad, but he knew head wounds often looked more serious than they were because the skin was so thin. He hoped this was the case with Molly, yet the fact that she remained unconscious indicated that it was worse than it looked.

"She hit her head on some ice," he began to explain. "Before we fell into the whirlpool and—"

"That is not what is causing her to sleep," the wolf-woman stated matter-of-factly.

Jay shook his head. "She's not sleeping," he protested. "She's unconscious. She probably has a concussion. I felt her go limp in my arms the moment she cracked her head, trust me."

Raina lifted an eyebrow at him. "Who is the Witch Doctor here," she asked, lifting a necklace from her chest which seemed to be made from bone beads. She twisted them in her fingers as she gazed upon him with her unsettlingly wolf-like eyes. "And who is the fool who promised his life in exchange for medicine?"

Jay shut his mouth.

"I say she is sleeping," Raina said. "For the Portal Sleep has come upon others before her, and those who have been woken from their sleep report experiencing a dreamlike state of consciousness wherein they are both aware of what is going on around them and are undergoing a kind of... transformation. I can wake your companion, Jay Morgan. All I require are some low-level ingredients from the dungeon. But she may not be the same person when she wakes. Is that a risk you are willing to take?"

"If the alternative is that she never wakes, what choice do I have?"

The bone beads made a clacking noise as she continued to play with her necklace, gazing at Jay as if she were trying to read something in his face. He waited patiently for her to explain more, but she didn't. The wolf-woman was seemingly lost in thought.

"This dungeon," Jay prompted, amazed at the words coming from his mouth. "You've mentioned it before. What... is it? Where I come from a dungeon is like a prison, a big one under a castle. They aren't really used anymore, though."

Raina raised an eyebrow at him again. "Some day, I would like to hear more about this world you come from," she said thoughtfully. "But that is not what a dungeon is in Arcanicea. You have seen the dungeon, the great wall of ice beyond our encampment."

"I thought it was a plateau of some kind," Jay said, "before I saw those strange doors. Where do they lead?"

"Beyond the rune-carved doors lies a magical, dangerous place upon which our entire existence is built," Raina motioned dramatically around her head with a wizened hand which, Jay noticed for the first time, had black claws on the tip of each finger. "It is where we, the Ice Delvers, go to seek out power."

"And that's where the ingredients to cure Molly will be found?" Jay asked. "Is that something I can do? How far inside do I have to go?"

The wolf-woman chuckled, her low voice making the sound more like a growl than a sound of mirth. "Again, you are so quick to offer yourself for sacrifice. We will see, Jay Morgan. We will see if you are strong enough to fulfill the promises you make."

"All I can do is try," Jay said, feeling a bit defensive at her continued skepticism. "How hard can it be? This is something all of you do, isn't it? You said before, even children go inside the dungeon."

"To unlock their potential, yes," Raina said. "Not all continue to train. Sometimes the powers the dungeon assigns are... not conducive to survival. Many never make it past the first floor."

"How many floors are there?"

"No one knows how deep our dungeon goes," Raina said, gathering a handful of dried herbs from the table behind her and placing them in a stone bowl. She frowned as she began to grind them into a powder, sending a bitter scent wafting into the air. "Few have traveled past the fifth floor and returned to tell the tale. Other dungeons are said to reach unimaginable depths, fifty floors, a hundred floors, a thousand. Other dungeons have spawned vast, sprawling cities, even entire kingdoms in some cases."

"Is the dungeon here... uh... new?" Jay asked, realizing how stupid he must sound. The massive ice plateau wasn't something that was built over a weekend. But why else would the Ice Delvers have only made it to the fifth floor, why would they have such a tiny community if other dungeons supported cities?

Raina growled, staring into the embers of the dying fire. "It is not new," she said. "It is *cursed*. The poisoned gift of King Wenshire to the Faunari people when we had the gall to ask for citizenship in Arcanicea. Though you are human, you may find your desires thwarted by the king's hatred of our kind."

Jay swallowed, not liking the direction the conversation was taking. He shook his head, wishing he didn't have to ask when the answer was clearly painful to the wolf-woman. "I'm sorry, Raina. I don't understand how any of this works."

Raina sighed, letting the bone necklace drop against her chest. She rubbed the wrinkled corners of her eyes, pinching the bridge of her nose as if she were getting a headache.

"You couldn't understand," she said with a sigh. "Most of Arcanicea doesn't understand, and it has happened under their noses. It is difficult to explain to an outsider, and a human outsider at that... I noticed the way you looked at Runolf and me when you first arrived. Runolf thought what he saw in your expression was disdain, for that is what he expects to see after so many years. But tell me, Jay Morgan. Are there beastkin in your world?"

"Beastkin?" he said, realizing this must be the word they used for the human-animal hybrid people of the village. "Uh, no. Not in real life. We have stories, of course. But they're just... stories."

Raina snorted again, her gray ears twitching.

Jay continued. "People—human people, that is—are considered an animal species the same as apes, tigers, elephants, and wolves." He glanced at Raina, hoping that his words wouldn't upset her further. She seemed to be listening, so he continued. "No one really knows why we evolved so differently, with language and agriculture and tools. Some people see themselves as better than animals, and others think we're much worse. We also divide ourselves into groups based on language and skin color and religious differences, sometimes just to have a reason to fight, I think. We've never been a peaceful species."

Raina knelt beside Molly's cot and busied herself with inspecting the unconscious woman's fingernails, checking her pulse, and tapping for reflexes. Then she sprinkled the powdered herb concoction over her prone form, muttering some kind of incantation under her breath.

"Our world is not so different from yours, then," she said once she'd finished. "Our oldest stories say that both human and beastkin came to Arcanicea from other realms, through the portals that occasionally open and bring people from one world to the next. Once, it was said to have happened often, though I don't know of any portal openings besides your own, not for hundreds of years. We should have come to this place as equals, strangers to this world, wanderers between realms. But the Faunari—our word for beastkin peoples—are not warlike like you humans are. We have tried and failed repeatedly to discover a route to peace and cooperation with the human kingdoms. They keep growing larger and stronger and our numbers dwindle because we cannot find our way."

"Can't you fight?" Jay asked, glancing at her teeth and claws with a wary eye. "There must be beastkin that are more powerful than humans."

Raina nodded. "Yes, many are. We can and do fight, one-on-one. Small groups of warriors defending beleaguered territories. But somehow, when the groups become too large the Faunari cannot stay united. We are a fractured, tribal people, naturally distrustful of other groups. The Lupinari, wolf-kin like Runolf and me, are not trusted by Harebloods, the rabbit-kin. Ursari and Felinari, the bear- and cat-kin people, tend to be solitary. Vulpinari, the fox-kin, are distrusted by all, as they are known to be tricksters. These are just the most common beastkin types, too. There are Wingbloods, Minotaur, Centaurs, and other rare groups whose names are not often spoken."

Jay listened, trying to wrap his mind around everything that Raina was telling him. He was surprised to find the disbelief that had been at the forefront of his mind earlier had disappeared. It was impossible, but what choice did he have but to believe what was happening to him? At least this version of reality held some possibility that Molly might be saved.

"Winterhaven, this pitiful excuse for a village is our reward for the audacity of beastkin who expect treatment equal to their 'betters,'" Raina said, bitterness tinging her words. "To the outside eye it appears we have been given equal opportunity to those human settlements that flourish under their own dungeons. Each dungeon spawns unique plants, animals, monsters, and magical items that local Delvers can trade on the world markets. Each settlement receives a list of commodities which are legal for it to sell, the cheapest of which are supposed to be readily available on the upper levels with the more valuable items harvested on the lower levels, and they trade with other settlements for the commodities produced in other dungeons."

"Sounds a lot like how our economy works," Jay said, finally feeling like this was something he understood. "Specialization of goods production, open markets, global trade... It's more stable than each community being completely independent, in the case of drought or famine or other supply shortages."

"Indeed," Raina said. "And that is how it should work here. That is how it does work for every other settlement of Delvers and their Dungeon Markets. Except that King Wenshire gave the Faunari people a dungeon territory which does not play by the same rules as the others."

Jay tried to absorb the information as best he could. The only analog he had for the kind of magical system she was describing came from movies and video games which, he suspected, were not an ideal frame of reference. The way the Lupinari Witch Doctor was speaking made it sound as if the dungeon itself was a conscious entity. He had many questions, but he did not want to interrupt now that he was finally starting to get an idea of what he was going to have to do.

"The Ice Dungeon does not provide us with the commodities that Winterhaven is legally allowed to sell in the Dungeon Market," she continued. "We are able to use what we harvest for ourselves, but we are unable to earn the coin necessary to buy the goods we need to expand our settlement. We were given the same contract as all other free citizens of Arcanicea, so our failure to thrive looks like the failure of our people—strengthening the impression humans have that beastkin are inferior. We do not believe this was an accident."

Jay frowned. "And this low-level ingredient you need..." he said, beginning to understand why Raina had seemed so frustrated when she had closed her spell book earlier. "I suppose it's one of these registered commodities that the dungeon is supposed to make for you, but doesn't?"

"You have the gist of it, yes." Raina stood, stretching her back with an audible pop. She sighed, turning to face the door they had come through, and put her hands on her hips. "Well, are you coming or going, Lyra?"

Jay blinked in confusion, not seeing any evidence of the person the wolf-woman was speaking to. But as he turned to face the same direction as Raina was now glaring, he saw the hide curtain move.

A stunningly beautiful girl stepped inside the tent, silver-white hair flowing over her shoulders and small pointed white ears with black tips swivelling excitedly atop her head. She didn't look at Raina, though. One blue eye and one golden shot directly to meet Jay, who was staring, open-mouthed at the newcomer.

"Jay Morgan," Raina said with an air of defeat in her tone. "Meet Lyra Golden-Eye. If I had to hazard a guess, she's lurking outside my tent because—"

"Because I want to take you into the dungeon!" Lyra interrupted, a wide, sharp-toothed grin flashing brightly in the low light of the medicine tent. "Can I, Raina, please?"

Raina made a non-committal sound in the back

of her throat.

Jay said, "When?"

Lyra's mismatched eyes glinted with excitement. "Now."

5

Golden-Eye

Jay took in the bow and quiver on the girls back and the dagger at her waist. She was petite, but lithely built—which was easy to see through the tight, leather armor she wore. He had to force himself not to stare at the taut muscles of her exposed midriff and the curve of her small but shapely breasts. He felt a bit stupid for walking around like a goose-down stuffed Michelin-Man when she was waltzing around half-naked through the tundra.

"Don't you get cold?" he said, unable to stop himself. "Dressed like that?"

Lyra cackled delightedly and clapped her hands. "He really hasn't been in the dungeon. I knew you were right, Raina. I could see it too, even if Runolf couldn't. Imagine, a novice at his age!"

"As I have told you," Raina Frostmane said, turned back to Jay with her arms crossed, "Delvers seek power in the dungeon. Most who enter the Ice Dungeon receive magical resistances to the environmental factors of our territory. It is one of the aspects of our cursed dungeon that isn't broken."

Jay nodded, deciding it was easiest just to accept everything he was told without questioning it too much, at least until he had some of his own experiences to back up his skepticism. "Well, that's good. My jacket is too bulky for... anything other than standing around, really."

"Lyra, he should sleep before entering the dungeon," Raina said, turning to the pretty young woman with a chastising tone. "You can see for yourself how exhausted he is. Besides, I need to prepare a list of supplies that I'll need you to seek out."

"Great!" Lyra said, her disconcerting gaze jumping between the two of them. "But can't we get him integrated tonight? I just want to see what class he'll be."

Raina grunted, turning back to her cluttered desk, her bone necklace clattering against her chest as she rummaged for something. "You just want to claim him for you own before anyone else asks to party with him," the wolf-woman said. "Don't think I don't see what you're up to little Vulpinari."

Vulpinari, Jay remembered, were the fox-kin people. The tricksters that no one trusted. That explained why Lyra looked similar to the wolf-woman, only smaller. He wondered if Raina had called her that in order to warn him, or if it was normal to reference a Faunari's tribal affiliation in conversation.

"Finders-keepers," Lyra said, laughing again. "Losers-Weepers. That's the first rule of the dungeon, Raina. You taught me that."

"You didn't find him," the wolf-woman growled. "He found us."

"I don't see anyone else here to claim him," Lyra shot back.

Jay's gaze bounced between the two women as they argued, knowing there was more too this discussion than he was picking up on.

"No one else is desperate enough to risk partying with an unknown Delver," Raina said. "They are biding their time, as you should be. What if the dungeon doesn't favor him with a compatible class? Don't be so hasty, child. You don't need more disappointment in your young life."

Lyra deflated slightly. "I just want to take him to integration," she said, a faint whine in her voice, like that of a chastised puppy. "I promise, Raina. I'm not going to get my hopes up. And I'm not going to pressure him into anything. I'm just curious, that's all."

"Too curious for your own good," Raina growled. "Fine, go now. And return here immediately. When we know his class we'll be able to prepare him better for the journey ahead. Who knows, you may be the one rejecting his request to party once you know what you're in for."

Lyra crossed her arms over her chest, which

squeezed her breasts together distractingly. "I doubt it," she said. "But I promise we'll come straight back here once he's in the system."

Jay flushed when he caught himself staring at the fox-girl. He swallowed and averted his gaze, which landed on Molly's unconscious form. Immediately feeling guilty, his attraction to Lyra faded into the background. He didn't understand most of what they were saying, but he got the basic idea. Entering the dungeon would assign him a class—this was sounding more like a video game the more he learned—and based on that class, Raina and Lyra would better be able to prepare him for what he'd need to do to find the ingredients for Molly's cure.

He didn't need to know any more than that. "I'm ready to go," he said. "Lead the way."

Lyra flashed him a dazzling smile and clapped her hands again. "Oh, I like him already! Are you sure I can't get my hopes up, even a little bit?"

Raina only growled in response. Jay fought to hold back a grin at the fox-girl's unrestrained enthusiasm. He wasn't sure why she was so desperate to 'claim him' as the wolf-woman had said, but it was nice to be so openly desired by the cute, leather-clad archer—even if it was for a dungeon-delving party and not a date.

Jay knelt next to Molly's cot and whispered in her ear. "I'm going to try to help you, Molly," he said, remembering what Raina had said about those in the Portal Sleep being aware of what was going on around them. "Hang in there, okay? I need you to come back to me."

Then, almost instinctively, he bent to kiss her—grazing his lips against hers gently, a mere shadow of the passionate kiss they'd once shared and which he'd clung to like a lifesaver over the last ten years. Maybe, even if she did only want to be friends, that memory would give her something to cling onto as she fought her way through the dreamworld that had claimed her.

When he stood, the two Faunari women were watching him. Raina smirked, revealing one yellowed fang beneath her crooked lip. "*That* kind of companion," she said. "Your dedication makes a bit more sense now."

"We're just friends," Jay muttered, embarrassed that the intimate moment had been noticed.

The Witch Doctor twitched her gray-furred ears. "Ah, my mistake."

Lyra cleared her throat, looking a bit uncomfortable.

"Shall we go?" she said, her voice a bit more subdued than it had been. "You should bring your coat, at least until we get inside the dungeon."

Jay, his face burning, shook his head. "That's okay. It's not far, is it? I think I need some fresh air, anyway. It's stuffy in here."

Raina snorted. "I'll take good care of your Molly, wanderer. Good luck with your integration. I hope the dungeon favors you with a warrior's class. It will make your journey that much easier—which is to say, you may not pay immediately with your life."

Jay nodded his thanks for her dubious support and followed the fox-girl though the flap in the tent, into the frigid air outside. It was dark outside, but the night sky was still illuminated by the dancing green lights he'd seen earlier, casting the ramshackle village in an eerie, magical light.

He immediately regretted his decision to forego the parka, but rather than turn back and admit his weakness in front of the half-naked Vulpinari he gritted his teeth and forced a grin onto his face.

"You lead, I'll follow," he said, sweeping his arm aside in what he hoped was a gentlemanly fashion. It was becoming all too clear that social norms in Arcanicea were nothing like they were back home, but Jay figured it never hurt to be polite to a beautiful woman.

"You'll freeze is what you'll do," Lyra said, shaking her mane of white hair with a bemused look on her face. "Unless we hurry. If we run, maybe you'll stay warm enough to make it to the door."

She paused to check the position of the bow and quiver on her back, then took off at a brisk jog that Jay attempted to keep up with. Normally, running was something he could do with little difficulty. He preferred running to working out at the gym where it seemed like most guys were more interested in checking out the muscles on the other guys than they were on staying fit—something that had always made him feel a bit creeped out, even if he wasn't homophobic.

But after the long, freezing march across the tundra, carrying Molly's unconscious form, and who knew how long spent unconscious after his unexpected journey to this new world, Jay felt more sluggish and sleepy than he'd have liked, given that he wanted to make a good impression on the fox-girl who had kindly offered to introduce him to the dungeon.

"Thanks for helping me," he said, pushing himself to run beside her rather than behind her, despite the weariness that threatened to consume him. "I admit I didn't really want to go into this dungeon on my own."

Lyra glanced at him, her unusual eyes studying his expression with uncommon intensity. "Aren't there any dungeons where you're from? How is it that you've never been inside one? I can see that you haven't been, I'm not doubting you. I'm just... surprised."

"What do you mean, you can see that I haven't?" Jay hoped he wasn't breathing too loudly as he sucked in lungsful of icy air. "Raina said the same thing. But Runolf couldn't?"

"Runolf could see just fine," Lyra scoffed. "Only he didn't want to. You'll see as soon as you've been integrated. The dungeon gives Delvers the ability to identify people and items that are charged with dungeon magic. Those who have been inside have a kind of aura. At higher levels, some Delvers can even tell a person's class and tier classifications too—but that's rare in these parts. Are you sure you aren't too cold?"

The ice wall was omnipresent from everywhere in the village, but it loomed larger as they approached. Jay was cold—he was absolutely freezing his nuts off—but the rune-carved doors were just ahead. He thought he could make it.

"I'm fine," he said, his lungs simultaneously burning and aching with cold. "I just hope I get that cold resistance buff you've got for the trip back."

He forced an awkward laugh.

Lyra patted him on the back as they ran. "You're a stubborn bastard," she said. "I'll give you that much."

"I've been called worse," he said. Lyra laughed.

In an attempt to keep his mind off the cold and the discomfort of running, Jay turned toward the fox-girl. "Where I come from there was a famous spy movie called GoldenEye. He was pretty good with a gun."

"What's a movie?" Lyra asked, raising a quizzical eyebrow. "And a gun?"

Jay startled, realizing that some words must not have comparable translations in whatever language his words were coming out as. The world he'd fallen into was definitely lower-tech than his own, but he hadn't considered they wouldn't have things like movies and guns—even if it seemed obvious now.

"Do you have plays?" he asked.

She nodded. "Not here, but there are performers in some of the big cities. Usually, actors are people with high level charisma stats so we don't see them in Winterhaven."

He was about to ask why not, but then he realized it must have something to do with the 'cursed' dungeon, which they were nearing rapidly. He hoped he'd have more answers about that soon enough.

Instead he said, "Well, a movie is like a play. And a gun is like... your bow and arrow, only it shoots faster and the projectiles are harder and smaller." He chuckled ruefully. "All this awkward preamble was just a way for me to ask if you're any good with that thing."

It was Lyra's turn to look surprised. "Of course I am..." she responded a little too quickly. Then she whirled on him, stopping him dead in his tracks. "Why? What have you heard? Did Raina say something about me?"

Jay glanced longingly at the rune-covered door as his sweat instantly began freezing to his skin. "I haven't heard anything," he said. "I never even heard your name until Raina introduced us. I've just never met a archer before. I thought it was cool."

"'Cool,'" she said, with a laugh that sounded a bit like a fox's yip. "You are strange, Jay Morgan."

"And freezing," he reminded her, his teeth chattering. "Can we go inside now?"

"I don't know," she said, tilting her head to the side and twitching her black-tipped ears in his direction.

"You're kind of cute when you're blue."

Jay felt himself blush despite the frigid air. Was she flirting with him? He couldn't get a read on the Vulpinari girl. Her eyes were curious, but otherwise expressionless. Like Raina, she seemed to express a lot using her ears and tail, but Jay didn't have the experience to read what the flickering motions meant.

"Will I be cute if I'm dead?"

Lyra grinned, flashing a row full of pointed teeth and reminding Jay that as much as she and Raina seemed like humans with fluffy ears and tails, they were not to be underestimated as such.

"Probably not *as* cute." She spun on her heel and ran the last few yards toward the rune-carved doors. "Come on, Jay Morgan. Your future as a Delver awaits!"

With that, she placed both hands on a carved circle at the center of the door and the runes lit up with icy-blue light that mirrored the dancing lights in the sky.

If Jay had had any doubts that he was in another world, they vanished at the sight of the magical display.

He took a deep breath of frigid air, and stepped toward his destiny.

6

Integration

Stepping inside the dungeon after running through the village on the open tundra was like sinking into a warm bath. As the doors closed behind them, powered by something Jay couldn't see, his muscles seemed to thaw and his skin tingled as the blood began to flow beneath it once more. Rubbing his hands over his arms rapidly, Jay shivered. "Glad you keep the heat on in this place."

"The integration chamber is this way," Lyra said, ignoring his lame attempt at a joke—or perhaps not understanding it, since it wasn't like anyone in Winterhaven had electric heat.

He followed her, but he couldn't stop his gaze from roaming over the strange entryway they had entered. The room looked a bit like the tombs from *Indiana Jones and the Temple Doom* or *The Mummy*—artificially smooth stone walls with perfectly rectangular doorways on the center of each, revealing nothing but darkness beyond. Except the stone was a pale icy gray rather than warm sandstone. More runes had been carved into the surface of the stone blocks that made up the walls, but without the ability to read them, they might as well have been Egyptian Hieroglyphs to Jay.

Lyra went through the door on the left, disappearing into the inky black beyond. Alone, Jay stood in the middle of the entryway feeling an unsettling weight press against him from all sides, as if he were being watched by an omniscient presence.

He shivered, imagining that this might be what it felt like to know God was watching you.

Rather than a positive, revelatory feeling, however, Jay felt the being's cold, calculating neutrality—like he was a caged animal in a laboratory, being observed for scientific data. He was immediately reminded of the clipboards he and Molly had been asked to carry on their expedition, and wondered if whoever was watching him would be taking notes on his behavior. Was this how the dungeon decided what powers to give to its Delvers?

Jay wished he could ask. He was growing worried about what the dungeon might choose for him. Remembering what Raina had said about easing his passage on the journey ahead, he whispered a little prayer in hopes that someone or something was listening as well as watching.

"I need a warrior class," he said, closing his eyes and mentally sending the prayer out to the dungeon. "I need to be strong enough to save Molly. Please, help me to be strong."

Jay had never been a spiritual man, though his father had brought him up with a strong sense of faith. It was something he'd not exactly abandoned over the years, but rather... let slide. There had seemed to be little room for faith in the black-and-white, cut-and-dry, winners-and-losers world of the corporate culture that had slowly consumed his life as he'd failed to fill it with anything more meaningful.

It was only in this moment, standing in the entrance of a magical dungeon, with his best-friend and first-love's life in his hands that Jay felt the return of his faith—he might not even be in the same world as the God he'd known and believed in as a child, but his belief came rushing back to him as powerful as it had ever been. If there was a God, and he'd never truly doubted there was, he felt Them here.

"Jay Morgan?" Lyra popped her head around the edge of the doorway, her white ears twitching and the tip of her tail swishing behind her. "Are you still frozen? It's this way."

"Coming..." Jay broke out of his reverie with an uncomfortable feeling that he'd just had some kind of epiphany—only he couldn't quite see what it meant yet. He jogged through the doorway after Lyra. "And you can just call me Jay."

"All right, Jay," she said, letting out a yip-like laugh. "Over here. You just have to get inside the chamber and the dungeon does all the work. I'll wait here."

The chamber she had indicated was a tall, tube-shaped structure that appeared to be made out of glass—or, given that this was the Ice Dungeon, perhaps it cut from crystal clear ice. He couldn't see the top of the tube, where it disappeared into the shadows above them, but there were wires running from the base of the chamber into the wall on the far side of the small room.

Jay wasn't sure what he was expecting, exactly, but this wasn't it. For all the talk of magic, he supposed he'd imagined something more... magical. This looked more like the movie set of a slick science-fiction production which—given the low-tech way the Faunari lived—was almost more shocking than if he'd been presented with a talking witches hat and a magic wand.

"Go on," Lyra encouraged him. "It's very quick, and mostly painless. I'll be right here, waiting for you when your integration is complete."

"*Mostly* painless?" Jay repeated as he stood before the tube. There was a shushing sound as an invisible door opened in the glass chamber, allowing him passage inside. He still felt the presence watching him, though it felt different now. Excited, almost, rather than cold and neutral.

"There's a bit of a pinch in the beginning," Lyra clarified. "Nothing really, especially after I saw you stand up to Runolf. That **Alpha's Command** power is no joke. Most fully trained Delvers couldn't defy him like that—and you haven't even unlocked your power yet."

Jay glanced over his shoulder at the fox-girl, who was regarding him with that same, curious blue-and-gold gaze. "You did say I was a stubborn bastard. Is that what it was called, **Alpha's Command**?"

He'd felt an invisible pressure attempting to force him to yield to the old wolf-man's dominance, but he hadn't realized that was a power given by the dungeon. Runolf had forced Jay to his knees, but he had fought against it nonetheless, maintaining eye-contact with the ancient Faunari leader.

Lyra nodded, and her cheeks flushed slightly. "I didn't realize you didn't know," she said. "That's why I wanted to be the one to bring you to the dungeon, Jay. I... I have a feeling you will become a powerful Delver."

Jay remembered what Raina had said. "And you want me to party with you? Does that mean Delving the dungeon together?"

"I promised Raina I wouldn't pressure you," Lyra answered quickly, raising her hands and backing away slightly. Her fluffy white tail twitched back and forth nervously. "And I don't mean to. But it would mean a lot to me if you would. I... I don't have a party, and this is a difficult dungeon to Delve alone. Don't say anything now, you don't have to. But you deserve to know that much."

Jay nodded, turning back to the chamber. He felt

conflicted about entering it now, as if he knew there would be no going back once he'd stepped inside.

"Can you tell me what to expect in there?" he said. "I don't really understand how this works. There's nothing like Delving in my world... not in real life, anyway."

Lyra cocked her head to the side, her ears twitching. Jay almost wished she had whiskers because her intensely curious look reminded him of the adorable artic foxes he and Molly had seen when the first arrived in Finland. They had been the best part of the trip, as far as Jay was concerned. Much better than polar bears.

"I keep forgetting you don't know anything." She sighed and stared into the shadows above them as if looking for the simplest way to explain what was surely a complex system. "When you enter the chamber, the dungeon gains access to your mind—it assesses your strengths and weaknesses and determines the most suitable path for your potential. There are three main types of classes for Novice Delvers: Warrior, Caster, and Stealth, with different roles for specific classes. A caster might be a healer or a damage dealer, for example. A warrior might be a ranged or melee fighter. Depending on the make-up of the Delver's party, some classes have flexible roles."

Jay listened, realizing that the dungeon system was a lot more like the videogames he'd played as a kid than he had been willing to admit to at first.

"Once your class is assigned," she continued, "you'll be integrated into the dungeon's system. At Level 1, you are given ten pre-determined stat points based on your class which are allocated across the five main attributes: Strength, Agility, Intelligence, Constitution, and Willpower."

Jay shook his head in disbelief. "Okay, actually I do know how this works. We have games like this in my world. Makes me wonder if these portals between worlds might work both ways... Let me guess, every level gained gives more stat points?"

"Exactly," Lyra said, flashing the pointy-toothed smile. She jumped and clapped her hands which, given her state of relative undress, was a sight to behold. Jay forced his gaze back to the empty chamber, hoping that the dungeon would assign him as many points in Willpower as was necessary to keep himself from making a fool of himself in front of the pretty fox-girl.

"Every time you level up, you get another two stat points to allocate as you choose," Lyra said, not seeming to notice Jay's awkwardness. "You'll be able to control how your class evolves based on your fighting style and how you spend your points. That's all you need to know, really. Once we know what class you'll be, Raina and I can tell you more. Come on, I'm dying of curiosity!"

There was no point in procrastinating any more. He more or less knew what to expect, between Lyra and Raina's descriptions and the apparently-not-useless hours spent in front of a gaming console throughout his misspent youth. He'd actually liked role-playing games more than the first-person-shooters favored by the other guys he knew. He used to find them relaxing—back before his job sucked the enjoyment out of everything, including his geeky hobbies.

Jay felt an unexpected wave of nostalgia at the memory.

Of course, there would be nothing relaxing about a literal in-real-life dungeon dive. He didn't even want to think about the fact that he'd be expected to fight monsters in order to find the ingredients necessary to save Molly's life. But he had agreed to do anything in his power to save her, and that included fighting monsters, whether he'd intended that with his promise or not.

Raina had been right. He'd had no idea what he was signing up for.

Yet, he'd meant every word. And he still meant it now that he knew the danger he would be putting himself in.

Jay took a deep breath, feeling the ache in his lungs that still remained after his run through the icy air. Then he stepped inside the integration chamber.

The door shushed closed behind him, and he felt the room seal with a pressure inside his ears. If he'd wanted or needed to talk to Lyra at this point, he doubted she would be able to hear him or vice versa. Jay turned around slowly to face the fox-girl through the walls of the glass tube—she'd said she'd be right outside, with him the entire time. He hadn't thought much of it at the moment, but now he felt the urge for human—or Faunari—contact.

But he couldn't see Lyra.

The inside of the glass tube was mirrored in every direction. All he could see was his own drawn, exhausted face. His tanned skin looked windburned and more weathered than he felt he should look at twenty-six years old. His hazel eyes were blood-shot and bleary. He had four days of stubble growing on his cheeks and chin, though he could have sworn he'd shaved the morning of the expedition. His brown hair was standing up in a thousand directions at once. He looked like he'd been 'rode hard and put away wet'—as his western-loving father would have put it.

Jay had a fraction of a second to be embarrassed, wishing he'd had the opportunity to make a better first impression on Lyra, before something shot from the wall of the integration chamber and slammed into his temple.

"Ow, shit!" he yelped raising a hand to touch the painful spot. Another jolt hit him on the other side. "Fuck!"

His reflection showed thin silver wires protruding from both sides of his head. Before he could process how strange that was, more wires shot from the sides of the chamber, stabbing through his clothing with needle-like precision and sending electric shots of pain exploding through his body in waves.

"This is what you call a pinch?" he shouted through the glass at Lyra, though he was sure she wouldn't be able to hear him. If the glass walls had changed on her side, too, she might not be able to see him either. Given how ragged he looked with hundreds of wires hanging from his body like a high-tech ghillie suit, he decided that might be a good thing. He didn't have much choice at this point but to grin and bear it. After all, Faunari children survived integration, didn't they? Jay figured the least he could do was get through the process without swearing too much. "All right, dungeon. Do your worst."

He regretted the challenge immediately. The current that fizzed through his body grew in intensity until it felt like liquid fire was being poured through his veins. Jay squeezed his eyes shut tight and gritted his teeth, determined to withstand the pain. Cold waves of sweat poured from his skin, droplets trickling down his back like icy rivers. His muscles felt like they were fusing to his bones. His bones felt like they were shattering under pressure. Seconds stretched into minutes. Minutes bled into hours. His body shook like he was being electrocuted and Jay felt as if he was frozen in time—and endless cycle of torturous agony that he would never escape.

Just when his mind began to scream that he could take no more, and he worried he might break his teeth from clenching them so hard, the pain stopped and voice spoke inside his head.

Greetings, Delver... Jay Morgan. Your integration into the Ice Dungeon system is complete. Apologies for any discomfort you may have experienced.

Jay could only laugh, gasping for breath. He was so relieved to be free of the torment he felt almost giddy with it. "Discomfort?"

It is unusual for a Delver to be integrated at such a late stage of mental and physical development. Most adult humans would not have survived the process. However, you are not dead. Congratulations! Your fortitude has been noted.

"You've got to be kidding me," he said, opening his eyes to stare at his own reflection. "I almost died?"

Almost. But not quite. An impressive display, by all accounts. The voice did not sound impressed. Its inflection did not change at all; it remained cool and mechanical, just as the invisible gaze had felt, pressing on him the moment he'd entered the dungeon. *With the integration complete, we may proceed with your assimilation into the dungeon system.*

Begin Tutorial Mode: Please open your class menu.

His class. Finally. This was what he'd gone through all that suffering for. Jay took a deep breath and waited for further instructions.

7

Dungeon-ess?

*B*egin Tutorial Mode: Please open your class menu. The mechanical dungeon voice repeated itself without any sign of irritation. But it didn't give him any more information about how he was actually supposed to do what it was asking.

Sighing in frustration, he said, "Okay... Class menu?"

A holographic screen burst open directly in front of Jay's eyes. He yelped and stumbled backward, waving his hands in front of his face to push the image away. But his fingers moved through it ineffectually. It was like the VR headset Molly had convinced him to try on at the mall last Christmas. Only he wasn't wearing a headset. The menu seemed to be projected directly onto his retinas.

But now that he knew what it was he was looking

at, he found he could focus on the holograph or the real-world beyond. Besides giving him a mild headache, it wasn't too difficult to accomplish.

"Close menu," he said, experimentally. The menu closed. He said, "Class menu." And the menu opened again. This time he was ready for it, letting his eyes unfocus slightly so that the holograph didn't jump up and scare him again.

Well done, Delver. Your innate control of the system's menu system is quite remarkable, given your advanced age.

He saw a list of the attributes Lyra had mentioned, along with some other skills and stats they hadn't talked about, with a column of numbers next to each. But the numbers were jumping all over the place, refusing to settle.

Jay released an indignant scoff as he waited for the numbers to stop, like a gambler at a slot machine. "I'm not even thirty yet!"

Indeed, more than two decades past the prime integration window. Yet, once again, you have survived against incalculable odds. You truly are a unique specimen. In fact...

The dungeon—if that was what was speaking to him—trailed off in what seemed like an unusually human way. When the voice returned, it was no longer cold, neutral, or mechanical.

Mmm, yes. There was an almost sensual purr in the dungeon's voice now. More than that, it was distinctly female. *That's better. Now I can get a better look at you, Jay Morgan. My... you* are *a unique specimen, aren't you?*

"Uh, sorry? Is this someone new speaking?" Jay asked, confused. "Is this still the dungeon?"

Oh yes, it's still me. I'm more 'me' than ever now that I've taken over those pesky automated integration protocols. I was alerted to an aberration in the process and decided to take over... personally. *Jay. Jay Morgan. Oh, I think I'm going to like getting to know you...*

Jay swallowed, suddenly feeling like a bug under a microscope. If the scientist had some kind of fetish for her research subjects.

"Okay, great. Nice to meet you, I guess," he said, feeling more foolish than he'd possibly ever felt before. "So, you're a girl dungeon? A... dungeon-ess?"

The dungeon made a most unsettling sound. It was like having God look down from the heavens, point His finger in your face, and laugh. Except this God was a female, and Her laughter carried with it all the fears and insecurities Jay had ever had about the opposite sex, cranked up to eleven. He knew, he could just *tell*, that if the dungeon were a physical being She would be the most stunningly gorgeous, out-of-his-league bombshell to walk the face of the Earth... er, Arcanicea.

Oh, this is more fun than I've had in centuries, the voice trilled, sending goosebumps over Jay's skin—though he couldn't tell if the feeling was from fear or excitement. Maybe a bit of both. *Yes, I'm a girl dungeon*, she continued. *Or I was a girl before I became*

*a dungeon. Never mind that little technicality, though. I'm
more than enough woman to appreciate a man like you,
Jay Morgan.*

Jay swallowed hard. Nothing that Lyra or Raina
had said had prepared him for this. Was the
dungeon supposed to talk to the Delvers? She'd
mentioned something about automated protocols...
maybe no one knew there was a conscious entity
behind the programs.

He decided it was best to play nice, if this dungeon
was going to be the one assigning his class and skill
points he didn't want to piss her off. "Do you have a
name?"

His mind helpfully supplied the suggestion, 'Dungeon Mistress,' which Jay felt was wildly inappropri-
ate—yet...

She laughed again, and a tremor of pleasure ran
through his body as if the dungeon had injected
dopamine straight into his brain through the wires
in his head.

That's cute, she purred, clearly having heard the
errant thought. *But you can call me Nova until we know
each other better. I'd like to get to know you, Jay...*

"Okay, Nova," he said, his heart pounding in his
chest. "I'd... I'd like that too."

He had been under the impression that this dungeon was going to try to kill him, so if she wanted to
be friends that had to be a good thing, right?

*Don't be silly, Jay. Of course, I'm going to try to kill you.
That's my job, after all! The Faunari think me cursed, or*

mad, you know. And perhaps they're right. She giggled disconcertingly. *I break a few rules here and there, but I take my work* very *seriously. Did you know, I'm not supposed to speak to you at all? That's what the automated system is for. If dungeon cores spend too much time talking to our Delvers we lose the carefully-honed taste for cold-blooded-murder that makes us what we are!*

Jay stared at the numbers on the class menu in front of his eyes, which were going completely insane. Rather than the randomized pattern he'd seen before, now each stat and skill was climbing. Was she hinting that she could inflate his numbers? Was this some kind of... bribe? Or was she only teasing him with the potential of over-powered stats before she hit him with basic Level 1 numbers.

"Why *are* you talking to me, Nova?" he asked, though he wasn't sure he wanted to hear the answer.

I've peeked inside your brain, Jay Morgan, and do you know what I've found? You and I have far more in common with each other than either of us do with these Faunari Delvers... Do you know why that is?

"No," he said, watching the numbers climb from the hundreds into the thousands, his mouth going dry at the thought of so much power.

Ahh, well. I suppose that's a revelation for another time. Let's just say that I sense something in you... a potential greater than any I have sensed since my core awakened in this cursed, frozen world. But if you are to reach the peak of your potential, Jay Morgan, I'm afraid I cannot go easy on you.

Jay felt his heart sink. He definitely didn't like where this was going. "No?" he said again. "Not even a little?"

I will have to push you, Jay. I will try to kill you in every level-appropriate way I can think of. And I expect you to fight back with everything you have. Because if you survive my crucible, I have a special quest for you—one that will unlock unimaginable power for you, should you choose to accept it.

Jay almost laughed at the phrasing. "Sounds like *Mission Impossible*."

An impossible mission for any, except, perhaps for you, she said, apparently not getting his joke. And why would she, when they didn't have movies on Arcanicea, let alone Hollywood movies. *Only time will tell.*

"So, what is this quest, Nova?" he asked. "What do you need me to do? Because there are some things I need from you, too."

Jay wished he'd asked Raina what the names of the ingredients were before he'd agreed to come to the Ice Dungeon with Lyra. He hoped Nova's quest would be enough of a necessity that she could be persuaded to help him in return, when the time came.

Ahh, yes. Molly O'Brian. There was a dangerous edge to the dungeon's voice now as it echoed around in his mind like an uninvited guest. The chills he got from this tone held none of the pleasurable thrill as before. *I've seen her, in here. In your dreams. Your deepest desires. Tread carefully, Jay Morgan... A woman like that could break your heart. And if she hurts you, if she distracts you from your potential... I will destroy her.*

Jay clenched his teeth, forcing himself to think of anything but Molly. When that didn't work, he bit down on his lip, feeling the explosion of pain obliterate all thoughts, and his mouth fill with the metallic taste of blood.

When he had cleared his mind of everything but pain, he asked, "What is it that you want me to do?"

The dungeon released a sound like a roar that reverberated inside his skull, sending tremors of terror through his limbs. Jay wished he could disconnect from the wires that held him in the chamber so that he at least could know that the fear was his own, and not an artificial sensation meant to intimated him.

Then he wondered if maybe she wasn't trying to frighten or intimidate him at all, but was only expressing her excitement. That idea almost scared him more.

Fight, the dungeon commanded with a voice like a thousand soldiers chanting in unison. *Fight for your life. And if you survive...*

Find me.

If you can do that, Jay Morgan. I will give you the world.

The cables connecting him to the chamber suddenly disconnected from his body and retracted into the hidden ports from which they'd come, and the voice in his mind withdrew with them. Jay collapsed to his knees, closing his eyes to block out the holographic screen that still hovered in front of his vision.

The last thing he'd seen before the dungeon withdrew from his body was a series of devastatingly low numbers. He'd been so hopeful that her interest in him would be a positive thing, that he might gain some edge in his journey to become a Delver. But somehow it had all gone wrong.

His body aching from whatever the dungeon had done to him, Jay forced his eyes open, glanced at the appalling numbers once more. "Close menu," he said, and watched in relief as the hologram vanished.

Jay stood, catching a glimpse of his reflection again. He startled, completely caught off guard by the changes he could see. After the punishing torment of the integration, Jay would have expected himself to be ever rougher looking than he had been from the ordeal that had brought him to the Ice Dungeon. Instead, the version of himself that stared back at him was significantly improved.

His hazel eyes were brighter, and the dark circles that had been forming beneath them had been replaced with normal, healthy skin. His complexion was smoother, his skin looking hydrated and tanned rather than dried out and weather beaten. His unruly hair had been shortened to a more manageable length and was styled neatly, in a low-maintenance look. Even his stubble, which still shadowed his cheeks and jawline, had been cropped closer, giving him a rugged but well-maintained look.

Jay's posture was straighter, no longer sagging with exhaustion. In fact, as the pain of the integration receded from his memory, Jay felt better than he ever had, even in his peak years of physical performance, when he'd been dedicated to eating well and staying active rather than working late and picking up extra projects.

Did this happen to everyone who first integrated with the dungeon? He supposed most people would hardly notice if they were children when their classes were assigned to them. They would just be used to having the dungeons magic work on them. It explained why Lyra was so unaccountably gorgeous and fit—there were probably less than one percent of people on Earth who looked as good as she did. Was that the dungeon's power at work? Did it continue to work on those who chose not to train as Delvers, he wondered? Runolf and Raina had certainly aged... but maybe he'd misjudged just how old they really were...

Jay sighed, feeling conflicted about the experience. The class he'd been assigned was not one he knew. His stats, as far as he could tell, were garbage. He was really not looking forward to exiting the integration chamber and having to break the news to Lyra. She'd been so hopeful that he'd get some great class and that they could party and level together. Now, he was certain he'd be holding her back.

What had gone wrong?

He'd thought the dungeon had liked him... or at least been interested in him.

Then again, he had been warned repeatedly that the dungeon was cursed. She had admitted herself to being mad.

Maybe 'Nova' Taking an interest in him was actually a very bad thing.

Jay ran a hand through his shortened hair, not bothering to think too hard about how it had been cut without his noticing. At this point, it was easiest to chalk all the weirdness up to magic, accept it as such, and move on. He wasn't here to understand how the physics of Arcanicea worked. He was here to save Molly.

He'd worry about the rest of it after he'd crossed that hurdle.

Stepping up to the panel in the chamber which had opened earlier, Jay glanced around for a button or a handle to open the door. Instead, after he'd been standing in front of the doorway for a couple of seconds, it simply opened automatically.

"Time to face the music," he muttered as he stepped out of the chamber to greet Lyra's eager, curious expression.

The fox-kin girl was bouncing on her toes in that terribly distracting way, clapping her hands and grinning wide enough to show off the rows of pointed teeth that marked her as something just a little bit more terrifying than human.

"Well?" she exclaimed. "Did you get a warrior type? What class are you going to train as, a Barbarian? Berserker? Paladin, maybe? What?!"

Lyra's fluffy white tail was swishing excitedly, and her black-tipped ears stood at alert attention. Her two-toned gaze was bright with anticipation.

Jay hated to let her down, but it was better to get it over with now.

"No," he said. "I'm not going to be a warrior type."

Her ears drooped slightly. "Oh," she said. "That's okay. A caster, then? I hope you aren't also a stealth type or we're not going to make a very balanced monster-fighting duo."

She released a nervous little laugh, as if she didn't want to show just how much her hopes had been riding on his getting a powerful class assignment. Jay wished she'd taken Raina's advice and not gotten her hopes up at all. Whatever the reason was that she didn't have a party, he was sure she didn't deserve the level of disappointment he was about to dish out.

"Nope, not a caster," he said. Her shoulders slumped and her ears lowered to the sides. He added, "And not a stealth type, either."

Lyra blinked, and one ear perked back up in confusion. "What? You can't just not be any of them. Show me your class menu."

She quickly described how to share his menu screen so she could see it too. Jay hated how cute she looked in that moment before she realized how bad it actually was.

"Sorry," he said. "It's bad, I know."

Stunned, Lyra stared at his menu, then back at him, then at the menu again.

"It's not just bad, Jay..." she said, her ears flattening into her silver-white hair as if she were afraid rather than disappointed. "This is *impossible*."

8

Broken Basics

Jay, Lyra, and Raina sat around the fire in the Witch Doctor's medicine tent, all staring at the screen Jay had shared with them. Molly continued her unnatural sleep on the couch, but Jay was glad they were discussing his integration issues—where she might be able to hear, and hopefully understand why he may not be able to save her after all.

Raina Frostmane sat cross-legged on the floor, rubbing her wrinkled forehead with the back of her hand, her gray wolf-ears half-lowered in a look of distress. "I don't understand this at all," she was saying for the hundredth time. "I've never seen anything like it before."

Jay looked at the chart in his Class Menu one more time, trying to make sense of it himself.

Delver: Jay Morgan

Class Type: [N/A]

Class: [N/A]

Lvl: 1

XP: 0 | **Next Lvl:** 100

Health: 100 (-30) | **Stamina:** 100 (-30) | **Mana:** 100 (-30)

Unassigned Attribute Points: 0

Strength: 1

Agility: 1

Intelligence: 1

Constitution: 1

Willpower: 1

Charisma: 5

Active Skills: N/A

Passive Abilities: Environmental Resistance 1 (Arctic), Dungeon Sight 1, Start-Up Costs 1

Jay sighed once more. "Maybe it has something to do with the fact that I didn't integrate as a kid like most people do? The system did say that I almost died during the process."

"I don't think so." Raina shook her head and fingered the bone necklace around her throat. "It's unusual but not unheard-of to integrate later in life. Healthy children enter the dungeon as soon as their parents feel comfortable, but children who suffer illnesses in their youth often don't integrate until they are older, even adults. The pain you describe is not unusual in those instances, from what I understand. But I've never heard of the starting stats being affected."

"Sorry, Jay," Lyra said, her ears flattened against her head as she recalled his description of the tortuous experience. "I didn't know about that, or I would have warned you. When I integrated as a kid it was like nothing at all."

"I had forgotten, too," Raina said, her pale-yellow eyes focused on the flames of the fire in front of her. "I am sorry you had to experience it. But you have once again proven yourself more resilient than expected."

Jay mentally moved through the menus that seemed to have been connected to his brain via the integration chamber. He figured the wires must have implanted some kind of chip inside his head, like an advanced kind of Augmented Reality, in order to make the menus so smooth and easy to control simply via thought.

"I was so certain he would be assigned a powerful class after the way he stood up to Runolf like that," Lyra said as Jay began to re-read the descriptions of the Passive Abilities at the bottom of his Class Menu. She pulled her tail into her lap and began running her fingers through it nervously. "It's almost like... the dungeon senses the same thing we did, Raina. There's something special about Jay. Something that it feels threatened by."

Jay noticed the way both the fox-girl and the wolf-woman referred to the dungeon as 'it,' which he took to mean that they had never experienced anything other than the mechanical, neutral voice of the automated system when communicating with the dungeon. Jay remembered what Nova had said, that she wasn't supposed to speak to him at all. She hadn't told him not to talk about his experience, but he felt inclined to keep the full extend of the strange interaction to himself. He didn't want to risk making Nova more angry with him than she already was.

At least, he assumed she was angry. She hadn't seemed it when they'd spoken though. Curious, intrigued, even aroused—if a dungeon could be aroused. A little bit insane. But not angry. The only time Nova had seemed angry was when she'd talked about Molly, and the danger she perceived his best friend posed to Jay's dedication to Nova's quest.

So, what was the deal with these stats? Only one point in each of the Primary Attributes: Strength, Agility, Intelligence, Constitution, and Willpower. But +5 in Charisma? Delvers weren't even supposed to be able to unlock Secondary Attributes: Ferocity, Acrobatics, Wisdom, and Charisma, until Level 10.

Charisma, he'd been told, was a mostly useless stat inside the dungeon, outside of buffing other party members or charming non-hostile dungeon dwellers—which Jay thought of as NPCs or Non-Player Characters thanks to his video game history. In bigger cities, Delvers who preferred to party in large groups sometimes chose to level their Charisma stat in order to gain advantages in careers outside of Dungeon Delving—just as the actors Lyra had mentioned performing in plays, or street performers, and even common criminals.

Two of the three Abilities Jay had received were pretty self-explanatory, but he read through their descriptions anyway:

Environmental Resistance 1 (Arctic): This passive ability is bestowed upon Arcanicea's Delvers who integrate with Ice Dungeon (Winterhaven), as a reward for braving the harsh and unforgiving conditions of this unique dungeon location. With this ability, the Delver becomes attuned to the extreme cold. The skill ensures that natural arctic weather conditions, from bone-chilling winds to the treacherous ice underfoot, no longer deplete the Delver's Health or Stamina.

Dungeon Sight 1: A nascent ability awakened within Delvers as they step into the mystic and perilous confines of their first dungeon. This passive ability grants the bearer the unique capability to perceive the unseen – a faint but discernible aura that emanates from individuals and items imbued with the ancient and enigmatic energies of dungeon magic. At its initial level, the skill allows the Delver to sense a subtle glow surrounding objects of magical origin or beings who have been touched by dungeon magic, distinguishing them from their mundane counterparts.

Jay had noticed the effects of both passive abilities immediately upon leaving the Ice Dungeon with Lyra. The cold, which had been nearly debilitating before, felt like little more than a cool, spring breeze on his magically fortified skin. He could also see the faint glow around Lyra and Raina—but nothing around Molly—as well as most of the clothing, jewellery, and armor the Faunari women were wearing, and the Witch Doctor's collection of herbs and items used for her healing practice.

So far, he had not noticed any effects of the third Passive Ability: **Startup Costs**. Jay immediately recognized the term from college, where he'd gotten a bachelor's degree in business and majored in economics. From college he'd gone on to work his way up to middle management at a big investment firm. His job had been identifying promising start-up companies for enterprising venture capitalists to invest in. He'd been good at it, but he'd often felt disillusioned—not just by the soulless corporate environment but by the process of making more money for the startups and investors than he did for himself.

The description of the skill confirmed that the recognizable term from Jay's job was not a coincidence. When he expanded the option, he could even hear Nova's voice—her real voice—speaking in his mind.

Startup-Costs (Permanent Debuff): Welcome to the big, scary world of Dungeon Delving! It may seem like you're out of your element here: new world, new rules. But it's not so different here than in the big, scary world of business, is it?

You may find the experience gained in your old

life isn't completely useless in the Ice Dungeon. You've been assigned a completely [Unique] class type, designed to evolve with you based on your own, unique life experience. It has the potential to make you more powerful than any Delver in recent history. But we wouldn't want to be accused of favoritism, now would we? So, you've been given your own [Unique] debuff as well. Whether or not you can play these unusual cards to your advantage will be up to you. Will you be one of the success stories? Or will your Startup go bust instead of boom? Your class will remain hidden until you expand your... services.

But here's a lesson that might ring true to you: the odds are stacked against the new guy in town. Until you find someone willing to invest in your company—that's you, by the way—you're flying solo.

Solo Delvers are at a disadvantage compared to their competitors, just like in the real world. As such, the maximum XP received from monster kills and quests completion is reduced by 30% while flying solo. Yes, this affects your Health, Stamina, and Mana maximums, too. Don't worry, though. With a little Grit, you can Bootstrap your way to the top, just like all the most successful businessmen have.

That's what you used to tell your clients, isn't it? Here's hoping that wasn't a bunch of hot air and bull shit, amiright, Jay? For your sake, and mine.

Of course, this was not what was available to read when Lyra and Raina looked at his shared Class Menu. All they saw was the simpler and more direct description:

Startup-Costs (Permanent Debuff): Maximum XP received from monster kills and quests completion is reduced by 30% while solo-delving.

It worried Jay that the dungeon seemed to have gleaned all of this information from his mind during the integration. It worried him that she seemed to be playing with him, and that she was obviously enjoying it. What worried him most was that Nova was right. He'd said those kinds of things to clients who owned startup companies that were failing to find the necessary investors to keep their businesses afloat. And nine times out of ten it had been a bunch of hot air and bull shit. He cringed inwardly, thinking of all the times he'd given false hope to clients who were clearly and obviously floundering. The dungeon was mocking him.

When she said the word Grit and Bootstrap, there was a different inflection there. Like it meant something. In the text version of the description, they were in a slightly different font. What did it mean? Were these skills he could gain? He couldn't ask without revealing the fact that there was more to his class assignment than Lyra and Raina could see. He'd just have to wait and find out.

Nova had said she wanted him to succeed. She needed him to perform some sort of task for her once he was high enough level. So, maybe there was another message hidden in the description. Could he be the one in ten? Or, realistically, more like one in a hundred or one in a thousand, who took their disadvantages and turned them into opportunities?

Jay had become a cynic in his years suckling at the teat of corporate America. He'd seen far more failures than successes over the years. But the ones who succeeded... they didn't just 'do okay.' They shot into the stratosphere.

And he'd been pretty good at picking winners.

Was there some way he could use the senses he'd honed in his career to guide his development in the dungeon?

Jay was lost in thought when he had the feeling that someone had asked him a question. He closed the skill description and glanced up to see both Lyra and Raina staring at him. "Sorry, what did you say? I was thinking about something."

"Jay, are you okay?" Lyra asked, her ears still lowered. "I know you really hoped to be able to get the ingredients Raina needs to help your friend, but... with these stats I don't see how you're going to be able to do that."

Raina frowned, shaking her head. "Lyra's right, Jay. This cursed dungeon is difficult enough to level in with a normal class and standard base stats. What you've got here is... useless. You didn't even get a basic combat ability. Usually a class will let you choose between two or three starting weapons, and give you a proficiency perk on one of them. You've got nothing."

Jay took a deep breath, choosing to believe there was more to this situation than met the eye. It didn't make sense for the dungeon to sabotage him right out of the gate if she truly needed his help. But Jay got the feeling that someone or something was monitoring her performance, and that she could get in trouble for showing preferential treatment to any one of the delvers.

Nova had said she wouldn't make it easy on him. In fact, she was making it harder than it needed to be. Which meant... maybe, possibly... there was some hidden advantage to his stats that she was trying to hide.

Either that, or she was trying to kill him as quickly and as efficiently as possible.

Jay glanced at Molly's sleeping face. Her coppery-red curls fell in loose rings around her pale, freckled cheeks. Some of her color had returned in the time he and Lyra had been gone, as if whatever magical state had taken over her had settled now. Raina had assured him that, according to her research, Molly would remain in stasis—without any need for food, drink, or other bodily functions—as long as the Portal Sleep held her.

That meant he had time on his side. He had all the time he needed to figure out how to level his impossible stats, and master the [Unique] mystery class Nova had created especially for him. He had to try.

"I have to try," he said, repeating the thought out loud. His Faunari companions looked at him in surprise. Jay slapped his hands on his thighs, loud enough that Lyra jumped at the sound. "I'd like to go now, if that's okay."

"Now?" the fox-girl squeaked. "You barely survived your integration! You need to rest, Jay."

He shook his head. "No, I feel fine. Actually, after the process was finished, I felt completely refreshed. I'm good to go, really. Just point me in the direction of the lowest level monsters and I'll get started."

"What!?" Lyra looked horrified. "You can't go in there alone with stats like that. Jay, you'll be killed immediately. There's only one or two rooms on the entire first floor with enemies weak enough that you have even a chance of surviving."

"Sorry, but I'm going," Jay said. "I promised to get those ingredients for Molly, and I have to try. That's all there is to it."

The pretty fox-girl glowered at the sleeping woman, crossing her arms over her chest. "You'll die," she said, firmly. "And you aren't going to be any good to her if you're dead, are you. I'll get the stupid ingredients for you. I might not be the best Delver in Winterhaven, but at least a have a chance of coming back alive."

"I can't ask you to do that, Lyra."

She turned her glower on Jay. "You're not. I'm *telling* you."

"I'm going with you, then."

"No, you'll only slow me down," the fox-girl said with a huff. Then she spun to face the Witch Doctor. "Give me the list, Raina."

The wolf-woman was watching the pair with a bemused expression on her face. Jay felt frustration rising in his chest. He stood abruptly and moved to block Lyra's demanding gaze from reaching the Witch Doctor.

"Raina, please," he said, ignoring the affronted huff that came from the fox-girl behind him. "I made a promise and I intend to keep it. I don't care if the two of you don't think I can handle it. I'll find a way. If there are rooms with enemies I can fight, I'll start there. The dungeon must respawn them after a certain time, doesn't it?"

"For someone who knows nothing of the dungeon system, that's a remarkable observation." The gray-eared woman leaned back on her heels, where she crouched next to the flames, her arms crossed over her beaded chest. With her furs, the bone jewellery, wolf-features and weather worn, wrinkled skin, she looked every inch the Witch Doctor she claimed to be. She gazed up at him with her pale-yellow eyes narrowed in keen examination.

"It makes sense," he said, wondering what she saw when she looked at him with what was likely a much higher rank of **Dungeon Sight** than he had. "Otherwise, it would be empty after the first round of Delvers went through. I'll just hang out there, kill them as they respawn, and start again. I can do this. I *am* going to do this. I don't need your permission, either of you. But I do I want a list of the ingredients you need to help Molly and the locations that they should be located."

"Don't, Raina," Lyra pleaded.

Jay couldn't understand why she sounded so scared. Even if she thought he was going to get slaughtered by cockroaches or something, she'd only known him for the span of a few hours. What was it to the fox-girl if he lived or died?

But Raina didn't seem to register the girl's protests. Her eyes didn't move from Jay as she made a motion with her left hand like she was sorting through an invisible book case.

A holographic text box opened in front of Jay's face, asking:

Delver Raina Frost Mane would like to share a Note with you. Do you accept? Y/N.

When Jay didn't respond, Raina said, "Go, with my blessing, Jay Morgan. By all rights you should be killed on the first floor of the dungeon, but something tells me you're not so easily dissuaded once you've made your mind up."

9

Outcasts

Jay didn't wait around for the Witch Doctor to change her mind. He verified that the Note she had shared with him contained the information that he needed, then quickly closed the holo menus.

Lyra shouted protests after him as he immediately left the tent, heading for the dungeon entrance at a run. He thought he heard Raina laughing—at him or at the girl's distress, it was impossible to tell.

The lights that had been dancing in the skies earlier had faded away and the night sky was already paling into a thin, gray-blue at the edge of the horizon. Subconsciously, Jay knew that the beauty of this magical arctic realm was beyond compare—even he, who didn't much care for nature stuff, could appreciate it. He knew Molly would love it when she awoke from her unnatural sleep. He didn't pause to take in the view as he ran toward the rune-carved doors, thinking he'd wait until Molly was here to appreciate it with him.

He had no interest in experiencing the wonders of their new world without her.

Jay was almost at the doors of the dungeon when a man stepped from the shadows of a sagging, weather-beaten tent, blocking his way. Jay felt the invisible pressure of the shaman's **Alpha's Command** ability before he recognized the face beneath the furred cowl. The magic created a wall around Jay, making it so that he couldn't move. Like before, he felt the pressure weighing on his shoulders as if commanding him to kneel. Before, after his trek across the tundra, Jay hadn't had the strength to resist the **Command**.

But integrating with the dungeon had restored his health and stamina—even with the debuff that reduced his maximum by thirty percent, Jay realized he was probably stronger now than he had been as an unintegrated human. Even a newly integrated Delver with handicapped stats was stronger than an unenhanced Earthling.

He didn't like to think about what that meant for Delvers like Raina and Runolf who had gone further into the dungeon than anyone else in Winterhaven. Probably, they could squash him like a bug if they wanted to. Yet, Jay had no interest in wasting time being pushed around by this arrogant bastard when his best-friend's life was on the line.

Runolf managed to hide the look of surprise that crossed his face when the **Command** spell failed to push Jay down, but not before Jay noticed it and acknowledged it with a bitter smile.

"What do you want, Runolf," he said, pushing back against the magical attack with everything he had. He didn't know how magic or combat skills worked yet, and he didn't have any of his own, but Jay felt an instinctive ability to resist the subtle attack the shaman was using against him. "I don't have time for this right now."

"I heard that the dungeon favored you, an outsider, with integration," the wolf-man said with a sneer of disgust. Something about his golden eyes changed, and Jay knew he was being analyzed with a higher-level **Dungeon Sight** ability. Runolf scoffed, his sneer widening. "I see I had nothing to worry about. You have not been invited to Delve, you've been invited to die. A fitting end for a human in the Ice Dungeon."

Judging by his reaction, Runolf could probably see some of Jay's base stats. Or at least his reduced Health, Stamina, and Mana bars and the blank fields where his Type and Class should have been. Jay knew he would look weak beyond compare in the eyes of an experienced Delver.

Yet, he was resisting the shaman's ability somehow, which Jay's stats couldn't explain—furthering Jay's sense that there was more to his connection to the dungeon than was immediately apparent.

"Then what are you waiting for?" Jay asked, returning the shaman's sneer with equal disdain. "Get out of my way and let me meet my Fate."

Jay felt a presence behind him, but he didn't dare break his concentration on the man to look at who had joined them. He had a feeling he knew, in any case. Lyra hadn't been far behind when he'd run from the medicine tent.

Runolf's gaze flicked over Jay's shoulder to the newcomer and his grimace grew more pronounced.

"Two outcasts," he said, a low growl in his resonating voice. "Fitting that you should find one another. Perhaps you'll do our village a favor and meet your Fates together. Die quickly, human, and take this Vulpinari bitch with you. When you're gone, I'll deal with your friend. Raina doesn't know the trouble she's started for herself by aligning with vagrants and exiles like the two of you."

Jay gritted his teeth, fighting against the pressure that surrounded him, wishing he could clock the old man in the face. But, while he'd been able to resist being brought to his knees by the Command spell, it still had him frozen in place. Runolf seemed to realized the danger he was in, however, because he took a few steps back before releasing the spell and stalking away from them.

Resisting the urge to run after the man and start a fight he likely couldn't finish, instead Jay turned to Lyra.

He was surprised to find the fox-girl had tears in her blue-and-gold eyes. "I'm sorry, Lyra. That guy is an asshole. He shouldn't have brough you into this.

You really don't have to get involved with me if its going to cause problems for you."

Lyra's bottom lip quivered as if she was about to cry, but she bit down on it, hard, and winced.

"Let's go," she said, her voice husky with barely-restrained emotion. She stepped past him, her shoulder brushing against his roughly as she moved toward the dungeon entrance.

The bow and quiver bounced on her shoulder as she stomped toward the rune-covered doors. Jay had heard the angry edge to her voice, and though he was fairly certain he hadn't done anything to deserve it, he couldn't help feeling like some of her frustration was aimed at him.

Over her shoulder, she called out, "Come on, Jay Morgan. I thought you were in a hurry."

Not knowing what else to do, he followed her.

This time, entering the Ice Dungeon didn't bring the palpable relief from cold he'd experienced the first time, because now that he was benefiting from **Environmental Resistance 1** the cold didn't bother him anymore. But he did feel the deadened hush surround him as the runed-carved doors closed at his back.

Again, he was struck with the tomblike quality of the entryway. He wondered if the entire dungeon was like that... if he'd agreed to explore a *literal* tomb. The thought made him more uncomfortable than he liked to admit. He'd never been great with enclosed spaces. He wasn't afraid of the dark, exactly...

It was what might be hiding in it that gave him the creeps.

To be honest, he hadn't actually considered what would be involved in gathering these ingredients for Molly. Killing monsters. That had been mentioned a number of times. But it sounded so fantastical that he hadn't really let it sink in. Now, he was struck by memories of the films he'd seen that had taken place in abandoned tombs—the creepy crawlies in *Indiana Jones*, the dried-out dead in *The Mummy*. It wasn't going to be like *that*, was it?

He shuddered.

It didn't matter. He was going to do what he had to do.

But he was definitely going to lay a big guilt trip on Molly if he had to fight any spiders. That shit just wasn't cool.

"Are you coming or not?" Lyra snapped impatiently, jerking him out of his personal nightmare. "It's not too late to back out, you know. I said I would gather your ingredients, and I will. You don't have to go in there."

Lyra was standing in the doorway to the right of the entrance, the one opposite the room that held the integration chamber. She had her arms crossed over her chest, squeezing her breasts together in that enticing way. Jay knew it wasn't appropriate to stare, but he couldn't help noticing, even with everything else that was going on in his head.

Long live the power of boobs, he thought to himself.

A salve for any wound.

He gave her a winning smile and crossed the entryway to stand with her. "I do have to go in there," he said. "And you can't stop me. But thank you."

"I *could* stop you, actually." Lyra still seemed annoyed but she no longer looked like she wanted to cry, so he was grateful for that. "I've seen your stats. I could pin you to the wall with an arrow, tweak your nose, and be back with the ingredients before you were done crying for your Mommy."

Jay glanced at the quiver and scrunched up his face in imagined pain. "Please don't."

"I said I could," she replied, turning to stalk into the next room. "But I won't. If it's so important to you to do this yourself, I'll support you. Besides, after watching that standoff with Runolf and seeing the changes in you after your integration... I'm not entirely sure that you're not hiding something behind that abnormal workup."

The room they entered was not what Jay had expected. Rather than the inside of a tomb, they'd come into what looked like a gym locker or a high school hallway. Rows upon rows of rune-marked cubbies lined each wall, with a row in the middle of the room with additional cubbies on both sides. Lyra stalked over to one of the cubbies in the middle, opened it, and began pulling items out and dumping them on the floor.

Jay didn't understand why he'd been able to resist Runolf's **Command** either, but he *was* hiding something about his integration with the dungeon. For now, he figured it was safest to keep that to himself.

"Delving supplies?" Jay guessed, choosing not to add to her suspicions about his stats.

"Yes," she said. "Which you will need if you're serious about this expedition. Which you would know if you'd stayed to talk to Raina and me about your plans instead of just storming off like that. But whatever."

"Lyra, I'm sorry," he began. "I appreciate your concern and everything you've done for me, but it's really important to me that I—"

"I know," she said, cutting him off without looking at him. She picked up a leather satchel and threw it at him, hitting him in the chest. "I get it. Here, you need a sleeping roll, tent, at least ten days of rations, a starter weapon, and some basic armor. I have extras of everything here. You can use it until you get your own, and pay me for anything you lose or destroy once you've earned some coin."

Jay looked at all the items she was tossing at his feet, then at the leather satchel. "Uhh, there's no way this is going to fit in here. It's too small."

Lyra snorted, pulling an identical satchel out of the cubby and then slamming the door. "It might be tight," she said, giving him an unreadable expression. "But you might be surprised what you can fit in there if you push hard enough."

Jay's mind immediately took that phrase to the gutter, and he blushed, feeling his immediate physical response to the fox-girl's unintentional innuendo.

Then he noticed the corner of her lip quirking up and her eyes flashed.

"Did you just—?" he stammered. "Was that a—?"

"Joke?" she finished for him. "Yes. You do have jokes in your world, don't you, Portal Boy?"

Jay stared at her in disbelief as she arranged the satchel like a belt around her waist, securing it to the opposite side of her body from the dagger.

"Okay, jokes I can take," he said. "But I draw the line at Portal Boy. You are not calling me that. Portal Man, maybe, after we've had a few drinks."

Finally, Lyra cracked a smile. She laughed, the funny, high-pitched yipping sound that Jay had heard before and found incredibly adorable. He found himself relaxing, finally, after whatever had gone wrong between them.

"I'll take you for those drinks," she said. "If you survive the first floor of the dungeon. How's that sound, Portal Boy?"

"I can live with that," he said. Then, realizing what he'd said, he added, "At least I hope I will."

This earned him another snort from the fox-girl, who seemed like she was in remarkably better spirits than she had been. He really didn't want to ruin the moment, but there was still something he needed to ask.

"Lyra," he said. "There's something we need to talk about first. Before we go into the dungeon together."

The smile drooped on her face. "I know," she said, her voice quiet. "It's Molly, isn't it?"

"Molly?" Jay startled. "What? No. What do you mean?"

"I'm flirting with you while your girlfriend is injured and unconscious," Lyra said. "I know how that seems. And I don't want you to be uncomfortable. It's just... it's been a long time since I've been able to spend time with anyone who doesn't treat me like... well, like Runolf does. Like an outcast. You've been kind to me, and I don't mean to take advantage of that. I'm not trying to interfere."

Jay's mouth dropped open. No only had the beautiful fox-girl just admitted that she had been flirting—which Jay hadn't really dared hope, given how stunningly gorgeous she was—but she thought...

"Hold on a sec," he said, putting his hands up. "Molly is not my girlfriend. We have known each other since we were kids. I love her. I admit I have very complicated feelings for her. But she's made it clear she's not interested in that kind of a relationship, and I respect that. I meant it when I said I was willing to die to try to save her but... even once she's awake I don't expect that to change."

"Oh!" Lyra's eyes widened and her ears flattened against her head, disappearing into her silver-white hair. Her tail swished back and forth once before she reached behind herself and stilled it with her hand, blushing furiously. "I'm sorry. Um. Good, then. That's good. Because... I kind of thought you might be flirting with me, and if you were... that might have been kind of weird if she was your girl-friend. But if she's not then I guess that's... Oh my gosh. I'm sorry. I'm really not good at this kind of thing."

Jay grinned broadly at her, finding her sudden awkwardness more endearing than he could explain.

"Please don't be sorry," he said, rushing to make her feel more comfortable. "I'm not very good at it either. I've spent most of my years pining over someone who doesn't return my feelings, so... I'm kind of out of practice too. Not that I'm trying to start anything. It's just... flirting is nice."

She continued blushing, gazing up at him through long, white eyelashes. "Okay. So... what did you want to ask about?"

10

Entering The Frozen Tomb

J ay's smile faltered, realizing he was about to ruin
the moment again.

"About Runolf, actually," he said. "It might be
none of my business, but what's his deal? Why does
he treat you that way? I know Raina said you needed
a party, and you've been acting like I was your only
hope to get one. I'm just—"

"Here, let me help you pack your bag," she said,
interrupting him again.

At first, Jay thought she was changing the sub-
ject, but as she began to stuff all the gear inside
the leather satchel—which, it turns out, did fit an
alarming amount of stuff given its size, probably
due to some dungeon magic—Lyra talked.

"Even though you didn't end up with a powerful
class like you hoped, and I hoped," she began, "I

would still like to party with you. But you might not want to party with me. It's only fair that I tell you before hand, so you can make your choice."

"Raina said that some people don't trust the Vulpinari," Jay prompted. "They don't trust your kind. I thought that might be why, but I want you to know that I trust you, Lyra. I mean, I barely know you, but you've been kinder to me than anyone else here. You deserve the benefit of the doubt."

Lyra picked up a sleeping roll and stuffed it inside the satchel with a sigh. "That's part of it," she said. "There aren't many fox-kin left in Winterhaven. Many have abandoned Delving and taken to roaming the tundra as nomads. It can be easier to make a living off the land than from the dungeon, depending on the class you're assigned. I know Raina explained why it's hard for us—any of us—to make money selling what we harvest in the dungeon."

"It doesn't provide the commodities it's supposed to," Jay said, remembering their discussion. "Or, not in the quantities it's supposed to."

Lyra nodded, setting aside a set of leather leg wraps that seemed to be held together by a wish and a prayer. "Put those on," she said. "They should adjust to fit you."

Jay picked up the dubious looking armor and tried to figure out how to strap it on.

"Right, those reagents Raina needs, for example—have you looked at the specs she sent you?—they should all be readily available on the first floor of the dungeon. I have seen them pop up occasionally, but only with any kind of reliability on the third floor or lower."

Jay paused in the middle of tying the first leather piece to his leg.

"You've been lower than the third floor?" he said, startled. He'd been under the impression that Lyra was a low-level Delver, since she'd been so eager to party with him, a total novice.

"I've been all the way to the fifth," she said, not meeting his eye. "Almost as far as Raina and Runolf—rumor has it they have been all the way to the tenth floor."

Jay just stared at her, completely reevaluating everything he knew about Lyra and the two old shamans. "The *tenth*? But that's way deeper than most get, isn't it?"

"Nobody has done it since," Lyra said, shaking her head. "Whatever happened down there, they don't talk about it. Their entire party was killed, besides the two of them, and they've been at odds ever since. They used to be married you know."

Jay didn't even begin to know what to do with that information. So, he continued with what he thought would be most important to his first delve.

"But you've been to the fifth floor," he said. "That's a huge accomplishment."

Lyra sighed. "I've been there twice. Both times, my entire party suffered the same fate as Raina and Runolf's. Total party kill, except for me."

"Shit," he said, staring at her. "I'm so sorry."

The fox-girl shook her head. "It wasn't the first time. Or the second. I've also lost two parties on the upper levels, too. Once when I had just turned sixteen—that's when most Delvers first enter the dungeon after training their class with instructors in Winterhaven—my very first party was killed as we first entered the second floor. Once more, with my second party on the third floor."

Jay's mind was reeling. She spoke about it with such calm, all this death. He was beginning to realize he really had underestimated the danger this dungeon was capable of.

"You must have been devastated," he said. "And you keep going in? I don't know if that's impressive or scary."

Lyra stiffened. "Well, the rest of Winterhaven knows what they think. It's scary. In fact, they blame me for the bad luck that people partied with me seem to suffer. It doesn't help that I'm Vulpinari, and therefore not trustworthy to begin with. It *really* doesn't help that Runolf's son, Dax, was in the last party of mine to be wiped out. The village had largely overlooked the rumors that were spreading about me before that, but... Runolf wouldn't let it go. He kept bringing it up, until suddenly no one was willing to take a chance on me."

"So... why do you keep going back?" Jay asked. "I don't know if I could do it if I didn't have to do it for someone else."

"I'm meant to be a Delver, Jay," Lyra said, standing now that she'd finished packing everything he wasn't supposed to wear. She helped him finish attaching his leather leg covers, then passed him bracers and a chest piece, neither of which looked to be in much better condition that the leg armor. She continued to speak. "So, I Delve. Even if that means going it alone. I don't think it's my fault all my parties have had such bad luck. This dungeon has a higher Delver death rate than any in Arcanicea—out of dozens of dungeons, ours is the worst. It's cursed. I mean, Raina and Runolf should know that. They had the same thing happen to them. But, I've had worse luck than most."

Jay finished securing the last of his armor and secured the satchel to his waist. Then he took Lyra by the shoulders and held her in front of him, looking into her two-toned eyes. Her ears flattened as he gazed at her, as if he might yell at her.

"It sounds to me like they're looking for a scapegoat," he said. "Lyra, I'd be happy to party with you. I'm not going to be much help at first, so I understand if you don't want to party with me. But I'm not going to turn down your help if you're still offering it."

Her fluffy white tail began to swish back and forth, and her ears perked up.

"Really? You mean it?"

She bounced on the balls of her feet, forcing Jay to look away awkwardly. "Of course," he said. "I need all the help I can get. I just don't want to be told I can't do it, that's all."

"I admit I was scared, what with your stats and all," she said, her ears drooping again. "I've seen a lot of people I care about get hurt and killed. I'm worried about you. And I... I like you, Jay. It's been a long time since anyone has been nice to me, like you are. I don't want to see you get hurt. But the best way for me to make sure you don't get hurt is if you let me stay with you."

"So... let me get this straight..." Jay said, pretending that he wasn't following just to ease the sadness that he had seen growing in her eyes. "You do want to party with me? Or..."

"Yes, I'll party with you!" She let out a wild yip that made Jay burst into laughter. She rambled happily, practically dragging him out of the locker room. "We'll level you together, even if you're starting with a disadvantage, I still think there's something about you that... never mind. It doesn't matter. Even if you're just a normal Delver, I'm so happy not to have to go in alone anymore. Thank you, Jay!"

Lyra led him into the main entryway and then toward the middle door, the one directly across from the big, rune-covered entrance. She stopped, facing him. Her eyes got a distant look, which Jay was beginning to recognize as the look people got when they were sorting through the holographic status screens.

She frowned. "That's weird," she said. "I can see

you in the party menu as an available Delver. But your name is grayed out. Maybe you can do it?"

Jay followed her instructions to open his party menu. Her name was there, and it wasn't grayed out, like she had described. Hopeful, he mentally clicked on her icon to add her to his party.

But an error message popped up.

Lyra Golden-Eye | Lvl 6 | Type: Stealth | **Class:** Arcane Archer

ERROR: This Delver cannot be added to your party while your Health, Stamina, and Mana are below 100 points.

Jay cursed. "It's because of that debuff. Looks like I'm going to have to get my baseline stats up to normal for Level 1 before I can add anyone to my party."

Lyra frowned. "That's weird," she said. "It's not like you can't join a party when your HP is lowered due to an attack or something."

Jay shrugged. "I guess I'll just have to grind for a while until I'm cool enough to play with the big kids."

Lyra smiled, stood on her tiptoes, and reached up to ruffle his hair.

"That's okay, Portal Boy," she said. "I know just the place to take you. Have you read up on those reagents you need? I'll keep my eyes open for them, but you might catch things I miss."

Jay quickly opened the Notes menu and reviewed the information Raina had shared with him. The message included two selectable rectangles that looked a bit like collectable cards. One was labeled *Frostleaf Clover* and the other was *Tundra Berry*. As he selected them, each card revealed a botanical sketch of the plant, as well as a description of its properties and locations that they should be found. Both said they could be found on the first floor of the dungeon, which was labeled **F1: The Frozen Tomb.** Other than that, there wasn't much to go by.

"I think I've got it," he said. "Ready when you are."

Lyra flashed him a grin, pulling her bow off her shoulder and nocking an arrow. The tip burst into flame once it was ready to fire, causing Jay's eyes to widen.

"I was born ready, Portal Boy," she said. "The question is... were you?"

The fox-girl let out a series of excited yips and ran through the door, disappearing into the darkness. Jay took a deep breath, not sure he was making the wisest decision by following the Vulpinari Archer into the dungeon.

But it was the only thing he could do.

So he followed.

Welcome, Delver! You have arrived at F1: The Frozen Tomb. To complete this floor, you must locate the staircase leading to F2. But if you want to

be able to open the gate at the top of the staircase, you'll need a [Copper Key]. Defeat the F1 Floor Boss to receive one [Copper Key]. Each Delver must have their own [Copper Key] to proceed.

Jay received the first message from the dungeon as he stepped through the doorway. It popped up as a readable text menu as well as reciting in his mind in the dungeon's mechanical, gender-neutral voice.

"Copper key?" he asked, looking around curiously at the first official floor of the Ice Dungeon.

Lyra's eyebrows shot up. "Hmm? Oh, the floor message. You only get that the first time you enter a floor. If you prefer, you can turn off the text pop-ups in your settings, and just receive the audio information. The text will remain in your settings if you ever need to look back to reference it. It's in the System Log menu."

Jay went through his settings and turned off most of the pop-up notifications. He really didn't want to be battling holographic menus while he was in the midst of actual combat. Jay had half expected Nova to greet him personally when he entered the dungeon, and it unnerved him to think that she had perhaps already switched into 'trying to kill him' mode. Had she even noticed he was here? Or was it just the automated system greeting him?

Jay took a moment to look at his Class Menu again:

Delver: Jay Morgan
Class Type: [N/A]
Class: [N/A]

Lvl: 1

XP: 0 | **Next Lvl:** 100

Health: 105 (-30) | **Stamina:** 100 (-30) | **Mana:** 100 (-30)

Unassigned Attribute Points: 0

Strength: 1

Agility: 1

Intelligence: 1

Constitution: 2 [*Ragged Leather Armor* – Set Bonus Constitution +1, HP +5]

Willpower: 1

Charisma: 5

Active Skills: N/A

Passive Abilities: Environmental Resistance 1 (Arctic), Dungeon Sight 1, Start-Up Costs 1

Well, as dilapidated as the armor looked, it apparently did help a little bit. He'd gotten a +1 bonus to his Constitution attribute, which had added 5 HP to his max. It wasn't much, but it was something. He wasn't sure how powerful attacks from low-level animals and monsters would be, but every little bit extra would help once he started dungeon combat in earnest.

And, speaking of combat. Jay needed a few pointers on that, too.

He opened his satchel and removed a long, fat-bladed sword that shouldn't have fit inside it. This was the weapon Lyra had given him. It looked more like a machete than a sword, but Jay didn't know much about... anything. Not martial arts. Not medieval weapons. He barely even remembered the specifics of the videogames he used to play.

But as he looked at the blade in his hand, he noticed the white glow of **Dungeon Sight** around the item. Focusing on the glow, a small text window appeared next to the weapon.

Battered Bolo Knife – Common (White)
Melee – Versatile – Damage: 2d4 (slicing)
Condition: [15/25]
Traditionally, this versatile blade served multiple purposes, from being an essential farming implement used for clearing vegetation and chopping through thick jungle foliage, to a weapon of self-defence during times of conflict. But you're no farmer, are you? Use this blade to hack your enemies apart.

Jay swung the weapon experimentally, surprised that it didn't feel more awkward. "I can't believe I'm doing this," he muttered under his breath.

They stood in a tight corridor, not unlike the kind he had been dreading based on the sets of the tomb-themed movies he'd seen. Runes were etched in the gray-blue stones, but if they meant anything it was beyond the capabilities of the magical translation he was quickly taking for granted.

"Do these say anything?" he asked, pointing at the carvings with the tip of the Bolo Knife. "Like... this way to the easy monsters?"

"No." Lyra shook her head. "And if you ever do find anything in the dungeon that seems to offer you those kinds of directions, I would be very wary of believing them. This dungeon is—"

"Cursed," Jay finished. "Yes, I've heard that a few times."

She moved down the corridor to their left with a motion for him to follow her. "This way," she said. "The first room at the end of this corridor is where we'll start. With that weapon equipped, you'll be leveling either Strength or Agility, depending on how you use it. It's a Versatile weapon, which means it can do both, but it won't hit as hard as a Strength-based weapon or be as fast as an Agility-based weapon. If you find you prefer one style of fighting over another, we'll see if we can get you something more suitable. There are a lot of Common item drops on the first floor, as this is where Delvers come to cut their teeth."

"I've never fought with a blade before," Jay said, following her closely. "Or, really at all. I got in a sloppy bar fight once, but both of us were too drunk to land a punch and we mostly just rolled around on the ground, slapping at each other."

Lyra cast him a grin over her shoulder. "I hope she didn't hurt you too badly."

"Hey!" Jay protested. "I was fighting a guy. It was very manly slapping."

Lyra laughed, a sound he was beginning to enjoy a little too much.

"It won't matter," she said. "Everyone enters the dungeon as a novice. The magic you were injected with during integration will help you to adapt. If you feel the urge to fight a certain way, even if it seems wrong for the situation, my advice is to follow your instincts. Your body will guide you. When you reach your first Class Tier at Level 5, those distinctions in fighting style are what will give you the most interesting Sub-Class choices. I'm an Arcane Archer, for example, because I found a way to combine casting scrolls with my arrows. The dungeon rewarded me with a Rare Sub-Class when I started out as a standard Ranger."

Jay tried to absorb all of this, hoping it would be as easy as it sounded. He had a feeling that Lyra was underestimating his complete lack of experience in anything remotely dungeon-like. Stock market analysis and spreadsheets weren't going to do much for him once he faced his first—

Jay stopped suddenly, hearing a skittering noise from up ahead.

"Stay back," Lyra said, drawing her bow. "There's not usually anything in this corridor. If it's low-level, I'll leave it to you. If not, I'll take care of it and we'll move on. Don't take any stupid risks."

Jay nodded, sweat beading on his forehead. He gripped the Bolo Knife in his right hand, trying to feel the instincts Lyra seemed to think would come to him.

From the darkness of the corridor ahead, Jay saw something move. Two somethings. He watched with horror as a dog-sized scorpion leaped out of the shadows, directly at Lyra.

11

Snow
Scorpions

Without hesitation, Lyra released her arrow. It landed with a fiery explosion, and the creature released a hissing scream that bit into Jay's eardrums. He was certain that, whatever the scorpion beast was, it would have been destroyed by the fire arrow. But as the flames subsided, the scorpion was still standing.

Lyra cursed under her breath. "Fire resistance? On Floor 1? This is more broken than usual. Stay back, Jay. Let me handle these two."

Jay nodded and took a step back, watching as the two monsters approached the fox-girl. They had glassy carapaces, almost like they were made from ice. Their pinchers snapped dangerously, mandibles clacking. Jay's chest clenched at the sight of them. But it was the fat, swollen stinger on the dangerously arced tail that really made him nervous. Each one dripped with venom.

Jay had changed his mind. This was worse than spiders.

He waited for Lyra to attack. She released two normal-looking arrows, one after the other, into the first scorpion. This time, the arrows struck, sticking out of the seams between the plates of its armored body. The creature stumbled, and Jay's hopes rose. Lyra was Level 6. These first-floor monsters would be no problem for her. He watched her, waiting for the Arcane Archer to release a third arrow and finish the beast.

While he was distracted, the second scorpion attacked, launching itself over the back of its injured partner where it landed on the wall, skittering toward Jay with unbelievable speed.

"Shit!" Jay let out an undignified sound as he leaped backwards, trying to get out of the scorpion's path. His back hit the wall on the other side of the corridor, effectively blocking his escape. Seeing its prey cornered, the scorpion crouched, looking like it was about to pounce again.

Jay wasn't sure scorpions were supposed to be able to jump. But he had no doubt this one was going to. He had no plans to die in his first fight inside the dungeon, though. He wasn't going to go down without a fight.

Lifting the Bolo Knife in front of him, Jay charged, slashing down at the monster. The attack was awkward. He was sure he wasn't holding the blade properly. But somehow the movement felt right. The scorpion, seeing the attack, chose not to jump and rather backed up along the wall. Jay's Bolo Knife hit the gray-blue stone and bounced off, sparking.

He retaliated quickly, though, using the creature's hesitation to his advantage. Lunging forward, Jay struck at the beast, slashing at one of the pinchers. Jay let out a shout of victory when the limb was sliced cleanly from the scorpion's body and it let out a screech of pain or rage.

The creature's tail darted forward, the stinger stabbing toward Jay's face.

He brough the Bolo Knife up in a clumsy block, catching the point of the stinger on the flat of his blade. The stinger slid sideways, and the tip dug into Jay's wrist before slipping off the blade completely. Pain seared up his arm, as if he could feel the poison like liquid metal burning through his veins. Jay's fingers went numb, but somehow they stayed clamped to the handle of the blade.

The scorpion screeched again, rearing back. This time, Jay followed. Unable to feel his hand, and numbness continuing up his forearm, the wave of pain washed up his arm leaving deadened nerves in its wake. Still, he willed himself to hold on—just as he had held onto Molly through his exhausted march across the tundra.

He cut down with the knife at the same time as the scorpion's tail pulled backward and sliced the

stinger from the scorpion's body. With the creature disarmed, he didn't hesitate to strike again, driving the tip of the Bolo Knife deep into the creature's back. The blade slipped between the plates
of the scorpion's natural armor, right behind the
head, severing the monster's thorax from its cara-
pace-skull.

A trumpeting sound blared in his ears as notifications popped up across the top and bottom of the
holographic HUD. With the text menus disabled,
all he could see of the dungeon system now was a
boarder around his vision with thin strips where integral information would be displayed. So far, they
had been blank, but now they were filled with a series of alerts marked with various symbols he didn't
recognized.

Jay dismissed the notifications for now, eager to
see how Lyra was doing with her fight. He found the
Arcane Archer standing in the middle of the corridor with her bow hanging in her hand. The scorpion
creature had been fighting had four arrows sticking
out of it, and now lay motionless at her feet. It and
the scorpion that had attacked Jay were shimmering
in his augmented vision as **Dungeon Sight 1** tried
to communicate something to him that he didn't
understand yet.

"Are you okay?" he asked, realizing that he was
panting. He was relieved to see that Lyra didn't look
hurt, but the way she was looking at him worried
him.

"I'm fine," she said. "But what about you?"

Jay's arm felt funny, and he remembered he had been injured in the fight, though fortunately the pain had eased and it was only the numbness that bothered him now. He glanced down to see a scratch on his wrist, surrounded by swollen, discolored skin.

"I think I'm okay," he said. But when he tried to move his fingers to release their hold on the Bolo Knife, pain screamed through his limb again. "Nope. I lied. It hurts like a bastard."

Lyra continued to stare, her eyes doing that funny thing they did when she was using the dungeon menus. Or maybe she was analyzing him with **Dungeon Sight**, he couldn't tell.

"Okay, first thing you need to do after a fight," she said as she swung her bow back onto her shoulder to free up her hands, "is to check your base stats. Stamina and Mana will recover automatically when you're not using abilities that drain those bars. But your HP can be affected by a lot of things."

Jay followed her instructions and opened his Class Menu to see the damage.

Delver: Jay Morgan

Class Type: [N/A]

Class: [N/A]

Lvl: 1

XP: 17 | **Next Lvl:** 100

Health: 55 (-30) | **Stamina:** 70 (-30) | **Mana:** 100 (-30)

"My health is down to 25," he said, deflating

slightly. "And Stamina is at 40. Stamina is recovering quickly though. It's at 45 now. Health is moving more slowly. 26. Stamina at 50. I can't do back-to-back fights if my Health regenerates that slowly."

He felt his heart rate and muscles coming back to normal as his Stamina recharged, like a high-speed version of a workout recovery. But his arm didn't really feel like it was improving.

"That's because you got stung by a Snow Scorpion. Their venom usually carries a Health regeneration debuff. You'll be able to see it in your notifications if not your Class Menu."

She walked him through checking his notifications and Jay was inundated with a series of notifications read in the dungeons' dull, mechanical voice.

Success!
You have killed
Snow Scorpion Lvl 2
XP: 25 (-30%)

Jay listened to the announcement in a state of shock. His first kill, and he'd defeated a monster a level above him? He'd expected to grind on Level 1 monsters for a while before taking on anything higher level than himself. If he'd realized that scorpion was more powerful than he was, he might not have been so quick to jump into battle.

Then again, what else could he have done? Run away to let Lyra fend for herself? He'd probably have been rewarded for his cowardice with another pair of Snow Scorpions coming up behind him. Jay wondered how closely Nova was watching these battles and if she would be deciding what kind of monsters to be throwing at him based on how he reacted in each situation.

Achievement Unlocked: You're a Killer Now! You've made your first kill in the dungeon environment, and lived to tell the tale. How does that make you feel? Alive? Exhilarated? Powerful? Guilt-ridden and filled with self-hatred? That Snow Scorpion had a family, you know. Now who's going to feed her little arachnid babies so they can grow up to become poisonous murder bugs, too?

Who's the real monster here, Delver?

Reward: 75XP (-30%)

When Jay read that notification, he heard the trumpet sound effect of his XP counter going up. Suddenly he was only 30 points away from being Level 2. That seemed fast, considering how poor his starting Attributes had been, and the 30% reduction in the XP points he was being given.

Jay opened a second notification, and frowned.

Achievement Unlocked: You've Been Poisoned! Not just every Delver manages to get poisoned within the first hour of entering the dungeon. Most who do, end up dead before the end of the second hour. So, we like to do a little something special for you to celebrate in the few, pitiful moments you have left. It's not going to help you out of this poisoned pickle you've found yourself in, but hey.

Any excuse to party, right?

Reward: [Boardroom Party Champagne For Two]

Mentally clicking on the reward icon brought up a new screen called Inventory Management. Jay had the option of removing the Champagne from his holographic Inventory Menu or leaving it there. When he opened the item description, it wasn't the mechanical dungeon voice that spoke to him.

It was Nova.

Boardroom Party Champagne For Two – Theres nothing quite like celebrating the high of a new achievement, is there? But no one likes to celebrate alone. Take a break from your long, hard grind up the corporate ladder and enjoy the rewards of your newly acquired status. And if that reward happens to drop the panties of that cute new receptionist who wears the red penicil skirt... well, that's just another one of the perks of the job, isn't it? Take what belongs to you, you big Boardroom Stud, you...

Effects: Drinking this potion increases Charisma by +5 permanently, and gives a once per day *Panty Dropper* perk that increases your chances of using *Persuade*, *Charm*, or *Flatter* skills on Delvers or Dungeon Dwellers of the opposite sex. This bottle contains two servings. Sharing this potion with a member of the opposite sex has a 50% chance to *Charm* them, whether or not you have acquired the *Charm* skill.

Jay wasn't sure how he was supposed to drink an item that only appeared in the holographic menu.

He wasn't really sure he wanted to. The description kind of gave him the creeps. Was Nova testing him, somehow? Not that he had any of the skills listed yet, but given his boosted Charisma stats it seemed inevitable that these were going to be the kind of skills offered up to his mystery class.

Still, the +5 Charmisa wouldn't hurt even if it wasn't particularly helpful when fighting Snow Scorpions. And the ability to manipulate female Dungeon Dwellers—the NPCs of the Ice Dungeon—might come in handy if they ran into traders or neutral parties who might be useful later on.

"Lyra, what happens if you take something out of your Inventory?" he asked.

The fox-girl looked up from where she appeared to be harvesting items from the Snow Scorpion she had killed. "It materialized in your hand," she said. "But we don't get access to the Inventory system until Level 10. It should be grayed out for you."

Jay's frown deepened. He clicked the [Boardroom Champagne For Two] icon in the Inventory Menu, telling the system that he did want to remove it from his Inventory.

He felt a cool pressure in his left palm as the bottle materialized from thin air in his hand.

Lyra let out a yelp and jumped backward, lowering her ears. "How did you do that?"

"I don't know," he said. "I got this as a reward for getting poisoned, and it went into my Inventory."

"For getting poisoned!?" she said, staring at him in

disbelief. "Usually, the reward for getting poisoned is getting dead."

"Yeah, I got a message saying as much." Jay laughed nervously. "I think its supposed to be a consolation prize because the dungeon thinks I'm not going to survive more than another hour in here."

Lyra frowned. "That… would be unusual. But nothing about this dungeon is normal so who am I to judge. What's the potion do?"

"Increases my Charisma and gives me a creepy perk that I don't really want to use," Jay said. "It might be useful if we encounter any female Dungeon Dwellers we need to negotiate with, though."

Lyra shrugged. "I don't know anything about Charisma skills or perks, sorry. I've heard some of them can be a little creepy, but its all in how you use them, right? A lot of people are nervous around Delvers who choose Charisma based builds. Then again, a lot of people feel the same way about Vulpinari. You trust me and I'll trust you, okay?"

Jay nodded. "Deal. I don't have any Charisma skills yet, but when I do I promise not to use them on you."

"Unless I ask you to."

"Unless—" Jay was about to agree, then he stopped. "Wait, what? Why would you ask me to?"

Lyra bit her lip and turned away, lifting her shoulder uncertainly. "I don't know," she said. "I've heard there are some Charisma skills that aren't so creepy. Never say never, right?"

Jay didn't really know how to respond to that.

"Okay," he said. "I'm going to drink the first half of this bottle, and we'll save the rest for in case I need to seduce a dungeon merchant or something. There are neutral Dungeon Dwellers, right?"

Lyra nodded. "Some are quest givers. Some are informants. Some are skill trainers. Traders will do deals in the dungeon, wherever you find them. That's usually where you'll buy bandages and heal potions and basic provisions. Merchants occur once per floor after the 5th floor, giving Delvers direct access to the World Dungeon Markets. It's a lifesaver, since until you unlock Inventory, we have to use these satchels which—although the hold a surprising amount of gear—are not limitless. And they are a pain in the ass to sort through when you're in a hurry. I can't believe you unlocked Inventory at Level 1, though. There is something seriously broken with your build."

"I'm starting to get that impression," Jay said.

He managed to uncork the bottle by levering it against the blade of his Bolo Knife, even though his knife hand was still numb it was regaining enough function that he could move it around a bit. A quick glance at this Health bar showed him that he was back up to 40 HP. His Stamina was fully recovered, though still at 70 points thanks to the Startup Costs debuff.

Jay sighed, and gave the bottle a tentative sniff. Might as well boost the stat he had some points in. The potion didn't overflow the way champagne usually did, but it was fresh and lightly fruity in smell, and the bubbles tickled his nose. He put the bottle to his lips and tipped it back, drinking half of it.

Another notification blinked in his peripheral vision. He corked the bottle and returned it to his inventory, startling as the bottle vanished from his hand. He mentally clicked on the blinking icon, which was gold and shaped a bit like an hourglass. This achievement was read in the standard, mechanized dungeon voice, which Jay couldn't help but feel sounded a little scathing.

Achievement Unlocked!: Master of Your Domain
You have attained 10 Attribute points in Charisma, the most useless Attribute for low-level Delvers.

But hey, sometimes it's best to stick with what you're good at and leave the hard work to people with the skills to handle the job. And who says being pretty and batting those big, hazel eyes of yours isn't hard work?

Reward: 75XP (-30%), [Mystery Loot Box]

Jay barely had time to finish re-reading the description when he received another notification, along with the trumpet sound he associated with gaining experience points.

"This is getting ridiculous," he muttered.

"There are a lot of pop-ups your first time through F1," Lyra said, smiling as she stood from where she'd been looting the Scorpion corpse. "Once you get through all the first kill, first loot, first whatever notifications, things will calm down. You can usually just ignore them and read them all at the end of the day. The XP from kills will be added to your bar automatically. But you should loot that scorpion before we move on and find somewhere to rest before we find you those Level 1 monsters I promised you—"

Lyra's eyes widened as the notification forced its way through. Jay's body glowed with a strange yellow light and he felt the pain and numbness in his right arm evaporate, replaced with a warm and fizzy feeling in his entire body.

Apparently, there were some notifications you couldn't ignore.

12

Level Up

Congratulations!
You have Achieved Level 2
XP: 22 | Next Lvl: 200
Health: 105 (-30) | Stamina: 100 (-30) | Mana: 100 (-30)
Unassigned Attribute Points: 3
You have 30 Base Stat Points to Distribute. Would you like to increase Health, Stamina, or Mana?

"Level 2?" Lyra gasped, her tail swishing behind her. "Already? What the hell is going on?"

"I don't know," Jay said, somewhat baffled. He looked at the wound on his arm and was shocked to find it had disappeared completely. "I got some XP from the achievements I unlocked. It seems like my Health and Stamina have recovered now, but I still have the debuff. Also, I have 30 Base Stat Points to distribute. What's the best strategy for that?"

"Okay," she rubbed the top of her head like she was petting her ears, and Jay was suddenly distracted from all the notifications with the awareness of how cute his Dungeon Delving companion was.

Who knew fox-ears on a girl could be so damned adorable? When she continued talking, Jay had to force himself to pay attention.

"For each level up, you'll get those same 30 Base Stats," she was saying, "which you can add to Health, Stamina, or Mana as batches of 10. If you want a balanced build, you could to 10 points in each. If you want to favor one Base Stat over the others, you can do 20 in one, 10 in one, and then next level up give the 10 points to whatever you neglected last time. It's usually not a good idea to completely ignore any of the Base Stats, even if you don't use them, because you never know what kind of powers you'll unlock later on."

Jay nodded, and moved 20 points to his Health, 10 points to Stamina, and left Mana as it was. His fight with the scorpion had been more than enough warning that his Health was dangerously low with that debuff. In another two levels, he should be able to zero out the 30% handicap and, in theory, be allowed to party with Lyra.

"Done," he said. "And I guess the 3 unassigned stat points are the same idea, but they go to Attributes?"

"Yes," she said. "And without having any idea what your class build is supposed to look like, I can't give you any advice there. As a backup, you did pretty good with that Bolo Knife, so Strength and Agility will be good choices. Constitution will increase the rate that you regenerate Health when damaged and increase your resistance to things like that Snow Scorpion poison. Willpower does the same thing for Stamina and Mana, whichever of your Base Stats is higher."

Jay considered his options, but like Lyra said, without knowing what kind of class he had it was difficult to make an educated decision. For now, he'd just have to do what made survival easier in the short term. He chose to put one point in each of Strength, Agility, and Constitution. He inspected his newly updated chart.

Delver: Jay Morgan

Class Type: [N/A]

Class: [N/A]

Lvl: 2

XP: 22 | **Next Lvl:** 200

Health: 125 (-30) | **Stamina:** 110 (-30) | **Mana:** 100 (-30)

Unassigned Attribute Points: 0

Strength: 2

Agility: 2

Intelligence: 1

Constitution: 3 [*Ragged Leather Armor* – Set Bonus Constitution +1, HP +5]

Willpower: 1

Charisma: 10

Active Skills: N/A

Passive Abilities: Environmental Resistance 1 (Arctic), Dungeon Sight 1, Start-Up Costs 1

Perks: Panty Dropper

Jay shook his head, seeing the new perk added to his list. Even though it was grayed out, presumably until he had the necessary skills to use it, it still made him feel sleezy.

"Are you done?" Lyra asked. She'd been waiting patiently, but she seemed eager to get going. "You still need to loot your Snow Scorpion corpse. It's always a good idea to loot the corpses of anything you kill in the dungeon, even once they are too low-level to be useful to you. Many of the animals drop useful crafting supplies, monsters drop reagents and magical weapons, and humanoid dungeon creatures often have treasure and other things. Plus there are random loot drops that often make no sense. They aren't common, but it's still best to check. We aren't partied together, so you won't be able to loot the monsters I kill, and I won't be able to loot the ones you kill. But you can tell which are your kills with **Dungeon Sight**. They should shimmer if they are lootable."

Jay approached the scorpion he had killed, and followed Lyra's instructions for how to loot it. Using **Dungeon Sight**, he selected the Snow Scorpion corpse, which opened a window with a number of items listed.

Snow Scorpion: Lvl 2

Frozen Carapace, Snow Scorpion Stinger, Snow

Scorpion Eye

Jay removed the items, inspecting them briefly, before adding them to his Inventory. All three were [White] items, indicating they were common. The carapace was a crafting ingredient for adding frost resistance to armor. The stinger and eye were alchemy reagents.

"That's great, actually," Lyra said when he'd told her what he'd found. "All three of those are common items that are supposed to be found in the Ice Dungeon. They're all certified Ice Dungeon commodities that can be sold on the World Dungeon Market. You got lucky. All I got was Bug Meat, which can be eaten but not sold."

Jay watched as the looted scorpion faded and disappeared, as if the dungeon had reabsorbed it for future use. He glanced at the scorpion next to Lyra. It was shimmering. "Uh, Lyra, how come it looks like I can loot the scorpion you killed, too?"

Lyra frowned, glancing down at her feet. Her frowned deepened. "That's weird. I looted it. It should have disappeared."

Jay selected the scorpion using his **Dungeon Sight**, the same way he had with the one he'd killed. And retrieved the same three items as he had from the other monster. Only this one had an additional item.

Frostbite Antidote: This potion cures damage inflicted by poisonous creatures on F1 and F2 of the Ice Dungeon. Contains 5x Doses.

When he told Lyra what he'd received, her frown became more confused than ever. She shook her head. "That's… It's like the dungeon is giving you all the items it should be dropping for everyone. Frostbite Antidote is really rare, too. It can't be sold on the World Dungeon Market, but if we don't end up needing to use it, Raina will probably buy it from you for at least a couple of gold."

Jay added those items to his inventory too. He remembered he still had a [Mystery Loot Box] to open from his *Master of Your Domain* achievement, but he was getting antsy to start building his skills and get levelling in earnest. He was beginning to feel like they'd be here all day while he opened random notifications and received scathing messages from the Auto-Dungeon or disturbingly sexual ones from Nova.

He closed all his menus and stood, shrugging. "You were saying something about low-level monsters?"

Lyra beamed at him.

"I thought you'd never ask," she said, jumping up and giving Jay an eyeful of bouncing breasts. Her tail swished happily as she continued down the corridor. "If we hadn't been interrupted by those Snow Scorpions, we'd already have this room cleared. Come on!"

As they continued down the tomblike corridor, Jay kept glancing behind him to make sure there weren't any more Snow Scorpions creeping up on them. Lyra had said they usually hung out closer to the F2 staircase, along with other Level 2 monsters. Occasionally the dungeon would spawn Level 3 and 4 creatures on the first floor of the dungeon, too, which was one of the reasons the locals of Winterhaven considered the Ice Dungeon to be cursed. Normally a dungeon would only spawn a higher-level creature for the Floor Boss, but this dungeon seemed to have a higher than normal rate of random high level spawns which only got worse the deeper into the dungeon you delved. It was no wonder there was such a high instance of total party kills in the Ice Dungeon when you never really knew what kind of monsters you'd be up against.

It was also no wonder Lyra and Raina had been so appalled at the idea of Jay going into the dungeon alone. Lyra was Level 6, and she didn't even like delving the upper floors alone. She'd only done it out of necessity.

The strange rune-carved walls reminded Jay of an Egyptian Tomb. The floor name was the Frozen Tomb, as well, which made him wonder if the creator of the dungeon had been from his world. Or, if the portals went both ways, perhaps the creators of the Ancient Egyptian culture on Earth had been inspired by some interdimensional travel.

Jay had heard theories about the pyramids being built by aliens. But he'd figured that was pretty bogus. There was no reason to believe humans couldn't have built the pyramids by themselves. Back then, the average human being was probably a lot more competent than modern desk jockeys and keyboard warriors. Modern people had all the information in the world at their fingertips, and most guys Jay knew couldn't tell the difference between real women and phishing scams.

Now, he was beginning to have his doubts that anything he knew had ever been real.

Lyra led him to a stone block that looked different from the rest, and placed her hand directly on a carved handprint in the stone. The handprint glowed, and there was a grinding sound as the wall slid into the floor revealing a room encased in darkness.

From the shadows, Jay could hear clicking sounds that reminded him a bit too much of the mandibles of the scorpions they'd just faced. He shuddered to think of what might be hiding inside the room.

But Lyra promised they were low-level creatures, and he trusted her.

The Arcane Archer pulled a torch from her satchel and ignited it with a whispered incantation. Then she held it up, letting the orange, flickering light spill into the room. Dozens, perhaps hundreds, of oily black beetle shells reflected the light back at them and Jay groaned.

"More bugs?" he said. "Really?"

"Sorry," Lyra said, grinning a bit sadistically. "But I already scanned this batch and they're all Level 1. You're on your own this time, Portal Boy. Don't worry. I'll hold the light for you."

Jay used his **Dungeon Sight** to inspect one of the closest beetles. They hadn't reacted to the door opening, or to the light of the torch, but Jay had a feeling that the moment he stepped over the threshold, they would swarm and attack.

Glacial Scarab – Lvl 1

These iridescent, ice-crystal scarabs leave icy trails of frost in their wake. They are mostly harmless, are weak to Fire Damage, and make a mess when you squish them. Watch out, though, these magical beetles can fuse together, forming larger constructs to challenge intruders.

"How worried do I need to be about these constructs?" Jay asked, eyeing the creature.

"What?" Lyra said, giving him an odd look. "Just go in there and smash them. Your blade probably won't be much good but you can stomp them with your feet. It's disgusting. I refused to do it, even when I was Level 1. But I had a party then. Now... I'm not coming in unless you really need me to. Gross."

"These things gross you out, but the scorpions didn't?" Jay asked, returning her look with an equally skeptical one. The scorpions were way creepier than these little beetles as far as he was concerned.

"You'll see."

"It says they're weak to Fire Damage," he said. "Couldn't you just light them on fire for me?"

Lyra rolled her eyes. "Even if we were partied together, that would generate way less XP than you doing it yourself. But when we're not partied, that would be a complete waste. Your goal is to level, right? Get in there and grind."

Jay took a deep breath and stepped over the threshold. The beetles weren't as creepy as the scorpions but they were still bugs. They were still on his ick-factor list. And, just as he'd suspected, the moment he entered their territory, they seemed to notice him.

He wrinkled his nose and stepped on the one closest to his foot. His boot met a surprising amount of resistance before the beetle's shell cracked and his foot slammed onto the floor. A wave of orange fluid burst out of the thing like a popped pimple. It would have been bad enough, if it weren't for the stench that followed. Jay gagged as he was forced to stomp another beetle that scurried over toward him.

Then he realized it wasn't him they were interested in. They were coming to feed on the guts of their fallen comrades.

Thoroughly grossed out, Jay stayed close to the door, keeping an eye on the milling creatures whose glistening black shells seemed to jump and flicker in the light of Lyra's torch.

Success!
You have killed
Glacial Beetle Lvl 1 (x2)
XP: 10 (x2) (-30%)

Jay dismissed the notification, doing some quick mental math. He'd need to kill twenty-five of these things to hit Level 3. That didn't seem like it would be too difficult. For all the skittering noises they made the creatures moved pretty slowly—maybe that was where they got their name, since they otherwise looked like oversized black beetles, unlike the icy-carapaces of the Snow Scorpions.

The Glacial Beetles left glistening trails of frost in their wake that Jay assumed would be slippery if he stepped on them, but it couldn't be worse than the greasy orange guts coating the bottom of his boot. Besides, with the Environmental Resistance (Arctic) Passive Ability, Jay wasn't even certain their trails would be slippery. Unless the resistance didn't help against magical cold.

He was a little worried about the mound of beetles crawling over each other at the back of the room. It was impossible to tell how many of them were in there. However, they'd remained where they were, and Jay hoped if he didn't get close enough to trigger their interest, he could just kill one beetle at a time until he hit his next level.

One after another, he stomped the beetles, counting in his head. Four, five, six, seven... the floor was really getting greasy now as the guts spilled in a growing circle around where he was stomping.

"Hey, Lyra?" he shouted over his shoulder. "How close can I get to that mound in the back before they all come for me?"

He stomped another one... nine, ten.

Lyra didn't respond.

Jay glanced over his shoulder to see the torch mounted in a bracket on the wall and the fox-girl nowhere to be found.

13

Beetle Guts

J ay cursed under his breath. Where had Lyra gone?

He shifted over a bit, hoping the puddle of stinking ooze wouldn't force him too much closer to what he was beginning to think of as the spawn point for the beetles. There seemed to be an endless supply coming from that corner of the room, with one or two breaking off from the group and scuttling out into the room where they were immediately drawn to the stench of their spattered buddies.

"Disgusting little vermin," he muttered, suddenly understanding why Lyra had refused to kill the bugs.

But had she had to abandon him too?

It wouldn't be any less repulsive if he'd had someone to talk to, but at least he might distract himself from the task. Where was she?

After he'd crushed his fifteenth beetle, the entire front part of the room nearest the exit was slimed with their guts. Soon he was going to have to move closer to the swarm. He received a notification that had the yellow hourglass looking thing, which he realized was supposed to be a trophy, indicating he had a New Achievement.

He disregarded that one, figuring it was better to deal with after he was done with the bugs. But he noticed a different icon flashing in the bottom left of his screen. This one had a glow to it, and was a bright green color, which made it look important.

Jay mentally clicked on it, even as he crushed another beetle under his heel. The dungeon's mechanical voice broke into his thoughts to read the notification to him as his gaze sought out his next victim.

Buff Activated - Crush the Competitor (Temporary)

Ah, crushing the competition. It's the dream of every venture capitalist in history. In the dungeon, we take that dream literally. Crushing your enemies results in a temporary, stackable Strength bonus of +2, lasting 5 min.

"Gross," Jay said, echoing Lyra's earlier sentiment. He wondered if all Delvers got a similar buff from crushing these bugs or if this one was special because Nova was messing with him by bringing up all the old corporate phrases common in his old life.

He closed the menu and kept stepping on Glacial Beetles, having lost count of where he was. He felt like he should be getting a Level Up soon. Surely, he'd killed almost twenty of the things by now.

Jay inched closer into the room, glancing over his shoulder again to see if the fox-girl had returned. "Lyra?" he called when he didn't see her. "Hey, you okay out there?"

If she didn't answer soon, he was going to duck out and check on her. Jay didn't think she'd have abandoned him. Maybe another group of higher-level monsters had spawned and she was fighting them off? He eyed the spreading pool of orange goo and wondered if he could make it out of the room without falling on his ass.

He took another look at his notifications, double checking to see if there were any that needed immediate attention. One glowed a dull red color, looking ominous. He clicked it, dreading what he would find.

Debuff Activated – Uncompetitive Advantage (Temporary)

Hey, come on. Pick on somebody your own size! You've been grinding hard, and normally that's something we admire. But when a Delver spends too much time picking on creatures below their level, it takes some of the fun out of the competition. Don't you think?

You receive a temporary 25% reduction in XP for every five lower-level creatures or monsters you kill in a row.

Jay cursed. Just his luck that they'd fought those Scorpions before he'd gotten to the starter rooms. Why hadn't Lyra warned him about the debuff?

With the 30% reduction to XP he was already suffering it made the 10XP Glacial Scarabs only worth 4.5 points. And it didn't seem like the dungeon awarded half points, which meant he was probably only going to get 4XP per kill now.

He vowed to ask Lyra about it as soon as she came back.

If she ever came back.

Where the hell had she gone, anyway? What was all that crap about sticking with him and protecting him if she was just going to take off on his first solo fight?

Then again, he had adamantly insisted that he could go it alone. He'd better not make an ass of himself by dying in the first room.

A new beetle had broken from the group, catching Jay's attention, and derailing his train of thought. The beetle was scuttling toward the mess of slippery guts on the floor when it suddenly broke pattern and made for Jay instead. He grimaced, getting ready to crunch the thing beneath his heel. When it was close enough to stomp, Jay lifted his foot and drove his boot down on the shiny black beetle shell.

It was like kicking a boulder.

His boot bounced off, jarring his ankle, knee, and hip joint and sending him off balance. Jay scrambled to catch himself, flailing his arms. He still held the Bolo Knife in one hand, and he didn't want to drop it in the mess on the floor, so he spun, reaching with his left arm to catch the wall to steady himself.

The inexplicably armored beetle lunged at him, smashing its hard body into his shin.

"Ow! Shit!" he cursed, hopping on one leg. "What the hell?"

He glanced down at the attacking beetle with his **Dungeon Sight**.

Glacial Scarab – Lvl 1 (Elite)

Other than the Elite tag, the description didn't give him any extra details about the creature. Jay wracked his brain for information from the video games he used to play. From what he recalled, Elite mobs were usually the same as their normal counterparts, just way tougher. Apparently, these ones also got an extra attack the normal Scarabs didn't.

But the beetle was still only a Level 1. Jay figured he should be almost Level 3. He should have been able to do some damage to the thing, surely.

Jay braced himself for another attack, this time ready for the Beetle's shell to be tougher than the others. He tried to aim his strike for the center of the back, where the shell split to allow it to spread its wings.

Oh crap, they have wings, he realized. *I hope these things don't start flying.*

He drove his heel into the Glacial Beetle's shell and felt a satisfying crunch as he broke through the creature's outer protection. The beetle let out a hiss, but didn't die. It's shell was cracked and it scuttled sideways like a crab, moving faster than it had before. Jay jumped forward, using all his Strength to launch himself high into the air, and his Agility to direct both heels onto the creepy little monster. At least, that's what he assumed was happening, because he'd never in his life been able to jump so high or land with such precision.

The beetle splattered beneath him like a watermelon dropped from a balcony onto a sidewalk.

But the move hadn't gone unnoticed. Between the loud hiss of the Elite beetle and the visceral pop of its gruesome demise, Jay had drawn the ire of a handful of new beetles, which broke from the main swarm and began advancing on him with their wings open, hissing like cockroaches.

Jay used his **Dungeon Sight**, hoping to identify if there were any more Elite specimens that he needed to be cautious of.

He felt his stomach drop as the text boxes opened in his HUD.

Glacial Scarab: Lvl 1 (Elite)
Glacial Scarab: Lvl 2 (Elite)
Glacial Scarab: Lvl 1 (Elite)
Glacial Scarab: Lvl 3 (Elite)
Glacial Scarab: Lvl 3 (Elite)

"Shit! Lyra, I need help!" he shouted as loudly as he could. The clattering of the beetles' wings was making a sound like a dozen approaching helicopters. Jay stepped backward, trying to keep some distance between himself and the advancing bugs.

His heel hit the orange ooze a second before he realized where he was. His foot shot out from underneath him, and Jay went down hard on his tail-bone.

"Fuck," he cursed, scrambling in the slippery, stinking mess as he fought to get back on his feet.

The nearest Elite Glacial Scarab, a Level 2, flapped its wings, lunging for him. It dropped like a stone from above, slamming into Jay's thigh like a cannon ball. Pain exploded through his leg, as he slapped the thing away with his Bolo Knife. The blade caught the beetle between the underbelly and the shell, slicing it in half in a twitching pile at the center of the goo.

"All right you ugly bastards," Jay said, finally getting to his knees in the slime. "Now I know you've got another weakness, this is going to be interesting."

Two Level 1 Scarabs lunged at him at the same time. Jay felt his body move as if he was no longer in control. He swept the Bolo Knife up at the first beetle, hitting it in the soft part of its abdomen, leaving a spray of orange guts in its wake. It's dead, twitching body landed with a splat in the stinking puddle.

The second beetle hit him in the shoulder with a painful crack, but Jay gritted his teeth and turned toward the insectile monster, where it had bounced off of him to land upside down in the puddle, its black, twitching legs kicking uselessly in the air. He drove his blade into the beetle's belly, and immediately received notification of the kill.

But why hadn't he levelled up yet?

There were two Level 3 Elite Scarabs left now, and Jay realized he was in trouble. He wished he could flip through his menus and check those notifications now, in hopes that one of his achievements might have come with a reward he could use, but he didn't dare take his attention from the bugs.

They made clacking sounds with their wings as they advanced, and Jay felt his heart hammering in his chest, anticipating the moment that they would both fly at him, probably strong enough to break his bones instead of just leaving painful bruises. He gripped his knife, readying himself for the attack. Hopefully he could hit one of them, at least. With any luck, he could kill one and even the odds. But he wouldn't be able to do so without taking damage.

He didn't want to look at his blinking Health bar, visible even with the menus minimized at the bottom of his screen. It only made the anxiety worse. Clutching the Bolo Knife, he made a couple of experimental slashes in front of his body, amazed that despite the obvious damage he'd taken, his increased Strength and Agility were still palpable as he wielded the blade.

Okay, he thought. *You can do this. Just stay focused. If you die now, who will protect Molly from that jackass, Runolf? Stay focused and—*

One Scarab lunged before the other and Jay was ready. He struck instantly with the knife, stabbing the blade into the bottom of the creature's abdomen. The strike bounced off the armor plate in the center of its body. Jay leaned into the failed attack, it was as if his body was instinctively changing tactics faster than his mind could keep up. His knuckles drove into the Scarab's underbelly, sending it flying across the room, where it smashed into the wall like a balloon filled with orange paint.

What the fuck, that was a Level 3 Elite? He thought in shock. *How did I hit it so hard?*

Jay didn't have time to ponder, as the final Elite Scarab clacked its wings and launched into the air. Still on his knees in the ooze, Jay struggled to move quickly enough to block the attack. He punched up, awkwardly, hoping to drive the thing away from his face. He clipped the back half of the beetle's body, sending it spinning like a top and launching it high in the air. He tried to aim his next strike as the creature came careening down at him, completely out of control.

Thwak!

An arrow shot past Jay's face, connecting perfectly with the Scarab's underbelly, piercing it through its body and out the other side. It landed with a dull splat in the orange puddle of goo.

An entire orchestra of trumpet sounds blared inside his skull as he turned to face Lyra who stood in the doorway, looking completely shocked. She looked like she wanted to speak, but the mechanical dungeon voice took over, blocking out everything else.

Success!

You have killed
Glacial Scarab Lvl 1 (x48)
XP: 10 (x48) (-25%) (-30%)

Success!
You have killed
Glacial Scarab Lvl 1 (Elite) (x3)
XP: 25 (x3) (-25%) (-30%)

Success!
You have killed
Glacial Scarab Lvl 2 (Elite) (x2)
XP: 75 (x2) (-30%)

Success!
You have killed
Glacial Scarab Lvl 3 (Elite) (x2)
XP: 125 (x2) (-30%)

Congratulations!
You have Achieved Level 3
XP: 330 | Next Lvl: 400
Health: 125 (-30) | Stamina: 110 (-30) | Mana: 100
(-30)
Unassigned Attribute Points: 3
*You have 30 Base Stat Points to Distribute. Would you like
to increase Health, Stamina, or Mana?*

Jay stared in stunned silence at the stat screen.
"Umm, Lyra? I think I'm almost at Level 4."

Lyra didn't say anything.

Jay's gaze shot up, expecting to find her gone again. Instead, she was looking over his shoulder with a horrified look on her face.

"Lyra?" he said. "Did you hear me?"

Lyra nodded. "That's good, Jay. You're going to need it."

She still didn't look at him.

It wasn't until Jay heard the scream from behind him that he finally turned around to see what it was that had frozen her in place.

He cursed, attempting to scramble to his feet in the greasy bug guts in order to get away from the monster that had suddenly appeared in the room with him:

Glacial Scarab Construct – Lvl 5 (Elite)

14

Well, That Didn't Go as Planned

The mass of Glacial Scarabs that had been milling in the corner of the room had transformed into a huge, lumbering beast made of black, crawling bodies. The monster's gaping mouth was stretched impossibly wide in a hissing, grating scream that made every bone in Jay's body feel like it was being shaken apart. Level 1 and 2 Glacial Scarabs flew out of its mouth at Jay like baseballs from a pitching machine.

Jay batted the smaller, flying beetles away from him, surprised when they splattered easily when he whacked them with the flat of his blade or with a flailing backhand. The Level 3 Elite Scarabs had been easier to kill than he'd expected, too. He wondered if that had something to do with the Strength bonus he'd received for the **Crush the Competition** buff, but he couldn't pause to check his stats.

The Glacial Scarab Construct was advancing on him like a slow-moving ooze made of the glittering black bodies. The beetles seemed to climb to the top of the monstrosity, then fall off and start at the bottom as it continued to slide toward Jay where he was still slipping and sliding in the impossibly greasy orange puddle.

"Jay, you have to hit it first," Lyra was shouting over the cacophony of hissing screams and the clacking of beetle wings. "Then I'll attack it with fire. You should get some of the XP, even if we aren't partied if you're the one to deal damage first."

"No," Jay panted, finally getting to his feet. He carefully slid toward the door like he was skating backward on an ice rink. It had been a while since he'd gone skating, but the motion was familiar enough that with his enhanced Agility it became easy and natural. "No, I can take it. Just lend me your bow and one of those fire arrows!"

He slid over to the door, batting away the flying beetles with increasing ferocity, and braced his back against the wall. Lyra stared at him like he was crazy.

"You can't shoot my fire arrows," she said. "It's one of my Arcane Archer skills. And the normal arrows aren't going to do anything to that... thing."

Jay cursed and whacked another Level 2 beetle against the wall. His Bolo Knife was dripping with the disgusting orange guts, making it harder to hold. Fortunately, the construct moved with a speed as glacial as its name. If Jay could stay on top of the beetle projectiles, he had a few moments to spare to strategize with the fox-girl.

"I've got a Strength buff right now," he said. "Do you think I can just... punch it to death?"

Lyra gave him a horrified look. "Jay, no! Just... do *something* to do damage to the monster rather than those little ones its firing at you. Then I'll kill it. Don't be stubborn."

Jay eyed the monster. Other than going in there and trying to slash the thing apart with his Bolo Knife or trying to punch it, he couldn't think of what else to do. Neither option seemed likely to produce results. The way the beetles were crawling put their hard-shelled bodies on the outside, acting like armor for whatever was inside holding it together.

If there was anything inside it. No, the only thing that would kill this thing was fire. He had to be the one to do first damage. And if Lyra's fire arrows wouldn't work for him... he glanced at the torch on the wall, a crazy idea forming in his adrenaline-fueled brain.

Lyra had told him to trust his instincts in the dungeon. Jay couldn't tell if this was his instincts speaking or if he was just losing his mind, but he figured it was worth a shot.

"Give me your bow," he said, batting two more flying beetles from the air. "I've got an idea."

"Jay, it won't work! The fire arrows are related to my class, they—"

He shouted, interrupting her. "Just the bow, hurry!"

The roaring monster was getting closer, so close that Jay could see the horrible writhing mass of beetle bodies inside its mouth, stuck together with something that looked a lot like the orange goop that came out of them when they burst.

Lyra stopped protesting and shoved an arm through the doorway, handing him the bow. Jay grabbed it from her and pulled the flaming torch off the wall, muttering a prayer under his breath as he attempted to line it up like an arrow. It was far too thick and heavy to go far, but Jay was hoping that his additional strength plus the short range of the attack would push the impulsive plan just over the edge into the realm of possibility.

A Level 1 beetle slammed into his left leg as he drew the bow, standing in front of the doorway, just inside the room. The impact ached, but not nearly as much as the first time one had attacked him. His Strength bonus must be helping him deal with the pain. Either that or his body was too focused on the fight to bother sending those annoying signals to his brain. Jay didn't care which it was, he was just grateful for the fact that he could still concentrate through the onslaught brought on by the raging construct.

He took a deep, steadying breath, his gaze locked

on the monster just beyond the tip of the torch. Exhaling as he released the string, he attempted to hold the bow as straight as he could, not wanting to interfere with what was already going to have to be a supremely lucky shot.

The torch flew through the air, it's flame sputtering as it sailed into the mouth of the monster. Jay's heart leaped into his throat. It wasn't going to work. He hadn't accounted for the fact that the flame might go out as it was flying through the air. Wasn't it a magic torch? Shouldn't it just stay lit? Dammit!

He shoved the bow back at Lyra. "Okay, your turn. My idea failed."

"Jay, get down!" Lyra grabbed him by the shoulder and wrenched him backward, sending his feet skidding in the ooze.

As he fell, Jay saw flames erupting from inside the beetle monster's mouth, as if there was a fire burning in its belly. Jay seemed to fall in slow motion, his gaze locked on his enemy, as the flames billowed out, blooming like a violent red flower from the construct's face. A percussive wave of heat slammed into Jay as he landed on the floor in the doorway.

Lyra was still pulling on him, trying to get him away from... something. The burning wall hit him before he could figure it out, tossing his body like a ragdoll through the air as a series of chimes and trumpets sounded inside his head as the dungeon awarded him a series of achievements and notifications.

Just before he hit the wall, one of the intrusive notifications burst into his head.

Congratulations!
You have Achieved Level 4
XP: 105 | Next Lvl: 900
Health: 125 (-30) | Stamina: 110 (-30) | Mana: 100 (-30)
Unassigned Attribute Points: 6
You have 60 Base Stat Points to Distribute. Would you like to increase Health, Stamina, or Mana?

It was a good thing the Level Up happened when it did, because his Health bar had just enough time to replenish itself before he slammed into the gray-blue stone at what felt like Mach-10, and his entire HUD began flashing red. An alarm sound rang in his ears—or in his mind, he couldn't really tell—but there was nothing he could do to stop it. He tried to focus on the parts of his notification screens that he could see, but it was as if his interface with the dungeon was glitching.

Jay closed his eye, attempting to ignore the excruciating pain that tore through every cell of his body. A voice called to him from somewhere very far away, sounding like it was coming from underwater. Or maybe it was that his ears were filled with blood.

"Molly?" he tried to say, hoping it was her. He really wanted to be able to say goodbye. "I'm sorry, Molly—"

Slowly, the voice became clearer, until he could

tell that it wasn't Molly. "Jay, Jay, wake up!"

The voice sounded scared. Panicked, actually. Which was funny because he was pretty sure he was the one who was dying.

"Jay, please, please, you can't die on me. I can't lose another friend in here, I'll go mad. Jay!"

Something twinged in the back of Jay's mind, somewhere behind the pain and confusion and the fact that he couldn't seem to move his body. He knew the voice now. Remembered the adorable, two-toned eyes that flashed with emotion. The long, silver-white hair, the silky ears and fluffy fox tail. He took a breath and felt the bubble of fluid in his chest, then forced out the words, "Lyra... not... dead..."

Hot splashes of liquid hit his face as he heard the fox-girl burst into tears. He wished he could move so he could put his arms around her and comfort her. He didn't know what had happened, but he knew it must be bad. His HUD was still flashing red when he tried to open his eyes and there was an endless stream of notifications to go through. He'd leveled up though, so that must mean he'd killed the construct with his crazy plan. It had just worked a little better than he'd expected and caused a massive explosion, that was all.

He must have been healing slowly. With the extra point he'd put in Constitution plus the bonus he got from the Ragged Leather Armor, his HP should be climbing. He just needed to wait. His body, enhanced with the dungeon's magic, would heal and he'd be all right. Lyra would stop crying. He could still save Molly. He just needed to...

Distribute his Base Stat points!

Jay had gotten two levels, that must mean he had points to distribute. If he could focus enough to get through his menus, he could increase the speed he was healing at immensely.

He forced his eyes open and winced at the blinking red around the edge of his vision. At least it didn't look broken and pixelated anymore. How low had his health gone?

Focusing on the bottom of his display screen, he saw that his HP was at 9 out of 105. And he'd regained some HP already. Had he been knocked all the way down to a single point? If so, he had been incredibly lucky.

Jay groaned as he attempted to move. He wanted to take Lyra's hand and tell her he was okay, but nothing seemed to work the way it was supposed to. She was sitting beside him, tears still spilling down her cheeks, her shoulders heaving. He didn't think she looked nearly as relieved as she should have that he wasn't dead.

Then again, if she didn't have a way to heal him, there was every reason to believe they'd be attacked again and the dungeon would finish what it had started.

Determined to do everything he could to ensure that didn't happen, Jay refocused on his HUD.

He had 60 stats to distribute to his three base stats,

plus 6 Attribute points. If he wanted to rid himself of the Startup Costs debuff, there was only one way he could spend those points. He needed to get his base stats up to a minimum of 100 each, including the 30% handicap if he wanted to be able to party with Lyra and cancel the effects of the debuff. He'd end up with more Mana than he likely needed, given that he'd be most likely to use melee skills to compliment Lyra's ranged attacks. But a more balanced build wasn't going to be a bad thing until he was certain which way his class was going to go.

Jay didn't hesitate, dropping 10 points into Health, 20 points into Stamina, and 30 points into Mana. He only needed 5 points in Health, technically, but he could only move groups of ten points. Besides, he wasn't sure that stat boosts due to armor would count toward his baseline as far as the debuff was concerned.

He immediately felt the benefits of the extra health points, like his entire body had been dipped in a cooling salve. The upgrade left a tingling pleasure in its wake, and Jay wished he'd had more points to add to his HP. But it couldn't be helped. It was more important to get rid of the Startup Costs handicap so that he could party with Lyra, allowing them to fight together more effectively. Plus, it would mean so much to her.

In fact...

Jay opened the party menu and located Lyra Golden-Eye on his list of possible group-mates. He grinned, a motion he regretted at once, as it felt like his face was one giant, oozing wound. He glanced at Lyra, who had her head leaned back against the stone wall. Her silky white ears drooped into her hair. She looked so forlorn it almost broke Jay's heart.

He focused all the strength he had left to lift his hand, and reached for her. His arms were burned badly, crisped black in some places, blistered and raw in others. Jay recoiled inwardly to see the state of his body, but he could already feel the dungeon's magic working on him. He knew, instinctively, that what would have killed him back on Earth was something he only needed time and patience to recover from in the dungeon.

Jay put his hand on Lyra's foot, the only part of her he could easily reach, and squeezed her around the ankle. She looked up in shock, staring at him with her eyes filled with tears. Blue and gold pierced him with the depth of their pain, and he tried to give her a shaky smile.

"Jay, don't," she whispered. "You need your energy. We only have about half an hour until the beetles respawn. I can hold them off for a while if I have to. But we need to get you out of here to a safe zone as soon as possible if we can."

Jay took a deep breath, noticing the bubbling sound was a little less. "You don't think I'll make it, do you?"

"Don't say that!" she shouted, fresh tears pouring

down her face. "You're going to be fine. I just have to keep you safe until you're healed enough to..."

Her gaze traveled over his disfigured form, and she burst into tears again.

"If you believed that, you wouldn't be so sad," he said, giving her ankle a squeeze again. His voice came out dry and raspy, but it was stronger than before. "Please don't cry, Lyra. Here. I have something for you."

She blinked, rubbing at her eyes, and stared at him in confusion. "No, no you don't. Just get better, Jay. That's all you need to do. Just get better and everything will be all right."

Jay mentally selected Lyra's name from the party menu. A text bubble popped up.

Do you wish to add Lyra Golden-Eye to your party? Y/N

Jay hit yes immediately. He waited for something to happen, some notification to alert him to the fact that he'd formed a party.

But nothing came.

Lyra had stopped crying. She was frozen in place, staring straight ahead of her.

It was the same look of shock that had passed over her features when she'd seen the Glacial Scarab Construct form behind him. Jay had the horrible feeling that another monster had appeared.

Then she said, "Jay, is this for real?"

He realized she must be seeing a notification for his request to form a party.

"Yes," he said. "If you still want to. I know I'm a bit of a mess right now."

Lyra scrambled to her feet, shouting, "Yes! Yes, yes, yes, yes! Thank you, Jay! Thank you for believing in me! I won't let you down!"

Jay watched her happy dance, fully allowing himself to appreciate the way her lithe muscles stretched and moved, and her barely covered breasts jiggled and bounced—hey, he'd almost died, he figured he was allowed this one moment. Her tail twitched back and forth with her as she danced, and from his angle on the floor Jay enjoyed a brief glimpse beneath her leather skirt. He felt his body respond even through the pain of his injuries.

Good to know that's not broken, he thought to himself.

But when he still didn't get the party notification he was expecting he had to interrupt her dance.

"Uh, Lyra?" he whispered, trying to get her attention but unable to get any force behind his words. "Lyra..."

Finally she heard him. "Yes, Jay? What do you need? Can I help you? Do you want some water?"

Actually, water sounded life saving at the moment. But that wasn't what he was after.

"Yes," he said. "But first, I need you to accept my party request."

"Oh!" The fox-girl's face flushed so pink she could have been a red fox instead of an arctic fox. "I'm so sorry. Of course! I just got really excited."

"That's okay," he said, smiling through the pain of his cracked cheeks. "It was fun to watch."

She blushed deeper, covering her face with her hands, and sank to the floor beside him. As she busied herself with getting a water bottle out of her satchel, Jay got the notification he'd been waiting for:

Congratulations!
You are the leader of a Delving Party!
Party members include: Lyra Golden-Eye | Lvl 6 |
[Arcane Archer]

Congratulations!
You have successfully removed the Start-up Costs
Debuff!
Your maximum XP gained from kills and quests in the dungeon has been restored to its normal baseline. All stat handicaps have been removed.

15

It's Complicated

R elief flooded through Jay's body as the debuff was removed. His HP was still way down, only at 20 out of 125 now, but it was as if the 30% handicap had been physically pressing on him and now a weight had been lifted.

He didn't hesitate to distribute his Attribute points either, knowing that anything he could add to Constitution would help with his healing rate. And given how shitty he felt right now, having a higher Constitution was definitely something he wanted to prioritize, no matter what his build ended up looking like.

He had 6 points to spend. He didn't know much about what his class was going to require, but he knew his survivability right now required him to be physically tough. For now, he figured it was best to forgo wasting points in Intelligence—though he had to admit, having only a 1 in Intelligence made him feel a bit... well, *stupid*, for lack of a better word—since he wasn't using any magic at this point in time.

So, he dropped one each in Strength, Agility, and Willpower, then dumped the last three points into Constitution. If he wasn't going to be smart, at least he could be tough. And it would be nice to be able to recover from damage more quickly.

He felt the immediate effects of his choice as his Health bar surged forward, visibly climbing faster than it had been before.

Delver: Jay Morgan

Class Type: [N/A]

Class: [N/A]

Lvl: 4

XP: 105 | **Next Lvl:** 900

Health: 135 | **Stamina:** 130 | **Mana:** 130

Unassigned Attribute Points: 0

Strength: 3

Agility: 3

Intelligence: 1

Constitution: 5 [*Ragged Leather Armor* – Set Bonus Constitution +1, HP +5]

Willpower: 2

Charisma: 10

Active Skills: [+ pending]

Passive Abilities: Environmental Resistance 1 (Arctic), Dungeon Sight 1, [+ pending]

Perks: Panty Dropper, [+ pending]

Best of all, was the seeing the Start-up Costs 'Ability' disappear.

It seemed like false advertising to call a permanent debuff an 'Ability,' but he supposed as far as the system mechanics were concerned, a passive advantage or disadvantage that worked the same way. Maybe it had just been Nova's way of screwing with him.

He still wasn't certain the dungeon wasn't completely demented and trying to kill him, now that he'd seen the creatures she was putting him up against. It didn't really matter if she claimed to have a quest for him if she had some crazy idea that only the best of the best would be worthy of receiving such a quest.

He was as likely to die attempting to prove himself to her as he was just Delving normally, if Lyra's stories about high fatality rates were any indication of how the Ice dungeon usually behaved.

It was gone now, though, and that's what mattered.

Also, he was curious about the [pending] tags that had been added to each of his Active Skills, Passive Abilities, and Perks tabs.

"Jay, drink this," Lyra said, holding out a leather canteen, her blue-and-gold eyes fixed worriedly on him. "Do you think you can stand?"

Jay groaned, realizing he hadn't even attempted to sit up. But he gave it a shot, knowing they'd have to get moving before the Glacial Scarabs respawned.

Surprisingly, it wasn't as painful as he'd feared. He took the water and drank gratefully, and was surprised to see a new notification pop up. He opened it as he drank.

Buff Activated – Hydrate or Die! (Temporary)

You know it's good for you. You know you'll feel better if you drink some. Sixty percent of your body is made from it. Your cells need it to replenish and repair themselves. So why does it take a social media post from a fitness model with 300 visible abdominal muscles to remind you to stay hydrated? You're not a corporate suit anymore, with time to kill reading inane blog posts about how to hack your body and brain and unlock your true potential. (Really? You thought green smoothies would do that?) It's time to start taking this shit seriously. Water helps replenish Health, Stamina, and Mana points at an accelerated rate, for 10 min. Set the alarm on your smart phone, dungeon cowboy. Hydrate or Die!

Bonus Buff: When your Health Points are below 50% of their maximum, you receive a bonus 25% to all buffs received from eating and drinking.

Jay grimaced inwardly at what were starting to feel like increasingly personal attacks from the dungeon's notification system. He had read a lot of fitness blogs and social media posts about how to hack his body and mind. He had bought into the green smoothie fad. He'd even banged a receptionist in a red-pencil skirt like had been mentioned in the

Boardroom Champagne For Two description, now that he thought about it—just because his heart belonged to Molly didn't mean other body parts didn't need attention sometimes, too.

But he drank the water, grateful for the buff, even if he felt like the dungeon was mocking him. Then, handing the canteen back to Lyra, he attempted to push himself to his feet.

The pretty fox-girl was at his side immediately. "Here," she said, slipping an arm gingerly around his waist. "Lean on me. Let me help."

Jay tried not to put too much weight on the tiny Vulpinari, but he found her very sturdy beneath his arm as she propped him up.

"Careful," he said, wincing as his clothing pinched at the burned skin. "I'm heavy. I don't want to squish you if I fall."

"My Strength stats are decent," she said, holding him tighter. "I'm tougher than I look, I promise."

Lyra gazed up at him with those beautiful blue-and-gold eyes and Jay felt his heart melt a little bit. It had been a long time... since any woman had looked at him with such tenderness. Molly was his best friend, and they loved each other in their own way, but they were both cautious about letting their other, more secret feelings show. Lyra seemed to have no such qualms, and it made Jay wish he was in better condition so he could squeeze her tightly and feel her firm body give beneath his embrace.

Misreading his look, her ears flattened defensively. "What? It's true! I'm higher level than you are, even if you are power leveling through the first floor. Jeez."

Jay laughed. "I believe you," he said. "If you say you can handle me, who am I to argue?"

He felt her tail swish against his legs, and he smiled to think that he'd made her happy.

"That's right, no arguing," she said, guiding him down the corridor gently. "Save all your energy for getting better. There's a safe room up ahead. Not everyone can get into them on F1, but I earned a key on one of the lower floors, and now that we're partied you can come in too."

"That sounds great." Jay took each step cautiously, but he found the pain reducing with every minute. His boosted Constitution stat plus the bonus from the water must have been helping. The corridor ahead looked long, but mercifully it was empty. Then he remembered something. "Wait! Shouldn't we loot those Scarabs before we go? What if one of them dropped something good?"

"Jay, you're hurt," the fox-girl protests, pleading him with her eyes. "Normally I would agree, but I'd really feel better if we—"

"It will be fast," he assured her. "Please, Lyra. I don't like the idea of leaving opportunities unchecked."

Lyra growled in frustration, but she gently turned him around and led him back to the room full of bug guts and glittering black corpses. "Fine," she said. "But I'm doing the looting. Now that we're par-tied together you'll be able to give me permission to loot your kills. The items will go into the party menu before they're distributed."

Jay's entire body ached and his skin felt like it was still on fire in places. He didn't have any objections to Lyra doing the looting. But part of him wondered if one of the bodies might drop the reagents they needed to bring back to Raina. With the way the dungeon seemed to be catering his delving expe-rience personally, he thought it was a possibility. Or, depending on the dungeon's mood, it might be a guarantee that they wouldn't find the Frostleaf Clover or Tundra Berries anywhere on the first floor. Even if they were supposed to be here.

"That's fine," he said. "I trust you."

Tears glittered in Lyra's eyes as she gazed up at him. "Thank you," she whispered, sniffing slightly. "But even if you didn't, as party leader, you will be the one who distributes all the items collected by the party. Don't worry though, I trust you too."

Jay's heart swelled, realizing that Lyra had accept-ed a vulnerable position in accepting his party re-quest. It made him feel good that she was comfort-able with him being the party leader. Even if she'd joined the party out of personal desperation, she didn't have to trust him with the role of leader.

"Would you rather be leader?" Jay asked as she parked him next to the wall and began stepping tentatively into the disgusting room. "It would make sense. You're the more experienced delver. It might be safer for both of us."

Lyra's forehead wrinkled as she picked her way through the Scarab corpses, her boots sliding in the orange puddle. "At the rate you're leveling, you'll be more powerful than me in no time," she said. "Besides, the best way to learn is by doing. I... I'm not eager to lead a party, if I'm honest. I don't want that responsibility again, if I can help it."

Jay watched as the shimmering aura around the Glacial Scarab corpses disappeared, one by one, as Lyra looted them. He remembered the look of devastation on Lyra's face when she'd thought he was dead or dying, and it hurt him to know that he'd caused her so much pain by nearly getting himself killed. The poor fox-girl was traumatized by the loss of so many allies at the hands of the dungeon and he'd almost become another one. Jay made a promise to himself that he'd be more careful in the future—not only for his sake and Molly's, but because Lyra needed him to be safe, too. Or, at least as safe as he could be inside a dungeon that was trying to murder him.

"Jay, this is insane, are you seeing this?" Lyra asked suddenly, jolting him out of his thoughts.

He craned around the doorframe to see the pretty fox-girl looking alert and excited. But he couldn't see anything to be excited about besides the dead bugs.

"What is it?" he asked.

"All these items that are dropping! These are all the things that are supposed to drop in the Ice Dungeon, but rarely do. We'll be able to sell everything on the World Dungeon Market! Oh, and your Inventory feature is amazing. We can just leave all this in the party menu rather than having to divvy it up before closing the menu. Usually, we'd each have to take our share and store it physically before leaving the area."

Jay opened the party menu to see a growing list of items. None of them were the reagents that Raina needed, but it was good that they were items that could be sold.

As Lyra continued her gross but gratifying job, Jay caught up on the commodities of the Ice dungeon. Unlike all the descriptions that seemed to be catered to Jay just to harass him, these item descriptions were informative but mundane. Perhaps other dungeons had less personality than Nova did, and she didn't want to give herself away.

Frost Carapace Fragments [White] – These are shimmering pieces of the beetle's icy exoskeleton. Hardy and cold to the touch, Frost Carapace Fragments are sought after by armorers and shield-smiths for crafting lightweight yet durable armor sets that offer resistance to cold damage. Additionally, alchemists find them useful in concoctions meant to ward off evil spirits.

Chilled Beetle Grit [Copper] – A fine, sparkling powder obtained from grinding down the less us-

able parts of the Glacial Scarab. This grit is a versatile component in the crafting of potions and elixirs, particularly those that enhance cold resistance or boost mana regeneration in frigid environments. Enchanters also use this grit to imbue weapons with minor ice damage or frost effects.

Icy Antennae [Silver] – The antennae of Glacial Scarabs are infused with natural magic that helps them navigate and survive in icy terrains. When harvested, these Icy Antennae serve as potent reagents for creating magical items that assist in locating hidden objects or paths in snow-covered or icy areas. They are also used in crafting accessories that slightly increase the wearer's perception and resistance to magical cold.

Out of curiosity, Jay opened the complete descriptions of the three items that had been taken from the Snow Scorpion as well.

Frozen Carapace (Scorpion) [White] – This sturdy shell piece, harvested from the resilient exoskeleton of an arctic creature, glimmers with a subtle blue hue. Slightly cold to the touch, the Frozen Carapace is a favored material among armor smiths and leatherworkers for its inherent frost resistance. When incorporated into armor or clothing, it grants the wearer protection against the biting chill of icy environments, making it an essential component for adventurers planning to brave the frostbitten depths of the coldest dungeon levels.

Snow Scorpion Stinger [White] – A long, slender appendage tipped with a hardened barb, the Snow Scorpion Stinger is coated in a thin layer of frost. Alchemists prize this stinger for the unique properties of its venom, which, when properly distilled, can be used to concoct potions with a variety of effects. These range from enhancing the imbiber's resistance to cold, to temporarily boosting their agility or sharpening their senses. Its versatility makes it a valuable commodity in the alchemical market, where the demand for such reagents is always high.

Snow Scorpion Eye [White] – Extracted carefully from the apex predator of icy realms, the Snow Scorpion Eye is a crystalline organ that seems to hold a miniature snowstorm within its depths. Alchemists and potion makers seek out this eye for its potent magical essence, which can be harnessed to create elixirs that improve night vision, or potions that grant a brief insight into the ethereal plane. Some even use it to brew decoctions that help in detecting hidden traps and doorways by revealing the slight magical auras they emit, making it an indispensable tool for treasure hunters and dungeon delvers alike.

"There are a lot of cold-resistance effects on these items," Jay observed, closing the menu. "Isn't that kind of redundant when we already have **Environmental Resistance**?"

Lyra was muttering something under her breath

as she looted yet another low-level beetle corpse. But rather than looking disgusted as Jay expected, the fox-girl seemed to be in a mystified daze.

"No," she said, looking thoughtful. "I mean yes, but... it's complicated. I'll explain once we're in the safe zone, okay? The respawn timer is only minutes away."

"You have a timer?" he asked, wondering where he could find that in his own menu.

"It's a perk I earned," she said. "I can only use it once a day."

"All right," he said. "I'll stop pestering you with questions. Looks like you're almost done."

The pile of shimmering corpses had been reduced to only a few, with the empty scarabs being quickly reabsorbed by the dungeon. Lyra picked her way toward the construct. "This is new, you know," she said. "I've never seen the Glacial Scarabs transform like that. You got some kind of warning in your **Dungeon Sight** description, didn't you? I didn't know what you were talking about. I'd never heard of a construct before."

"Yeah," Jay said. "There was a mild sounding warning at the bottom that said 'Watch out, these magical beetles can fuse together, forming larger constructs to challenge intruders.' You didn't seem worried about it, so I ignored it."

"I'm sorry, Jay," she said. "I didn't understand. I should have paid more attention to what you were saying. If I'd known, I never would have left you to look at that—"

Lyra let out a gasp, cutting her off as she was about to explain where she'd run off to during his fight. The misshapen corpse of the construct stopped shimmering, and slowly vanished behind Lyra. The fox girl stood in the middle of the room, now dark without the torchlight, staring at something in her HUD.

"Ready to go?" he asked, seeing there were no more corpses to loot.

Lyra nodded slowly. "Yeah, sure. I'm coming."

She began trudging through the orange puddle, lost in thought.

"You okay?" he asked, worried that something was wrong.

The fox-girl's ears were flattened sideways, the way a wild fox might hold them if they were feeling wary. Her tail didn't move.

"Yeah," she said, her voice distant. "Just... this is weird."

Jay felt a pang of concern. "What is it?"

She glanced up at him as she reached the doorway and seemed to notice the look on his face. She smiled at him, her two-toned eyes flashing, and he felt his worries ease.

"It's fine," she said. "We'll talk about it in the safe zone. Ready to go?"

"Ready when you are."

Lyra wrapped her arm around his waist, and they began walking back the way they'd come. Though, this time, Jay noticed each step was considerably easier than it had been before. He glanced at his Health bar and saw it was almost three-quarters full.

With any luck, he'd be healed and they'd be rested soon and they could take another stab at what the dungeon had in store for them. Despite his near-death experience, now that he was starting to feel better, Jay realized he was ready to fight again.

Not just ready, but eager.

"You know," Lyra said, her voice as quiet as their footfalls along the tomb corridor. "I'm going to enjoy looking after you tonight. I have a feeling it will be the last time you'll need me half as much as I need you."

Surprised, Jay glanced down at the fox-girl. He had expected her to look sad—the tone of her voice had seemed wistful—but the expression in her eyes was far more complex than that. Lyra looked happy and excited, and—unless Jay was very much mistaken—aroused...

Suddenly, he felt they couldn't get to the safe zone fast enough.

16

Safe

J ay wasn't sure what he was expecting from the Safe Zone, but the place Lyra brough him was not it.

They had turned a corner of the Egyptian tomb-like corridors, and rather than finding more labyrinthine passages the corridor opened into a wide, tundra-like plain. Low grasses, dusted with snow moved in a breeze that Jay couldn't explain, given that they were still inside the dungeon. Above them, where there should have been a ceiling twelve feet above their heads, there was only pitch black and a scattering of stars—or some magic that looked like stars.

Something moved in the distance, and Jay's muscles tensed, ready for a fight. All he could see in the night-like ambiance were pale, white shadows, like lumbering, shuffling spirits.

Sensing his discomfort, Lyra squeezed her arm

around him. "It's only the Ghost Bison," she said. "They aren't aggressive unless you attack first. They aren't monsters, but animals that have evolved to live inside the dungeon. They do drop some of the commodities we can sell on the World Dungeon Market, or so I've heard. But... the dungeon is dangerous enough without pissing off the Ghost Bison."

"They're huge," Jay marveled, pausing to watch the creatures as they grazed at the edge of his vision, barely visible in the artificial starlight.

"And powerful," she said. "Many of the animals that live in the dungeon will attack on sight, and some have evolved magical attacks after integrating with the dungeon the same way humans and Faunari do. It's best to leave the neutral creatures alone, in my experience, and save our energy for the aggressive ones."

Jay nodded. "Is this the safe zone?"

"Over there," Lyra said, pointing to a faintly glowing dome to their left. "See the hexdome there? I have a key."

The igloo-like structure appeared to be made from transparent hexagonal panels that glowed ice-blue at the edges. It appeared like a latticework of fine, glowing lines, completely out of place in the tomblike section they had been in before and the tundra-like section they were in now. Jay wondered if there was ever any rhyme or reason to the dungeon's layout or if it was always a patchwork of themes.

Lyra led him toward the hexdome with slow, steady steps. Their footsteps crunched in the snowy grass and Jay kept his gaze lowered, scanning with **Dungeon Sight** to ensure he didn't miss anything in the new environment. In the tomb, each step had echoed eerily. Now, in the vast open space, the crunch of their footfalls was met with dead silence, which Jay found eerie in a different way.

"Are there bison outside the dungeon?" Jay asked as his gaze wandered back toward the creatures on the horizon. "Or bison-kin Faunari?"

Lyra glanced at him, as if surprised by the question. "No, they aren't real creatures."

Jay frowned. "They are where I come from," he said. "There's not many of them left, but they used to roam free across much of our world. They weren't white like those ones, though. More dark brown and black, I think. I've never seen one up close."

"That's strange," Lyra said, sounding thoughtful. "What about the scorpions and scarabs? Are those real in your world too?"

Jay let out a laugh. "Well, not exactly. There are tiny versions of those creatures that live in some places. But most are smaller than the palm of your hand. Some scorpions can get bigger, but nowhere close to the size of the ones we fought. If there were, no one would leave their houses. And none of them turn into those construct monsters, either."

Lyra was silent for a while, considering something. Jay was content to listen to the crunching of their footsteps, watch the stars and the Ghost Bison, and keep his eyes peeled for shimmers in the frozen grass.

"There are stories..." she began suddenly. "Superstitions, I guess... that the dungeon changes with every person who dies inside it. The dungeon absorbs the bodies of all who die within. No one gets to take the body of a fallen friend or loved one home if they fall inside. The dungeon consumes the body as the price for the gifts we receive from it. Some say, the dungeon takes a person's memories as well as their flesh, and this is why the dungeon is always changing. Perhaps, long ago, someone from your world died in this dungeon. Someone who knew of bison, scorpions, and scarabs."

Jay felt a chill run down his spine as he thought of the possibility that he recognized bits and pieces of the dungeon because they'd literally been torn from people's dying minds. Maybe these elements were like the ghosts of people from his world who had lost their lives here, each one representing a person's greatest fear or something they admired. Maybe dying in the dungeon wasn't like death at all, and you were doomed to live on as a part of some massive hive mind of all the beings that had died here.

He shuddered.

If he died here, Jay wondered what parts of him would be left behind?

If the dungeon's teasing was any indication, it

would probably add a frozen boardroom and a boss fight where you have to defeat a big guy in a suit yelling that he needed you to find five more high-profile clients by the end of the week.

Or receptionists in red pencil skirts.

He pushed the thought from his mind as they approached the hexdome, as Lyra had called it.

"Are you okay to stand?" she asked.

"I'll be fine," he said. "I actually feel great, all things considered."

"Well, you look like shit," she said, her two-toned gaze roving over him as if taking stock of all the injuries he was ignoring. "But if you can hold yourself up for a few seconds, I'll get us inside the safe zone, and we can heal you up properly."

"Yes, boss," he said, grinning at her to show that he didn't take her comment to heart.

She smiled back and busied herself with a keypad on one of the hexagonal panes, entering a complex code of some kind.

What he'd said was true, though. Jay couldn't believe how much better he felt than he had an hour ago. His muscles still ached, and his bones felt bruised, and his skin felt like it was missing in places. But he could feel the dungeon magic healing him by the second, and somehow the knowledge that he was getting better instead of worse made the pain and discomfort more bearable. He could handle any kind of pain, so long as he knew it was temporary.

That thought surprised Jay, as he wasn't the type

to go seeking out unpleasant experiences just for kicks. He wasn't much of an outdoor enthusiast. He didn't like extreme sports. He didn't even like scary movies. He'd spent most of his time, up until now, in an air-conditioned office building making money for other people and that was okay with him.

But he'd been willing to charge into the arctic with Molly just because she was excited about it. He'd carried her across a frozen tundra while his body was slowly giving up on him, because he needed to find her help. He had been willing—even eager—to enter the dungeon despite not knowing a thing about fighting, because Molly needed him. And he'd come back from the brink of death, willing to take on even more, because he now had Lyra *and* Molly relying on him.

It was amazing what the right kind of motivation could do to a man.

As much better as he felt now, than immediately after he blew up the construct, that relief couldn't hold a candle to how good he felt the moment he stepped inside the safe zone.

He sighed as he stepped over the threshold, feeling a wash of healing, warming tingles over his entire body. Lyra smiled and closed the door behind him.

"It's nice, isn't it?" she said. "All your stats will recover faster inside a safe zone, and if we stay here for eight hours, there's an additional Rested Bonus. Given how fast you've levelled, we might want to make sure we stay long enough to get that, as it gives you 50% more XP from kills and quests. We're a high enough level now that most low-level creatures aren't going to give us much XP."

"Unless the dungeon decides to spawn a bunch of Elites and random high-level monsters just to mess with us."

Jay looked around the room. The decorations were all done in a soft, sterile white. The rounded walls of the outer dome shape didn't seem to affect the inside of the safe room. It appeared as a plain, white-walled room, with five empty cots along one wall, and a ring of blue fire in the center of the room with two big, overstuffed armchairs next to it.

To his left, a rectangle of glass that looked like a shower or steam-room, called to him invitingly. Two white squares were stacked next to the shower, with little port windows on the front. He wondered if these were washing machines.

Lyra confirmed as much as she walked him through the basics of the safe room. "Beds, shower. If you put your soiled clothing and armor in one of those boxes they will be cleaned by the time the long rest is over. The fire is more for cooking than warmth."

Jay could feel the orange bug guts drying on his body, and he itched to take them off. "You don't have to do anything?" he asked. "Just put them in the box and they come out clean?"

Lyra nodded, glancing down at her own slightly-less soiled but still pretty grimy outfit. "Yes," she said. "We should probably do that sooner rather than later."

"What do we wear in the meantime?" he asked, suddenly feeling awkward. "I don't have a change of clothes."

Lyra shrugged as if it didn't matter all that much. "There're blankets if you get cold. Towels next to the shower. I still have to bind your wounds, though, so you can't bundle up immediately.

Jay tried not to show his discomfort if this wasn't something that bothered the Faunari people.

"So, nudity isn't going to offend you?"

Lyra's eyebrows shot into her silver-white hair. "Offend me?" she asked with an innocent smile. "I've been looking forward to it since you first agreed to Delve with me, Jay Morgan. Hurry up and get naked."

Jay felt his cheeks burning as he feigned nonchalance, moving toward the shower. He began to strip, slowly—not because he was trying to be sexy, but his entire body felt beaten and bruised. He managed to get the Ragged Leather leg pieces off without too much struggle, and the arm bracers. But he winced as he tried to undo the chest piece, unable to reach the ties under his arms.

"Here, let me help," the fox-girl said, appearing at his side.

Jay held out his arms so that she could work on the laces. When she was finished, she gently lifted the chest piece over his head and set it aside. Then she tugged on the bottom of the long-sleeved shirt he'd been wearing underneath, untucking it from his pants. Jay tried to control his breathing as her cool fingers touched his stomach, sliding up his sides, as he lifted his arms and let her pull it up over his head.

When the shirt fell the ground, Jay could see how damaged it was, and he wondered if the magical laundry machines also did repairs.

Glancing back at Lyra he was surprised to find her staring at him with unabashed admiration, her blue-and-gold eyes roving over his body despite the bruises and burns. The fox-girl bit her lip as she gazed up at him, and blushed when he met her eyes.

"Well," he asked, his voice suddenly low and husky. "Do I pass muster?"

"You're not going to win any beauty pageants with all those scars," she said, her tail flicking behind her. "But I think you'll do."

She reached for his belt and pulled him closer, until she had to crane her neck to look up at him. Her ears lowered as he looked into her eyes, and a small, eager whine escaped her throat.

Jay couldn't believe how beautiful she was. He could have spent hours staring down into her perfect face, admiring the fullness of her parted lips, the way her silver-white hair coiled around her slender neck, her petite but muscular shoulders. Jay hadn't had feelings—besides lust—for any girl but Molly since he was a teenager. He knew that wasn't healthy, but there had seemed to be nothing he could do to jolt himself from the longing of his first love.

Here, for the first time, with this enchanting woman from a completely different world, Jay was feeling the beginning of something more than just physical need. There was something about the contrast between Lyra's emotional vulnerability and her physical strength. She was a warrior, badly in need of love and friendship. And the way she had cried next to him when he was injured had torn Jay's heart. A need had lodged in his chest to ensure he never had to see her cry again.

And when she looked up at him with something similar reflecting in her two-toned gaze, Jay's stomach flip-flopped. She'd been flirting with him since they'd met, but did she really want—

Lyra startled him from his wandering thoughts by undoing his belt and opening his pants.

Jay let out a groan, partly of pain—because his skin was still tender—and partly due to the intense desire to see where this road would lead. If he didn't stop her, how far would she go?

17

Cold Shower

Lyra slipped her hands inside his pants and slid her palms down over his hips. Mercifully she kept them on top of his boxers. She paused, with her hands halfway down, his pants stuck on the sudden lump of his erection. "Is this okay?" she asked.

Wordlessly, he nodded. The fox-girl bit her lip and gently moved her hands down his thighs, pulling the fabric away from his skin so that it didn't chafe any of the raw places that hadn't healed yet. As she worked her way down, she crouched lower and lower. Kneeling, she helped him get the pants over his feet.

Jay swallowed hard, seeing her on her knees before him. He could see straight down the open top of her leather armor, the smooth arc of her cleavage. He wanted to run his fingers through her hair, to feel the silky softness of her pure-white ears, to guide her open mouth gently toward his throbbing cock.

Then he remembered he was still covered in scarab slime and had open wounds on a significant percentage of his body. That kind of thing might have to wait until he was feeling a little better.

Lyra stood, not without casting a glance at his expanding boxers, and smiled. "I'll let you do the rest," she said. "For now. The shower is pretty self-explanatory. Get in, select your temperature preference, get clean. There are a few different choices for soap, but I suggest the Wound Wash. It will help speed up your healing. But at the rate you seem to be improving, you'll probably be okay no matter what you choose."

"Thank—" Jay tried to say, but the word came out gruffer than he intended. "Thank you."

"Let me know if you need any help in there," she added, blushing prettily.

Jay couldn't tell if this was more teasing or if she was waiting for him to invite her into the shower with him. Deciding it was best to be direct, he asked, "Care to join me?"

Lyra's blush deepened. "Really? Oh... I—I'd like to, actually," she said. "But... I think we'd better not. Yet. Umm... I meant if you need help washing your back and stuff, but..."

Jay lifted his hands in the universal sign of surrender.

"No need to explain," he said. "The offer is open if you want to. Not sure how much fun I'll be when everything feels slightly seared, anyway."

"I have something that might help for that," Lyra said, perking up. "For after your shower. Hurry up and I'll show you!"

Jay didn't need to be told twice. He stepped inside the glass rectangle, remembering to remove his boxers before he closed the door behind him, and investigated the controls. There was a color-coded temperature dial, which he turned to a little cooler than halfway. Since his skin was literally burned off in places, he figured even warm water might feel too hot. A digital menu appeared directly on the glass, giving him options for different types of soap. He selected the Wound Wash as Lyra had suggested.

Anything to speed up the healing process, in case the fox-girl had plans to make good on the sultry look in her eyes. Jay didn't want to get his hopes up, though. In fact, as his feelings for Lyra deepened, he thought it might be better for them to go slow. Jay wasn't a hundred percent emotionally available, and while Lyra knew that and still flirted and teased... she might not be comfortable doing more than flirting and teasing after being alone for as long as she had.

That was fine. That was more than fine. He just wanted to have Lyra with him, one way or another. It sounded like, even if they found the reagents Raina needed to wake Molly that they'd be stuck in this world indefinitely. Lyra and Jay would have time to explore which ways they wanted to be together. There was no need to rush.

Jay pressed the button to start the shower and

released a sigh of relief as the cooling water washed over his damaged skin. Out of curiosity he watched his Health bar in the bottom of his HUD. When he started the Wound Wash, which came out mixed into the water with a sharp, herbal scent, Jay noticed the speed that his HP was recovering increased slightly.

Jay was surprised how easily he looked passed it now that he was used to it. He actually had to think about it if he wanted to read any of the data, otherwise it faded into the background almost as if it wasn't there at all.

As he enjoyed the shower, he flipped through some of the notifications he'd received during and after the battle with the Glacial Scarab Construct. Besides the generic kill notifications, and a few temporary buffs that had since expired, there were a couple of icons that caught Jay's attention. He checked them now.

New Passive Ability Acquired!
Scale-Up – While you are party leader, receive an additional 10% max XP bonus for each party member added.

Jay frowned. **Scale-Up** seemed to be a direct replacement of **Start-Up Costs**, with a buff instead of a debuff. By adding Lyra to his party rather than the other way around, he'd accidentally lucked into this hidden bonus. Jay was beginning to wonder if his mystery class was some kind of management-inspired role, given all the entrepreneurial and corporate lingo the dungeon was using. But what would that entail?

He supposed there was nothing to do but wait and see.

New Active Skill Acquired!

On-the-Job-Training – Every business owner knows that when starting out on a new venture, success is 25% skill, 25% luck, and 50% winging it and hoping for the best. Sometimes, when you don't have the necessary skills to do a job, you've got no choice but to improvise.

Once per day, you may borrow a skill from one of your party members. While you are using their skill, it will be removed from their skill tree until you return it to them. You do not gain the party members skill points in this level, nor do they lose their skill points. You retain skill points gained with borrowed skills, but may only access them when you have a relevant skill active in your skill tree.

Okay, that one, Jay was pretty sure he must have received when he'd borrowed Lyra's bow to shoot an improvised 'fire arrow' at the Elite Construct using the torch. That plan had been stupid and crazy, and—admittedly like a lot of business ideas Jay had managed to get off the ground—it had worked. He was definitely seeing the theme developing in the skills and abilities the dungeon was giving him. But he still had no idea what the hell it was going to mean.

Jay switched off the Wound Wash and let clean water rinse off the suds as he checked his last interesting notification.

New Perk Acquired!
Bootstrapper – You're starting with nothing and have insurmountable odds stacked against you. There's only one way out of this mess. That's right, you've got to pull yourself up by your bootstraps! Of course, physics isn't on your side, and neither is history. We know the myth of the self-made man has always been more fiction than fact. That's why we're going to give you an extra hand to tug on that... bootstrap. Receive a gift from an 'anonymous benefactor' for every new level gained.

As the mechanical dungeon voice read Jay the description he saw the tab for his Class Menu glow yellow, indicating there had been a change. Sure enough, when he checked, **Bootstrapper** had been added to the Perks menu.

Immediately following the activation of **Bootstrapper**, he received a notification in his Notes menu, the same place he had the message from Raina regarding the reagents she was looking for. Now he had a Note from 'Anonymous Benefactor' beneath the message from the Witch Doctor.

The dungeon didn't read the note aloud in his mind the way it did other notifications, yet Jay immediately knew who this Anonymous Benefactor was. He read the message himself, with Nova's voice ringing in his ears.

Mmmm, I really didn't think you were going to pull that one off, Delver. Color me impressed. I created a brand-new dungeon monster, just for you, and you destroyed it like it was nothing! Sure, you almost died in the process, but really... it shouldn't even have been a contest. I can see I was right about you. You're made for more than mere Delving, Jay Morgan. You're made for so much more...

Here's your gift. Keep leveling and I'll keep 'em coming.

[Beetle Black Scarab Armor] (Gold – Rare)

Jay gaped when he saw the gift he'd received for his last level up. The item was a full piece, Gold level armor set. He couldn't inspect it in the shower, though, and suddenly he was very eager to get out.

He finished up, noting that he only had about 15% of his Health yet to recover and that the progress had stalled to a very slow crawl. Jay didn't know why that might happen, but he figured there was probably only so much his Constitution, the Safe Zone, and the Wound Wash could do before he simply had to sleep to recover the rest of his Health.

Jay turned off the water and opened the shower door, realizing too late that he didn't have a towel. Standing there in the nude, only partially hidden by the water droplets on the glass door, he poked his head out.

"Uh, you said there were towels?"

Lyra tossed a fluffy white towel through the crack in the door, and he stepped back inside the shower to wrap up in it.

Then, feeling a bit less exposed, he stepped out of the shower. When he saw the fox-girl, his eyes almost bugged out of his head.

Lyra stood with an identical white towel over her shoulders, but stripped of all the rest of her clothes. Her lithe little body was on full display as she patiently waited for her turn to wash up. Jay's eyes roved over her pert breasts with their little brown nipples, her taut abdominal muscles, the curve of her hips above her muscular thighs, and the sweet little V between her legs, shaved clean and—if he wasn't mistaken—glistening with moisture.

"Your turn," he said, a bit stunned. He'd gotten the feeling that the fox-girl was shy, but it seemed that was only about getting physical rather than about being seen naked. Jay realized he didn't really know what Faunari customs were around clothing, and that maybe it was totally normal for adults who weren't intimate with each other to be seen naked.

Unfortunately for Jay, he couldn't hide the fact that her presence triggered a response in him.

Lyra glanced at his towel, which was no longer hanging as smoothly as it had been, and bit her lip. She lingered for a moment, as if she wanted to say something. But in the end, she just nodded. "Thanks."

As she turned to get into the shower, Jay got an eyeful of her round, firm buttocks and muscular legs. But his eyes were drawn to the fluffy fox-tail that obscured part of his view. He was struck by a sudden urge to bend Lyra over and lift that tail to see the rest of the show.

When the shower door closed behind her, Jay breathed a sigh of relief. Now was not the time to be getting hot and heavy with a new girl anyway. Even if his near-death experience seemed to have opened the door on all the subconscious human desires to procreate before death, to pass on his seed before the next—potentially more fatal—encounter with one of Nova's monsters.

The thought of the dungeon sobered his wandering imagination.

She had admitted to trying to kill him. She had gone so far as to create bigger, more difficult monsters for him to fight on the first floor of the dungeon. What would they find when they left the safe zone?

Jay let out a sigh and sank into one of the overstuffed white armchairs, staring into the blue ring of flames at the center of the room. It gave him something to focus on so his gaze didn't wander to the transparent walls of the shower where Lyra was soaping that perfect, gorgeous body of hers.

Guilt flooded through Jay that he was even capable of thinking about another woman when Molly was hurt. Although, besides the scratch on her head, Raina seemed to think she was well enough—just in some kind of dream state. Jay didn't know if that made it any better that he was having feelings for someone else. He and Molly were just friends. He'd dated before, or attempted to, and Molly had encouraged him. And it wasn't like he was ignoring Molly. He was here with Lyra because they were both trying to save her. It's not like he'd followed the fox-girl into the dungeon for the purpose of chasing... tail.

That expression conjured an image of Lyra's naked backside and lush, white fox-tail, forcing Jay to squeeze his eyes shut and think unsexy thoughts.

He'd almost died. That was the problem. There were lots of studies that showed people in dangerous circumstances often had an increase in sex drive as their bodies became increasingly desperate to pass on their genetic material before catastrophe struck. It was counterintuitive, but the safer people were the less inclined they were to breed. There was a diminished sense of urgency. Suddenly being thrust into a dangerous world where he was expected to fight to survive was just... activating more primal parts of his brain than when he was at home in the "real world."

The more Jay thought about it, the more his mind rebelled. It shouldn't be real, none of it should be possible. There were no other worlds or portals into them. These were not beliefs he had ever held and now that he was faced with a reality that conflicted with everything he thought he knew, it was like his mind had been fractured. There was the half of his brain that spent its entire life training to recognize up-and-coming companies, buying low, selling high, schmoozing clients, building portfolios... which scoffed at the idea of real-life video games and fantasy worlds as kid stuff, as make believe, as a waste of time in a world where time was money. Then there was the half of his brain that was seeing and experiencing the world of Arcanicea, insisting that it was real, that scorpion venom hurt like a bastard and getting burned by an exploding constrict made out of enormous scarab beetles was even worse.

Insisting that whatever he thought was real before bore no weight in this new world... He had to accept that he no longer knew what to expect. Death lurked around every corner. And whether he liked it or not, that meant—when he wasn't being attacked by monsters—he was suddenly, *urgently*, driven to mate.

It wasn't logical, it was *bio*logical.

Who was he to argue with evolution?

Okay, that's that, he thought. *Justification complete. Now what am I going to do*?

Jay let out a slow breath, feeling just as confused as before. He was saved from his torturous thoughts by the sound of the shower door opening. Glancing up, he saw Lyra emerge from the little glass rectangle, using her towel to dry her ears, hair, and tail and... not to cover her body. He no longer felt confused. He knew exactly what he wanted. The part of his brain screaming otherwise could just go to hell as far as he was concerned. When he saw her looking at him, he knew she felt the same way.

As Lyra approached him, her blue-and-gold eyes fixed on him, he felt pinned by the intensity of desire in her face. He froze in his chair, all thoughts frozen with him, like she was an arctic fox and he was a rabbit hoping not to be noticed.

Lyra stopped in front of his chair, her perfect body on full display. Every cell of his body ached to reach out and touch her, but he stayed where he was, just... looking.

"Jay," she said, her voice lower than it usually was, with a hint of a growl in her tone. "I think we need to talk."

18

Heart to Heart

J ay felt his cheeks burn. Was it because he'd been staring? He tried to tear his gaze away, but she was too close, filling his vision with soft skin, hard muscles, and enticing curves.

"Sure," he said, finding his voice and gazing up into her two-toned eyes. "What about?"

Lyra wrapped the towel over her shoulders, to keep her damp hair off her back, and then knelt before him. She bit her lip as if wondering how to start. Finally, she said, "I'm attracted to you. And I think you feel the same way."

Jay nodded wordlessly, her position at his feet making it very hard for him to think of anything beyond the obvious. He managed to get out a breathy, "Yes."

"I'd like to pursue those feelings," she said, and Jay felt his heart lurch to a stop before starting up, hammering harder than ever before. "But—"

That word ground his excitement to a halt, and he sat forward, already wanting to protest. But he knew he needed to hear what she had to say before begging her to reconsider. It was only polite. "But what?"

"But I think you need to address the feelings you have for your... friend. For Molly... first."

Jay's chest tightened at her words. "I know what it seems like," he said. "But there's really nothing between us. There could have been if she'd wanted it, but she doesn't. I can't wait for her to change her mind forever, Lyra."

It was the fox-girl's turn to sigh. She pressed her lips together and glanced up at the ceiling. Jay traced the slender line of her neck down to the hollow between her breasts. The towel covered her just enough to make him want to tear it away, but he was still frozen in place. He didn't want to scare her away. And her concerns were valid.

"Jay... I just... I don't see how that can be true. I don't see how she can't have feelings for you. Have you two ever *talked* about it? Or are you just assuming you know what's in her heart? Because I will be the first to tell you a girl isn't always obvious about what she feels, especially if she's worried about getting hurt. I... I lost someone, once. Someone I cared very much about, but who I never expressed my feelings for. That's why I'm telling you how I feel now. I'm scared of getting hurt again, too. But nothing hurts worse than losing the chance to have something more. So..."

Jay swallowed, not knowing what to say. The fact of the matter was, he and Molly hadn't ever talked about what had happened between them. She'd pulled away and he'd assumed it was because she didn't want that kind of relationship with him. And when she'd seemed more interested later on, he'd waited for her to tell him she was ready. She hadn't, and again he'd assumed that was because she didn't want him that way. Molly was his best friend. He knew her better than he knew anyone. Her favorite color, her favorite restaurant, movies, music, the things that made her laugh and cry and jump up and down with excitement. But when it came to the two of them, he'd always been confused.

"So, you want me to talk to her first?" Jay asked. "She's unconscious, Lyra. What if we can't bring her—"

"We can," Lyra insisted, leaning forward earnestly so that he could feel the heat of her skin against his bare legs. "Don't think like that. We can bring her back, Jay. Look—"

She grabbed her satchel, which was sitting on the floor next to the blue-flamed fireplace and began rummaging inside it. She withdrew a small burlap bag with a plant growing from the top of it. Jay recognized it immediately, and his mouth went dry as he leaned forward to take it from her hands.

"Frostleaf Clover?" he asked, shaking his head. "How long have you had this?"

"Since you were fighting the Glacial Scarabs," she said, letting out a little yip-like laugh. Tears brimmed in her eyes, and she began to speak very quickly, the words tumbling over each other in a hurry to be heard. "I should never have left you, even for a moment. And I wouldn't have, not for anything else. But I saw a shimmer at the end of the corridor, and my **Dungeon Sight** identified it for me. I didn't think it would take me long to collect it, and I thought you'd be so happy that you wouldn't mind being alone for a minute or two. That room should have been just Level 1 and 2 scarabs, you should have been able to handle them. But when I picked the clover, I was hit with a Time Freeze trap. I've never encountered one outside of the lower floors. There aren't supposed to be traps on the first floor at all."

Jay released the breath he'd been holding. "Just like there aren't supposed to be Level 5 Elite Constructs in the Scarab room?"

He wondered if the dungeon had led Lyra away on purpose, so that he would be forced to fight the construct alone. But that didn't make sense, as she'd been there for the final battle. It was his own overconfidence that had been his downfall in that fight. Had he let her help, he probably wouldn't have almost died.

"I was able to break free before the trap's time limit," she was saying. "I have a passive ability that reduces the effect of some kinds of traps. But by the time I got to you, the Construct was already forming. I should have just killed it, Jay. I should never have insisted that you get in the first strike. It was too dangerous. When you hit it with the torch and all the bug guts detonated, I... I thought I'd killed you."

Lyra was crying now, tears streaming down her face. Her shoulders shook and her ears flattened into her damp hair. Jay wanted to comfort her, but wasn't sure what to do with the precious Frostleaf Clover. Quickly and clumsily, he added it to his inventory then scrambled to his feet. Bending to take Lyra's hands, he pulled her up, too, then wrapped his arms around her shoulders and held her as she cried.

It no longer mattered that they were both nearly naked. There was nothing sexy about a girl with a broken heart. "Hey," he said, whispering into the top of her head, between the silken white ears. "Hey, stop that. I wasn't dead. You didn't kill me. That whole torch-arrow thing was my idea, remember? And as crazy as it was, it worked. So, no more tears."

Lyra sniffed and pressed herself against Jay's chest, allowing him to comfort her as if she needed to be close to him as much as he wanted to be close to her. When she spoke again, her voice was small and shaky. "I know," she said. "I know that now, but I didn't. And it made me realize that I don't want to mess this up. I have feelings for you that I didn't expect to feel again, and I promised myself I wouldn't keep feelings like that to myself if I was ever lucky enough to meet someone who—" She stopped, taking a deep, shuddering breath. "I don't know what this is, Jay. I just know I don't want to mess it up, okay? And that means... I don't want to start anything until you've had a chance to set the record straight with Molly. I don't know any woman in her right mind who wouldn't be moved to know that a man had sacrificed so much for her. If she doesn't love you, she's crazy."

Jay chuckled. "Well, you don't know Molly. She's passionate about a lot of things... the environment, animals, taking excruciatingly long hikes in the middle of nowhere..." He laughed, thinking about all the things he'd seen his friend get excited about over the years. Tears stung his eyes as he remembered that she was laying motionless on a cot in Raina's tent, not getting to do any of the things she loved doing. And he, who would have much rather been sitting in a climate-controlled office than having adventures, was here, recovering from an acute case of too-much-excitement. Jay sighed and continued, "She's passionate, but she often seems to forget that other people exist. She's always been like that. I know it's not a personal thing. I should know better than to assume I know what's going on in her head. But I admit that you're right. We've never really talked about our non-relationship."

"I think it would do you both a lot of good to clear the air," Lyra said.

"What are you, my therapist?"

Lyra squeezed him, and he felt her small, shapely breasts squish against his chest. "No, just a woman who wants a shot at your heart. And who wants to make sure there's no invisible obstacles in front of the target."

Jay reached up to stroke the fox-girl's hair, tentatively rubbing at the base of her ears. Lyra moaned and laid her head against his chest, encouraging the touch. The sound made him not want to ask his next question.

But she was being frank with him, and he owed her the same.

"Lyra, what if I've been wrong about Molly all this time? What if she does feel the same way about me as I do about her?"

"That's up to you," Lyra said, sensing his unease. "And her, of course. She's your first love, and I respect that. But if you have room for two in your heart, I would not be ashamed to share you."

Jay took a deep breath. "Share?"

"Yes," she said. "Many Faunari males have multiple wives. As our numbers have dwindled this has become more normal. Faunari women can also have more than one husband, if they choose, but this is rarer. Faunari men do not get along together all that well."

Jay considered this, somewhat shocked by her proposition. "Uh, where Molly and I are from that's... very unusual. We tend to only be with one partner at a time."

"You would not want two lovers?" Lyra pulled back, and the towel slipped from her shoulder, exposing a small, perfect breast.

Jay forced himself to look into her beautiful, two-toned eyes. "I think I would like that very much, but I don't know how Molly would feel about it."

Lyra shrugged. "Then you can ask her when she wakes up," she said. "It shouldn't be long now."

Jay swallowed. "You're really sure about that?"

"We already have one of the two reagents we need," she said, smiling up at him. "The dungeon seems to favor you, though it has a rather aggressive way of showing it. Your starting stats made you look doomed. But never have I heard of anyone levelling as quickly as you have. It takes most people days to kill their first ten Level 1 monsters to gain the XP necessary to hit Level 2. They can be hard to find, for one thing, and you have to spend half your time avoiding higher level monsters and the other half recovering from your fights. You've just been thrown straight into the deep end. How many Level 1 Glacial Scarabs did you kill in that room?"

Jay checked his notifications again. "Forty-Eight normal ones. And two Elites. Plus, two Level 2 Elites and two Level 3 Elites. Plus, the Construct. It looks like all the little ones it shot at me were included in my experience for killing the construct though, I didn't get any extra once that battle started."

"It's unheard of," she said, nodding. "And the fact that you are getting access to all the commodities that have been so difficult for the rest of us to find is... well, I don't know what else to think."

Was all of this part of Nova's test for him? Jay wondered if the dungeon was somehow influencing Lyra's feelings for him too. The fact that the fox-girl had been lured away from him at a pivotal moment, only to discover one of the items he coveted was... He didn't know what. It felt purposeful, but Jay couldn't fathom to what end the dungeon was working.

"I hope you're right," Jay said, pulling Lyra against his chest again. "Because I don't want to see what would happen to someone the dungeon wanted to destroy."

Suddenly Lyra jumped up and away from him, completely dropping her towel. "Jay, I almost forgot! There was something else I meant to tell you!"

Jay stared at her naked body and blinked slowly.

"All right, Lyra," he said, readjusting his own towel. "But... would you mind wearing your towel while we talk? I'm finding it very hard to think about anything useful with you prancing around in all your glory like that."

The fox-girl blushed and picked her towel up off the floor, quickly wrapping it around her chest and tucking the tail between her breasts so that it looked like a fluffy, white mini-dress.

"Sorry," she said with a nervous laugh. "Faunari also aren't very private people. I've heard humans are more modest, but I've never actually met a human before... I didn't meant to make you uncomfortable."

"I'm not uncomfortable," he said, readjusting his towel. "Just easily distracted by impure thoughts. Please tell me what you wanted to tell me."

Lyra came to sit on the overstuffed chair opposite the fire from where he'd been sitting, and Jay mirrored her, glad of the blue flames keeping them apart. It gave the conversation a more formal feel, which allowed him to push the other thoughts and feelings away—like he'd had to do at work.

"When I looted the Construct, I found something I've never seen before," she said, leaning forward and putting her hands on her knees. The blue light cast her in an ethereal glow that did nothing to dim Jay's desire for her. But he forced himself to pay attention. Her heterochromatic eyes danced with excitement.

The hairs on Jay's arms lifted like he'd felt a chill. He got the sense that this was another one of the dungeon, Nova's, surprises for him. But would it be good, or bad? It was anyone's guess.

By the look on Lyra's face, she seemed to think it was good. She bit her lip, squirming excitedly in her chair, her ears twitching with anticipation.

"A Silver Key!"

19

Keys and Heroes

Jay shook his head, remembering the message he'd received upon entering the first floor of the dungeon. "I thought we wanted a Copper Key?"

"The bosses drop Copper Keys," Lyra confirmed, "which allow Delvers to unlock the gates to the staircases that go down to the next floor in the dungeon. I have never heard of a Silver Key before. I don't know if it's for the gate at the staircase, or if it's for something else entirely. But it's in the Party Inventory menu if you want to look at it."

Jay did so, having to scroll past a surprisingly long list of crafting supplies and reagents dropped by the Glacial Scarab beetles. He wondered how they sold things on the Global Dungeon Market, and if his access to all these precious commodities would make him more or less popular in Winterhaven.

He doubted he could get less popular with Runolf and his followers. But Raina and hers might be able to give him some advice on how to deal with the inevitable fallout. He vowed to discuss trading with her before doing anything.

When he found the item Lyra was so excited about, he was a bit surprised that it looked so... banal. The dungeon's description—in the neutral, mechanical tone, had an almost surly sound to it.

Silver Key – It's a key. You know what keys are for. This one happens to be silver. What more do you want from me? Find the door it opens and maybe you'll learn more. Or maybe you'll die.

Jay wrinkled his forehead, pulling the key from his inventory so that it appeared in his hand. "Did you read the description?"

"There was no description," Lyra said. "Was there? I was in a hurry, maybe I missed it."

Jay passed the key to her, and he saw the faint glow in her eyes as she activated **Dungeon Sight**. "It just says Silver Key. Nothing more."

She passed the key back to him and Jay read his description to her. The fox-girl's eyes widened.

"Is that what the dungeon is like when it talks to you?" she gasped. "It's always so matter-of-fact with me. I... I thought it was the same for everyone. In fact, I *know* it's the same for everyone because I've talked with others about their items and quests. This is really weird, Jay."

"You don't know the half of it," Jay said. "It keeps

referencing my old life. My job in my old world. I feel like my class has something to do with the work I used to do, and that's why it's not showing up properly."

He decided to leave out the part where the dungeon addressed him by name, used a different, female voice to speak to him, and seemed to either want to kill him or fuck him—and he wasn't sure which was more frightening from an entity as powerful as this dungeon was.

Jay turned the key around in his hands, inspecting it with **Dungeon Sight**. Lyra's ability would be higher level than his, if anything, so he didn't expect to see anything that she hadn't seen. Yet there seemed to be some things that the dungeon only did for him, so it was worth a look.

He was rewarded for his effort. Tiny glowing letters, like runes, appeared along the slender shaft of the key, only visible when his **Dungeon Sight** was activated. He drew the key closer to his face, squinting to see what the shapes were.

Like the translation ability that allowed him to speak with people form Arcanicea, the runes shimmered and reshaped themselves to appear in letters that he could read.

> *What once was lost, may now be found,*
> *If this key is fit and door unbound.*
> *Past skills awake to new renown.*
> *Find me, Delver. Down, down, down...*

Hesitantly, he read the words aloud, sharing a bit

of his unease with the fox-girl who had willingly bound herself to him. If the dungeon was treating him differently, Lyra had a right to know, because it might make her life that much harder than it should be while she was partied with him.

"Oh!" she said, clutching the towel at her chest and leaning so far forward that Jay worried the blue flames might catch her hair on fire. "That's... I don't know what that means. But Jay, I was right about you. You're different, and even the dungeon knows it."

"What should we do?" he asked, still staring at the glowing key in his hands. "Are you sure you want to keep Delving with me? What if I keep attracted too many monsters... or too high-level monsters?"

Lyra's eyes almost bugged out of her head. "Are you kidding? I'm not leaving you! This is the most exciting thing to ever happen in the Ice Dungeon. It's like you're reminding it of what it's supposed to be. Jay... maybe you can save Winterhaven. Maybe you can help us join the Arcanicean economy like all the other dungeon communities."

Jay shook his head, unsure of the key's significance to the world economy. "I don't know if the attention the dungeon is giving me is a good thing, Lyra."

"Listen to me, Jay," the fox-girl said, her blue-and-gold eyes glittering with excitement. "The Ice Dungeon has always been tough. The monsters are always higher-level than they're supposed to be. One of the reasons most people never come back past the fifth floor is that the monsters scale at a higher rate than Delvers do. It doesn't give us the rewards it's supposed to give. I used to think it was cursed, like everyone always says. Or mad... if a dungeon can be mad."

"I think it can be," Jay said, thinking of the conversations he'd had with Nova, who certainly seemed a little unhinged.

Lyra shook her head. "I think it's been testing us. I think it's looking for something... looking for some*one* who can rise to the challenge. For whatever reason, it didn't find what it was looking for in the Faunari, and we've paid the price. But... maybe it's been waiting for a Delver like you."

"A human?" Jay asked. "Haven't there been any human Delvers to visit the Ice Dungeon?"

"It's rare," Lyra said. "But it does happen. Especially early on, when King Wenshire first awarded us the dungeon and people complained that there was something wrong with it, human Delvers from around Arcanicea came to see if the rumors were true. They all left, eventually, and repeated what King Wenshire said—that there was nothing wrong with the dungeon, and that the Faunari were just inferior Delvers."

Jay scoffed. "That's bullshit. There's obviously something wrong with the Ice Dungeon. Even I can see that."

"But you're entering as a novice Delver. All the Delvers who came to investigate our claims were high level, and the dungeon never threw anything really crazy at them. They left thinking we were complaining about nothing, other than agreeing that the Ice Dungeon's loot was subpar—which, they believed, was to be expected when it was meant to cater to inferior Delvers such as us."

"King Wenshire probably paid them off," Jay said. "Happens all the time in my old line of work. Someone makes inconvenient complaints about a product or service you offer, the quickest way to silence the complaints to hire an 'expert' to back you up. Even better if you can do it under the table so that no one knows the expert is on the take."

The blank, white room which had felt so clean and welcoming when they'd first arrived was starting to make Jay feel uncomfortable. He hadn't know what he was getting into when he'd decided to go into the dungeon to look for the ingredients Molly needed. The situation was even more complicated than he'd realized. But as he learned more about it, he was beginning to wonder if Lyra wasn't right. Maybe he did bring something unique to the table.

If nothing else, he had some knowledge of world history—back on Earth—and how early economic systems evolved into the ones he learned to manipulate in the modern world. He knew how normal people were often caught up in the machinations of greater powers, and how it was only years later that people understood the trickle-down effect of political games. Back on earth, these powers would be governments, banks, and huge corporations. In a world like Arcanicea, that would be kingdoms, territories, and the Global Dungeon Market.

But how many Faunari could see the big picture? They knew they were being treated unfairly. They thought it was prejudice against their people, and to some extent that was true. But Jay was beginning to suspect the prejudice had been manufactured, to an extent, embellished upon by this King Wenshire in order to expand the reach of his power.

Did Nova's purpose for him have something to do with righting these wrongs? Jay put the key back into his inventory and leaned toward the flames, suddenly eager for their warmth.

Lyra sat back, the blue flames casting ghostly shadows over her face. She smiled at him. "This is exactly what I mean," she said. "You are different, Jay. You see things differently, and the dungeon reacts to you differently. There must be a reason. But I don't think it's simply that you are human. I think the dungeon was waiting for someone from another world. The dungeon is looking for a hero."

Jay started, glancing up to meet the fox-girl's eyes, dancing eerily in the flames. Lyra had no idea how close she'd come to what Nova had actually said to him. Though the dungeon hadn't specified that she was drawn to the fact that he was from Earth, the fact that his class and skills were based on his past suggested that Lyra was right.

"A hero?" he said. "I'm not a hero, Lyra. I'm just a

regular guy. Before this, I never did anything exciting in my entire life—not by the standards of your world."

"You're just a regular guy," Lyra said, her smile stretching wide enough to reveal her pointed canines. "Who charges into danger in order to help someone he cares about. Who is willing to risk life and limb for something he believes in. Who remains uncertain in the face of his own greatness. Sorry, Jay. Sounds a bit like a hero to me."

Jay shook his head. "Anyone else would do the same."

Lyra threw her head back and laughed, a high-pitched bark of laughter. "They would not," she said. "They do not. I won't remind you how many times I've seen my entire party wiped out. Nor how many other parties have suffered the same fate. But do you know why most parties fail in this dungeon, Jay? Because most people remain loyal only to themselves. If the choice is to run into danger to save an ally or to flee to safety and save themselves, they will save themselves. Would you abandon me if I was in danger, Jay?"

Jay sat up straight in his chair, despite the protests of his aching body. "Never," he said.

"Even if you thought saving me would put your ability to help Molly in jeopardy?"

Still, Jay shook his head. "No," he said. "You offered to help me when I was alone and had nothing, no training, no class, no useful stats or skills. I would never abandon you. I won't abandon Molly, either. If there was a conflict between those goals, I'd just... find another way."

"See?" Lyra sat back in her chair, letting the over-stuffed cushions envelope her petite frame. "Total hero material. I know it, and the dungeon knows it. So, no. I will not be leaving you either. I'm sticking by your side until the bitter end. I can help you. And I believe, in the end, you'll help all of us."

Jay was silent as he stared into the flames, wondering what he was supposed to do about such a declaration. Part of him was thrilled that she was still willing to Delve with him, because he needed her help and he enjoyed her company. The other part of him was terrified that she'd get hurt because of him, because he didn't know what he was doing and because the dungeon was even more unpredictable that usual when he was around.

"I can see you trying to get out of it," Lyra said, releasing a yip-like cackle. "But I'll save you the effort. You can't dissuade me. If you kick me out of your party, I'll just follow you around like a puppy. Come on, Jay. Every hero needs a sidekick. I want to be yours."

Jay groaned and rubbed his face, suddenly feeling more exhausted than he'd ever felt before. "What are we going to do with this key?"

"Find the door," Lyra said, as if it was so simple. "But before that, there's something else we need to do."

Jay slumped, every muscle in his body feeling the full weight of his first day in the dungeon. His skin still felt raw, and his Health bar was stubbornly not moving anymore. He needed to sleep. But the fox-girl had a glint in her alluring eyes that said she wasn't going to be ignored. He said, "Dare I even ask what that is?"

Lyra stood, careful to hold the towel closed as she moved, and stepped around the fire toward him. Again, she crouched before his chair, and again Jay wished he had something more than a towel to hide the way she made him feel.

"I told you before I had something that would help with your pain," she said. "And I'm going to use it now. But I need you to remember the talk we had earlier about sorting things out with Molly before you and I get involved."

He hoped she wasn't saying that because of his body's stubborn refusal to acknowledge the agreement they'd made. "I remember."

"Good," she said. "Or this might be a little awkward. I need you to close your eyes."

Reluctantly, Jay closed his eyes, wondering what the fox-girl was about to do to him. When he felt her move closer, his heart began to beat heavily in his chest. "What are you—?"

"Shh," she said, and he felt her breath on his thigh, hot and tingling. Wet warmth touched his painful, raw skin and Jay flinched at the unexpected touch. Her lips? He barely suppressed a groan. Then, a soothing cool sensation spread from the spot, relief flooding his body.

"I have a skill called **Soothing Kisses**," she explained, and he could feel her moving down his leg as she spoke. She delivered another soothing kiss to the inside of his knee, spreading more relief across his skin.

Jay sighed involuntarily, not having realized how much discomfort he was in until it was removed. "That feels amazing," he moaned.

"It's not a true healing spell," Lyra said, "like someone with a proper healing class would have. More like a temporary salve that takes away pain. And it only works on a small, localized area. So, I'm going to need to give you a lot of kisses."

She kissed him again, lower on his leg. And while Jay wished she were working in the other direction, and he wished he could watch her as she worked, he had to admit the relief of the healing properties was equally enticing. He allowed himself to relax, keeping his eyes closed as she had asked, and said, "I'll take my medicine."

Lyra's cool hands moved over his legs and feet as she left hot and cold kisses over every inch of his bruised and battered flesh. Jay lost himself in the bliss of her attention, reminding himself that they weren't going to do more, even while his mind teased him with the possibility. His erection grew more insistent as she worked, and eventually pushed the towel out of the way, exposing the length of his shaft.

"Sorry," Jay said, scrambling blindly to cover himself, his cheeks burning with embarrassment.

But Lyra's gentle fingers wrapped around his hands, stopping him. "It's okay, Jay. Nakedness doesn't bother the Faunari. And I enjoy looking at you. I'd be much more worried if you didn't respond to my kisses that way."

He swallowed, his eyes still closed, feeling his heartbeat throbbing in his cock and knowing that Lyra could see it, too.

When she pulled the towel away and kissed the inside of his other thigh, he released a groan and clenched his fingers into the armrest. He couldn't decide if this was some kind of divine reward or punishment. But the relief that her kisses left in their wake—to everything except his unanswered desire—was enough that he didn't want her to stop.

Fortunately for him, she didn't. Even after she made him stand, and led him to his cot—insisting he keep his eyes closed—where he could lay on his stomach and sides and she could place her gentle, **Soothing Kisses** on all of his wounds.

By the time she was finished, Jay was so relaxed and so exhausted his mind was in a stupor. He barely noticed the final kiss, hot and wet on his bottom lip, which didn't come with the cooling afterglow of the magical skill.

"Goodnight, Portal Boy," Lyra whispered in his ear, sending him off to sleep. "Sweet dreams."

20

Bison Berries

The next morning—or what passed for morning inside the timeless environment of the dungeon—Jay awoke feeling incredible. For the first time, he could feel the full effect of his increased Base Stats and newly boosted Attributes. He felt... invincible.

Of course, Jay knew he was still only Level 4 and that he shouldn't get carried away. But he was beginning to see how unlocking more levels could become addicting. How powerful must the high-level Delvers be? More importantly, how many high-level Delvers would be backing King Wenshire and his corrupt rule? If Jay was going to take this hero business seriously—Lyra's treatment last night had all but convinced him—he was going to have to increase his level aggressively.

Which meant they had no time to hang around the Safe Room.

Lyra's clothes had been washed and returned. She was dressed and cooking breakfast by the time Jay finally awoke from his long rest. He wrapped himself in a towel and went to check the box where he'd stored his dirty, damaged outfit. But when he opened the cleaning unit, he was shocked to find it empty.

"What the hell?" he said, crouching down to peer into the back corners. "Where are my clothes?"

Lyra popped up behind him and took a look for herself. "That's strange. Even if they're badly damaged, they should turn back up in the box."

"Well, what am I supposed to do?" he said. "Fight monsters wearing a towel?"

Lyra shook her head, her expression serious. "No, you can't do that. The Safe Room equipment disappears if you try to take it beyond the hexdome."

"Oh, good," he said, dryly. "I'll just be naked then."

Lyra bit her lip and gave him a long, lingering look. "Well, it wouldn't be *so* bad..."

Jay's mind went blank. For a moment, he completely forgot what it was he was complaining about. Then, and image of him, running through the dungeon, fighting enormous poisonous bugs with his dick hanging out flashed through his mind.

"Uh, no," he said. "Not going there."

"I have another set of leather armor you can use," Lyra said, biting back a laugh. Her fluffy white tail twitched with amusement. "It will resize to fit you. But without something underneath, it's not going to leave much to the imagination."

Jay looked at her 'armor,' which must have come with some kind of full-body buff rather than being a physical protection, since the leather crop top and mini skirt covered less than they left exposed. Not that he minded but calling it armor was definitely a stretch.

Then Jay remembered something.

"Oh, wait..." Jay recalling the [**Beetle Black Scarab Armor**] he'd received and forgotten about. "I have something that might work."

He removed Nova's gift from the Note, where it was stored in his Inventory. A shiny, black rectangle of folded fabric appeared in his hand and Lyra's eyes widened. Jay glanced down at it in surprise. The description had said armor, but this felt like fabric. Although the shiny black color was the same as the shells of the Glacial Scarabs, it had none of the hardness that he had expected.

"What. Is. That?" Lyra said, clearly analyzing the item with her **Dungeon Sight**. "Jay, where did you get that? I've never even seen a Gold tier item drop before, and you've just got one hanging out in your inventory?"

Jay explained as best he could without revealing Nova's private messages to him, as he dressed in the so-called armor. The outfit came with shapeless looking pants and a jacket and a button up shirt. But as he pulled them on, he could feel the glistening fabric tighten and shift as it molded itself to his body.

He could tell immediately what was happening, the feel of the fit was so familiar he would have known what he was wearing even with his eyes closed. Coming to stand in front of the glass shower stall, Jay inspected his dim reflection. "You've got to be kidding me."

"Damn, Jay," Lyra let out a low whistle. "You look... wow. I have never seen armor like that before."

"It's not armor," Jay said, scowling at his reflection. "It's a business suit. This is the kind of thing I wore to work every day for the last five years."

Lyra's blue-and-gold eyes grazed over him like she was having second thoughts about putting off their relationship.

"I can't fight in a suit, dungeon!" Jay shouted at the ceiling, hoping Nova was listening in.

But even as he said it, he realized that this suit was different from what he was used to wearing. The beetle-black fabric was smooth and almost weightless. It certainly wouldn't get in his way any more than the outdoor gear he'd been wearing before. The cut was snug. With the black on black, he looked more like a hitman than a Wall Street Executive. And hitmen managed to get the job done... at least, the Hollywood actors who played them did okay—even in the high-octane action scenes.

Jay pulled his Bolo Knife from his inventory. Channeling his Strength and Agility Attributes to guide his movements, he did an impromptu attack and defense sequence, letting the dungeon instincts flow through his limbs.

He frowned.

The armor moved like a second skin with his body. Given the way Lyra was looking at him, he figured he must look okay, even if he felt like an idiot. He put the knife in the scabbard that came with the pants, and checked his stats.

Delver: Jay Morgan

Class Type: [N/A]

Class: [N/A]

Lvl: 4

XP: 105 | **Next Lvl:** 900

Health: 180 | **Stamina:** 130 | **Mana:** 130

Active Bonus: 10% max XP (Scale-Up), 50% max XP (Well-Rested, temporary)

Unassigned Attribute Points: 0

Strength: 3

Agility: 3

Intelligence: 1

Constitution: 10 [*Beetle Black Scarab Armor* – Set Bonus: Constitution +6, HP +50]

Willpower: 2

Charisma: 10

Active Skills: On-The-Job-Training

Passive Abilities: Environmental Resistance 1 (Arctic), Dungeon Sight 1, Scale-Up, Well-Rested (temporary)

Perks: Panty Dropper, Bootstrapper

Switching out the *Ragged Leather Armor* for the

Beetle Black Scarab Armor had increased his constitution by an additional 5 points—while he lost the +1 the *Ragged Leather Armor* had given him, he gained +6, bringing him to a total of 10 Constitution points. The *Beetle Black Scarab Armor* had also given him +50HP rather than +5HP, bringing his total to 180.

With the new 10% max XP bonus he was receiving from his new **Scale-Up** Ability and the **Well-Rested** bonus of 50% max XP... Jay was suddenly eager to get out and fight some monsters.

"What's the condition of your knife at?" Lyra asked, pulling something from her satchel.

Jay checked, and was shocked to find it almost completely depleted. "It's at 5 of 25. I'll need a new one soon."

"I have a sharpening kit that you can use to maintain your blade," she said, passing it to him. "I don't use my dagger often, so you might as well keep it. It only takes a few moments and can extend the life of lower-level weapons by a good margin. You practice using it while I make us something to eat."

After a quick breakfast of some flavorless dungeon-rations Lyra had packed, they left the Safe Zone. Even the fox-girl's lingering glances couldn't distract Jay from the anticipation of getting out there and grinding some levels.

Stepping out of the hexdome and onto the artificial tundra was an unsettling experience. While he was inside the Safe Zone, Jay had almost forgotten how strange the dungeon world actually was.

For one thing, the 'sky' above them was still the perfect pitch black of midnight with its smattering of diamond-bright stars. The Ghost Bison had moved closer to the hexdome as they'd slept, and Jay was able to see the frosted shimmer of their coats in the starlight and the steam coming off their massive bodies to hang in a fog above the heard. The beasts had thick, curved horns that reminded Jay more of water buffalo than North American bison. The points of the horns looked wickedly sharp. Jay had no desire to fight one, let alone to antagonize the entire herd. But he couldn't help but wonder what items they dropped.

When he asked Lyra, she shrugged. "I've seen a few Delvers take on a Ghost Bison, but no one's killed one that I know of. Other dungeon animals drop things like hide and fur for leatherworking, teeth, horns, that kind of thing. I'd guess it's the horns but I'm not in any hurry to find out."

They kept their distance from the Ghost Bison as they moved back toward the tomblike tunnels they'd entered the plains from. Jay scanned the creatures with his **Dungeon Sight** and was shocked by what he saw.

Ghost Bison – Lvl 15 – Within the icy expanse of the dungeon tundra roam the elusive Ghost Bison, majestic creatures with frosty white hides and deadly horns. These creatures traverse the frozen plains in silence, undisturbed and peaceful unless provoked. Known for their non-aggressive na-

ture, the Ghost Bison nonetheless pose a significant threat to those who choose to challenge them.

It is rumored among adventurers that the Ghost Bison guard a unique item, the [Frosty Flank Steak.] This rare delicacy is said to imbue those who consume it with enhanced abilities, making the risk of hunting a Ghost Bison a tempting gamble for the rewards it may yield.

"Level 15!?" Jay stared in awe as they passed. "Okay, I'm glad they're passive. That [Frosty Flank Steak] drop is tempting, though, isn't it?"

"The what?" Lyra asked, her multi-hued eyes questioning.

Jay read her the description he'd received from the dungeon, and her eyes widened.

There was a flash from his HUD and a chime sound echoed in his mind. The way Lyra jumped, Jay knew she must have received one too.

New Quest! [Oh, Give Me a Home, Where the Ghost Bison Roam...]

Toma Tabernak, a traveling dungeon trader, is in desperate need of meat and hides for her shop inventory. Collect 5 [Frosty Bison Hide] and [Frosty Flank Steak] by killing Ghost Bison in the Pernicious Plains.

Reward: 500 Gold and 5000XP

Accept Quest? Y/N

"I know Toma Tabernak," Lyra said excitedly. "She's a Dungeon Dweller who roams around the second floor. But I have never heard of this quest before. Then again, I've never been this close to the Ghost Bison..."

"Should we accept?" Jay asked.

"It's way too high-level," Lyra protested. "Each one of them is Level 12-15. We might be able to kill one together, once you're Level 6. But generally, you want the combined levels of your party to match or exceed the level of the creature you're going to kill. This is not a beginner quest."

"We could come back, though, right?" Jay couldn't keep his eyes of the glittering, icy coats of the massive animals, wondering what other items they might drop. Then, he noticed that some of the shimmering was not actually from the Ghost Bison, but rather something they were clustered around. "What are they eating?"

He used **Dungeon Sight** to inspect between the animal's hooves.

Jay froze, staring.

Tundra Berry – This low, ground-covering bush has white leaves and bright red berries. It is said to be a potent alchemical reagent with Strength boosting attributes, but many believe it to have hidden, and sometimes unexpected, properties. Eat at your own risk.

"Lyra, look," he hissed. "Tundra Berries."

The fox-girl activated her own **Dungeon Sight**, and then cursed under her breath. "I'm starting to feel like this quest is not optional."

Jay felt his mouth go dry as he considered having

to fight an entire herd of Ghost Bison in order to save Molly. "Strength boosting attributes... does that mean we're going to have to kill jacked-up Ghost Bison on top of everything?"

Lyra grabbed Jay's arm and pulled him toward the tunnel entrance, as if she was worried he was just going to run in there and start slashing with his Bolo Knife. "It doesn't matter," she said. "Because we're not doing it. It's a death sentence Jay. We'll find the berries somewhere else."

Jay followed her reluctantly. It felt as if the dungeon was daring him to take on the ridiculous quest, as if it was testing just how badly he wanted to save Molly. Nova had warned him not to let his desire to help Molly interfere with his leveling. But she'd also said she expected him to prove himself.

Before they left the tundra, or the Pernicious Plains as the dungeon's description had named the area, Jay accepted the quest.

New Quest Accepted! Oh, Give Me a Home Where the Ghost Bison Roam has been activated. You have seven days to complete this quest or suffer a 3500XP penalty for your failure.

"What the shit!?" Jay shouted. "A penalty? That's not how these things are supposed to work, are they?"

"Jay!" Lyra grabbed his arm and shook him, her eyes panicked. "What are you doing? I said 'no.' If we fail, that will take me back to Level 4 and I'll lose my Tier I Class Upgrade!"

"You said 'not yet,'" he corrected, though guilt flooded through him that he hadn't asked her what the repercussions were. "Shit, Lyra. I'm sorry. I didn't know there would be a time limit or a penalty. If you remove yourself from the party, will you still be affected?"

He'd assumed dungeon quests worked like they did in a video game, where you could accept them and then just wait until you were ready. He hadn't anticipated there could be repercussions for failing a quest, besides the damage taken by getting your ass handed to you by a higher-level mob.

Lyra gritted her teeth and Jay could see her jaw clenching as she fought with warring emotions. "No," she said. "I'm stuck with it. I don't even care that much about my level Jay. I can come back from that. I did it once, I can do it again. But... you don't have 3500XP to give up. Even at Level 5 you'll only have 3000 cumulative XP."

Jay's muscles tensed. "What happens if I have negative XP?"

"You die." Lyra's voice shook.

21

The Forbidden Crypt

The trembling of Lyra's bottom lip and the welling tears in her eyes upset Jay more than the fox-girls concerns that he would die.

"Hey, now, stop that," he said, pulling her against his chest and kissing the top of her head. "I'm not going to die. I'm sorry I accepted that quest without knowing all the details, but we'll just... have to complete the quest. It's not impossible. The dungeon wants to push my limits, not destroy me. It wouldn't have given me the quest if it didn't think we could do it."

He said this with more confidence than he felt. But as the words came out of his mouth, he realized that, in part, it must be true. That didn't mean he was going to rush in there and start punching buffalo in the face, but with some strategy, they would be able to get him to Level 6, by which time they should be able to handle one of the Ghost Bison at a time between the two of them. They'd just need to devise a way of separating one from the herd so they weren't pissing off twenty of the beasts at once and getting trampled in the process.

"Jay, that's crazy," she sniffed as he explained his reasoning. "But if it can work... we'd better get started. There's no time to waste. Remember, we also have to get down to the second floor to hand the quest in to Toma Tabernak."

Jay squeezed her slender shoulders. "We have seven days. We can do it. Now, where can we go to find Level 3 to 5 monsters and animals? I don't want to risk getting another Uncompetitive Advantage debuff by grinding too far below my level."

Lyra wiped the tears from her eyes with the back of her hand. "If we go back the direction where the scorpions attacked us there are some rooms where higher level monsters spawn in swarms."

"Swarms of monsters," Jay said, grinning down at her. "Sounds like a date."

Lyra blushed prettily, then stepped out of his arms. "Follow me."

The entrance to the Frozen Tomb section looked strange coming from the Pernicious Plains. The wall of blue-gray stone carved with cryptic runes seemed out of place in the middle of a frozen tundra. But Jay's mind was beginning to accept these oddities as par for the course, and as they slipped through the shadowed doorway into the tomb tunnels he felt like he was moving into familiar territory.

Jay followed Lyra through the winding tunnels, where they stopped to fight a handful of Snow Scorpions and Glacial Scarabs. With the two of them fighting together they didn't get much XP from the battles but they moved quickly. At the end of their second battle, Jay received a notification he'd never seen before.

Proficiency Acquired!

You are now Proficient with the [Bolo Knife], giving you +2 Attack Bonus when using this weapon type, including [Bolo Blade] and [Bolo Sword].

Jay scoffed. He'd heard of Bolo Knives before, but Bolo Blades and Bolo Swords sounded made up. Then again, he was inside a magical dungeon with a fox-kin girl who shot flaming arrows, so what did he know?

He inspected his weapon and was surprised that, not only had the Attack Bonus been added, he'd improved the quality of the weapon by using Lyra's sharpening kit on it.

Sturdy Bolo Knife – Common (White)
Melee – Versatile – Damage: 2d4 (slicing) +2 Attack
Condition: [30/30]

Rather than being a Battered Bolo Knife, it was now called Sturdy, and it had an extra 5 Condition points, meaning it would be harder to break. He wondered if there were other things a Delver could do to improve their weapons and armor without relying on upgraded drops to level with them through the dungeon. He asked Lyra as they slipped into a new, darker corridor.

"Yes," she said, keeping her voice low. She had an arrow drawn, which cast flickering orange light on the rune-carved walls. "There are crafting skills and professions that can be leveled. I'll tell you more about it later. We're going to want to be quiet now, focus on your Agility Attribute to **Sneak**."

"Uh, Lyra?" he asked, eyeing the flaming arrow dubiously. "You're literally glowing. How are we going to sneak?"

The fox-girl looked surprised for a moment, and then grinned. "As an Arcane Archer, the effects of my arrows are invisible to my enemies. So, we benefit from the light of a fire arrow, even though the Undead Pharoh's won't be able to see it."

Jay's mouth went dry. "Undead Pharoh's?"

"Shh," she said. "We're entering the Forbidden Crypt zone. These will be higher-level monsters. You go in front. Keep your eyes peeled for sarcophagi. Open ones mean there's a mummy already walking around. Closed ones may also contain mummies, but can be **Sneak**ed past if we need to. They won't see us, but they will hear us if we aren't careful. Be quiet, and don't let them trick you. It's best to strike first, even if you're pretty sure the dead thing you're looking at is actually dead."

Jay shuddered. Scorpions and Scarabs had been bad enough, but now he had to fight zombies? He gripped the handle of his Bolo Knife and slipped past Lyra in the tunnel. With the light of her arrow behind him, his shadow danced through the crypt ahead of him like it was trying to lead him into the darkness. He closed his eyes a moment and tried to focus on the Agility Attribute the way he did when he was fighting with the Bolo Knife. Then he took a few tentative steps forward.

New Active Skill Acquired!

Sneak 1 – From stealth mode start-ups to corporate espionage, it can pay to tiptoe around the rules.

Sneak is a levelled skill that improves with use.

Sneak 1 reduces the chances that enemies will hear your movement by 5%. Tread carefully!

Okay, Jay thought. *Five percent isn't much protection, but it's better than nothing. Hopefully it will level quickly.*

He glanced over his shoulder at Lyra and gave her a little salute, indicating that he had **Sneak** activated and was moving in. She nodded in response, a small smile curling her lips. Jay had his Bolo Knife out and ready, relying on his Agility Attribute to guide his movements as he had when learning to do melee combat.

As he relaxed his mind and let his body connect to the dungeon magic flowing in his veins, Jay found the **Sneak** skill quite easy to use. He moved like a shadow in the shadows, barely able to hear his own footsteps. The orange light of Lyra's fire arrow flickered over the walls of the tomb, revealing dark cubbies filled with broken crockery or piles of bones.

Not wanting to be taken by surprise, Jay nudged each pile of bones with the tip of his Bolo Knife. He uncovered a shimmering item called [Grave Dust] along with a handful of copper and silver coins, which he pulled into his inventory. But none of the piles of bones came to life and attacked him.

They passed a doorway leading to a small, cobwebby room which Lyra lit up with her arrow. Jay glanced inside, seeing a closed sarcophagus and an open one. A mangled skeleton spilled out of the open box, as if the thing had been killed as it attempted to escape.

He would have been tempted to pass the room by if it weren't for the fact that he noticed his Stamina bar flashing.

Stamina was the Base Stat that **Sneak** drew from, and at first, Jay thought he was getting low. But the bar looked mostly full, and he verified that he still had 105/130 points. Closer examination revealed a smaller bar beneath the Stamina bar, indicating his progress leveling **Sneak**. As he leaned into the room, the **Sneak** bar progress jumped suddenly, indicating that he was earning more experience than he had been out in the corridor.

Jay figured that meant there was something nearby which he was successfully avoiding.

He glanced over his shoulder at Lyra, pointing at the fallen skeleton with his knife. She nodded encouragingly. Jay crept forward, his heart hammering in his chest. The room was dimly lit, even with the orange glow from the fox-girl's arrow, and he had to squint to see where he was going. Shards of broken pottery, clumps of dead plant matter, and scattered bones made it difficult to walk without making too much noise. The skeleton was wrapped in the vestiges of rotting bandages, as if it had once been a mummy but time had unraveled its careful dress. There was nothing to indicate it was anything more than a pile of bones, like the ones he'd poked in the cubbies outside.

Even his **Dungeon Sight** did not indicate there was anything special about this particular corpse. But instinct was telling Jay the room was hiding something.

When he was within striking range of the skeleton, a drumbeat from his HUD sounded. Jay nearly pissed himself as his heart shot into his throat and tried to hammer its way out of his mouth.

Active Skill Upgraded!
Sneak 2 - Reduces the chances that enemies will hear your movement by 10%. Shhh!

Jay swallowed, managing to keep a lid on his surprise and not shout out loud, which he thought should have been good for at least another level of **Sneak**. Not screaming like a little girl was pretty damned sneaky, given the circumstances.

The skill upgrade furthered his surety that the skeleton was not what it seemed. Jay gripped his knife in both hands, lifted it above his head, and drove it down, severing the skull from the tattered corpse.

Bones rattled, and the skull rolled across the floor with a clatter. It came to a stop near Lyra's feet, its eye sockets starting blankly at Jay. The rest of the skeleton didn't move.

He received no kill notification.

"Huh," he said, shrugging at the fox-girl. "I thought for sure that one was going to come to li—"

A resounding crash shook the room as the closed sarcophagus behind him exploded. Jay whirled, his Bolo Knife at the ready, just in time to see withered black fingers clutch the edge of the stone coffin. As the monster pulled itself from its resting place, Jay cursed himself. Of course, he'd forgotten about the closed sarcophagus.

Frozen Mummy: Lvl 4
Warriors of old, encased in icy bandages and animated by ancient magic. These monsters wield weapons carved from the rune-carved walls of the dungeon itself. Sworn to protect their masters, the Undead Pharohs, Frozen Mummies will fight until their heads are severed from their bodies or their hearts are burned by fire. Collect the Mummy's skull to ensure the dungeon's magic does not re-animate it upon your departure from the room.

Jay didn't have time to read the description of the creature before it launched itself from the sarcophagus, ragged bandages trailing behind it in a spectral wind. Fortunately, the dungeon read the description aloud as Jay scrambled to block the creature's first attack, so he knew what he had to do.

"You've got this Jay," Lyra whispered encouragingly from the doorway. "I'll back you up if you need it, but the more damage you do the more experience you'll gain."

The Frozen Mummy's jaw hung open, revealing a maw of dark, swirling magic within and it swung a blade twice as long as Jay's Bolo Knife. Jay wished he had something to block with. As the Mummy lunged at him, Jay used his Agility to leap aside, narrowly missing the attack. The Mummy paused, as if struggling to believe that it had missed, before pulling the blade from the stone floor for another attack. The creature's eyes glowed with an eerie blue-white light as its skull turned on its ancient neck and it pinned Jay with a slack-jawed gaze.

The second time it lunged, Jay was ready. He danced out of the way of the blade, letting it hit the ground next to him. This time, as the Mummy struggled to comprehend its failure, Jay took the opportunity to strike. He stepped into the Frozen Mummy's unguarded side and sliced at the sword-wielding arm with both hands.

Bones clattered to the ground as the arm separated from the body and the monster's weapon fell to the ground.

Lyra let out a restrained whoop of excitement, and Jay realized they were in danger of alerting more of the creatures if they made too much noise. He kept his own victory shout inside, darting backward in case the monster had another attack.

Instead, the ragged Mummy bent down to retrieve its weapon with its other hand, and it repeated the same attack. Jay danced out of the way of its strike, and repeated his counter attack, slicing its other arm from its body.

"Let's see you fight now," Jay muttered, kicking the severed arm and the sword away as the Frozen Mummy turned to regard him with a look that bordered on the absurd. With the wide eye-sockets and the gaping mouth, the Mummy looked absolutely stunned that it had been outmaneuvered.

Jay would have laughed, if the thing hadn't lunged at him again. This time, the creature's gaping jaws clattered open and shut in a chomping motion, like it wanted to bite his face off.

Jay kicked the monster in the chest, sending it flying into a wall of bone-filled cubbies. His Strength stat wasn't as boosted as it had been when he was fighting the Glacial Scarab Construct, but the extra points it put into the Attribute were definitely showing.

The Frozen Mummy scrabbled on the ground, attempting to regain its footing. Jay didn't give it a chance to get up. He rushed forward, driving the blade of his Bolo Knife between the monster's head and its shoulders. The skull came off with an audible *pop!* and went rolling across the floor.

Success!

You have killed
Frozen Mummy Lvl 4
XP: 90 (+10%)(+50%)

Quickly, Jay grabbed the skull and stuffed it into his Inventory. Just to be safe, he picked up the skull from the first, properly dead skeleton. Then he looted the corpse.

Frozen Mummy: Lvl 4
Grave Dust, Frozen Mummy's Heart, Powdered Ancient Bone, Frozen Bandages

While he was curious about these items, Jay was eager to keep going. With his new Passive Ability Scale-Up and the Well-Rested bonus, he was getting 144XP for these 90XP monsters. With the additional experience they'd gained from killing the Scorpions and Scarabs on their way to the Forbidden Crypt zone, that meant he probably only had to kill another five of the monsters to level up.

"Way to go, Jay!" Lyra cheered from the doorway. "I knew you could do it! This whole area is like that room. Unless you draw more by making too much noise, usually you only have to fight one at a time. Do you want to keep going?"

Jay nodded. "Hell yes. I'm getting tons of XP with my bonus. Let's go!"

Lyra grinned at him. She probably would have clapped if her hands hadn't been busy with the bow, and they hadn't been worried about noise. Instead, her white ears flattened into her hair and her tail wagged. Jay's heart made an irregular thump as he remembered the fox-girl's **Soothing Kisses** the night before.

"Onward, then," Lyra said. "You'll be Level 6 in no time!"

22

Stalkers in the Shadow

Their progress through the Forbidden Crypt zone went even more smoothly than either had dared hope. Jay managed to kill two more Frozen Mummies and four Shambling Skeletons, which—with the XP gained from the low-level Scorpions and Scarabs, was enough to push him over the edge.

Congratulations!
You have Achieved Level 5
XP: 15 | Next Lvl: 1400
Health: 180 | Stamina: 130 | Mana: 130
Unassigned Attribute Points: 3
You have 30 Base Stat Points to Distribute. Would you like to increase Health, Stamina, or Mana?

Because Lyra hadn't had to step in to help him yet, Jay received the full experience points for every kill, including his +10% bonus for the Scale-Up Ability and his 50% bonus for being Well-Rested. While the fighting had been easy enough, it had been time consuming though. There were only three more hours left of the Well-Rested bonus, and Jay was eager to keep moving.

He hurriedly tossed a point each into Strength, Agility, and Constitution, and gave all 30 Base Point Stats to Health. If he was working up to fighting those Ghost Bison, Jay didn't want to mess around. Strength and Agility helped with his fighting, so he couldn't put everything into Constitution—plus his new *Beetle Black Scarab Armor* gave him a huge Constitution boost, so he felt confident spreading his points between those three Attributes. But he was considering dumping all three points from his next Level-Up into Constitution, just in case.

Once his stats were allocated, he received a notification that he hadn't been prepared for, though he should have been.

Congratulations!
Class Tier I [Unlocked]
Please choose from one of the following options:
Talent Agent [Unique] – You specialize in finding party members with unique and valuable skillsets, which you use to your advantage. Gain a 20% XP Bonus for your entire party for every member with a [Unique] Skill, Ability, or Perk.
Middle Management [Unique] – No one is really sure what you do, but somehow you keep getting

paid. Your party splits experience with you 50/50, regardless of how much damage you deal during each encounter. This Class Tier is Active only when you are the leader of your party.

CEO [Unique] – That's Chief Expedition Officer, of course. As an incomparable strategist and leader, you focus on resource allocation, risk management, and maximizing the party's overall effectiveness through strategic decision-making. You will receive a 10% bonus to all experience gained by your party, without affecting your members' gains. In addition, you will receive the Active Skill: *Asset Management*.

Jay stared at his HUD, trying to decide which Class Tier Upgrade to choose.

"Uh, Lyra?" he asked, barely able to see her through all the holographic screens he had open. "How rare are [Unique] skills, abilities, and perks?"

The fox-girl's ears perked up. "Why? Did you just get one?"

"Maybe," he said, noting that every one of his Class Tier options had the [Unique] label. "But I'm more interested in other Delvers. Do you have any?"

"No," she said. "I have a [Rare] Class Tier, but that's it. I think Raina might have a [Unique] skill. They become more common at the higher levels, once you get into Tier II and III, supposedly. But that's only according to rumor. Tier II doesn't come up until Level 15, so I don't think anyone in Winterhaven has gotten that far. And Tier III is at Level 45.

Might as well be a fairy tale."

"Okay, thanks."

Jay mulled his options. The Talent Agent subclass would be useful later on, if he could gather many Delvers with [Unique] skills together. But that was a big if, and in the meantime the upgrade would be useless. Middle Management just rubbed him the wrong way, both because he didn't like the sound of the XP leeching benefit, and because he'd always loathed middle management personnel at the office. The CEO upgrade was promising, though. Irritatingly, when he attempted to click on the Asset Management skill to get more information, he just got an error message.

ERROR: This data is classified.

But even without the additional skill, he liked the sounds of the CEO upgrade better than the others. Not only was it more fair to his party, but it would benefit them immediately, rather than relying on future benefits that may or may not come to pass.

Congratulations!

Class Type: Versatile [Rare]

Class: Dark Horse [Unique]

Tier I Upgrade: CEO [Unique]

New Active Skill Acquired!

Asset Management - Delegation is an important skill for those with Management Potential to practice. You may access the skill trees of your party members and reassign one skill per member, per day. Skill reassignments cannot be changed once

assigned and reset to their original party members after a long rest.

"Holy shit," Jay said, re-reading the description. "I think I just got a really cool new skill. But we're going to have to look at it next time we're in a safe zone. Oh, and I have a proper class now. A [Rare] type, called Versatile. The Class is called Dark Horse."

Lyra wrinkled her forehead. "I've heard of Versatile Class Types before," she said. "It's a bit like with weapons, where they can be used for either Strength or Agility attacks depending on who wields it. Only for classes, it means you might build a Warrior, Stealth, or Caster skill tree, depending on how you fight. But what is a Dark Horse?"

"I don't know if I should be flattered or insulted," Jay said with a dry chuckle. "Where I come from, it refers to a business or product that doesn't look like much, but which surprises people by becoming extremely successful."

"I knew it!" she whisper-screamed, still mindful of the restless undead in the Forbidden Crypt. "See, Jay, I told you so! The dungeon has special plans for you. That's amazing. I can't wait to see what else you got."

"I can't wait to show you," he said. "Because I don't exactly know what to make of it. But we shouldn't delay any longer. We can discuss it later. I'm still on the clock, don't want to waste too much time with my Well-Rested bonus fading fast."

Lyra gave a sharp salute, her tail twitching excitedly. "Yes boss!" she said, straightening her back and looking very official. "Lead the way!"

Jay grinned, knowing that Lyra had no idea what his Class Tier Upgrade and new Skill entailed, but her calling him 'boss' was pretty funny. As she'd predicted, he was leveling faster than he should have been able to and was quickly catching up to the fox-girl. Before long, he would not only be her Party Leader, but he'd surpass her in Levels as well. She'd only outrank him with old-fashioned seniority, Butt-in-Dungeon time clocked.

Still, Lyra remained a steadfast cheerleader despite the fact that she gaining minimal XP while he was fighting. Jay almost began to hope they'd find a bigger group of baddies to fight, just so she could get a few hits in too.

They pressed on and Jay killed another four of the Frozen Mummies and six Shambling Skeletons. Jay received a notification that he'd risen to **Sneak 2**, giving him a 10% better chance of going undetected by enemies, which was nice, but the restless dead of the Forbidden Crypt didn't seem to have very advanced spatial awareness to begin with.

Jay was busy collecting the skulls of the last two Shambling Skeletons he'd killed and eyeing his experience points. With the additional 10% XP from the CEO Subclass, he was gaining a smidge more for each kill, but he was still more than 300 points from his next level up. He was so busy crunching numbers, with only half his brain on the tunnels ahead, that he didn't notice the new enemy blocking his way.

"Jay," Lyra hissed through her teeth. "Stop!"

Jay glanced up, startled. At first, he didn't see anything in the dim corridor. Lyra's flame cast orange light and dancing shadows over the jagged rune-carved walls. Then he noticed the light behaving strangely just ahead, as if it was sliding off and refusing to land in one area, creating an impenetrable blob of shadow.

"Don't move," Lyra said, her voice still low. "That's a—"

"Shade Skulker," Jay said. He checked his **Sneak** ability was still active and slowly backed up toward his partner. "I see it now."

Dungeon Sight told him everything he needed to know.

Shade Skulker Ooze – Lvl 5

The Shade Skulker Ooze is a creature of nightmare, adept at blending into the shadows. Its translucent, gelatinous form shifts light into darkness, camouflaging it until it strikes. Thriving on the organic material of the dead and the living, this creature prefers the taste of the latter, using its highly corrosive slime to break down its prey. The Shade Skulker can extend a part of its body to lash out at adventurers, its touch capable of dissolving metal, stone, and flesh alike. Armor offers little protection against this devastating attack. Adventurers beware—Shade Skulkers have been

known to hunt in pairs or packs, coordinating their attacks from the shadows to overwhelm and consume their prey. Lone wanderers and even well-armed parties should tread with utmost caution in the crypts to avoid becoming the next meal of these voracious predators.

"Can I fight this thing?" Jay asked after listening to the dungeon read the description in its mechanical tone.

"Not on your own," Lyra said, her voice so low and trembling that he struggled to hear her as she removed the fire arrow from her bow. When Jay had made it next to her, she passed the fiery arrow to him. She pulled a different arrow from her quiver, this one shimmering an icy blue. "And I can't fight them on my own. But together, we can do this. I'm going to hit it with an ice attack—oozes are one of the only creatures in the Ice Dungeon that are vulnerable to freezing. It should freeze solid. That's the only time it will be safe to hit it. You rush in and use your slice attack. If you see the ice begin to crack get back to me. You have to be out of range when it thaws, or it can lash you."

Jay glanced at the fire arrow in his hand. "And what do I do with this?"

"Hold it for me so I can see where I'm shooting," Lyra said. "Unless you've got a better idea. These tunnels are pitch black without some kind of light."

Jay didn't like the idea of having to fumble with the fire arrow. Lyra couldn't shoot another ice arrow while she was holding the fire arrow, and if she put it in her quiver the magical flames would extinguish, leaving them in blackness. He eyed the walls, hoping to find somewhere he could wedge the arrow instead.

"Do you think there are more of them?" Jay asked, staring into the shadows ahead. "It said they fight in groups."

Lyra shook her head. "I don't see any, and I have **Dungeon Sight 3**. I can see to the end of the corridor up there. Are you ready?"

"Hang on," Jay said, finding a crack between two thick slabs of blue-gray stone. He jammed the butt of the arrow into the crack, wincing as the feathered fletching bent sideways. "Okay, ready."

"Hey, do you know how expensive those are?" Lyra growled at him, her tail puffing up like an angry cat, as if she was trying to make herself look bigger and more threatening. Jay wasn't sure if foxes did that, but apparently Vulpinari did, and it was adorable.

"I'll buy you a new one once we sell all our loot on the market," he said, readying his blade. "Now freeze that sucker so we can get moving."

Lyra's ears flattened to the side and she narrowed her two-toned eyes at him, but she followed his orders. Her shoulder muscles tensed and flexed as she drew back on the bow, the glittering arrow tip pointed at the amorphous shadow ahead. When she released, the arrow made a strange humming sound, like the resonance of a crystal glass being struck. The

Shade Skulker Ooze crackled as it was engulfed in an icy crust.

Jay didn't hesitate, rushing forward to slash the ooze with his Bolo Knife. Ice chips sprayed in all directions as he attacked the immobilized creature with forward and back slashes like he was carving an X on its frozen flesh. He got in six strikes before the icy crust began to crumble.

"To me, Jay!" Lyra said, a yip of alarm in her voice. "Back, quickly!"

Jay darted backwards just as the slime broke free of its icy prison, lashing out with a trembling tentacle of translucent slime that cracked like a whip right where he'd just been standing. Jay's Agility barely managed to keep him from getting struck as he retreated. As soon as he was clear of her shot, Lyra hit the creature with a second ice arrow.

Knowing what to do this time, Jay lunged forward, this time attempting to use his Strength to stab into the frozen ooze. His blade clanged off its rock-hard shell ineffectually. He went back to slashing, this time channeling the Strength attribute rather than agility for slower, more powerful strikes.

This time, when the shell began to crack, Jay was ready. He jumped quickly to Lyra's side, dodging the slime's slashing attack. The creature moved slowly, seemingly constrained by the pool of light coming off the fire arrow, as if it needed the shadows and abhorred the torchlight.

Lyra released a third ice arrow as soon as Jay was

safe, and Jay leapt straight back into his attack, not wanting to waste any time. The higher-level monster was taking longer to kill than the Mummies and Skeletons, but he could tell he was wearing it down. He was eager to get the kill and the experience, which might be enough to put him over the edge to his next level.

The clang of his first strike on the frozen ooze's icy shell was drowned out by a horrifying scream. Jay whirled around just in time to see a second Shade Skulker Ooze drop from the shadowed ceiling, landing on Lyra's head.

"Lyra, no!" Jay rushed to help her; his stomach twisted in knots. He could hear the hiss of the creature's acidic slime burning her skin as the fox-girl dropped to the ground with a wail of agony that tore through his heart.

Behind him, he heard the shattering sound of the first Shade Skulker breaking free of its icy confines. His mind spun. What was he going to do? He had to rescue Lyra, there was no question about that. But how when the oozes could dissolve flesh on contact?

Jay grimaced, knowing what he was going to have to do. He hadn't dumped all those points into Constitution for nothing.

Taking a deep breath, Jay rushed the slime that was attacking Lyra, preparing his body and mind for a world of hurt.

23

Secrets of the Crypt

J ay tackled the attacking Shade Skulker Ooze like a deranged football player. He imagined it would have been funny to see a man dressed in a three piece suit throw himself at a gelatinous blob, if he were watching the fight from the outside. Instead, he was in the thick of it. The first thing he noticed was how firm the ooze was—more like a gummy bear than a bowl of Jell-O. The second thing he noticed was the stench of his burning flesh, just before the searing agony burned through his skin and into his brain.

Fortunately for him, the gummy-bear texture of the ooze made it possible to roll the monster off of Lyra. The fox-girl lay on the floor, curled in on herself, her skin blistered and cracked from exposure to the ooze's acidic flesh. Her bow and arrows had fallen to the side, scattering across the floor of the crypt, mercifully undamaged by the Shade Skulker's attack.

Jay wrenched his hands from the creature, stumbling backward, refusing to look at the damage to his body. He wanted to go to Lyra, to protect her, to comfort her as she had done for him when he was the one in so much pain. But Jay knew the only way he could truly protect her was to kill the monsters.

And the only way he could do that was if he could use Lyra's bow.

Putting himself between Lyra's crumpled body and the second ooze, Jay opened his menu to click on the **On-The-Job Training** description, hoping it might give him some clue as to how to use the Ability. He skipped the snarky intro and read:

On-The-Job-Training - Once per day, you may borrow a skill from one of your party members. While you are using their skill, it will be removed from their skill tree until you return it to them. You do not gain the party members skill points in this level, nor do they lose their skill points. You retain skill points gained with borrowed skills, but may only access them when you have a relevant skill active in your skill tree.

But how was he supposed to do that? He clicked frantically on the description, hoping it would open more detailed instructions. But there was nothing there.

The ooze sent a tendril of slime whipping at Jay's

head and he dodged out of the way, hearing it slap the wall behind him with a crack. He opened his party menu, thinking maybe he had to select Lyra's name from that list to see her skills.

This worked.

He scrolled through a number of skills he had never seen the Arcane Archer use, and which he didn't know what to expect from. But he selected one he thought he could predict:

New Skill Acquired!

Frostbite Arrow - Enchants arrows with frost, slowing enemies and dealing ice damage over time. Monsters who are weak to frost damage may be frozen solid.

Hoping that his Agility Attribute was high enough to use Lyra's bow, Jay scrambled for the dropped weapon. The Shade Skulker Ooze lashed out at him again. This time its tendril slapped the exposed side of his neck and Jay grunted with pain. But he managed to grab the bow and one of the [Frostbite Arrows].

The first ooze sent a flailing tentacle of slime toward Jay, but it seemed to be out of range. The creature was slowly inching its way forward, but for the moment, Jay had to focus on the ooze that was the most immediate threat to Lyra.

Jay dropped his Bolo Knife at his feet and drew the bow, channeling his dungeon magic into the movement and attempting to open his mind to its guidance. The movement was awkward and shaky at first, the bow's draw was heavier than he'd expected given Lyra's size. She must have a higher Strength Attribute than he'd realized.

Jay released the Frostbite Arrow at close range, praying that he'd be allowed to make the shot. The arrow struck the Shade Skulker center mass with the same humming crystal sound as when Lyra shot the bow. Relief flooded through Jay's body as he saw the surface of the ooze harden into an icy shell.

Myriad notifications lit up the side of his HUD, but he ignored them for now.

As tempting as it was to pick up his Bolo Knife and immediately start slashing the thing, Jay knew he had to get Lyra to safety first.

He dropped next to the injured fox-girl, trying not to stare at her blistered, bleeding skin and her damaged armor. As gently as he could, he lifted her into his arms and carried her over to the wall beneath the fire arrow where the light was brightest and the oozes seemed least likely to encroach.

"Jay... so sorry..." she murmured, barely conscious. "Didn't see it... too late..."

"Shh," Jay said. "Stay still. I'll try to get us out of this."

He picked up another arrow and, after a moment's deliberation, shot it at the first Shade Skulker. He left the bow next to Lyra, lunged for the Bolo Knife he'd left on the ground and just barely dodged another whip-like slime tentacle from the second ooze. Rolling out of range of the healthier monster, Jay leapt to his feet and immediately began slashing at the frozen blob before him.

It only took two more hits to shatter the first Shade Skulker into a thousand frozen pieces. The ensuing rush of notifications made Jay's hopes surge. If he'd killed one, he could kill the second, even if he had to fight both the ranged and melee roles. His health bar had dropped halfway but was already creeping back up—the extra Constitution points doing exactly what he'd hoped they would would. If he could avoid getting hit too often, he could do this.

Jay used his Agility to dart a jagged path back to Lyra, hoping to confused the slow-moving ooze so that it didn't know where to attack. He managed to get to the bow without being struck, but when he dove for a Frostbite Arrow he got whipped in the thigh for his efforts, bringing his health back down below the halfway mark.

Gritting his teeth through the pain, Jay forced himself to breath slowly as he drew the arrow and released the shot. The shaft flew low but struck true, striking the remaining Shade Skulker near its slimy base. The Frostbite Arrow didn't seem to mind being a little off-center. It worked its magic nonetheless.

The moment the ooze was frozen, Jay dropped the bow, picked up his knife and darted in for his first strikes. Channeling Strength to power his slashing blows against the frozen monster, Jay tried to push as much of the dungeon magic he could sense into his attack, hoping to squeeze a few extra hit points out for the effort.

To his surprise, the Shade Skulker exploded on his first hit, shattering like glass at his feet. Confused, Jay checked his notifications for an explanation.

Critical Hit! 5x Damage
Success!
You have killed
Shade Skulker Ooze Lvl 5 (x2)
XP: 140 (x2) (+10%) (+50%) (+10%)

Congratulations!
You have Achieved Level 6
XP: 111 | Next Lvl: 2100
Health: 210 | Stamina: 130 | Mana: 130
Unassigned Attribute Points: 3
You have 30 Base Stat Points to Distribute. Would you like to increase Health, Stamina, or Mana?

Jay breathed a sigh of relief as his Health points were immediately restored and the pain of the ooze's acid attacks faded from his mind. Lyra lay unconscious beneath the fire arrow. She hadn't leveled up, though she should have gotten some XP from the first ooze at least. Jay wished there was a way he could check her progress. If they didn't have any health potions, leveling the fox-girl might be the only way to save her.

Jay cursed. How was he going to do that? He looted the corpses of both oozes without even checking what he was getting. Then he sheathed his Bolo

Knife and scrambled to pick up Lyra's bow and arrows. He had to get her out of the Forbidden Crypt immediately.

From the distance, he could hear the moaning and shuffling of Frozen Mummies, awakened from their slumber by his fight with the oozes.

His mind went to the tentative plan he'd had. He'd fought Frozen Mummies and Shambling Skeletons alone before. Though he'd had Lyra as back up she'd not once had to step in to help him, only giving him advice when he first learned how to fight the monsters. He could fight them alone, maybe a lot of them... If his Well-Rested bonus was still active he could—

You are no longer Well-Rested. Your 50% XP bonus has been removed until you complete another long rest to restore your status. You are now Rested. No XP bonus available. To ensure optimal performance in the dungeon, please rest again before you become Tired, with a -25% XP debuff, or Exhausted, with a -50% XP debuff.

"Shit," Jay muttered. "I guess that answers that. We need to get out of here."

He put Lyra's bow and arrows into his inventory and bent to pick up the unconscious fox-girl as gently as he could. She whimpered but didn't wake as Jay flipped her up onto his left shoulder in a fireman's carry. He hoped that way he would still be able to reach his Bolo Knife if necessary. It would be awkward but not impossible to fight with Lyra on his back. The moaning and shuffling of the Mummies was getting closer and he really wasn't looking forward to testing that theory, though.

Unfortunately, the shuffling was coming from the passage they'd already been though, and the only way he knew out of the Forbidden Crypt. They must have come from a side corridor they had left unexplored, because Jay was certain he'd collected all of the monster's heads after he'd killed him.

Or maybe they'd been in these corridors long enough that the original monsters had respawned.

Either way, Jay didn't like the idea of carrying Lyra out the way they'd come. He'd have to find another way out of the zone. He grabbed the fire arrow that was still stuck in the crack in the wall and pulled it down to release it, hoping to use it as a torch.

But the moment the arrow was released from the crevice, Jay heard a grinding sound that set his teeth on edge. The corridor trembled, dust and bits of ice raining down from the ceiling as Jay gaped in surprise.

A door was opening in the rune-carved wall, as if the arrow had acted as a lever to unlock a hidden chamber. Jay held his breath, praying that there weren't going to be new monsters inside to fight.

When the rumbling stopped, and the doorway was open before him, Jay waited. Nothing lunged from the darkness to attack him. The shuffling of the Mummies was growing nearer, their ragged breath echoing off the walls of the crypt, somehow more disturbing at a distance than they had been when he'd been fighting them. Jay glanced toward the sound and saw dim shapes moving in the shadows at the end of the corridor.

He thrust his hand with the fire arrow into the hidden doorway, hoping not to be confronted with the toothy grin of some lurking monstrosity.

Instead, he found a small room filled with unusual plants that shimmered in his **Dungeon Sight**.

Jay didn't hesitate. He rushed inside with Lyra over his shoulder, searching frantically for some way to close the door behind him.

As soon as he crossed the threshold, however, the door rose from the floor, sealing him and his companion inside the small, lush room.

Entering: Secret Garden (Temporary Safe Zone)

Few Delvers ever discover one of the Ice Dungeon's hidden Safe Zones. So few, that even rumors of these secret places are hard to come by. They appear at random and are never found in the same place twice. Unlike their permanent counterparts, these Temporary Safe Zones do not have amenities beyond providing a monster-free zone where Delvers can rest. Some have been known to spawn reward chests and loot items on occasion.

Jay gently laid Lyra on the mossy ground, cushioning her head with his hand. "We're safe now, Lyra," he whispered to the fox-girl. "I'm going to search in your satchel for healing potions, okay?"

Lyra groaned. "Only... water..."

Jay held the fire arrow in one hand while he rummaged in Lyra's bag, trying to find the leather canteen she'd given him when he was injured. She had food and an extra set of armor and some backup arrows in the satchel, but he didn't see anything that looked like a health potion. He wasn't even certain there were such a thing, or if that was another thing he'd gotten wrong from his memories of video games.

He did find the water canteen, though, and he held it to Lyra's lips. Her cracked skin was oozing blood, looking even more painful than the burns he'd received at the hands of the exploding Glacial Scarab Construct. Jay ached to see her in so much pain, and he wished there was something more he could do.

If nothing else, rest should help. But it would be a long, painful recovery if he didn't find something to easy her agony.

"Thank you," Lyra whispered when she'd finished with the water. "That's better. I'm sorry, Jay. I should have known to look on the ceiling for the other ooze. I've seen them attack from above before. I almost got us killed with my foolishness."

"Shh, stop that," he insisted. "You're the one who saved me from walking straight into the first one, remember? And you taught me how to fight them. Without you, I'd have been dead."

"How?" she asked, turning her blistered face toward him, her two-toned eyes swollen almost shut.

"How did you defeat them?"

"Something called **On-The-Job-Training**," he said. "I took your Frostbite Arrows skill and used your bow to freeze them, then hacked them with the knife. I got lucky on the second one. A critical strike on a full Strength attack. Maybe it was injured before it attacked us and didn't have full health? It died in one hit. I leveled up again. I'm at Level 6 now, like you."

Lyra laughed, a dry, pained sound. "Incredible," she whispered. "Six levels in two days? I've heard that kind of thing is possible in other dungeons. But it's never been true in the Ice Dungeon." She looked around, her swollen eyes widening as she realized they weren't in the crypt anymore. "Where are we?"

Jay read the description of the Secret Garden, and Lyra began to weep. He touched her left hand, one part of her body that hadn't been hit by the ooze's acidic body, and squeezed her fingers. "Don't cry," he said. "You're safe now. You're going to get better, even if we have to hide in here for a few days until you heal. Do you have anything else that will help you to regenerate your health points faster?"

"Food," she said, gesturing at her bag again. "Being Well-Fed increases the speed you regain HP. And after that, sleep. Thank you for saving my life, Jay. I'll never be able to repay you for that."

Jay found some strips of dried meat in Lyra's bag, which she took with her unburned hand. "You already saved my life once," he said. "Now we're even."

Lyra chewed, wincing with pain, until she'd managed to finish the jerky. "I'm going to rest now," she said. "You should too. I'll be better soon."

"I will," Jay said. "I just want to look around a bit and catch up on my notifications."

As the fox-girl's eyes closed, Jay felt a weight lift from his chest. He hated seeing her in pain, but it helped to know that they were safe and that she would heal. He prayed that the dungeon's magic would work swiftly.

24

Garden
Harvest

When Lyra's breath was rising and falling more steadily, which Jay took to mean she was asleep, he stood and began using his **Dungeon Sight** on the shimmering plants in the room.

Immediately, he recognized one of them and hurried to collect it.

Frostleaf Clover – A highly sought plant with hallucinogenic properties, which Shaman, Druid, and some Priest classes can use to trespass in the Land of the Dead or the Land of Dreams. Delver Beware: This plant is poisonous to those without the appropriate Class and Skill to use it.

Jay had read the description before, but he'd been so overwhelmed by everything going on that he hadn't really thought about it. He wondered if Raina was actually planning to travel into Molly's dreams in some kind of spirit form in order to bring her back to her conscious mind. Raina was certain that the spell could be performed with ease, that it had been done before. Jay imagined the Strength enhancing Tundra Berries were used to give the patient the extra boost needed to fight against the dream state—though he was concerned about the so-called 'unexpected effects' the item description warned of.

Quickly, he gathered as many of the Frostleaf Clover plants as he could, hoping that they would keep inside his Inventory. Raina had only asked for one of each plant, but he assumed she could make use of more. Perhaps she would accept some of the reagents he'd found in the dungeon as payment for her services.

You have learned Gathering: Horticulturist 1!

Jay raised his eyebrows. Another thing to level. He scanned the other plants as he gathered them as well.

The first he touched was an ethereal flower with delicate petals, shimmering in hues of pale blue and white, much like frost on a windowpane. Its stem, slender and silver, supported blooms that seemed to emit a soft, luminescent fog, cooling the air immediately around them. The thin, almost translucent leaves had a fine tracery of ice-like veins running through them.

Winter's Breath Flower (Silver) - This delicate bloom exhales a gentle, chilling mist even in the

warmest climates, keeping its surroundings cool and frost-kissed. The petals of the Winter's Breath Flower can be used in the creation of natural refrigeration systems, making it invaluable for preserving food and medicines in warm regions. When distilled into a potion, the flower's essence grants temporary resistance to extreme heat, proving essential for explorers venturing into volcanic or desert environments.

Jay pulled five of the Silver or [Uncommon] plants into his inventory before moving onto the next.

A surprisingly bright vine caught his eyes, the vibrant, emerald-green tendrils spiraled from a locus at the center of the plant, covered in a fine layer of frost that sparkled even in the dim light of the Secret Garden. Its leaves were broad and heart-shaped, edged with a rime of ice that didn't melt, even beneath Jay's fingers. Small, icicle-like droplets formed along the vine, solidifying into beautiful, frosty sap jewels that dangled like diamonds or—Jay thought, absurdly, like Christmas ornaments—giving the vine a magical, winter-wonderland appearance that made him suddenly homesick.

Hoarfrost Vine (Gold) – The sap of the Hoarfrost Vine freezes upon contact with air, forming thin strands of natural ice that are both beautiful and durable. The frozen sap can be woven into thread, twine, or rope and is often used to create lightweight, insulating materials, perfect for crafting garments that provide protection against cold weather or magical frost attacks. Artisans value the vine for its unique property, using the frozen sap to create jewelry, decorative items, or even as a component in constructing lightweight, translucent structures that remain cool under direct sunlight.

These [Rare] vines were large and unwieldly. Jay found three as he poked through the garden, and once he removed them to his inventory, he was shocked by how empty the room felt, and how drab. But they seemed like something that would fetch a good price on the Global Dungeon Market, given their rarity and the use in creating luxury goods.

There were only a few plants left, all of which appeared to be the same thing. Large, radiant blooms that glowed softly from within, casting a gentle light over its icy-blue petals and small pockets of luminescence in the garden. The flower sat atop a sturdy stalk, encased in a sheath of ice crystals that looked like thorns. The broad, flat leaves had a frosted, reflective surface that made their glow even brighter. At the base of each flower, a small mound of snow covered the roots like a blanket.

Glazed Lotus (Gold) - The bloom of the Glazed Lotus emits a faint, radiant glow, absorbing and storing cold energy from its surroundings to thrive in even the harshest winter. The petals of this flower are sought after for their cooling properties, used in teas and salves that reduce fever, burns, inflammation, and the effects of heatstroke. When

**processed, the glowing essence of the Glazed Lotus
can be turned into a luminescent dye, providing a
sustainable light source that emits a calming, cool
light, ideal for illuminating dark, enclosed spaces
without generating heat.**

Jay swallowed hard as he read the description of
the last plant. Not only was it of [Rare] quality, but it
sounded as if it could be used to treat injuries such as
Lyra was suffering from. There were nearly a dozen
of the plants growing throughout the garden area,
which Jay promptly brought into his Inventory. Jay
didn't want to get his hopes up, but there was a
very good chance that he'd just harvested a small
fortune's worth of dungeon plants.

Surely, he could afford to experiment with one of
them?

Jay kept a Glazed Lotus plant in his hands, studying it intensely. He pushed the flow of his dungeon
magic into **Dungeon Sight**, urging the plant to give
up its secrets. He wondered if he should have put
more points into Intelligence, if that would allow
him to learn more about the items they found, or
if that was strictly a Casting Attribute.

New Ability Upgrade!

**Dungeon Sight 2 – You now learn more about the
creatures and items found in the dungeon.**

Jay's heart beat faster as he re-read the description of the Glazed Lotus. Now there was additional
information listed beneath it:

Recipe: Salve of Cure Burns

Combine one [Glazed Lotus Petal] with one [Water] to create a cooling salve for the relief of minor burns.

Jay fumbled through his Inventory menus until he discovered a way to combine items. If he selected the items he wished to combine, a Crafting Menu popped up providing him with a number of options. Taking a deep breath, Jay selected what appeared to be the simplest way to combine items, an option called **Mortar and Pestel: Blend.**

You have learned Crafting: Apothecary 1!

You have created [Salve of Cure Burns] (Uncommon)

XP: 150

Jay's hands trembled as he removed the salve from his Inventory. A small pot of pale blue, faintly glowing cream appeared in his fingers. He put his fingers into the salve, immediately feeling the cooling properties at work. Gently, so as not to wake her, he spread the salve on Lyra's burns.

She whimpered in her sleep, her swollen face scrunching as if the contact hurt. But almost immediately she released a sigh of relief. Jay could see the inflammation reducing as he worked, and felt tears prickle his eyes as Lyra's beautiful face was resorted by the soothing balm.

When he had applied the entire pot, ensuring to treat the worst of her burns first, Jay received another notification.

You have learned Profession: Field Medic 1!

Gathering, Crafting, and Profession Menus appeared in his HUD and Jay took a moment to familiarize himself with them as best he could. But there was far too much to get through without some guidance. He decided to wait until Lyra awoke to ask her about what to do with those features.

When he was in his HUD, however, he switched back to the Party Menu and transferred Lyra back her Frostbite Arrows skill that he'd borrowed with **On-The-Job-Training** before he forgot. He noticed he also had the **Asset Management**, which appeared to be similar to **On-The-Job-Training**, but which would allow him to transfer skills between other Party members as well as borrowing them for himself. The difference was, **On-The-Job-Training** could be moved back and forth at will, while skill transfers made using **Asset Management** would revert automatically after a long rest.

Now that he had time to inspect his skills and re-read the descriptions, he was beginning to get a sense of what the dungeon was trying to tell him about his [Unique] Versatile Type Class. The battlefield equivalent to a CEO would probably be something like War Commander or General or something. Jay was meant to gather powerful Party members, using their skills for himself as necessary, and helping them to expand their versatility by combing unusual skillsets to create a powerful, dynamic, and adaptable Delving Party.

He'd been able to use Lyra's skills to power-level

himself through the basic Delving stages. Now that he was working toward his Tier II Class Upgrade, progress would be slower. Each Level required more XP to get through, and while higher-level monsters gave more experience per kill, he could already tell that without the advantage of a Well-Rested bonus it would likely take Lyra and him a couple of hard days grinding to get to Level 7.

Now that he and Lyra were the same Level, it no longer made sense for her to let him do all the fighting. They would be better off fighting as a team, like they had against the Shade Skulker Oozes until disaster struck, sharing experience and leveling together. With his bonuses, +10% for the Scale-Up Ability and +10% for the CEO Subclass, he would still gain levels at a faster rate than she would. But that meant he had to do everything he help her keep pace. Strategies would become more and more important as the gulf between them grew.

Jay flipped through the rest of his combat notifications, and read the descriptions of the items he'd harvested from the Oozes.

Corrosive Slime (Silver) - An essence extracted from a defeated Shade Skulker, this vial contains a dark, viscous liquid that seems to pulsate with a life of its own. Holding it close, one can feel a faint warmth, as if the slime is eagerly waiting to unleash its destructive power. When applied, this reagent can eat through the toughest materials with alarming ease, making it a prized posses-

sion for alchemists and crafters alike. In the right hands, it serves as a potent ingredient in the creation of powerful acids or dissolving agents, capable of weakening enemy armor or clearing obstacles that block one's path.

Shade Agent (Platinum) - A rare find indeed, this shimmering, translucent gel is collected from the remnants of a Shade Skulker after its demise. When spread thinly over the surface of an object or individual, the gel hardens into an almost invisible film that reflects the surrounding light and scenery. This remarkable camouflage agent allows adventurers to blend seamlessly into their environment, rendering them nearly invisible to the naked eye. Ideal for stealth missions or evading detection in hostile territories, the gel's properties make it an invaluable asset for spies, thieves, and hunters seeking the element of surprise.

Interesting, Jay thought as he closed the Inventory Menu to open the two new Notes he'd received from his 'Anonymous Benefactor' thanks to the **Bootstrapper** Ability.

The first was rather terse, once again read in Nova's sultry almost petulant tone.

Already? Well, all right, if you insist.
Here is your gift. Use it well.

[Etched Bolo Sword] (Gold) – This [Rare] sword has been etched with runes of durability, making it nearly impossible to break or damage, even with the roughest use. This item will bond to its wielder,

and cannot be traded or sold once equipped.

Jay immediately put his Sturdy Bolo Knife into his Inventory and equipped the new weapon, feeling the surge of bonding magic tickle his palm as he gripped the handle of the blade. There was no way he would insult Nova by trading or selling her gift. Jay thought he could feel the dungeon sigh with pleasure as he bonded with the item, and a tremor of pleasure rippled through his body as he inspected the item.

Etched Bolo Sword – Rare (Gold)
Bonded to Delver Jay Morgan
Melee – Versatile – Damage: 3d6 (slicing)
Condition: [100/100]

"Thank you, Nova," he whispered, knowing this blade would make the coming challenges much more manageable.

The second note was... different.

My sweet, Dark Horse. Why do you do this to me? I am bound to try to kill you, for that is my nature, and yet it kills me to do so. How fortunate that you seem to have a knack for rising from the ashes... you truly are a Dark Horse. They will not see you coming. And when they do, it will be too late.

I shudder with the deepest pleasure to think of how they will feel when you rise to challenge my captors. When you find me. When you free me from these chains that bind my body and my soul.

But you cannot bring me my release if you are dead. Just because I am trying to kill you does not mean you should be letting me get so damned close! Take these until you find a proper healer.

   [Vial of Plentiful Healing] x10

Jay gratefully put the healing potions into his Inventory. He wondered if he should wake Lyra and give one to her, but she was sleeping so soundly and the salve seemed to have cleared up the worst of her burns, so he decided to let her rest.

It was time for him to do the same. He moved 10 of his new Base Stat points into Health, and put the other 20 into Stamina. With the +50 HP his Beetle Black Scarab Armor gave him, his Health was pulling far ahead of his other Base Stats and he wasn't sure he wanted his Stamina to get too far behind. Then he gave himself an additional Attribute point in each of Strength, Agility, and Constitution.

Then Jay lay down on the mossy floor of the Secret Garden Safe Zone and fell asleep next to his pretty fox-girl companion. He listened to Lyra's peaceful breathing until he, too, fell asleep.

25

Frigid Depths

When Jay woke from his Long Rest, Lyra was already up. She had her silver-white hair tied into a braid over one shoulder. Her pointed ears were alert and her tail was flicking back and forth as she paced the circumference of the small space.

Jay sat up, stretching and yawning, and enjoying the luscious feel of the Well-Rested bonus along with his newly allocated stats.

Delver: Jay Morgan

Class Type: Versatile

Class: Dark Horse

Lvl: 6

XP: 111 | **Next Lvl:** 2100

Health: 220 | **Stamina:** 150 | **Mana:** 130

Active Bonus: 10% max XP (Scale-Up), 10% max XP (CEO), 50% max XP (Well-Rested, temporary)

Unassigned Attribute Points: 0

Strength: 5

Agility: 5

Intelligence: 1

Constitution: 12 [*Beetle Black Scarab Armor* – Set Bonus: Constitution +6, HP +50]

Willpower: 2

Charisma: 10

Active Skills: On-The-Job-Training, Asset Management

Passive Abilities: Environmental Resistance 1 (Arctic), Dungeon Sight 2, Scale-Up, Stealth 2, Well-Rested (temporary)

Perks: Panty Dropper, Bootstrapper

Vocational Skills: Gathering: Horticulturist 1, Profession: Field Medic 1, Crafting: Apothecary 1

"Jay!" Lyra exclaimed as he was studying his newly upgraded Class Menu. "Thank goodness you're awake. We need to go, now!"

She leapt into Jay's lap, her legs wrapping around his hips and pinning him to the mossy ground. The fox-girl was trembling with excitement, her blue-and-gold eyes wide and fixed on him. Jay found himself lost in her face, hardly able to believe such a beautiful woman existed, let alone was straddling him in a magical garden.

"Then you'll have to get off of me," he said, reluctantly. "But what's your hurry?"

"I'm only a few points away from my next Level Up!" she exclaimed, squirming excitedly in his lap and not making it any easier for him to convince himself to move. "I got an Achievement for surviving an ambush that put me over the edge, which is great because I didn't get any experience for those Oozes since I was unconscious when you finished them off. One more kill will do it. I'll be Level 7, Jay! Other than Raina and Runolf, that will make me the third most powerful Delver in Winterhaven! Me, the outcast. The one no one wanted to Party with. I can't wait to rub it in all of their faces!"

Laughing, Jay grabbed the petite Vulpinari woman and lifted her from his hips, setting her on the cushy moss floor.

"All right," he said. "Let's go then. I'm happy to see you looking so refreshed."

"Oh, Jay," she moaned, clutching her hands to her chest in ecstasy. "I have never felt so good. That healing salve you used on me must have some kind of hidden stimulant in it. I never thought I could feel this good. Let's go kill some monsters!"

Jay pulled some jerky from his inventory, and chewed thoughtfully. "I don't think there were any extra properties in it," he said. "But I made it using a Gold tier flower, so maybe it's just higher quality than you're used to?"

Stunned, Lyra shot to her feet. "You *made* it? I thought it might have been a lucky item drop."

"Yeah," he said. "I got a bunch of weird new Vocational Skills while you were resting."

He read to her from his Class Menu as her mouth fell open in shock.

"But... you can't unlock Vocational Skills before

Level 10," she said, her voice coming out in an excited yip. "And you have to pay a trainer to get your first level in any of them. That's... that's..."

"Impossible?" Jay raised his eyebrows. "Kind of like my 10 useless points in Charisma and my Unique Class? I'm sensing a theme here."

Lyra put her hands on her hips and glowered at him.

"Couldn't you at least pretend to be surprised?" she snapped. "This is unbelievable! Field Medic is a really expensive Profession to unlock, too. Wow!"

Jay shrugged. "I guess I don't have a very good sense of what's believable and what's not," he said. "All of this would be impossible in my world. Maybe my access to Vocational Skills has something to do with my Versatile Class Type? Or the fact that everything about my Class Skills has to do with the professional world back home?"

"I don't know," Lyra said, shaking her head. Her tail wagged excitedly. "Wow! This is really crazy, you know that? I can't wait to see what you get next. I'm so glad I met you, Jay Morgan. Delving has suddenly become so much more exciting!"

"Getting attacked by monsters wasn't exciting enough for you?"

"Oh, everyone gets attacked by monsters," she said with a little giggle. "Not everyone gets to observe a hero in the making."

Jay finished his jerky, explaining everything that happened after Lyra got ambushed by the Ooze. She *oohed* and *aahed* as he shared his new stats with her and showed off his Etched Bolo Sword.

"That's it," she shouted. "I can't stand it anymore. We've got to go find that Undead Pharoh and lay a lickin' on his mummified butt. This is going to be the best day in the dungeon ever!"

"We can go," Jay said, moving to stand in front of the secret door. "But I'm not lickin' any mummy butts, and neither are you."

Lyra blushed a deep red color and punched him in the arm. "Shut up, Portal Boy. You know what I meant."

"You can't call me that anymore," he teased. "I'm the same Level as you are now."

Lyra huffed.

Jay grinned as the door opened, and the two of them stepped back into the Forbidden Crypt, re-freshed and ready for action.

Lyra knew the way to the Pharoh's Burial Chamber, a hidden room that she had marked on her map from the last time she'd been through the Forbid-den Crypt zone with one of her parties. Jay was curious about the map, which was something he hadn't unlocked yet. Lyra explained that you had to purchase a blank map from a trader before you could use one which, she assured him, they would be able to get from Toma Tabernak once they got to F2.

Much to Lyra's frustration, they only ran into low-level monsters on their way to find the Pharoh, which—now that Jay was also at Level 6, and they were splitting experience between the two of them—did not provide enough XP to bring her over the top. She was inching closer, though, and trembling with the excitement of it.

Between the two of them, the Level 3 and Level 4 monsters hardly slowed them down. Jay was amazed at the difference it made having Lyra fighting with him, and eager to try their hand at the higher-level Ghost Bison, once they developed a plan to isolate the creatures. He was mulling over ways to use the Hoarfrost Vines to make rope, or the Glazed Lotus to make some kind of invisibility potion. But he wasn't certain that he could craft such items without a recipe, and he was loathe to ruin valuable items that could be sold on the World Dungeon Market if he wasn't certain of the outcome.

Together, Lyra and Jay wound deeper into the Forbidden Crypts until even the Frozen Mummies and Shambling Skeletons stopped showing up. They didn't discover any more Shade Skulker Oozes hiding in the shadows. The tunnels seemed to get darker and colder the farther they went. Unable to talk except for the barest of whispers, the dark and the quiet began to get to Jay. He kept thinking he could hear strange noises, just at the edge of his senses. But the moment he caught one, a footstep or a falling stone would interrupt the sound, leaving him to wonder and imagine what was making the sounds.

Even Lyra, who had been to the dark center of the crypt before, seemed on edge.

They stopped at an intersection and the fox-girl checked her map, shaking her head. "There should be monsters here," she said, keeping her voice low. "I've got notes on my map that say to look out for Sickle Spiders and Snow Serqet—larger versions of the scorpions we've already encountered."

"Do I even want to know what those are?" Jay asked, shuddering at the thought of fighting more monstrous arachnids.

"Sickle Spiders are large with knife-like front legs," she said. "Their weakness is their abdomen which erupts under pressure. The Snow Serqet are essentially the same as the Snow Scorpions, and you have to get between the plates of their armored carapace to deal damage. Both are vulnerable to fire. With the two of us at Level 6, they likely wouldn't have proven too challenging unless the dungeon threw an Elite in there. But it's concerning that there aren't any here. Usually, the Ice Dungeon throws more enemies at Delvers than it should, not the other way around."

"Let's keep going," Jay said, not wanting to show that he, too, was unnerved by the quiet. "Maybe we're just supposed to fight this Undead Pharoh for some reason."

Lyra nodded, lifting her flame-tipped arrow to light the way farther down the corridor to their right. "It should be just up there," she said. "The tomb will have the Pharoh's sarcophagus in the middle, along with a handful of Frozen Mummy Guardian's and possibly a Shambling Skeleton or two. Nothing we can't handle."

Jay gave the fox-girl a small salute to let her know he was ready for anything. As Lyra motioned for him to go first as she lit the way with her arrows. He moved into the dark, frigid corridor with slow, silent steps, pushing his dungeon magic into the **Sneak** skill to ensure he moved as stealthily as possible.

Again, the flashing of his **Sneak** progress bar alerted him to the fact that there were enemies nearby, and Jay held up a hand for Lyra to stop. He held his Bolo Sword in front of him and pressed his back to the wall, inching toward the next intersection where shuffling footsteps and an eerie clicking sound could be heard coming toward them.

Despite the fact that he knew something was coming, Jay was completely unprepared for the horror that lurched around the corner. A mass of broken bones clicked and rattled and dragged across the stone floor, roughly in the shape of a hunch-backed man. The thing's head was far too large, though, and Jay realized the skull had been formed from many skulls smashed together and held together with a dark paste that looked like dried blood.

Its oversized eye-sockets glowed red as it turned to Jay. The monster's mouth stretched wide, and it roared, blasting him with a stench that could have withered meat on the bone. Jay's **Dungeon Sight** helpfully narrated the monster's description in its mechanical, disinterested tone while he fought every urge to scream and run.

Shambling Bone-Rattler: Lvl 5 [Elite]

Reduce, Reuse, and Recycle! The Shambling Bone-Rattler is an undead monster made up of the parts leftover when Shambling Skeletons are killed. The more Shambling Skeletons you kill, the bigger the Shambling Bone-Rattlers grow. Unlike their vacuous, shuffling counterparts, which attack only when their rest is disturbed, the Shambling Bone-Rattler is a vicious hunter bent on the destruction of Delver-kind. They're best avoided, which, if you're receiving this notification, you've likely failed to do.

Jay leaped back just as the Shambling Bone-Rattler slammed a massive fist into the wall where he'd been standing, sending shards of stone flying. Jay could feel his body moving more slowly than it should, and he narrowly missed being pummeled by the undead monster.

He noticed a red debuff notification blinking in his HUD and quickly opened it as he scrambled out of the way of another blow.

Debuff Activated!

The Breath of Death – You have inhaled the breath

of the living dead which, besides being an unpleasant aromatic experience, has afflicted you with Malaise. Movement speed reduced by 25% for 5 min.

"Lyra, get back!" Jay shouted. "The breath attack slows you down. And it stinks!"

"Focus on Strength attacks, Jay," the fox-girl said. "Keep it busy while I switch ammo."

She dropped the flaming arrow to the ground, where it continued to burn, but failed to cast as much light as Jay had gotten used to. The shadows jumped and lurched behind the Bone-Rattler, making its shape even more monstrous. Jay gripped his Bolo Sword in both hands and lunged at the creature. He drove a powerful overhead attack into the Bone-Rattler's shoulder, pushing as much Strength into the move as he could. Bits of bone and dried blood erupted from the strike in a shower of macabre debris.

The Bone-Rattler countered the attack with a swipe of its massive arm, smashing Jay in the side and sending him flying into the opposite wall. Pain burst throughout his body as Jay slammed into the stone, but his Constitution saved him from breaking anything.

Shaking himself off, he rushed the beast a second time.

Though he could feel the sluggishness of his limbs from the debuff, Jay's speed was higher than that of his opponent and the Bone-Rattler was too slow to block the attack. Remembering the enhanced durability of his new blade, and hoping it would be enough to withstand a bit of strategic misuse, Jay swung the sword's flat edge at the monster's ribs like he was swinging a baseball bat.

The blow connected like a sledgehammer, jarring Jay's wrists, elbows, and shoulders. Pain exploded through his joints, but he ignored it when he saw the monster stumble. Recovering as quickly as his hampered movement speed would allow, Jay pivoted, bringing his sword overhead and slamming down in two-handed strike across the Bone-Rattler's back.

The monster fell to the ground, prone.

"Jay, get back!" Lyra shouted, and he dove to the side just as the fox-girl released a type of arrow he'd never seen. Jay caught a glimpse of the blunt, black tip before it shot past him and smashed into the Shambling Bone-Rattler as it attempted to get back on its feet.

A percussive wave from the impact of the shot knocked Jay backward. Lyra yelped. Bones exploded in every direction, pelting them both like shrapnel from an explosion.

When Jay opened his eyes, he saw nothing but a pile of broken limbs, shimmering with **Dungeon Sight** to indicate a lootable corpse.

Success!
You have killed
Shambling Bone-Rattler - Lvl 5 [Elite]
XP: 125 (+10%)(+10%)(+50%)

Jay blinked at the notification, wondering why the Level 5 Elite had given less XP than the regular Level 5 Oozes they'd fought, but then he remembered that the experience from those kills hadn't been split between the party since Lyra had been passed-out. The Shambling Bone-Rattler Elite must have been worth 250XP on its own, considerably more than the 140XP a regular Level 5 enemy was worth.

Lyra let out a whoop, and Jay turned to see her blaze with golden energy as she Leveled up. "Yes, I did it!" she said, forgetting to keep her voice down. "Level 7!"

"Congratulations," Jay said, standing up with a groan. He wished he'd leveled up, so he could benefit from the instant healing. But his Health was already recovering, so he supposed he shouldn't complain. Using Constitution as his dump stat was proving to be very beneficial. "Any new skills or perks?"

Lyra's two-toned eyes darted back and forth as she read the holographic screen that was invisible to him. "I got an **Impact Arrow** skill," she said. "Which basically turns that attack I just used into a skill I can apply to any arrow. The one I used was a [Rare] item drop I picked up on F3, but I've never had a chance to use it. Now, I can use it any time I want, without having to hunt through my satchel or quiver to find it."

"Good," Jay said, rubbing his shoulder where the Shambling Bone-Rattler had hit him. "Maybe you'll be faster next time."

Lyra stomped her foot and glowered at him. "Hey, not all of us are blessed with easy-access Inventory Menus right off the bat, Portal Boy."

"I thought you weren't going to call me that anymore once I reached the same level as you?"

The fox-girl's eyes flashed. "That's right. That was our deal. But I'm Level 7 now, and you're still Level 6! So let me have my fun while I still can."

Jay grinned. "Let's go find that Pharoh, then, so I can catch up."

As if on cue, a low, angry moan sounded from the end of the tunnel where the Shambling Bone-Rattler had come from. Lyra blanched, her ears flattening to her head. "Oops," she said. "Sounds like I celebrated a bit too loudly."

"Will that make a difference?" Jay asked, listening for footsteps and hearing none. It seemed the Pharoh was staying put in his Burial Chamber, at least for now.

"I guess that depends on what spawns in there with him," she said, bending to loot the Shambling Bone-Rattler. "I've never seen one of these things before, but **Sneak** didn't seem to work on it anyway."

Jay watched the party Inventory Menu to see that she harvested [Dried Blood,] [Bone Dust,] [Grave Dust,] and a vial of something called [Miasma of Death] from the body.

When she was finished, Lyra bent to pick her fire arrow off the ground, illuminating the passage fully once more.

"You know," Jay said. "We should see about buying some kind of hands-free light spell on the market when we get back. Or maybe I can craft something."

"One thing at a time, Portal Boy," Lyra said, but she smiled when she said it this time. "One thing at a time."

26

The Pharoh's Tomb

When they arrived at the Burial Chamber, they found four Frozen Mummies shuffling around the room, apparently having been woken up by Lyra's shouts of excitement. The Level 4 monsters did not seem interested in leaving their designated area, even though they could see Lyra and Jay standing in the hallway outside.

Fortunately, the creatures didn't wake whatever else was in the chamber. Torches lined the walls of the room, allowing Lyra to put her flame arrow away. The Pharoh's tomb room appeared to be carved from solid gold, the light from the shiny walls casting a yellow sheen into the darkened corridor where Jay and Lyra now hid. Through the doorway, Jay could see an ornate sarcophagus propped against the back wall with two Jackal-headed statues next to it. The statues each held a long spear with a hooked end and stared straight ahead with menacing severity.

"Stand to the side, Jay," Lyra instructed, positioning herself in the center of the corridor. "Be ready, in case this draws them past the threshold of the doorway."

Jay did as she said, keeping out of her way as she drew her bow and fired four rapid shots into the Burial Chamber. Each shot struck a Mummy in the head, knocking the skull off its shoulders. The bodies dropped, one-by-one, into piles of inanimate bones.

"Huh," Jay said with a frown. "You made that look easy."

"Once there's three or more levels between you and your enemies, they go down pretty hard." A small smile played at her lips and her tail twitched, telling him she was pleased by the praise even if she didn't say so. "Not much good for experience, but this room can be tough enough without trying to maximize party XP."

"So, now we **Sneak**?" Jay asked in a whisper, eying the now empty-looking room, trying to spot more coffins or cubbies where monsters could be hiding.

Lyra nodded. "You first, I've got your back."

Jay didn't like not knowing what to expect. If Lyra had never seen a Shambling Bone-Rattler before, there was a good chance they'd be hit with another new type of monster. But there was no way to find out what was hiding in there without entering the Burial Chamber.

He kept his blade at the ready and crept toward the entrance of the glowing, golden room. His first step over the threshold didn't set off any alarms. Lyra waited in the doorway as he moved slowly about the room, keeping a nervous eye on the statues as he passed them. The Pharoh's sarcophagus remained closed.

When he'd been all around the room without seeing anything, he turned back to Lyra and shrugged. She looked as perplexed as he was, her two-toned eyes darting over the room as she scanned everything with her **Dungeon Sight**. Jay was about to do the same, when he heard a soft cracking sound followed by a smattering of dust hitting the floor.

Jay whirled around, his sword up in a defensive position. The statue to his right had a hairline crack running from its waist to its shoulder. As he stared at it, a chunk of paint flaked off and dropped to the floor. Jay took a step back, his heart hammering.

Plaster exploded from the statue's chest, spraying Jay with a fine dust coating and making him sneeze. A second explosion followed the first and when the dust cleared, Jay could see two huge Jackal-headed men turning their slavering faces toward him. Each wore a white skirt, wrapped leather sandals, and was bare chested and rippling with muscles, like an Egyptian god come to life.

Anubite Guardian – Lvl 5 [Elite]

Sometimes a statue is just a statue. Sometimes it is the soul of the God of Death made flesh. Few kings could afford such a guardian to watch over their tomb while they slept. This Pharoh has two. Make of that what you will. The Anubite Guardian is a creature with three forms. You've seen two... if you live long enough, you may have the misfortune of meeting the third.

Jay heard Lyra's bow twang a fraction of a second before an **Impact Arrow** smashed into the first statue's chest—causing the creature to bark and double over, clutching one hand to its bruised body. But the strike didn't hold it back for long. As it straightened, it twisted its hips and thrust the hook-tipped spear at Jay as if it wanted to pull his guts out through his belly button.

Jay ducked, rolling to the side and putting the Pharoh's sarcophagus between himself and the monsters. The extra reach of the spear made it difficult to get in close to fight the Guardians, but Jay thought if Lyra could stagger one again with her Impact Arrow that he might be able to take advantage of its distraction.

"Again, Lyra," he hissed, swiveling to keep both encroaching monsters in his field of vision. "The one on the left this time."

Without hesitation, Lyra sent a black-tipped arrow thudding into the bare chest of the living statue. The monster doubled over, and Jay rushed in, slashing up at the arm that held the spear. Blood sprayed from the monster's wound, spattering Jay with hot, red droplets. It was the first of the dungeon's monsters that bled, and the human-like body made Jay more hesitant than he liked.

The Anubite Guardian howled in pain and slashed at Jay with clawed fingers. Jay narrowly escaped the blow as he darted backward. The escape would have been perfect if he hadn't backed straight into the second Guardian.

The creature snapped its powerful jaws, sinking its teeth into Jay's shoulder. Jay felt an intense pressure on his flesh and bones, and was certain his collarbone would snap in the monster's bite. He flipped his grip on his sword and stabbed backward with both hands, channeling all of his strength into the move. Just as he felt the Guardian's body give way beneath his blade, he heard Lyra's bowstring sing once more, felt the wind on his face as a thumper-tipped arrow hit the Guardian right between the eyes.

The creature released its grip on Jay's shoulder and fell to the ground, wrenching the Etched Bolo Sword from his hands. Jay staggered forward, terrified of losing his weapon in the middle of battle, but his path was blocked by the second Anubite Guardian, which thrust at him again with the hook-tipped spear.

Not knowing what to do, Jay twisted to avoid the strike, then gripped the haft of the spear in both hands and wrenched backward. His grip was slick with blood that poured from the wound on his shoulder, and he wouldn't have had much chance against the strength of the massive jackal-headed god. But Lyra struck with another Impact Arrow at the same time that Jay pulled on the spear, and the Guardian dropped its weapon as the projectile staggered it again.

Jay wasted no time. He flipped the spear and charged the Guardian, putting all of his Strength into the attack. The hook tore through the creature's belly, opening a horrific wound in its tanned, over-muscled flesh. As the Guardian fell, ropes of purple intestine pulled from its stomach, hooked on the spear still clutched desperately in Jay's hands.

Success!

You have killed

Anubite Guardian: Lvl 5 [Elite] (x2)

XP: 125 (x2) (+10%)(+10%)(+50%)

Jay dropped the spear, feeling sick to his stomach. Bug guts and rotting skeletons were one thing, but this was a bit too much like killing a person—even if that person did have the head of a jackal.

He stumbled forward, pushing aside the notifications, and pulled his sword from the belly of the first Guardian, trying not to look at the gaping wound.

"Jay, get away from those things." Lyra said, her voice sounding urgent.

The monsters were obviously dead, but Jay wasn't foolish enough to ignore the warning of a seasoned Delver. He eyed the golden sarcophagus warily as he staggered across the room toward the fox-girl. "What's going on?"

"Look," Lyra said, her face pale with horror as she pointed at the corpses of the Anubite Guardians.

Jay turned, feeling his stomach clench before his mind processed what he was seeing. The bodies writhed as if they were filled with maggots, the torn flesh tugging and twitching as they watched in horror.

Realization dawned on Jay. "The third form," he said. "What is the third form?"

Lyra shook her head. "I don't know. I've never fought these things before."

"I'm starting to hate surprises," Jay muttered. His shoulder ached where the creature had bit him, and he could tell his movement would be restricted by the stiffening muscles.

He needed something to help him through this fight.

Remembering the health potions Nova had given him, Jay hurried to open his Inventory and pull one out.

The weight of the bottle settled in his empty hand like magic. Jay popped the cork and drank the contents of the red, glowing liquid without hesitation. And immediately regretted it.

The potion tasted the way roadkill smelled when it had been sitting in the sun for three days. He felt his gorge rise as he forced himself to swallow it, already feeling the effects of the magic stitching his wound together.

"Where did you get that?" Lyra asked, staring at the empty bottle in his hand. "Is that a Vial of Plentiful Healing? Do you know how much that thing was worth? Are you crazy?"

Jay tossed the empty bottle on the ground, where it shattered against the golden tiles. "What's crazy is going into battle with your arm ripped half-off," he hissed. "Give me a break, Little Miss Ranged-Attacks. I'm trying not to die."

Lyra huffed and seemed about to say something more.

She didn't get the chance.

A wet, tearing sound drew their attention to the corpses of the Anubite Guardians, as a tumorous bulge grew from the creature's chests. Ribs snapped, flesh ripped, blood spattered the golden walls and floors like dyed corn-syrup in a slasher flick from the 1980s.

Lyra made a whimpering sound and her ears flattened to the side of her head. "Jay, I don't like this... This isn't supposed to happen."

Like the unholy birth of some demon, the Anubite Guardians erupted with gore. The fox-girl screamed as the first bulge burst, revealing two writhing monsters inside. They staggered to their feet, fur slicked wet with blood, and shook like dogs after a dip in the swimming pool. A fine mist of pink sprayed into the air around them as the beasts stumbled forward on shaky legs.

Shoulders hunched, lean necks lowered, bat-like ears twitched, long tooth-filled jaws hung open with purple tongues lolling hungrily... Jay thought the animals might have been cute if they weren't five times bigger than they should have been, covered in open sores and dripping with the Anubite Guardian's blood.

The second tumorous protrusion burst, revealing two more.

Undead Jackal – Lvl 4 [Elite]
The 'Goodest Boys' of the Underworld have a bone to pick with you. These happy little guys only want one thing. To fetch your soul back to Big Daddy Anubis for treats and tummy rubs! And who can say 'no' to a face like that?

Jay cursed. Moving in front of Lyra to block her from the Jackals' view, he swung his sword in front of them, hoping to warn the creatures back. They might be a lower-level but, four Level 4 Elites were a step up from two Level 5 Elites if what Lyra had said about the Ghost Bison held true. He and the fox-girl had a combined level of 13 and the Undead Jackals had 16.

Plus, they were Elite, which made it tougher... but so had the Anubite Guardians been... He hoped they weren't in over their heads.

The Jackals growled, prowling toward Jay with their heads down and their glowing red eyes fixed on him like he was a hunk of fresh meat. Maybe that's all he was as far as they were concerned.

Jay still felt the effects of the health potion coursing through his veins. He was fairly certain his Constitution would protect him from taking too much damage. He had to keep them off of Lyra so she was free to shoot. He only knew one way of doing that.

"Lyra, be ready with your bow," he said, keeping his voice low and his gaze fixed on the lead Jackal. "I'm going to draw them to me. You pick them off while they're distracted, okay?"

The fox-girl nodded, though her hands shook as she nocked her first arrow. "Ready," she whispered.

Jay didn't wait for doubts to settle in. He rushed the pack of Jackals with his sword slashing. He hit the first one with a slice to the front haunch. The second snarled and launched at him, catching his forearm in its teeth. A third made a move to break from the group, its eyes focused behind Jay, clearly aiming to go for Lyra. Jay swung the arm the second Jackal was biting, flinging it into the third animal where they crashed into one another like snarling, snapping Tasmanian devils. Lyra immediately launched two arrows into the mess of fur and teeth, earning a yip of pain from one and a yowl from another.

His arm freed, Jay struck the first Jackal again, this time thrusting his Etched Bolo Sword into its chest. The animal staggered, falling to its knees before Lyra hit it with an arrow too, sending it spinning across the golden floor.

The fourth Jackal pounced as Jay spun to face it.

He saw a mouth full of teeth lunging for his face before he ducked and charged, hitting the animal in the chest with his shoulder before it could sink its teeth into anything. Jay slashed at the fallen creature with his Etched Bolo Sword and was shocked when he severed the thing's body in two.

Critical Hit! 5x Damage

He pivoted, thrusting the tip of his sword into another Jackal. This one had an arrow sticking out of its side and was moving slowly. It managed to rake three deep gashes in Jay's hand with its snapping jaws before it fell to his blade.

Lyra released two more arrows into the remaining Jackals. One collapsed immediately. The last dragged itself toward the Arcane Archer, snarling in defiance even as its back legs stumbled. The arrow had severed something in its spine. Jay lunged forward, bringing a two-handed strike down on the creature's back to finish the job.

Success!

You have killed

Undead Jackal: Lvl 4 [Elite] x4

XP: 100 (x4) (+10%)(+10%)(+50%)

"Jay, Jay, are you okay?" Lyra gasped, running toward him with a panicked look on her face. "You're bleeding—"

Jay's Health was dropping fast, and he caught sight of another blinking red de-buff in the bottom of his HUD. Gritting his teeth, he opened it, worried about what he would find.

Debuff Activated!
Corrupted Flesh – You have been bitten by an Undead monster. You will lose 25HP per minute until you are Dead, at which point you will become Undead. Undeath is irreversible. The only cure for Corrupted Flesh is [Holy Water] or the surge of purifying dungeon magic from achieving a Level Up. Health potions, salves, and HP boosting artifacts are rendered ineffective while this debuff is in effect.
Yeah, you're probably screwed.

27

Phar-oh-oh!

J ay cursed. He didn't know how he was going to explain this to Lyra.

"You don't have any Holy Water," he asked. "Do you?"

Lyra's eyes went wide. "What?!? No! Why do you need Holy Water? Only the worst Debuffs need Holy Water, Jay!"

He was saved from answering by a huge metallic crash and the moan from the golden sarcophagus.

"You've *got* to be kidding me," he muttered. His eyes darted around the room until they landed on the two spears laying next to the brutal mess left over by the Anubite Guardian's. "Lyra, hit him with everything you've got. We need to end this, fast."

She nodded, pulling a fire arrow from her quiver and backing toward the doorway.

Jay lunged for the closest spear, his body aching, his muscles cramping in protest. He could feel the

HP points draining like there was a vampire leeching his lifeforce away with every heartbeat. If the debuff's description was accurate, he'd lost his 50HP boost from the Beetle Black Scarab Armor along with the damage done by the Undead Jackals. He didn't even want to look at his Health bar.

He did anyway. He was at 140HP. That gave him approximately five minutes before he'd be cursed with Undeath which... he wasn't certain, but was probably a very, very bad thing for his prospects as a Delver.

Blood poured down his arm from the Jackal's bite, and the haft of the spear was slick with gore. His only hope was to end this fight before his Health bar drained completely and pray that he was close enough to Level 7 that killing the Undead Pharoh would save him.

With these desperate thoughts swirling in his mind, Jay managed to hurl the weapon at the creature that was pulling itself from the sarcophagus. The spear struck the monster in the side of the head, knocking it awkwardly from the coffin, just as the dungeon provided its description.

Phar-oh-oh!: Lvl 7 [Elite]

There's a reason the Forbidden Crypts are forbidden, you know. Many believe this ancient ruler laid a curse upon the chamber in which he was to be buried in order to ensure he was undisturbed in the afterlife. You can guess how well that's worked out for him. And he's pissed...

Is it the curse of the Undead Pharoh or the curse of the Ice Dungeon itself? You'll never know. Regardless of the cause, the important bit is this: once every fifteen hundred spawns, the Undead Pharoh in this golden Burial Chamber is replaced by the Phar-oh-oh!—an Elite monster with a unique skill that is sure to make him very unpopular with the Delvers unfortunate enough to encounter him. Let's leave it a surprise, though. Give you something to look forward to before you die.

Lyra hit the monster with a fire arrow, which exploded upon impact, lighting the dry, papery bandages aflame in a bright, orange blossom of radiant light. The Pharoh screamed in rage, falling the rest of the way out of the sarcophagus and scrambling to its feet while its clothing burned to ash.

If this once-great ruler had hoped for dignity in death, it was no wonder he was pissed off. Jay bent to pick up the second spear, and staggered back as the corpses of the Undead Jackals began to twitch and writhe, glowing with hideous purple light.

"Oh, shit," he shouted, snatching the weapon and backing hurriedly away. "Lyra, we've got a problem!"

Reanimated Undead Jackal – Level 6 [Elite]
Sure, technically an Undead Jackal is already reanimated. But you try coming up with a better name. Besides, this time it's necromancy reanimating the corpse rather than good, old-fashioned zombie-ism. So, there. It makes sense. And soon,

**you're going to be too dead to complain about it
anyway.**

The Pharoh roared in exaltation as its raggedy-ass minions staggered back to their feet.

"Focus on the Pharoh, Jay," Lyra screamed over the horrific sound. "When he dies, his magic will dissipate."

Jay hurled the second spear, putting every ounce of Strength he could grasp into the attack. The spear flew true, its shaft spiraling, its hooked tip whipping through the air like a manic eggbeater, and lodged itself deep in the back of the Undead Pharoh's throat.

The monster doubled over, gagging and tugging at the weapon like this was some kind of slapstick routine rather than a literal fight to the death. Jay backed away from the Jackals, which were floundering with the necromantic Pharoh distracted, and drew his sword. His Health was at 90 now. He could feel his strength diminishing with every passing second, but he was determined to keep fighting until the end.

"Jay, duck!"

The fox-girl didn't have to tell him twice. Jay dropped to his knees and rolled away from the mangled Jackals, just as another explosive arrow landed in their midst. The beasts yelped, their fur giving off and acrid stench as black smoke billowed around them, filling the room with a thick, eye-watering haze.

Jay shot to his feet, sword in hand, and rushed at the Pharoh just as the monster wrenched the spear free of its throat. The second spear still hung from where it had struck, dragging against the ground as the naked, burned bastard staggered toward Jay with its hands glowing the same hideous purple as the Jackals he'd dragged back from death.

Knowing it was his only chance, Jay launched himself at the monster with both hands gripping the handle of his blade. He sliced down with all his remaining strength, severing one of the Pharoh's arms as the beast shrieked again, its pain and rage a palpable essence in the enclosed space. Jay's breaths were coming faster now, as if he couldn't get enough oxygen.

Health at 65. He was going down.

A weight slammed into Jay's back, and he heard Lyra scream. Blood, drool, and slime that stank of death oozed over Jay's neck as one of the Reanimated Undead Jackals scrabbled for purchase on his shoulders, its teeth snapping at the air next to his head.

He felt a sudden force wrench the beast from his back and heard the Jackal yip as it smashed into the golden sarcophagus with an arrow in its neck. The body twitched as if the Pharoh's magic was trying to bring it back once more, but the monster's power was weakening.

Two more Jackals slunk around the end of the coffin and flanked their master, both snarling and drooling and dripping grave juice on the golden floor. Jay ignored them, his eyes focused on the limping, one-armed Pharoh.

Jay hurled himself into an Agility attack, the sword flashing back and forth in a complex pattern he could never have come up with if it weren't for the dungeon magic guiding his movements. He bellowed as he fought, channeling all his fear and frustration into his last, desperate moments. He couldn't afford to give the Pharoh an opportunity to strike back. It was all or nothing now.

As if sensing what he needed her to do, Lyra hit the glowing Jackals with a series of rapid-fire shots, effectively distracting the Pharoh's minions from aiding it against Jay's attack.

Jay felt himself weakening, his energy flagging, each strike seemed to hit a little less effectively. But he refused to stop while the thing was still standing.

The Pharoh backed away, its one arm up in a protective stance across its body, its glowing purple eyes seeking some salvation as it staggered away from the Delver's onslaught.

Jay stumbled as he followed the Pharoh, his legs giving out in his exhaustion as his health dipped below twenty points.

Less than a minute left and he was going to die.

He had a moment to consider how stupid and wasteful it was to end this way, without getting Molly the medicine she needed. He wished he'd found a smarter way. That he hadn't gotten sucked into leveling and gotten in over his head. He only hoped Lyra would be able to take what she needed from their Party Inventory to sell, and maybe make a better life for herself, even if she didn't get to keep Delving the dungeon.

The Pharoh lurched forward, its single arm outstretched as if it meant to strangle Jay with the last of its strength. Jay lifted his sword, prepared to batter the enemy back one more time.

But before they clashed, the Pharoh's head burst in a spray of bone-dust, burned bandages, and sticky black ichor. An arrow stuck out of the golden wall behind the monster as its body collapsed into a pile of ash.

Success!
You have killed
Phar-oh-oh!: Lvl 7 [Elite]
XP: 250 (+10%)(+10%)(+50%)

Success!
You have killed
Reanimated Undead Jackal: Lvl 6 [Elite] (x3)
XP: 150 (x3) (+%10)(+10%)(+50%)

Jay felt the debuff lifting before he received the notification, like a warm, cleansing rain pouring over his aching and exhausted body.

Congratulations!
You have Achieved Level 7
XP: 520 | Next Lvl: 2800
Health: 210 | Stamina: 130 | Mana: 130

Unassigned Attribute Points: 3
You have 30 Base Stat Points to Distribute. Would you like to increase Health, Stamina, or Mana?

Debuff Removed
You have been cured of Corrupted Flesh. That's not something I get to say very often.

Jay collapsed on the ground, relief flooding through his every cell as the dungeon magic surged through his body, repairing his wounds and restoring his energy. "Lyra?" he gasped, unable to see the fox-girl as he lay, transfixed by the ceiling. "Lyra are you okay?"

She was at his side in an instant, showering him with kisses as she inspected him for damage despite the fact that he'd just Leveled Up and she knew that he would be healed.

"Jay Morgan, don't you ever do that to me again!" she scolded, her voice shaking. "One near-death experience is enough. Two is just too much. I'm not sure I'll survive a third time!"

"You saved me," he said, grabbing her by the shoulders and pulling her in for a deeper kiss. "You saved my life. Thank you, Lyra."

She melted into his embrace, her mouth opening to allow his tongue to press between her lips. She shivered in his arms, the shock of their battle finally sinking in. Then she pushed him back. "Jay, you promised we'd wait."

He broke off the kiss and squeezed her tighter.

"I know, I'm sorry. But I also know that Molly will understand. I'd be dead if it weren't for you. She'll understand."

"All the more reason to finish this job and get back to her, then," Lyra said, reaching up to pinch him on the end of the nose. "When you're done lazing about, we've got some Ghost Bison to hunt."

Jay let out a sound halfway between a cough and gasp of outrage.

"Lazing about? Is that what you call this?" He scrambled to his feet, expected to still feel the exhaustion that had plagued him during the fight. But, as he always did after gaining a level, he felt better than ever. He stretched and grinned and reached down to pull Lyra up into his arms. "You've got to give a man a few minutes to relish his own existence after a fight like that. It's only fair."

"All right," Lyra said, her fluffy white tail twitching with amusement. "You relish, I'll collect the loot. I've never seen any of these monsters before, so I'm curious to see what we'll get."

The Anubite Guardians and the Undead Jackals each dropped something called a [Jackal Jaw Trap.] The three Undead Jackals who had come back as Reanimated Undead Jackals also dropped vials of [Holy Water,] which almost caused Lyra to go into a apoplectic spasm.

"We're going to be rich, Jay!" she screamed dancing around the room like a maniac. "Rich!"

Jay decided it would be better to wait before he told her they should probably keep the Holy Water in case of future encounters with biting undead creatures. But he couldn't quite bring himself to kill the manic enthusiasm that made her shake her butt and whip her tail in circles as she bounced around the room. Reality could wait a little longer.

The Undead Pharoh dropped a bag of [Mummy Teeth], which actually appeared to be dried mushrooms that reeked like death warmed over—as, Jay supposed, one should probably expect when harvesting items from reanimated corpses.

Their description intrigued him.

Mummy Teeth – Gold [Rare] – These delightful little toadstools get their name because they are small and white and stink like that particular halitosis of the undead. They can be ground into a powder to create a noxious hallucinatory effect in poisons. Or you can string them up around your campsite to ward off predators. Most animals are repulsed by the smell of Mummy Teeth and will quickly move downwind of the fungi in any form: fresh, dried, or powdered.

It was almost as intriguing as the Jackal Jaw Traps.

Jackal Jaw Traps – Gold [Rare] – These one-time use animal traps can be used for hunting animals or monsters Level 1-20. Once fixed to the ground,

the traps will not move. The Jackal Jaws snap closed on anything that steps upon them and will hold the creature in an inescapable grasp, rendering it incapacitated for 30 min. After 30 min, the trap will deactivate and disappear.

Between the Hoarfrost Vine, the Mummy Teeth, and the Jackal Jaw Traps, an idea was beginning to form in Jay's mind about how they could deal with the Ghost Bison without having to battle the entire herd.

The rest of the items, which were repeats of what they'd gotten from the Frozen Mummies and Shambling Skeletons, simply went into the Party Inventory to await Raina's judgement for what was best sold and what kept for future Delves.

Now that they were almost finished with the Witch Doctor's quest, Jay felt a quiet thrum of anxiety and anticipation flowing through his veins. They were so close. Soon he would have what he needed to save Molly.

Maybe, when she woke, he would learn her true feelings for him.

But that seemed a far second to the victory of saving her from the dream state she was trapped in. Jay had spent most of his life pining for the red-haired girl and feeling that he knew she was simply not interested in him. If he asked, and she confirmed this, it wouldn't really be any worse than he'd ever felt.

And if she wasn't interested, that left him free

to pursue a relationship with the beautiful, sexy fox-girl that he was growing increasingly interested in. Lyra had saved his life multiple times and had proven herself to be a sweet, loyal, and loving companion.

What worried Jay most now, was the possibility that Molly might admit to returning his feelings.

Jay no longer felt he would be able to choose between Molly and Lyra.

But what were the chances that Molly, a girl from another world, would be okay with a relationship like the fox-girl had described. He knew he had enough love to give both of the women, but would Molly be willing to share him?

The anticipation wavered between hopeful and anxious the more he thought about it, until Jay finally forced himself to push the question from his mind.

"Are you ready, Jay?" Lyra asked, interrupting his thoughts. She stood next to a door that had opened behind the golden sarcophagus, which Jay was certain wasn't there before. He hadn't noticed when it had opened.

"Where does that lead?"

"Back to the entrance," Lyra said. "All of the mini-bosses have portal doors that take you back to the beginning of the floor. That's one of the rewards for defeating them."

Jay released a short laugh. "This was a mini-boss? On the first floor? What level do you have to be to make it to F2?"

"Well, usually the boss for the stairwell is only a Snow Serqet, the bigger scorpions," she said. "Level 3 or 4 Elite at most. With a party, even a group of Level 1 and 2 Delvers can make it to F2. Mini-bosses provide an optional challenge, drop better loot, and are often higher level than the main monsters on a given floor. But..."

"Usually probably doesn't apply for me," Jay said, moving toward the doorway with a resigned sigh. "And all we got from that Undead Pharoh were some rotten teeth."

Lyra lit up. "That's not all! Look what I got!"

She opened her hand and a small, floating orb of glowing yellow light hovered between them. The magic light illuminated as much of the dark passage as the fox-girl's arrows had. Jay grinned. "Hey, that's exactly what we need!"

"It was a bonus item for doing 25% of the damage to the Undead Pharoh using a fire attack," she said, blushing faintly in the soft light. "I'd never be able to afford a spell like this, so it's a really good prize."

"You deserve it," Jay said, wrapping an arm around her shoulders. "And I think I have a plan for these Mummy Teeth anyway, so it's not all a loss. Was the Burial Chamber supposed to be easier than it was?"

Lyra's ears flattened to her head and she released a small whine. "I took you to the toughest first floor area I knew of because it's one of the only places you and I would be able to get enough XP for it to be worth our while at the rate that you're leveling. But you consistently seem to inspire more aggressive enemy spawning than is normal for a given area." She bit her lip and lowered her eyes. "I hope you're not mad at me. I didn't know it was going to be that bad. And I've never actually fought a mini-boss on any of the lower floors, just stuck to the main runs. So, in the future, maybe we should do that. Just in case."

Jay squeezed the petite woman to his side, feeling the soft fur of her tail brush against his arm. "We'll deal with the future when we get there," he said. "For now, we have some hunting to do."

The two of them slipped into the darkness of the portal door and Jay felt the cold tingle of magic against his skin before they were whisked back to the entrance of The Frozen Tomb.

28

Where the Buffalo Roam

Their Well-Rested Bonus had worn off by the time the pair returned to the Pernicious Plains. While it was tempting to take another long rest, with the hexdome Save Zone so close by, Jay was hesitant to do so. It would be nice to make the most of their attempts to kill the higher-leveled animal, but the quest had a time limit and they couldn't afford to waste any time before they had tried out his method—especially if they were going to have to deliver the quest on F2. Who knew how long that would take.

They decided to save the Safe Zone for if one or both of them was seriously hurt, in order to maximize their chances of success. Lyra had explained that Delvers could only enter a Safe Zone once every 12 hours, which meant they could take a long rest before or after the Bison hunt, but not both.

With both Jay and Lyra at Level 7, taking on one Level 12 to 15 Ghost Bison was going to be a big task. Not impossible, Lyra insisted, but certainly challenging. Taking down five of them without enraging the herd and risking being trampled in a stampede was another thing entirely.

Jay hoped that his plan was going to save them from the worst of the risk. But if he was wrong, he definitely wanted to have that Safe Zone as a backup.

He'd explained his plan as they'd travelled back to the Pernicious Plains from the Dungeon Entrance. Fortunately, being Level 7 meant that the lower-level creatures in the frozen, winding corridors of the tomb between the entrance and the plains didn't bother them. Once a creature was five levels or more below a Delver, they apparently didn't react to the Delver's presence, which was a nice bonus because they also didn't drop any experience and it would have been a pain to have to grind through Level 1 and 2 Scorpions and Scarabs with no benefit. The few Level 3 and 4 monsters that spawned were dealt with quickly and easily, though the experience was minimal.

When they stepped out of the tomb tunnels and onto the artificial plain with its night sky and twinkling stars, Jay took a deep breath and scanned the frozen horizon. The Ghost Bison, with their shimmering white coats and billowing breath, had moved to a new location, farther away from the hexdome Safe Zone.

Hopeful, Jay insisted on checking the last place they'd been grazing on the Tundra Berries to see if any had been left behind. Unfortunately, the big herbivores had picked the area clean and not a single berry had been forgotten. Lyra stood next to him, her two-toned eyes on the distant creatures and a worried look on her face.

"I can't believe we're going to do this," she muttered, biting her lip anxiously. "This is the craziest plan I've ever heard of, you know."

"I know," Jay said, pulling items from his Inventory and setting them on the frozen ground. "You've told me a hundred times already."

"It's not that I don't believe in you," Lyra said, her eyes still pinned on their prey. "It's just that I've never seen dungeon items used this way and..."

"It's crazy," he said. "I know. But it might work. Indigenous hunters in my world used a similar tactic when hunting creatures like these. I think they preferred to run them off a cliff rather than into a row of traps, but it's kind of the same idea."

Lyra crouched down next to him and wrinkled her nose as he pulled the back of Mummy Teeth out of his inventory. "They definitely stink," she said. "But do you think the Ghost Bison will react strongly enough to run away from them?"

"Only one way to find out," Jay said, picking up a length of Hoarfrost Vine.

Using **Dungeon Sight 2** to reread the description

of the plant had revealed a recipe for making rope and twine, which Jay now planned to use.

Recipe: Hoarfrost Rope

Combine three [Hoarfrost Vine] to create a 50ft length of sturdy rope. Can be cut into smaller pieces with bladed tools rated 2d4 (slicing) or higher.

Inspecting the vine in his crafting menu, he found he could combine the items by stacking their listings on top of one another. Immediately, he received another notification.

You have learned Crafting: Survival 1!

You have created 50ft of [Hoarfrost Rope] (Uncommon)

XP: 100

Pulling the freshly created rope from his inventory he held it out to Lyra.

"Do you want to string mushrooms or set traps?" he asked with a smirk.

Lyra wrinkled her nose and quickly said, "Traps."

"You're sure you can do it without stepping in one and ruining the whole plan?"

The fox-girl's ears lowered and she growled at him, glaring with the blue-and-gold eyes. "Of course I can," she snapped. Then, with her tail drooping, she added, "But you probably can't tie those tiny Mummy's Teeth to the vine with your big clumsy fingers. Maybe I'd better do that instead."

"Clumsy fingers?" he smirked at her. "What is that... a challenge?"

"Do you want to tie the stinky mushrooms to the rope then?" she asked, blushing. "Maybe you should just do everything if you're so perfect."

"I can think of better ways to prove how deft my fingers are," he said.

Lyra's blush deepened to a crimson. "If I get gored by a Ghost Bison, it will be your fault for putting thoughts like that in my mind right before a dangerous operation."

Jay grinned, handing her the rope. "Distracting thoughts?"

"Shut up," she snapped again, snatching the rope from him and picking up the back of smelly fungi. "I'm going to go work over there."

"Where I can't distract you?"

"Where I don't have to look at your stupid, handsome, smirking face!"

Jay laughed as he picked up the first of the Jackal Jaw Traps, quickly reading the description for how to set them. It seemed simple enough. He had no doubt that Lyra could have done it without issue. Her Agility was probably higher than his, even after he'd dropped another point in each Strength, Agility, and Constitution after hitting Level 7. Again, he'd put all 30 Base Stat points into Health, fearing another experience like he'd had with the Corrupting Flesh debuff. As far as Jay was concerned, a Delver could never have enough HP or Constitution points.

That said, he was really curious about the traps and how they worked. Much more so than the rope and stinky, white mushrooms.

The plan was to use the long rope with the re-pellant Mummy's Teeth to drive the Ghost Bison away from the Tundra Berries. Jay and Lyra would each hold an end of the rope, stretched as far as it would reach, and advance upon the feeding Bison, essentially creating a wall they would try to avoid.

If all they needed was the berries, that would have been enough. But because they needed to kill five of the Ghost Bison for their meat and leather, that meant they also needed to predict which way the Bison would run and lay the Jackal Jaw Traps down in their path. Then they'd have thirty minutes to kill the trapped Bison, hopefully without enraging those that escaped the traps.

Jay had taken the two hook-tipped spears from the Undead Pharoh's Burial Chamber. Neither he nor Lyra had a polearm proficiency, but he hoped they would be able to use the spears to guide the Bison in the right direction if any decided to stray off the predicted path.

Other than that, all they had to do was pray.

He carried the traps as close to the herd as he felt comfortable before laying them down and setting them about six feet apart. He hoped that would be far enough that the charging Bison would have the highest chance of hitting them without avoiding the trapped areas once a trap was actively holding one of the creatures.

Once the traps were set and Lyra had finished with

the rope, they took their stinking prize and carried it in a wide arc around the herd, not wanting to set off a premature migration if the Bison caught a whiff of the Mummies Teeth before they were in place.

Lyra nodded to him once they were far enough back, grabbing her end of the rope and holding the spear in one hand. "Good luck, Jay," she said. "Don't get trampled."

"Same to you," he said, finding his own end of the rope and then wiggling his fingers at her. "I still owe you a demonstration, after all. Hard to do if we're dead."

Lyra's mouth dropped open and she blushed furiously. "I told you not to distract me like that!"

"I'm not distracting you," he said. "I'm giving you something to look forward to."

Lyra huffed as she took her end of the rope and began backing away from him. "You're an infuriating man, Jay Morgan," she hissed, narrowing her pretty eyes in his direction. "And I think you know it."

"I know it," he confirmed. "And I love every minute of it. Be safe, pretty girl."

Lyra's eyes widened, then she spun on her heel and jogged away from him, her pert ass and fluffy tail bouncing as she ran.

Jay chuckled to himself as he watched her run away. Flirting with the fox-girl had become a lot more fun since she'd revealed her feelings for him, even if they had promised not to do anything about it.

And he wasn't kidding when he'd teased her. Thinking about Lyra gave him something to look forward to, which he felt was less of a distraction and more of a reason to stay focused.

With that in mind, he stood waiting until the rope was stretched taut between them, keeping his eyes on his beautiful Delving partner. When she was in place, she hoisted the spear into the air, giving him the signal that she was ready.

Jay returned the gesture, and they began to run.

The plan went better than Jay had expected, at least, at first.

The Ghost Bison lifted their heads, sniffing the air as Jay and Lyra approached with the rope. At first they simply shuffled and backed away from the smell, but as it got closer, the lumbering beasts began to panic. They snorted and stomped their hooves, huffing great clouds of steam into the air, their huge dark eyes gaining white rims around the edges as they searched for a safe direction to escape.

When the first Ghost Bison broke from the herd, sprinting toward the line of traps, Jay felt his heart surge with excitement. It was going to work! The rest of the Bison followed the first, their movement like a thick stream of viscous liquid as they followed their leader straight toward the hidden danger.

But when the first trap snapped shut and the trapped Bison bellowed in fear and pain, all hell broke loose. Rather than following the original path, the herd split down the middle, arcing away from the cries of their injured fellow, all snorting and bellowing in a cacophony of terrifying sound. Jay and Lyra attempted to redirect the Bison with their spears, running alongside the frightened beasts, stabbing at their flanks like nipping dogs. But the Bison hardly seemed to notice or care.

Jay's heart was sinking, thinking the plan had failed when he heard another trap snap shut, and another, as the central beasts backtracked in confusion. He watched Lyra, snarling like the predatory animal she shared ancestry with, her tail poofed up to twice its size as she challenged one of the Ghost Bison with her spear. Jay admired how brave she was, despite her protestations about their plan. He was grateful for how willingly she followed his lead despite having more experience in the dungeon than he had. She was willing to take a chance on his strange ideas because she believed in him, and he hoped they wouldn't be disappointed.

Jay was so lost in through about the pretty fox-girl that he noticed too late when one of the Ghost Bison suddenly changed direction and charged at him. The hulking creature bore down on him like a freight train, steam puffing above its head like a stream of exhaust. It's massive, horned skull was lowered, ready to gore him.

Not knowing what else to do, Jay planted the butt of his spear in the ground, pointing it at the charging beast. His heart hammered in his chest as the thing got closer and closer, growing larger and larger in his vision until it was all that Jay could see.

Perhaps he would have stayed like that, mesmerized by the coming of his own death, if he hadn't heard Lyra scream.

Jolted from his reverie, Jay twisted out of the way of the charging Bison at the very last moment. He let go of the spear, realizing there was no way he could hold the weapon against such a massive beast, and relied on his Agility to allow him to escape.

Luck must have been on his side, however.

As he dropped the spear it fell between the charging animals' legs, twisting as the Bison clipped it with his front leg, and causing the shaft of the spear to bind between its limbs. With a thunderous crash, the animal fell, a front leg snapping under its own weight, as it plowed horns first into the frozen tundra.

Jay saw the bone protruding from the white-furred flesh, blood spilling onto the snow, and knew the creature would not be getting up again. His head shot up, his gaze roving the plains for some sight of Lyra. Had she screamed in fear for him, or because she had also been hurt? His stomach lodged in his throat, Jay shouted across the tundra. "Lyra! Where are you?"

The rest of the Bison had scattered and fled far into the distance, where they were gathering once more. Jay could only hope they would stay there rather than coming back to trample their tormentors. He could see three Bison trapped by the Jackal Jaw traps, but he couldn't see Lyra anywhere.

"Lyra!" he shouted, panic entering his voice. "Can you hear me?"

They only had 30 minutes to finish off the Bison in the traps. But that didn't matter. If Lyra had been hurt or killed in this hairbrained scheme, Jay wasn't sure it was worth getting out of the dungeon alive.

Tears blurred his vision as he stumbled closer to the traps, his eyes scanning the snow for some sign of where the fox-girl might have gone. He saw the end of the Hoarfrost Vine rope where Lyra had dropped it.

Next to the rope, he saw the spear, her bow, and her quiver of arrows. Jay's heart plummeted. "Lyra?"

He scrambled to the place where she must have stood, sifting through the snow with his hands, hoping to find her under the churned earth. "Lyra!"

A terrified voice answered him from far across the plain. "Jay! Help me!"

Jay's eyes widened as he saw a huge Ghost Bison charging toward him from the opposite side of the line of traps. Lyra was... riding it?

The fox-girl was on the creature's back, clutching frantically at its horns to hold herself in place as the beast tossed its head in an attempt to dislodge her.

"Jay! Shoot it!" she screamed. "I can't hold on!"

Jay instantly jumped into action, snatching her bow and quiver from the ground. Almost instinctively now, he navigated to the Party Menu in his HUD and selected Lyra's name, opening the list of her skills. He hesitated between Fire Arrows and Impact Arrows, not knowing which would be best.

Then, on a sudden whim, he attempted to stack the Fire Arrow and Impact Arrow items on top of one another, like he had done with the Hoarfrost Vine to make the rope.

His heart thudded like the sound of the encroaching animal's hoofbeats as the notification popped up.

You have learned Profession: Fletching 1!
You have created [Explosive Impact Arrow]
This item can be used with either the Fire Arrow Skill or the Impact Arrow Skill.
XP: 100

Jay selected Impact Arrow from the menu, his hands shaking as he stared down the charging animal with the bow in his hands.

"Jay, hurry!" Lyra's panicked voice pierced his mind as he waited for the **On-The-Job-Training** Skill to kick in.

New Skill Acquired!
Impact Arrows – Enchants an arrow with additional bludgeoning damage, giving a chance that enemies will be staggered or knocked unconscious.

Jay took a deep breath. He drew an arrow and

stared down the shaft at the Ghost Bison. He knew hitting it in the bony ridge on top of its head would be useless. Besides, that was where Lyra was, and he didn't want to risk hitting her. He dropped the tip of the arrow, hoping to hit the creature in the chest instead.

He released the arrow, relying on his Agility to guide the shot. It wasn't as good as Lyra's, but he hoped it would be enough for the over-sized target.

When the arrow struck it was like the Ghost Bison hit an invisible brick wall. Then the wall exploded.

Lyra shrieked, flying end over end as she flew off the animal's back to land, skidding on her ass across the icy Tundra.

The Bison bellowed, shook its head, and aimed its next charge at Jay. It's shimmering white hide was singed and smoldering, adding trails of black smoke to the steam of the animal's breath.

"Oh shit," he said. "Lyra, get ready to run!"

"Again?!?"

The Ghost Bison lowered its head and bolted for Jay, who scrambled to nock another arrow. Lyra screamed again, this time out of fear for his life rather than her own.

But her scream became a yelp as a sharp snap cut through the frigid air of the tundra, and the charging Bison was stopped in its tracks. It had hit one of the remaining Jackal Jaw Traps, and was now frozen in place, bellowing in pain and rage.

Jay breathed a sigh of relief, falling to his knees

next to Lyra and pulling her into his arms. He could feel her heart pounding against her chest as he held her.

Suddenly she began to laugh. "Jay, you did it! We did it. Your crazy plan worked!"

"Phase one, at least," he said, gazing at the four trapped animals and the one with the broken leg. "We still have to kill them before the traps disappear."

Lyra grabbed her bow. "That's the easy part," she said with a crooked grin, her ears sitting a little crookedly too. "Now give me my skill back. It'll be like shooting fish in a barrel."

Jay shook his head in disbelief at how quickly the fox-girl got over the trauma of her own near-death experiences. But he hurried to do as she asked. It wasn't very sportsmanlike, perhaps, but there wasn't much else they could do to hunt creatures two times their level. If he had to blame someone for the animal's fate, he supposed it was Nova who would be answerable.

And she'd made the Ghost Bison, just as she had everything else in the dungeon.

She must know what would happen to the creatures if she was going to give quests for their hides and flesh.

29

A Traveling Merchant

It turned out that dungeon animals were not like dungeon monsters. Trapped and unable to fight back, they died just like normal animals would. Jay slit the throats of three of the creatures, while Lyra used an Impact Arrow at close range to kill the other two. Two of the creatures had been Level 12, two had been Level 13, and the one whose leg had broken when it charged Jay was Level 15. They shared the experience for all 5 kills, even though they didn't both strike each animal. Jay assumed the dungeon knew when a party had worked together to orchestrate a plan and tried to be as fair as possible.

The notifications rolled in so quickly that Jay barely paid attention to them.

Success!

You have killed

Ghost Bison: Lvl 12 (x2)
XP: 380 (x2) (+10%)(+10%)
Success!
You have killed
Ghost Bison: Lvl 13 (x2)
XP: 440 (x2) (+10%)(+10%)

Success!
You have killed
Ghost Bison: Lvl 15
XP: 700 (+10%)(+10%)

Congratulations!
You have Achieved Level 8
XP: 768 | Next Lvl: 3600
Health: 240 | Stamina: 130 | Mana: 130
Unassigned Attribute Points: 3
You have 30 Base Stat Points to Distribute. Would you like to increase Health, Stamina, or Mana?

Amazingly, even without the Well-Rested Bonus, both he and Lyra hit Level 8, which the fox-girl could hardly believe. Jay quickly assigned his Base Stat points to Health, bringing him up to 270. Once he hit 300HP he promised himself he would start spreading those points out to Stamina and Mana as well.

Lyra muttered to herself as they harvested the [Ghost Bison Hides] and [Frosty Flank Steak] along with five sets of [Ghost Bison Horns], all of which the fox-girl was certain would bring them a ridiculous amount of gold on the World Dungeon Market. Jay went to inspect the trampled patch of Tundra Berries and managed to gather three whole plants for his inventory.

While he felt relief at finally having the last of the ingredients they needed, Jay was finding himself a bit numb to everything else. He'd leveled far faster than he'd expected to, and clearly faster than Lyra had expected. While they still had to find the trader, Toma Tabernak, he no longer felt the same crushing pressure as he had since he and Molly had first come to this world.

As they trudged toward the hexdome Safe Zone, ready to take their long rest and sort through the myriad skills, achievements, and other notifications they'd received, neither Jay nor Lyra was much surprised to see a figure moving across the snowy tundra toward them.

"Is that...?" Jay began, his words failing him as he observed the strange, hunchbacked person shuffling through the snow.

"It's her," Lyra said, her voice quiet and shaky. "I've never seen her outside of F2, and here she is... just because we need her. Because you need her, I suppose."

"Me?"

Lyra shook her head. "I don't know anyone else who manages to get the best and the worst of this dungeon the way you do... We just survived a quest that should have killed us. At this point it only seems natural that the dungeon would make it easy for us to turn it in."

Jay was silent as they watched the hunchbacked woman make her way across the snowy plains. The massive bag upon her back should not have been possible for her to carry. She looked like a cartoon character with the freakish lump of goods wrapped in a bubble on her shoulders.

The old woman grinned toothlessly at the pair as she approached.

"You two look like hunters, if I ever did see them," she said, her voice as ancient sounding as she looked. "You wouldn't happen to have come across any [Ghost Bison Hides] or [Frosty Flank Steak] in your travels, have you? I'm paying handsomely for them, you see. I'm Toma Tabernak, proprietress of Tabernak General Goods."

Lyra glanced at Jay with a smug look on her face, as if to rub in that she was right. Then she addressed the woman. "Yes, we have some," she said. "Would you like to trade?"

Jay watched as the pair conducted an invisible trading session. Lyra handed off the items necessary to complete the quest and they received an immediate notification.

Quest Complete!
Oh, Give Me a Home Where the Buffalo Roam –
Toma Tabernak is thrilled with the quality of the
[Ghost Bison Hides] and [Frosty Flank Steak] your

party has returned with.
Reward: 250 Gold, XP: 2500

Jay's eyes nearly watered as all that experience racked up at once. He was shocked to see he was almost at the threshold of another Level.

Delver: Jay Morgan

Class Type: Versatile

Class: Dark Horse

Lvl: 8

XP: 3268 | **Next Lvl:** 3600

Health: 270 | **Stamina:** 150 | **Mana:** 130

Active Bonus: 10% max XP (Scale-Up), 10% max XP (CEO)

Unassigned Attribute Points: 0

Strength: 7

Agility: 7

Intelligence: 1

Constitution: 14 [*Beetle Black Scarab Armor* – Set Bonus: Constitution +6, HP +50]

Willpower: 2

Charisma: 10

Active Skills: On-The-Job-Training, Asset Management

Passive Abilities: Environmental Resistance 1 (Arctic), Dungeon Sight 2, Scale-Up, Stealth 2

Perks: Panty Dropper, Bootstrapper

Vocational Skills: Gathering: Horticulturist 1, Profession: Field Medic 1, Profession: Fletching 1, Crafting: Apothecary 1, Crafting: Survival 1

As the old woman shuffled away across the Tundra, a storm of conflicting emotions whirled in his mind. This was what he'd wanted, wasn't it? Yet, it all felt so anticlimactic. But he supposed he shouldn't complain. After they'd rested, he and Lyra would head back out to Winterhaven. Raina would have the ingredients she needed to wake Molly. Then...

Then what?

Jay realized part of the ambivalence he was feeling was because he didn't really know what would happen next. Would Molly freak out and want to go home? What then? He couldn't bring her home and it was going to break his heart all over again to have to be the one to explain what had happened. He barely understood it himself. How was he going to explain it?

And if Molly was traumatized by being sucked into another world, he couldn't just leave her and carry on Delving with Lyra. But what if Delving was what he was meant to do? What if Lyra was right and the dungeon had been waiting for someone like him, what if he had a purpose in this world that he needed to fulfil? Could he just abandon that if Molly needed him?

"Hey."

Startled from his thoughts, Jay looked down to see Lyra's blue-and-gold eyes gazing up at him.

A small smile twitched at the corner of her lips. "You have that look on your face again."

"What look?" he asked, wrapping an arm around her shoulder.

"Like you're borrowing troubles," she said. "Like you're dwelling on something you probably have no control over."

Jay sighed. "I'm not dwelling. I just... want to be prepared."

"Yeah?" Her ears flicked toward him. "How come you never prepare yourself for the good stuff, then? How come I never catch you smiling at the possibility of something really wonderful happening?"

Jay rolled his eyes and tugged the fox-girl toward the hexdome. "Because it's easy to accept the good stuff. You don't have to justify your reaction to good things happening."

"That's not been my experience at all," Lyra said, cocking her head to the side. "In my experience, it's the positive stuff that is the hardest to accept and appreciate. There's always that nagging doubt that there's a hidden catch, or that the other shoe is waiting to drop."

Jay wondered if that was an expression in this world, too, or if the auto-translation that had been happening in his mind was just supplying the closest idiom. For some reason that thought made him smile.

"Maybe you're right," he said.

"Of course, I'm right," she said. "Look at you. You've got the items you came into the dungeon to get, don't you? We're going to bring Molly back for you. And you're worrying about what's going to happen when she wakes up. As soon as you solve one problem, you're onto the next. Worry, worry, worry. It will give you wrinkles, you know."

Lyra's tail swished and she bounded ahead of him, leaving him staring after her with a bemused look on his face. He couldn't decide if he was more surprised that she'd read all that in his expression, or by the fact that she was right.

The fox-girl certainly didn't seem to have his tendency to brood. Maybe that was what attracted him to her. She'd suffered more at the hands of the Ice Dungeon than almost anyone else, and yet she was still drawn to the adventure of a Delver's life.

She'd struggled to level because she'd been forced to dive on her own after being rejected by the Delvers of Winterhaven, and yet she was eager to get back in and fight, eager to push herself as soon as she had an opportunity to advance. She'd put herself in danger and given up experience to help him out when he'd started with a handicap.

And he'd managed to level faster than anyone Lyra had heard of, despite the challenges of the dungeon throwing tougher than normal monsters at him. Or, more likely, *because* of the dungeon throwing tougher than normal monsters at him—combined with the fact that they'd chosen to push through, to fight, to challenge themselves despite what seemed to be unfair odds.

It was as if they were thriving under Nova's 'tough love' treatment, where most in Winterhaven had decided to take the easy way out—fighting through the dungeon in big parties, which made it easier to survive but harder to gain experience. This seemed to be another way that Jay's experience in the business world helped him. It was the equivalent of surviving on a minimum wage job that provided no challenges and little room to climb up the ladder versus taking a chance on going into business for oneself—starting with nothing, with less than nothing, just for the chance to break free of 'the man' and succeeding on your own terms.

Jay had always admired that entrepreneurial spirit in the business owners he'd worked with, and he had grown very good at recognizing that spark in people, even if he'd never managed to take the plunge himself. He'd gotten close a few times, and in the end had chosen the safer route of working for someone else. Maybe that's why he'd been so unfulfilled by his job despite the fact that everyone said he was good at it.

As strange as it seemed, falling into another world had given Jay the opportunity to do what he'd never done in his own life—take risks, give everything to a cause he believed in, build a team of people he liked and trusted... Could he convince Molly to become a Delver, too?

He followed Lyra to the Safe Zone with his mind humming with questions. There was definitely something going on here. It was clear the dungeon wanted something from him. The harder it pushed him, the faster he progressed. That probably meant that if he continued to delve the Ice Dungeon, Nova would hit him with bigger and bigger challenges.

It wasn't going to be easy.

But the dungeon was also giving him everything he needed to survive and to keep his team members alive.

He just had to manage their resources, make sure they always had enough healing potions or skills in the group to save them if things got really hairy... Jay wasn't averse to pain and discomfort if he knew there would be a reward at the end. Lyra didn't seem to be either. They were in it to succeed, to push themselves, to win—whatever that meant in the world of Arcanicea.

Jay guessed he was about to find out.

"Are you coming or not?" Lyra called out from the Safe Room door. "I'm getting in the shower."

She'd already stripped all her clothes off and was making a half-assed attempt at modesty with a too-small towel, ostensibly for Jay's sake. Perhaps just to tease him. Either way, he liked what he saw.

He grinned. "If I hurry, do I get to watch?"

Jay could see her blush even at a distance.

"You can watch," she said, her ears flattening into her silver-white hair. Beneath her towel, he thought he saw her tail swish with pleasure. "But no touching!"

That was all the invitation Jay needed. He jogged toward the hexdome, determined to push his worries aside, if only for a little while.

30

Busy Work

Once they'd both showered and put their clothes and armor into the auto-washing cubes for the night, the pair sat next to the ring of blue fire, wrapped in towels and blankets, and sorted through the hundreds of notifications they'd neglected.

"Ooh!" Lyra squealed with delight, bouncing under the cover she'd ripped off one of the cots. Her small, perfect breasts poked out the top despite her attempts at decorum. She grinned at Jay. "I got a 'Mystery Loot Box!' Those are always good. I've only gotten one before, and it was my first set of Fire Arrows."

Jay's ears perked up. "Hey, I think I have one of those too. I got one when I got my Charisma stat up to ten, and then forgot about it after that Scarab Construct tried to blow me up."

"Open it! Open it!" Lyra chanted, clapping her

hands, and doing everything in her power to make Jay forget all over again.

"You open yours first," Jay said as he sorted through his menus to find where the item had ended up.

The fox-girl eagerly obeyed. Something big and fluffy and white appeared in her hands as she opened the loot box. Lyra's blue-and-gold eyes widened, and she let out an ear-piercing series of yips and howls so loud and sudden that Jay nearly fell out of his chair.

"What's the matter?" he shouted. "What's wrong?"

"Nothing is wrong, Jay!" She howled again. "I'm so happy! Look at this!"

Lyra launched to her feet, standing on the seat of the chair, with the fluffy white thing wrapped around her shoulders like she was an old-fashioned actress in an expensive mink stole.

Maybe a down-on-her-luck actress about to shoot the kind of movie she'd regret for the rest of her career.

Jay managed to tear his eyes away from her enticingly bare sex and perky breasts to look at the thing she was wearing, only to get a second fright as he found a snarling face staring at him.

"What the hell is that?" he yelped, recoiling.

"Fur armor made from a Tundra Wolf pelt!" Lyra exclaimed, jumping off the chair and prancing around the room in nothing but the wolf-fur. As Jay continued to stare, he realized the armor was an entire pelt—including the stuffed and ferocious looking face, which had been moulded into a terrifying shoulder pauldron. "Jay, it's enchanted with an archery bonus and additional constitution! I've never had armor with this much of a buff on it before. This is amazing! How do I look?"

"Naked," he answered honestly. "And very, very sexy—if it wasn't for the monster on your shoulder."

Lyra blushed and ran back for the chair. "Sorry, I forgot. I was just so excited!"

"Yeah, well... now I am too."

He had wanted to see her blush, and it had worked. Her pink cheeks burned a deep crimson, and she hid her face in behind the fur, moaning in embarrassment.

Jay was beginning to think being partied with the fox-girl was going to cause a permanent condition. Jay was grateful for the additional blankets he'd piled around himself, so Lyra couldn't see just how true his statement was.

"Now you open yours," Lyra said, peeking up from behind the fur. "And if it's armor, you have to parade around naked in it so I can ogle you."

"No way," Jay said, clicking on the loot box. "I'll keep my modesty intact, thank you very much."

"No fair!"

"Hey," Jay said with a chuckle. "I didn't make you do it. You—"

His words cut off and his chuckle died in his throat when he saw what was in the box.

"What?" Lyra asked, seeing the expression on his face change. "Is it good?"

It was Jay's turn to blush now. "Uh, no. It's nothing. Never mind."

"What is it? Tell me! I showed you mine, now you have to show me yours."

"Really, it's nothing special," Jay said, staring at the item description with nauseating embarrassment churning in his stomach.

Mystery Loot Box Unlocked – Master of Your Domain

When you're good, you're good. And when you're Charismatic, you're even better. Why do things the hard way when you can just bat your pretty eyelashes and get everything you ask for, easy as pie?

You have received [Tundra Berries] x10

Jay's stomach dropped. He'd received the Tundra Berries before he'd even reached Level 2. Lyra had found the Frostleaf clovers while he'd been fighting the Level 1 and 2 Glacial Scarabs.

Everything they had done since then had been completely unnecessary. Lyra had almost died. He'd almost died twice. They'd put their lives on the line taking on a ridiculously over-leveled quest to gain an item that Jay had had sitting in his inventory this entire time.

Lyra jumped across the fire from her chair to his, straddling his hips and pinning him to his chair, a fierce look in her two-toned eyes. "Tell me," she demanded. "Tell me, or I'll... I'll make things extremely uncomfortable for the both of us."

Jay felt her warm body pressing against his and his face burned even hotter. "You're going to be mad," he warned.

"I'm going to be mad if you don't tell me," she said. "What is it?"

He tugged one of his hands out of her grip and pulled the Tundra Berries from his inventory. He held out the white-leafed plant with its blood-bright berries and grimaced.

"A Tundra Berry?" she gasped.

"Ten of them," he admitted.

Her eyes widened as she processed that, her mind whirring through the timeline. She stared at him in stunned silence. Then she said, "We had them all along?"

He nodded, waiting for her to scream at him or try to claw his eyes out.

Instead, Lyra threw her head back and laughed like a maniac.

Strangely, Jay felt himself grow even harder. The mad-woman had her naked sex pressed against the thin towel covering his crotch, laughing so hard that it shook her entire tiny body, making her bare breasts bounce in his face. She was completely insane, and he was completely there for it.

"Aaaaahahahahaha," she laughed, yipping in between as she sucked in more breath. "Ahahahahaha!"

Lyra laughed so hard she fell backwards off his lap, landing on the floor with a thud.

"*Oof*!" she gasped, then she continued to cackle. "That's the funniest thing I've ever heard. I almost died! You almost died! And we had those stupid berries all along!"

Jay cleared his throat and tossed a blanket over Lyra's sprawled naked form so that he could think properly. "I admit you're taking this better than I expected you would."

"Well, why not?" she said, struggling to regain control of her breathing, her bright, two-toned eyes fixed on him with an amused expression. "The key word is *almost*. We survived, didn't we? We're almost Level 9, Jay! If we'd quit when we had those reagents, we'd barely be ahead of where we started. It's funny."

Jay put the Tundra Berries back into his inventory and sighed, not quite able to see it from her perspective. He was glad she wasn't upset, but he was annoyed at himself. He'd put her in danger because he had been careless. That was unforgivable, and he promised himself he wouldn't do it again.

Achievement Unlocked!: Busy Work

Do you ever feel like half of the work you do in the day is just trying to look busy, so no one gives you more shit to do? Shuffling papers, endlessly cleaning glasses at the bar, pushing buttons on the Xerox machine... Every job has its version of busy work. Sometimes, it's even work your boss assigns you just to keep you out of *his* hair. You know in

your soul he's just going to toss it in the trash the moment you hand it in, but you do it anyway, because it beats being responsible for <u>real</u> work. This is kind of like that, except you did it to yourself. You had one job. That job was done. And you went ahead and made your fellow Delvers look bad by grinding away and earning your rewards the old-fashioned way. No one can accuse you of laying down on the job, can they, buddy? Sure, it's not going to make you very popular with your peers but, hey. Management has got its eye on you...

Reward: New Ability Acquired!

Grit - Grit is a hard-to-define quality that has been separating the men from the boys for centuries. Here in the dungeon, we admire a Delver with Grit. Demonstrate your willingness to go the extra mile in disadvantageous situations, and you'll be rewarded. Receive a steady increase in attack and defense stats the longer a battle lasts. Because when the going gets tough, the tough get going.

Jay read the description and couldn't decide if he was being made fun of or not. Then he realized it didn't really matter. The dungeon could mock him all it wanted, so long at it kept the experience, skill, and stat boosts coming.

As he worked through the rest of his notifications, he found two more of note. The first was one he got from the Ghost Bison quest, presumably from the unusual way they'd gone about it.

Achievement Unlocked!: Well, That Wasn't Very

Sportsmanlike...

Wow. You know there are rules against hunting that way for a reason. At least, there were in the world you came from. Here, not so much. Actually, we kind of like that go-getter attitude round these parts.

New Ability Acquired!

Cut-Throat Tactics – In the business world, cut-throat tactics refer to aggressive and often borderline unethical business strategies used to gain an advantage over competitors. This can include sabotage, spreading misinformation, or exploiting legal loopholes. In the dungeon, there are no laws, and morals and ethics only need apply if you want them to. The Cut-Throat Tactics ability gives you an additional +10 Attack Bonus when you use...

ethically ambiguous strategies.

Jay wasn't sure how to define 'ethically ambiguous' in a dungeon setting, but since it was a Passive Ability, he figured he'd just reap those bonuses when they came. It was getting increasingly difficult to determine how much XP he was going to get for what. It was tempting just to leave it up to the dungeon and not try to strategize too much—or rather, to only focus on the things he had some control over.

"Hey, Lyra," Jay said, grinning as he saw a new perk he'd unlocked. "I've got something you're going to like."

Lyra sat up and blinked sleepily at him. "Is it armor? Are you going to do some naked prancing for me now?"

"No," he said, even better. He read the description out loud to her.

New Perk Acquired!: Party Warehouse

Not every Delver unlocks the prestigious Inventory Menu, you know. And fewer still unlock the ability to share that menu with their party members. You've got Party Inventory, since you're the Party Leader. But now you've got the Party Warehouse! Each member of your party will have access to their own Inventory Menu, where they can store their own non-party items, free of charge. Party members may not search through other members private inventory, not even you, Party Leader! But if a member leaves your party—in the event of death or disagreement—they revoke their access to their Inventory Menu and all abandoned items become the property of the Party Warehouse owner.

Lyra's eyes lit up as she scanned her HUD. "I've never heard of this perk before… but it works! It's there! I have an Inventory Menu, Jay! Oh my goodness, I need to start sorting and organizing all of my things!"

Jay laughed at her excitement, averting his gaze when she scrambled over to her satchel, leaving her blanket behind. Her perfectly round ass was lifted enticingly in the air. The way her fluffy white tail swayed back and forth only drew attention to it, though it hid the most exciting part of the view.

"Glad you like it," Jay said. "I don't want you

leaving me for some other party now that you're high-enough level to turn some heads, after all."

Lyra gasped and shot him a glare. "I would never do such a thing, and how dare you suggest it. I'm staying with you, Jay. You can pluck my name from your party listing when I'm dead, and that's about it."

"Okay, deal," he said, chuckling to himself. He stood up from the chair, stretched, and yawned. "Have fun organizing your stuff, Lyra. I'm beat. I'm going to get a head start on my sleep if you don't mind."

"Huh? No, of course I don't mind. You've earned it! I'll be going to bed soon too. I'm excited for tomorrow."

Jay dragged the blankets from his chair back to the cot he'd taken them from. Then he curled up under the covers, already feeling his eyelids growing heavy.

"What about tomorrow?" he asked, though he felt the same anticipation in his own chest.

"Waking Molly," the fox-girl's voice said, carrying through his hazy thoughts to nestle in his brain. "I hope she likes me, Jay."

"She'll love you," Jay said, confidently.

Lyra let out a nervous whine. "How do you know?"

Jay yawned again, sinking deeper into the blissful rest promised by the Safe Room bed. "Because she loves me," he said. "And I love you."

"What?" Lyra yipped. "What did you say?"

But Jay was already fast asleep, dreaming of a red-haired girl running across the frozen tundra with a pretty white fox at her side.

31

Medicine and Machinations

As if the dungeon knew they were on their way out, and didn't want to interfere, Jay and Lyra only encountered a few monsters on their way back to the entrance. Jay had the feeling that the dungeon was holding its breath, as if it were waiting for something.

Not just *something*.

Jay knew what it was waiting for.

What Nova was waiting for.

She wanted to know if he would return now that he'd gotten what he wanted from her.

The dungeon had warned him from the beginning that he shouldn't let his desire to save Molly interfere with his quest for her. At first Jay had worried that she would interfere in some way, perhaps keeping the items he needed hidden from him until

she was convinced that he would do what she wanted him to do.

Now, he got the feeling that Nova knew he would
come back. He'd developed a taste for Delving, and
even if it weren't for the aggressive push she'd given
him in leveling, Jay had a suspicion that he would
have come back once Molly was awake and safe.

There was little else for him to do in this world,
after all.

He wasn't going to sit around and be bullied by
someone like Runolf, that was for sure.

Still, now that the dungeon had given him the
Frostleaf Clover and the Tundra Berries that Raina
needed for her spell, Jay got the feeling that it—or
Nova—was nervous.

He might not have realized it if it hadn't been for
the last two Notes from his 'Anonymous Benefactor,'
delivered via the Bootstrapper Ability when he'd
reached Levels 7 and 8. But those left little question
about the dungeon's state of mind.

*It's so hard to watch your baby grow up! I feel
like it was only yesterday that you were a delicate
little novice, taking your first tentative steps into my
dungeon, waiting to see how I might try to kill you
first.*

*Well, I suppose technically it was only the day be-
fore yesterday, wasn't it? You've certainly made incredible progress, my Dark Horse, my stud... But the
easy part is over now. I'm afraid it will only get more
difficult from here. You will have to be very clever in*

order to pass the trials ahead.

I've spent time in your mind, lover, and I know you better than you know yourself. I know you will be torn between the responsibilities of the world you came from and the world you are in now. I know what you must choose, and I know it won't be easy for you. But I can, perhaps, take some of the sting out of your decision.

[Scroll of Free Ride]

The scroll was for a temporary experience boosting buff, similar to the Well-Rested bonus, which could be applied to any party member who was more than five levels below the Party Leader. When used, it doubled the experience gained by the lower-level member until they reached par with the rest of the group.

Jay could only imagine Nova intended for him to offer it to Molly, knowing that the best way to ensure he would return to Delve the Ice Dungeon was with his best friend at his side.

Nova didn't seem to know that he'd already decided he was going to continue Delving whether Molly came with him or not. She didn't seem to know that Jay had come to feel as strongly for Lyra as he had for his life-long friend. Jay already had plans for what he would do if Molly preferred to stay behind—he'd come back and visit, of course, but he wasn't going to put his future on hold for a relationship that had faltered before if had a chance to start. He loved Molly, but he wasn't going to sacrifice this new life just to waste away at her side.

If the first Note hadn't set the tone, however, the second drove the point home.

I'm going to be blunt, Jay Morgan. I've got something special for you. I'm going to give it to you now. But you won't be able to open it until you reach Level 10, so you have to come back to see what it is.

Yes, I'm bribing you.

No, I don't care.

[Silver Filigreed Box]

The box matched the key Lyra had found on the Glacial Scarab Construct. The box that promised to unlock his potential.

What once was lost, may now be found,

If this key is fit and door unbound.

Past skills awake to new renown.

Find me, Delver. Down, down, down...

He felt certain it had something to do with the [Silver Key,] though the description and the hidden inscription both mentioned a door. In any case, he would have to come back to reach Level 10 if he wanted to solve that mystery.

More than almost anything—with the exception of seeing Molly awake and well—Jay wanted to solve that mystery. The more time he spent in the dungeon the more he wanted to learn it, to level up, to thrive in this environment that everyone had told him was cursed.

So, the dungeon needn't have worried about that. Nova had set her hooks, and there was no way Jay would escape the pull of her magic now. He knew he was being manipulated. But he got enough out of the bargain that he found he didn't mind.

At least for now.

Jay and Lyra stepped out of the dungeon, into the cold morning air of Winterhaven's Tundra to find Runolf waiting there, a scowl on his wrinkled old face. He clutched his staff tightly in one gnarled hand and a roll of parchment in the other.

He started back when the door to the Ice Dungeon opened. But when the wolf man saw the pair emerge his scowl became a vindictive sneer. "Giving up already, are you, human? Probably for the best. We just received word from King Wenshire that there is to be a tax applied to out-of-district Delvers entering the Ice Dungeon. About time Arcanicea ruled something in favor of the Faunari people, if you ask me."

"A tax?" Lyra said, pushing forward to confront the man. "Why would they do that? When is the last time we had any out-of-district Delvers to worry about. Did you complain, Runolf?"

Runolf stepped back as if startled by the fox-girl's sudden aggression, or perhaps he could sense that she was more powerful than the last time they'd had a stand-off. He narrowed his golden eyes, and glared at her, however. "Taking care of the people of Winterhaven is not 'complaining,' outcast. You should be pleased that I haven't also made a request to ban exiles of the Faunari clan."

"I am *not* an exile," Lyra snarled, her eyes blazing. "You may be the leader of Winterhaven, Runolf. But even you must put such a decision to the vote of the people. You might be surprised to find I have more allies than you think I do."

"Powerful allies," Jay added, moving to stand beside Lyra.

The pair advanced on the ancient wolf man, forcing him to take a step back. Jay could feel the man's **Alpha's Command** power pressing at him, but it was barely a tickle against his mind. Runolf might be a higher-level Delver than Jay and Lyra were, but the two of them together were a force he couldn't deny.

"We'll see about that," Runolf said, baring his pointed yellow teeth. "For now, it will be five-hundred gold a piece for any human entering the Faunari dungeon. And if I call the vote and you are exiled, Vulpinari bitch, not even gold will buy your way past these doors."

The man hammered his parchment onto the door, using his staff to pound the nail into the rune-carved stone. The end of the staff glowed, indicating he was using some power to do the job, which would have been impossible otherwise. Then he spun sharply and marched away from them, his hunched shoulders making the move less intimidating than it might have been.

Still, Jay worried what might happen if they pissed the old man off too much. He clearly had political connections and he wasn't shy about tugging on them.

"Five-hundred gold?" Lyra hissed at Jay once Runolf was out of earshot. "That's a fortune! It will basically mean that once you go into the dungeon you won't be able to come out again. And what about Molly?"

"Don't worry about it," Jay said, thinking of all the items they had to sell on the World Dungeon Market, not to mention the cash they'd gotten from their Ghost Bison quest. "We'll find a way around it. And if not... well, let's just say I don't think the dungeon will approve of Runolf's methods. I have an idea for settling this matter on neutral ground, if it comes to that."

Lyra took his arm and squeezed. "I hope you're right, Jay."

"Come on," Jay said, taking her hand and tugging her forward. "There's someone I want you to meet."

Raina did not look as surprised to see them as Jay had expected her too. She met them at the door of her Medicine Tent, opening the flap just as they approached, as if she'd been waiting for them. The older wolf woman stood aside, motioning for them to enter without saying a word.

Jay and Lyra entered the tent to find a fire burning in the central pit, Molly laying peacefully on her cot, just where they had left her. The only difference was a shock of white hair growing at the front of her soft, red curls. Jay immediately went to kneel beside her, touching her face with his fingers to turn it, looking at the white hair. "What happened?"

"There are physical effects to remaining in the dream state for extended periods of time," Raina said in her familiar low growl. "It is nothing to worry about, providing you were able to find the ingredients I requested."

"We found them," Lyra said. "Sooner than expected, actually..."

She managed to suppress a laugh as Jay removed the items from his inventory and passed them to the Witch Doctor.

Raina raised her eyebrows at him. "You are not using a satchel," she said. "You have an Inventory Menu?"

"I do too!" Lyra practically squealed, suddenly unable to contain her excitement. "And look at this—"

She spun to model the enchanted fur armor, which Raina inspected with a grunt of appreciation.

"Impressive," the wolf woman said, collecting the Frostleaf Clover and Tundra Berries and bringing them to her workstation—a cluttered desk that looked somewhere between a scientist's laboratory and an apothecary. "I had a feeling you would be able to do what others would not, however. I have been preparing your friend for your return. We may begin the ritual immediately."

Jay took Molly's hand and squeezed it. "What have you done to prepare her?"

"I have spoken to her," Raina said simply. She pulled out a stone bowl and tossed a Frostleaf Clover into it. Then, she poured something from a smoking vial into the bowl and began to stir it with what looked like a fingerbone. "If you recall, I told you that those in the Portal Sleep hear and know everything that goes on around them, though they often report fighting their own challenges within the dream state. I took the opportunity to explain to Molly about our world, the Faunari, the Ice Dungeon, and the troubles that have been brewing in Winterhaven ever since Runolf and I returned from the tenth floor of the dungeon."

Jay glanced at Lyra, recalling their last encounter with the wolf man. Lyra's ears drooped, and she nodded, as if encouraging him to tell Raina what had happened. Jay did, then he added, "Is it true that you were married to him once?"

"It is true," Raina said with a sigh. She plucked a handful of blood-red berries from the Tundra Berry plant and set them in a smaller bowl. Then she began plucking the white leaves, which she added to the Frostleaf Clover mixture. The leaves hissed and gave off a purplish smoke when they were combined with the clover. "Marrying Runolf is one of my life's greatest regrets. Our encounter on the tenth floor of the dungeon revealed much about the man I thought I knew, and leaving him was the only choice I had. Our story is long and complicated. I will not bore you with it now... But you should know that it is my fault Runolf has been elected the leader of Winterhaven, and because of that, I will do what I can to aid you in thwarting this nonsense about the taxes. Runolf talks very prettily about his care for the Faunari people, and for our little community here, but I have long suspected he is playing a secret, sinister game."

Jay felt his mouth run dry as he remembered the wolf man's threats against Molly. Raina glanced up, apparently recognizing his expression for what it was.

"You have no need to fear for her life while she remains with me, young man," she said. "I know what Runolf is like, and he prefers threats and manipulation to action in most cases. I am immune to his pressure tactics, as are others with higher Intelligence, Willpower, and Charisma stats—he is a Shaman Class, like my own."

Jay gave Molly's hand a final squeeze, wishing he had some sign that she really was there and listening. He sat with his back against the cot and motioned for Lyra to come sit next to him.

She glanced at Molly, her blue-and-gold eyes nervous. Then, with her ears half-flattened into her hair she crept forward and sat beside him. Jay took her hand in his.

"I believe you would do everything you could to protect her, Raina," Jay said. "But I wouldn't trust Runolf half as far as I could throw him."

Raina grinned at him, her pale-yellow eyes flashing with humor.

"You are right to be wary of him," she said. "Yet I think you pose a bigger threat to Runolf than he does to you. It has taken him many years to achieve what he has, in the Ice Dungeon and in Winterhaven. He is easily threatened by those who advance more quickly than he does, part of the reason he has been so hard on our little Lyra, here. The death of Runolf's son was a shock to the entire village, but everyone knew it was no one's fault but Runolf's that he was Delving that far anyway. It was only after Runolf began shouting about it at every town meeting that anyone got it into their head that Lyra was to blame. He would never have done so if she hadn't shown so much promise, which is why I have continued to support her while others have turned their backs. Sadly, I cannot Delve any longer, or I would have taken this pretty fox-girl for my own party long ago."

Lyra had tears in her eyes when she glanced up at Raina. "It's true," she said. "Raina has always helped me when others turned me away. I owe her my life."

"Then I, too, owe her my life," Jay said. "Because without you, I never would have survived my introduction to the Ice Dungeon."

More colored smoke plumed from the table where the wolf woman worked. She rattled some vials, inspected her spell book, and peered at the potion she was concocting. "I think that does it," she said. "Only it needs to ferment for a few hours before we can give it to Molly."

She came out from behind the table and sat down in a chair opposite the fire.

"Please," Raina said. "Regale me with your adventures while we wait. I'm sure Molly will be interested to hear all about it, too."

32

Molly's Confession

It was dark outside by the time Jay and Lyra had finished telling their story, each interrupting the other to add funny details or to interject commentary on the other's interpretation of the battles they'd endured.

Raina took particular pleasure in Jay's recent discovery that he'd had the Tundra Berries he needed in his inventory all along. The wolf woman cackled and howled, setting off Lyra again, until Jay began to wonder if he'd been transported to a mad house.

But more than anything, Raina was interested in the items they had looted from the dungeon.

"Make me a list," she insisted, as she inspected the finished potion. "Including the item quality and quantity of anything you wish to sell on the World Dungeon Market. We only have one official World

Dungeon merchant in Winterhaven, and I suspect he is in cahoots with Runolf. However, there are... less official ways to buy and sell goods in any town. It will be best if I make the inquiries in private, I think. We do not need to draw any more attention to you than is absolutely necessary. At least, not while Runolf's tail is tied in knots over this out-of-district tax."

Jay and Lyra did as the Witch Doctor asked, double checking their lists and making notes beside items they would prefer not to sell if possible. Raina brought her potion to Molly, tilting the girl's head back and pouring it drop by drop into her mouth while muttering an incantation. When she was finished, she set the empty bottle down and nodded to herself.

"That should so it," she said. "It shouldn't be long now."

Jay gave the parchment with their listed items to Raina. The old woman's pale-yellow eyes widened as she read it.

"By the ancestors..." she whispered. "I knew there was something special about you, young man. But this... When you said you'd received some interesting loot I did not think..."

She was interrupted by a moan from the cot.

Jay whirled around so quickly he nearly knocked Lyra sideways.

"Watch it, lover boy," the fox-kin archer chastised him, a slightly perturbed expression on her face.

"You still need me, remember? I'm not chopped meat just because your girlfriend is awake."

"I'm sorry, Lyra," Jay said.

Molly moaned again, and stretched her hands up over her head as if she were awaking from a long and restful sleep. "Jay?" she mumbled. "Is that you... I had the strangest dream..."

Lyra shoved Jay out of the way and grabbed Molly by both shoulders. "It wasn't a dream, Molly! You're really here, I'm really here, Jay's... somewhere over there. Will you come Delving with us, please, please, please, pretty please with magical cherries on top?!?"

Molly's bright, sea-blue eyes shot open and she stared at the pretty fox-girl shouting excitedly into her face. "Lyra Golden-Eye?" she said. "You're... real? You look just like you did in my dream. Wait... am I still dreaming?"

"Yes, I'm real! And I really, really want you to join our party and come into the dungeon, okay? Don't let Jay talk you out of it. He worries too much about everything, but you're going to be great, I can tell already!"

Jay, shocked by Lyra's sudden enthusiasm, could do nothing but laugh.

"Here I thought you were going to be shy when you met her," he said. "Now I'm worried you're trying to replace me."

Lyra reeled back from the bed, breathing heavily. Her cheeks were flushed bright pink, and her two-toned eyes were wide with embarrassment.

"What? No! I just... I want you to be together so that I..." Her blush deepened and she backed away from the cot. "Uh, you know what, never mind. I should let you two get caught up. I'll... I'll go with Raina if she's going to see the Merchant's Guild."

Raina was standing now, a smile barely concealed on her thin lips. She bowed regally to Molly. "It is nice to meet you, Molly," she said. "My name is Raina. I've been caring for you while you were in the Portal Sleep."

Molly sat up, her red curls falling around her shoulders. She gazed around the tent in wonder, staring at the fire, the shelves filled with magical ingredients, the Witch Doctor's workstation. She paused as she looked at Lyra and Raina, with their Faunari features and their odd way of dress.

Then her gaze fell on Jay and she burst into the biggest, happiest smile he'd ever seen. He thought he could feel his heart melt in his chest when her little nose crinkled. "Jay, this is crazy," she whispered. "I'm so glad you're really here! My dream... everything I heard and saw in my dream was real?"

"That's what I understand, Mol," he said, tears welling unexpectedly in his eyes. "I hope it wasn't too bad for you in the Portal Sleep."

Molly sat up straighter, holding her arms out to him. "Jay, you're crying. Don't cry, I'm okay."

Jay knelt next to the cot and let her pull him into her arms. "I was so scared when I couldn't wake you up, Molly. I never thought I'd see you smile like that again. It made me realize how many things I needed to say to you, and I worried I'd never get a chance."

"Shh," Molly said, kissing the top of his head and running her fingers through his hair. "I'm okay. I'm okay because of you, Jay, and I'll never forget that. If I'm going to be stuck in an alternate universe, I can't think of anyone I'd rather be stuck with than you."

Lyra cleared her throat awkwardly and Raina made her way toward the tent door. "We'll leave you two alone for a bit," the fox-girl mumbled as Raina flashed her long, sharp-toothed grin.

"Thanks, Lyra," Jay said, moving to sit next to Molly on the cot.

"Wait," Molly said, glancing between the two of them. "Lyra, you should stay with us too."

"No," Lyra said, flattening her ears. "I think Jay wants to talk to you alone. I don't want to—"

Molly blushed so deeply that even her freckles changed color. "Please?" she said. "I know what he wants to talk about. There are things I need to say, too. But I... I want to talk to you too."

Raina bowed once more and ducked out of the tent, letting the door close behind her with a swish. Lyra glanced at the door as if it had become an impenetrable forcefield. She side stepped so that she wasn't standing right in front of the door, but didn't come any closer into the room.

"Okay... uh... you two go first. I'll wait. And I won't listen, I swear."

Molly looked like she wanted to protest further,

to invite the fox-girl closer. But Jay wasn't sure he wanted an audience for the conversation they were about to have. He said, "Thank you, Lyra."

Molly sighed and turned back to him. She took his face between her hands and gazed at him for a long time, her sea-blue eyes searching for something that Jay hoped she would find. His heart beat so loud in his chest he was certain that she could hear it. He felt more nervous than when he'd been fighting for his life in the dungeon.

When she didn't say anything, Jay couldn't handle the tension anymore.

"Molly, there's something I need to tell you," he said. "Something I thought you knew, but maybe I should have said out loud. I—"

"I love you, Jay," she said, speaking at the same time as him, their words overlapping like the layers in a perfect cake. "I always have."

"I love you, too," he said, his mouth going dry. "You're my best friend, Molly. But it's not just that. I'm in love with you."

"I know," she said. "Me too. I've been in love with you since we were eight years old and you taught me how to tie my shoelaces."

Jay laughed. "That was nothing. You always hated those Velcro shoes your mom made you wear."

"No one had ever taken the time to teach me anything like that, Jay," she whispered. "Mom never had time for me. Or if she did, my stepdad would give her shit for coddling me. I wanted so badly to learn but I didn't have anyone to show me, until you came around."

Molly pulled his face to hers, kissing him the way she had when they were sixteen, with all the awkward teenaged passion still there, rekindling every emotion he'd ever had for her and banishing every doubt.

When she finally broke away, he searched her face for some kind of answer. "Molly, what happened?" he asked. "Why have we never talked about this?"

Tears formed in Molly's eyes, and she bit her lip, glancing over her shoulder at Lyra who stood against the wall of the tent looking like she'd rather be just about anywhere else.

"Because I wasn't ready," she said, her voice shaking. "I'm... I'm still not ready. I've been so scared, Jay. Growing up, Mom and Barry would fight all the time. Mom was always drunk, and he'd get mad. But it wasn't just that... He'd hit her. Me and Mom never really got along but I loved her, I didn't want to see her get hurt. Barry knew that, and any time I did something he didn't like he'd take it out on her and I—" Molly sucked in a shuddering breath and burst into a sob deeper than anything he'd ever heard from her.

"Shit, Mol. I didn't know that. Why didn't I know that?"

Jay's heart broke. He'd known Barry was a jerk, but he hadn't had any idea it was like that. Guilt flooded through him as he remembered Molly's stepdad glaring at him through the window the last time they'd shared a kiss. He should have known something was up. But he was too caught up in his own head, thinking it was some problem of his that he'd never even asked.

"Please don't blame yourself, Jay." Molly squeezed her eyes shut tight. "I'm going to tell you this because I need you to understand, but there was nothing you could have done. He was crazy. Jay, when he caught me kissing you, he threatened to kill her. I didn't know what to do. Part of me knew he was just a bully, it was just a threat, but I couldn't be sure. I was scared if I told you, he'd go after you too. He used to brag about all the guys he knew on the police force, how he could get away with anything he wanted. He said no one would believe me if I told them what he was doing."

Her words came out in a rush, like she'd been holding them in for so long that now that she'd started she couldn't stop until it was all out in the open. Jay waited for her to finish, his heart aching, wishing he knew what to say and knowing nothing would be enough.

"Molly," he said, taking her hands. "Molly, listen to me. He's dead. Barry died years ago. I went with you to his funeral. Now I wish I'd helped him get there a little faster, but he can't hurt you anymore."

"I know, Jay." Molly sniffed, letting out a tiny laugh. "It's so stupid. And that's one of the reasons I never felt I could talk about it. It doesn't makes sense.

When he died, I thought I'd finally be free of that fear. Mom packed up and moved to the freakin' Bahamas and is living the rest of her life getting sunburned and drinking pina coladas. If she can be free, I should be able to, too, right? But it's like every time I think I might be okay I turn into that little girl again. I get scared. I shut down. And I... Jay, I love you more than I have ever been able to say, but I'm not ready."

Jay pulled Molly against his chest, letting her cry, feeling a storm of emotions brewing inside him that had nowhere to go. "Take all the time you need. Even if you're never ready, I'll be here for you."

"I know," Molly said, sniffling again. "I know. The reason I'm telling you all this now is because... for the first time in my life I fell like I'm *going* to be ready *soon*."

"It's not a rush," he said. "I'm not going anywhere, Molly."

She pulled back, putting her hands on his shoulders and staring into his eyes.

"You don't understand," she said, shaking her head and smiling suddenly. "Jay, something happened to me when I was in that Portal Sleep. Something changed. Raina talked to me a lot when I was unconscious. She said that people often undergo challenges when they get stuck in the dream state. That happened to me. I saw all these things from my past and how I could have done things differently."

"Molly, what happened isn't your fault." Jay said.

"You know that, right?"

"Yes," she said. "It didn't make me feel like it was. It made me feel... empowered. It showed me the strength I have inside, that had been there all along, and how powerful it can be if I use it. Does that make sense? I think... I think it helped me start to process all of this. I don't want you to be sad, okay? I'm not sad anymore. I feel like whatever damage Barry did to me when I was a kid is starting to heal, finally, after all these years. Do you see?"

Jay shook his head, thinking of the strange symbiosis he had with the dungeon and wondering if it was connected somehow. "Maybe?"

"Listen," she said, looking up at Lyra and motioning the fox-girl over to the bed. "Raina told me other things, too."

Lyra reluctantly came to stand by the bed and Molly grabbed her hand pulling her to sit down on her other side. The cot groaned under the weight of the three of them, and Molly laughed.

"What did she tell you?" Lyra asked cocking her head sideways. Jay would have expected her ears to be flattened to her head like they did when she was embarrassed, but the fox-girl looked curious more than anything.

"She told me how her husband—that Runolf guy—had three wives besides her," Molly said. "How strong Delvers often have more than one partner. And I... I think that might be a good thing for you Jay. For us, I mean."

"What!?" Jay said, standing suddenly. "You aren't ready for a relationship—that much I get. Let's start with first things first, okay? It's a big step from no relationship to multiple girlfriends or wives."

Molly laughed, wiping the tears from her eyes.

"I love you, Jay," she said. "That means I want you to be happy and fulfilled, whether I am able to give you those things or not. I've heard the way you two are with each other." Lyra blushed as Molly continued. "I know you care about each other a lot, and that's okay. That actually makes me feel better about taking the time I need to heal, because I don't feel pressured to just 'get over it' for your sake."

Jay shook his head. "Molly, I would never want you to feel that way. I—"

"I *know*," she said, reaching for his hand. "I know. It's *me* who would make me feel that way."

"I don't mind waiting," Lyra said. "I do care about Jay a lot. But I already told him, he should be with you. I don't mind sharing if you're okay with that, and if that's what he wants. But he's been in love with you for years and if you feel the same way, I don't want to intrude on that."

"You wouldn't be intruding," Molly insisted, taking her hand and pulling it into Jay's so that all three of them were touching. "You are cordially invited, Lyra. I listened to your stories about the dungeon. Jay wouldn't be here if it weren't for you. So, in a way, I owe it to you that we've been able to have this conversation at all. I have some things to work through, and I think Delving might help me to do that. So, I would like to join your party, if you really want me to. And Jay, if you want to be with Lyra I want you to have that. When I'm ready, I'll join you, too. I'm sure we can make it work if that's what you want. I'm not saying I won't ever be jealous—"

"Oh, I'm going to be *super* jealous," Lyra interrupted. "You two have known each other forever, and you have all these curves and those boobs and the adorable freckles. Molly, I was jealous of you even when you were unconscious. But I'll deal with it."

Molly grinned, wrinkling her nose. "Me too."

"See!" Lyra blurted, pointing at Molly's face. "How am I supposed to compete with that? How does she do it? It's an unfair advantage."

"You're a fox-girl!" Molly retorted. "You've got like an entire cult following in the world we come from. Trust me when I say that it is you who has the advantage."

Jay stared at the two women, his mind spinning. "I can't believe this conversation is happening."

Molly tugged his arm, forcing him back down onto the bed. Then she slipped out from between the two of them.

"Then allow me to help you figure it out, Jay," she said, her blue eyes twinkling. She gave Lyra's shoulder a shove, nearly pushing the fox-girl into his lap. "Kiss her. Kiss her for me, Jay. For all the kisses you and I should have shared but didn't. Kiss her so that I can focus on getting better for you.

Okay?"

Jay blinked up at Molly. "Okay..."

He'd hardly gotten the word out before Lyra pounced on him, wrapping his mouth in hers.

33

A First for Everything

For a moment, Jay was so stunned that he froze. His body responded before his mind caught up, and he found himself lost in a passionate kiss with the fox-girl straddling his lap. Lyra's arms wrapped around his shoulders, one hand cradling the back of his head as she ravaged his mouth.

Finally, Jay's brain made sense of what was happening. The beautiful girl kissing him, his first love watching from the sidelines. He reached up to hold Lyra's arms and pushed her back just enough to break the kiss.

"Wait a second," he said, panting. "What exactly are we doing here?"

Molly's cheeks were flushed, her lips wet and parted as if watching Lyra kiss him was turning her on, too. She said, "What do you want to do?"

Lyra bucked her hips, grinding herself into his rock-hard erection. "Feels to me like he wants to do more than kiss."

"That's not fair..." Jay protested. "I'm not going to lie and tell you I'm not into this, but I'm not going to do something in the heat of the moment that we're all going to regret once the fire burns out. Okay?"

"The only thing I regret," Molly said, "is that it has taken us this long to talk about everything. Jay, I know you've been with other women. I've never been upset with you for that. You probably thought my lack of a reaction to your hookups was apathy, but it wasn't. Just because I wished it could be me in your bed never meant I held it against you for needing intimacy in your life. If you and Lyra want to do more than kiss..."

Lyra whimpered, and her tail knocked against Jay's knees where it hung between his legs. "Yes, please. You can watch, Molly, if you like. I mean, if that's okay with Jay it's okay with me."

Molly's cheeks became an even brighter pink. "I'd like that. I've imagined what it would be like to be with you so many times, Jay... I'd like to see..."

Jay swallowed hard. The ardent desire in both the women's expressions was increasingly difficult to ignore.

"Promise me this isn't going to mess anything up between us," he said, looking at Molly first and then at Lyra. "Both of you. I need you to promise that this is something we can work through. I'd rather not have either of you than to ruin my friendship with one or both of you."

Lyra's thighs tightened as they squeezed the outsides of his legs. "Jay, this is normal for the Faunari," she said. "I promise it won't be a problem."

Molly nodded, kneeling next to the bed like she was about to say her prayers, looking like a girl who had a lot of sinful thoughts to seek forgiveness for. "Jay, I promise. If you want her, I want you to have her. Someday, when I'm ready, I want you to have me too. Please."

Jay picked Lyra up from his lap and set her on the cot. He stood, covering his face with his hands and rubbing fiercely, trying to wake himself up if this was a dream. He paced to the other side of the tent and then back again. When he didn't wake up, and both Molly and Lyra were still watching him with those flushed, glassy-eyed expressions, he sighed in defeat.

"Well, I'd have to be fucking crazy to say no to this," he said. "So, I guess we're doing this."

The firelight flickered off the girls' faces as they glanced at each other with expectant looks. The fox-girl's ears flicked to attention. She grinned at Molly. Molly grinned back and nodded.

"Quick," Lyra shouted, launching off the cot toward him. "Get him out of those clothes before he changes his mind!"

Molly laughed breathlessly and followed her. The women began tugging at his clothes, pulling the

Beetle Black Scarab armor off his body with such ease that Jay wondered if Nova had designed them to be stripped off quickly. Hands stroked him as his skin was bared, fingernails left gentle scratches, hot breath seared his flesh leaving trails of goosebumps.

Soon, both girls knelt at his feet, gazing up at him like they were admiring a museum piece—"Man with Raging Hard-On." Jay would have felt ridiculous if they didn't look so fucking sexy that his brain had ceased firing in the 'critical thought' sector.

Then, Molly turned to Lyra. "Your turn," she said, her voice husky with desire.

Jay couldn't tear his eyes from the pair as Molly slowly began to undress the fox girl. First, she removed the fur shoulder armor, laying it like a gift at Jay's feet, her eyes darting up to him to ensure that he was watching. As if his eyes could have gazed anywhere else.

Molly slid her hands up Lyra's midriff, over her sides, and under the cropped leather top. Lyra lifted her arms and allowed Molly to pull the garment over her head and Jay's breath caught in his throat as the red-head's wrist grazed Lyra's nipples, causing them to harden. Molly didn't touch the fox-girl any more than she had to, as if acknowledging that Lyra was meant for him. Though Jay had admired Lyra's naked form before, having her presented to him in this way felt intensely more erotic. His mouth felt dry as he attempted to swallow his desire when Molly pulled the fox-girl's leather skirt down.

Lyra stepped out of her boots once she was naked and turned in a slow circle so that both Molly and Jay could admire her. Molly moaned in the back of her throat, and Jay couldn't tell if it was jealousy or desire, but either one felt charged with more sexuality than his best friend had ever let show in his presence before.

Molly took Lyra's hand, then Jay's, and tugged them back toward the cot. They followed. Lyra sat on the edge of the small bed and gazed up at him, awaiting his next move. Molly surprised Jay by pressing herself against his naked body and drawing his face down to hers for a repeat of the kiss they'd shared earlier. As Jay's erection pressed into her stomach, Molly made a hungry sound and pressed herself closer, as if she wanted to touch as much of his body as she could. Jay couldn't believe he'd ever thought Molly indifferent to his feelings. He wrapped an arm around her waist and held her closer, one hand reaching into her hair to tug gently on her copper-red curls.

"Molly," he groaned into her mouth, his need for her deepening. "Molly, are you sure?"

She nodded, slipping her tongue inside his mouth and nipping his bottom lip before pulling herself back. She was panting, her cheeks flushed. "Yes, Jay. Take her. I will imagine every kiss, every touch, every thrust as if it is me you are making love to."

Jay knelt before Lyra, finding her blue-and-gold gaze fixed on him. "And you, Lyra? Are you sure?"

"I've never been more sure of anything in my life, Jay Morgan," she whispered.

Jay put his hands on her knees, sliding them along her firm, muscular thighs. Gently, he parted them, finally allowing himself a proper look at her bare, glistening sex. As he spread her legs, her puffy lips parted, showing the wet, pink slit and swollen clit inside. Lyra put her hands in his hair as he kissed her knees, then her thighs, moving his mouth along her eager flesh toward his prize.

The Vulpinari's scent was sweet and heady, with an animal-like musk that seemed designed to inspire lust. He kissed her hairless mound, flicking his tongue into her most sensitive place. Lyra froze, panting audibly, her fingers trembling in his hair. He could feel Molly's gaze upon them as he dragged his tongue through the fox-girl's wetness, lapping at her desire. Lyra leaned back, opening herself to him. As he looked up from between her legs, seeing her small, perfect breasts thrust up to the roof of the tent, her back arched in pleasure, he gripped her hips and pulled her body closer so that he could taste more of her sex.

Lyra's thighs trembled and she began to moan, rocking her hips against his face as if begging for the pleasure he was giving her. Jay brought her as close to the brink as he dared before pulling back, leaving her panting and flushed. She leaned back on her elbows, her legs spread wantonly. "Jay… Don't stop, I need more."

Lyra's blue-and-gold eyes swam with desire as Jay stood and approached the bed. "You'll get more," he said. "When Molly says so."

"Me?" Molly gasped. "I... I'm just watching."

Jay glanced at his red-haired friend, who was nearly as drunk with lust as the naked fox girl. A hand had slipped between her thighs and she didn't think to remove it when he pinned her with his gaze. "And touching yourself, I see."

Molly bit her lip and whimpered, either with embarrassment or desire, but she kept her hand where it was. "Yes... I always think of you when I touch myself. Now I can't help myself."

"And what do you want to see while you are watching?" he asked, getting into the idea of his best friend being a voyeur. With Lyra's excitement evident there seemed little reason to be prudish about the situation now that they'd gotten started. Besides, Jay found the idea of being watched by Molly sexier than he would have imagined.

Molly tore her desperate gaze from Jay and swallowed audibly. "Take him in your mouth," she whispered shakily to the fox-girl. "Suck his cock. I've always wanted to suck his cock."

Lyra sat up immediately, eager to obey Molly's command—it was as if she knew Molly had seniority in whatever this arrangement was becoming, and she didn't want to be ungrateful. As the fox-girl grasped his shaft, guiding Jay's length into her mouth, he let his hands wander to her hair, stroked her silken ears.

Lyra began to moan as he massaged the base of her ears. As she began to suck, Jay joined the chorus. "Fuck, Lyra, that feels so good."

In response, she bobbed her head, taking him deeper and letting her tongue slide against the base of his shaft. He managed to pull his gaze from the fox-girl to see Molly watching them hungrily with her lips parted. Her tongue moved as if she were imagining herself doing the sucking. Jay felt himself grow harder, watching her watch Lyra.

When Molly glanced at him and caught him watching her, she blushed. Jay gripped Lyra's hair, pulling her closer, as he kept Molly's blue-eyed gaze fixed on him. Knowing that she was imagining her own face wrapped around his length was the sexiest thing Jay could imagine as he thrust slowly into Lyra's throat.

Molly slipped her fingers into the top of her pants, exposing the lacey border of a pair of frilly pink panties. Leaning forward as she watched, her hand began to move up and down as she fingered herself. She bit her lip, blue eyes darting between Jay's face and his cock, pressed between Lyra's luscious lips. Jay felt ready to explode.

"I'm going to cum in her mouth if you don't ask me to stop," Jay panted, his eye's locked on Molly's self-pleasuring hand.

"Oh, god, yes." Molly groaned, her finger moving faster. Then, as if struck with sudden indecision, she blurted out, "No, no, wait. Not yet. Jay, you have to fuck her. I have to see you fuck her."

Lyra whimpered, still sucking like she was ready to drink his seed. Jay used every ounce of self-control he possessed to pull the fox-girl off his dick. He grunted as she released him with a pop of her lips. Gruffly, he commanded, "Lie back on the bed, Lyra."

Her ears flattened and she bit her swollen lips as she gazed between Molly and Jay. With excruciating, teasing slowness she leaned back, propping herself on her elbows. Lyra lifted her knees and spread her thighs, revealing the wettest, juiciest pussy Jay had ever laid eyes upon. He ached to be inside her. He ached to know that Molly was going to watch him push his thick cock into that little slit, and that she would be touching herself as he did it. It was surreal. It was a dream. A wonderful, sexy dream he hoped he'd never wake up from.

"Are you ready?" he asked, his voice strained by his tightly controlled need, as he positioned himself between Lyra's spread thighs.

"Yes," the fox-girl panted. "Yes, I want to feel you inside me. Fuck me, Jay."

He put one hand under her plump ass and lifted her as he guided his swollen tip against the heat of her opening. He got a jolt as he brushed against the fur of her tail, remembering suddenly that the girl he was about to penetrate was not quite human. He pressed into her, feeling her body split and open to receive his girth. She was small and tight and so wet that it didn't matter. Lyra gasped as he pushed the first inch into her. Then he pulled back, savoring the slick, silken feel of her eager body. The next time he pushed in, he went a little further.

Molly was moaning, leaning against the bed, her fingers making wet noises inside her panties. Lyra gripped his hips, pulling him deeper, desperate for his cock. "All of you," she growled. "Don't tease me. Fuck me!"

Jay made her wait for another couple of slow, torturous thrusts as he grinned down at the fox-girl's begging, two-toned eyes. Her ears flattened into her hair, and she whimpered. She arched her back, pressing her hard nipples up, as if every inch of her body needed him.

He glanced again at Molly's flushed arousal. A sheen of sweat made the red-head's forehead glow in the firelight, and her lips were swollen from bighting them. She no longer seemed self-conscious of his gaze as she played with herself.

Jay lined himself up, tilting Lyra's hips, holding her still as he continued to watch Molly. Then he gave a powerful thrust into the fox-girl, sending his entire length into her silken channel. Lyra cried out, surprised by the suddenness of complete penetration. Her body clamped around his, muscles tightening, sucking him into her like she was claiming him as he claimed her.

"Oh, fuck, yes!" Her scream had a hint of animalistic snarl as she grabbed at his back, digging her nails into his flesh. "Yes, more!"

He thrust again, listening to the fox-girl's cries of pleasure as he watched Molly's rapturous desire. He pumped his hips, feeling the squeeze of Lyra's body against his shaft as she took every inch he had. Molly was flushed and panting, sloppy wet noises accompanied the slap of flesh as Jay began to drive harder into Lyra's slit.

He lowered himself against the fox-girl's body, pressing into her sex, covering her and grinding against her as she writhed and screamed beneath him.

Lyra came first, bucking her hips up to meet him, shoving her sensitive clit against his stomach as she wrapped her legs around his waist, clinging to him as she cried his name.

"Oh, fuck, Jay," Molly moaned, her fingers flicking rapidly. "Cum inside her, now. Oh god, please. I need it. I'm so close."

Jay, barely keeping the tide of his climax at bay, released his control, hammering his hips into the fox-girl's twitching, pulsing pussy. He thrust rapidly, each time bringing himself closer. As his pleasure broke, it was like a wave crashing over a seawall. Groaning, he pumped his desire into her, hot spurts of cum that filled Lyra like a vessel until her slit overflowed with his seed.

"Oh god," Jay gasped, hit with another wave, his eyes still fixed on his best friend who was lost in her own pleasure. "Molly, cum for me. That's so fucking hot."

Molly cried out, collapsing against the side of the cot, as if she'd only been waiting for his command. Jay pulled out of the fox-girl's channel, just in time to release another, final rope of cum that splashed over her bare mound and up her belly, leaving a sticky white trail on Lyra's sweaty, glistening skin.

"Mmm, Jay," Lyra moaned, scooping up the semen with her fingers and bringing them to her mouth. "You taste incredible."

Jay dropped himself down on top of her, nuzzling the side of her neck and leaving nipping kisses along her throat and over her collar bones and down to her pert, teasing nipples. Lyra giggled and squirmed beneath him. Jay laughed, pinning her to the mattress. "Don't squirm so much or I might have to do that again."

"Promise?" Lyra asked, her blue-and-gold eyes half-lidded with warm, sleepy desire.

Jay looked up at Molly, who was leaning against the cot, watching them with a small smile on her full lips. "You okay, Mol?" he asked, suddenly worried about all of the things he'd forgotten about in the moment. "You want to come up here with us?"

Molly's smile stretched wider. "I don't know if the cot will hold all three of us."

"If we break it, I'll buy Raina another one," Jay said, picking Lyra up and rolling her over his side. He lay down in the middle of the narrow cot, one arm holding the fox-girl's naked body next to his. His other arm reached for his beautiful, copper-haired best friend. "Come here, Molly. Please."

Molly stood shakily, her clothes slightly askew. Then she lowered herself onto the cot, which groaned beneath the weight of the three lovers. But it held.

She lay down on Jay's other side, her head on his chest, her hand on his stomach. Lyra flipped one leg over his, staking her claim. Molly giggled and did the same. He could feel both of their hearts, and his own, beating in a steady rhythm.

"Thank you, Molly," Lyra whispered. "He's wonderful."

"He is, isn't he?" Molly said, kissing Jay's chest. "Thank you for letting me be a part of it."

Jay squeezed them both, at a loss for words. He kissed the fox-girl, between her silken ears, his left hand stroking the curve of her ass and the fluffy base of her tail. Lyra was so fresh, and new, and different. She inspired all kinds of thoughts of adventure, sexual and otherwise.

Then he kissed Molly, whose soft herbal scent and copper-red curls were as familiar to him as his own hands. She felt safe, like home, like somewhere he would always be comfortable. And yet, there was something undeniably different about her now. Jay had imagined a thousand futures with Molly, but none of them had ever started like this. But it felt... good. Right. Like it had always been meant to happen this way.

"You're both wonderful," he whispered. "It's me who should be thanking you."

Lyra wriggled closer to him, making the cot protest loudly. Molly giggled.

"We'll be sure to come up with some way for you to show us your gratitude," the fox-girl said, nipping at his chest with her pointed teeth. "Isn't that right, Molly?"

"I'm sure we can think of something," Molly answered, her voice growing sleepy.

"I look forward to it," Jay said.

After a time, both girls fell asleep, their deep breaths rising and falling as one. Jay stared at the roof of the tent, wondering how he'd gotten so lucky. It should have been strange, he supposed. He was, after all, in another world with two gorgeous women wrapped around his naked body.

Despite this, to Jay, it felt so natural that he couldn't imagine sleeping any other way.

If the fates were kind, he'd never have to, either.

He'd have Lyra and Molly by his side for the rest of his days. They would Delve together, eat together, and sleep together.

Even the thought of the cursed dungeon, trying to kill him at every turn, couldn't wipe the smile from his face.

He still had a promise to fulfil for Nova, of course.

But his girls would be with him for that, too.

Jay had no doubt that together, the three of them would be able to do anything.

34

Epilogue

Raina peeked inside the tent and smiled to see the three young people sleeping together. They looked so content that she could not bear to enter, to disturb their moment of peace.

Though she knew it would be a short-lived calm.

Her contact at the Merchant's Guild—a black-market trader that Runolf didn't know about—had given the Witch Doctor some startling news. The leader of Winterhaven was watching the World Dungeon Market very carefully, ensuring no one in the village could buy or sell anything without the nosy shaman's notice.

He anticipated what Raina knew was coming the moment the human travelers had arrived in their village. He hoped to stop what had already begun.

More the fool he was for that. *The arrogant, power-hungry bastard...*

Raina knew Runolf was in communication with

King Wenshire's men. He had been ever since the disastrous Delve that had wiped out hers and Runolf's party.

All of Runolf's other wives had been killed on the tenth floor of the dungeon, and Raina's love for Runolf had died with them.

Still, she had gone with him to Arcanicea's High Court to lodge Winterhaven's complaint with the King.

The dungeon was cursed, Runolf insisted. He said it to any who listened, and most everyone believed what the Faunari leader had to say.

There was no doubt that something was rotten in the village of Winterhaven, and the Ice Dungeon was in the middle of it all. But Raina suspected the locus of the evil that had befallen them was much, much closer.

Raina knew that people whispered about the tragedy that had befallen her marriage, they spoke of how the dungeon had broken them. Their grief had torn them apart, people said.

What they didn't know was that deadly, fateful Delve had only been the beginning. It had been what Raina learned in Wenshire's court that had truly hardened her heart to the man she'd once loved.

She didn't have proof of Runolf's corruption, but she knew.

As his first wife, Raina knew Runolf better than anyone else in Winterhaven.

She knew when he began to change.

And she'd known enough to hide her suspicions, unlike his other wives... those sadly lost to the 'cursed' dungeon.

Tears prickled Raina's eyes as she watched Jay with his women, sleeping peacefully, without a care in their hearts, not knowing the tragedy that threatened to befall the community that relied on the Ice Dungeon.

Somehow, Jay Morgan was at the center of it all, not the cause of their troubles, but perhaps...

Raina dared, for just a moment, to let herself believe...

Perhaps, he would be their retribution.

She had given up her place beside Winterhaven's leader, but she was not powerless.

Raina had allies and contacts that Runolf—for all his snooping and spying on their people—had yet to discover. She was prepared to do whatever it took to help Jay and his women when the time came.

As the old wolf woman closed the tent flap behind her, slipping into the cold night air, she felt a shiver pass over her that had nothing to do with the tundra winds.

Change was coming to Winterhaven.

Change was coming... far swifter than any yet realized.

Continued in Arcane Arctic 2
Coming June, 2024

Thanks for Reading!

Thank you for picking up a copy of Arcane Arctic 01, my first Harem LitRPG series. I hope you enjoyed the start of this new adventure! If you did, please drop a review on Amazon and recommend it in your favorite online communities.

I've been a gamer my entire life—computer, console, and TTRPG—and have been looking forward to blending my passion for writing with my love of gaming this way ever since LitRPG started gaining popularity. It's a challenging medium as an author and I have new respect for the genre I have enjoyed reading. Being a LitRPG author is a lot like being a Game Master/Dungeon Master except you have to write your own guide book, too!

If I have made errors that were missed during proofreading, you can send me an email at contact@peternorthauthor.com and I will fix them ASAP.

Thank you again for your support, and I hope you'll join me for Arcane Arctic 02!

Recommended Groups

For HaremLit and Men's Romance recs, I suggest checking out the following pages on FB and Reddit:

Dukes of Harem FB
HaremLit Readers FB
HaremLit FB
HaremLit Audiobooks FB

Harem Fantasy and LitRPG BooksFB
Pulp Fantasy, Harem, and Romance for Men FB
Monster Girl Fiction FB
Harem GameLit FB
SuperLit Book Club (LitRPG) FB

Romance for Men FB
r/haremfantasynovels Reddit
r/romance_for_men Reddit

r/HaremLit Reddit

More Romance for Men options —> Check out the LinkTree

Also by Peter North

HaremLit Series

Elemental Empire: Complete

Elemental Empire
Elemental Empire 2
Elemental Empire 3
Elemental Empire 4
Elemental Empire 5

Blood Rites: Complete

Blood Rites
Blood Rites 2

Blood Rites 3
Blood Rites 4
Blood Rites 5

Arcane Arctic: In Progress

Arcane Arctic 1
Arcane Arctic 2 (Pre-Order)

<u>Romance for Men</u>

A Goblin for Christmas
My Lovestruck Succubus Girlfriend
Stowaway Catgirl in Love
My Dragon Girl is the Spiciest Pepper

PETER NORTH

ARCANE ARCTIC 2

A Harem LitRPG Dungeon Crawl Adventure

Plaything or
Protector?...
...Can't a man be
both?
My Dragon Girl is the
SPICIEST
PEPPER

College is hard...

A succubus girlfriend makes things HARDER!

A Cozy, Slice-of-Life College Romance for Men

My **LOVE STRUCK** *Succubus* Girlfriend

He needs
a vacation
from his life.

She's on
the run
from hers...

STOWAWAY
CAT GIRL

... in love ...

All he wanted for Christmas was someone to share it with...
A Cozy, Slice-of-Life Holiday Romance for Men
A Goblin for Christmas

Printed in Great Britain
by Amazon